PENGUIN BOOKS

Meg Bignell grew up in a sprawling garden on the banks of the Derwent River in Tasmania's Derwent Valley. She now lives with her husband and three children on a dairy farm at Bream Creek on the east coast of Tasmania. She is the author of *The Sparkle Pages*, *Welcome to Nowhere River* and *The Angry Women's Choir*.

www.megbignell.com.au

Meg Bignell

Welcome to Nowhere River

PENGUIN BOOKS

PENGUIN BOOKS

UK | USA | Canada | Ireland | Australia
India | New Zealand | South Africa | China

Penguin Books is part of the Penguin Random House group of companies
whose addresses can be found at global.penguinrandomhouse.com

Penguin
Random House
Australia

First published by Michael Joseph in 2021

This edition published by Penguin Books in 2022

Cover illustrations by Shutterstock
Cover design by Louisa Maggio © Penguin Random House Australia Pty Ltd
Map by Ice Cold Publishing
Typeset in Adobe Garamond by Midland Typesetters, Australia

Printed and bound in Australia by Griffin Press, part of Ovato, an accredited
ISO AS/NZS 14001 Environmental Management Systems printer

A catalogue record for this
book is available from the
National Library of Australia

ISBN 978 0 14377 757 1

penguin.com.au

MIX
Paper from
responsible sources
FSC® C009448

We at Penguin Random House Australia acknowledge that Aboriginal and Torres Strait Islander
peoples are the Traditional Custodians and the first storytellers of the lands on which we live
and work. We honour Aboriginal and Torres Strait Islander peoples' continuous connection
to Country, waters, skies and communities. We celebrate Aboriginal and Torres Strait Islander
stories, traditions and living cultures; and we pay our respects to Elders past and present.

If we never get lost, we can never be found.

Mudlark (noun): a person who scavenges in river mud for objects of value

Gongoozle (verb) (dialect): to gaze lazily at water or boats

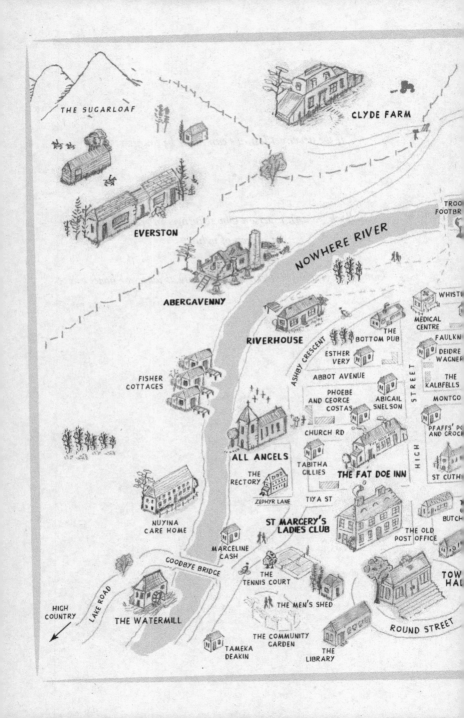

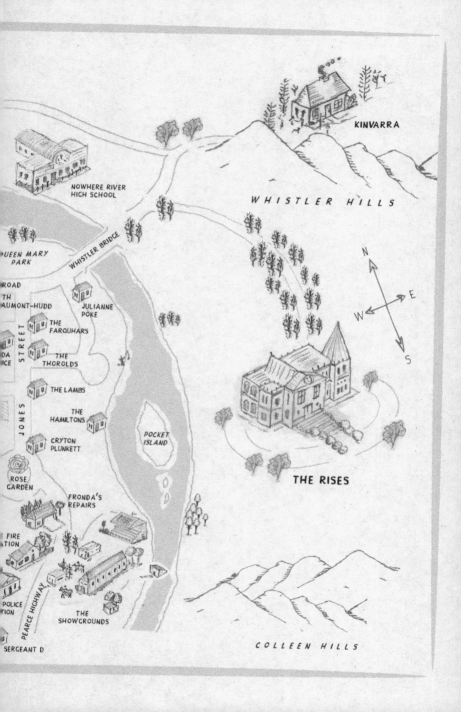

Chapter 1

Carra Finlay stood under the clothesline and watched in dismay as all her dreams blew away in the wind. In linty little pieces they whirled up, up and all around. Some landed in her hair, others collected cheekily in the folds of some drying knickers before shimmying skywards, and one very bold piece danced right into her gaping mouth. By misfortune of reflex, she spat the tiny scrap of paper onto the lawn, then stared at it in dismay, wondering which particular fragment of which dream it might have been.

'You will go,' said Carra to the fleck of paper, 'to the place where all the broken dreams go.'

She spent a moment wondering what a place filled with broken dreams might look like, and just as it was starting to take on a familiar shape in her mind, the corner of a sheet whipped her smartly in the face.

'Ow,' Carra said to the wind, rubbing her cheek. She flushed with rage, but quickly saw that being cross with the wind was unfair. It was, after all, her fault for leaving the list of dreams in the pocket of her jeans. It was she who had put the jeans in the washing machine. She inspected again the bits of notepaper dotted on the lawn in case they might be reassembled, and leaned down to pick up a few mushy flecks. The grass, by contrast, was brown and crisp. The warm spring wind buffeted her ears before blustering away towards the hills. Carra looked up at the dun, threadbare hills and let her anger return.

'Sod off, you bastard wind.'

In response, the wind flapped the sheets again, as if to remind Carra of its usefulness.

'Sod off,' she said again, but quietly this time, because fast-drying sheets could help the day catch up on itself. It had got unruly, the day. As usual.

Carra berated herself for being so slapdash about the laundry. Once, she had found great satisfaction in viewing her neat lines of clean washing: tiny, bright white socks and wafty, softened muslins. Now she couldn't remember how to care. And evidently nor could she remember to remove things from pockets. Not two months before, she'd presented her husband, Duncan, with the sodden pieces of his pocketbook and said meekly, 'Um, I'm hoping this didn't have all your passwords in it.'

Duncan had drawn one of those deep breaths with a significant pause before the exhale, which is how Carra could tell he was cross. She wished he'd yelled about it, though. She didn't know what to do with such a tiny hint of anger, couldn't yell back about doing his own goddamn washing or checking his own pockets. She could only feel guilty. The little notebook had been filled with reminders, contact details, jottings to enter into patient files, details of committee meetings . . . all the hallmarks of an active and conscientious community member, good friend and diligent GP. He had reason to be grumpy about losing it, but, as always, Duncan's temperate nature prevailed.

From under the clothesline, Carra wondered whether some intractable part of her had known the notebook was in his pocket. And whether that same part had also sabotaged her list of dreams. She surveyed again the last of the flecks in the grass – all that remained of her considered, bulleted list, titled with the earnest declaration

Things I Really Want. The first of these Things (Carra recalled) was *To create a wonderful garden admired by people far and wide.* This was followed by a less confident *Maybe make a name for myself??* and then a grumpily scrawled *Use my degree!!!!*

This was a perennial source of disquiet for Carra, the fact that she had attained first-class honours for her Bachelor of Landscape Architecture and worked as a council gardener and then, for the sake of marriage to Duncan, a move to the country and the arrival of twin babies, ceased gainful employment altogether. There had been a dismaying but grounding period between marriage and pregnancy in which she had dreamed up a landscape design service and shop for the Nowhere River High Street, but her detailed business plan had been met with rather pat, dismissive responses ('What a romantic idea', 'How sweet', and so on) and a feasibility study had rendered it absurd.

Be a better mother had been another item on the list, followed closely by *Be a better wife.*

Those two had then been struck through with heavy-handed lines and replaced with *BE A BETTER PERSON.*

The words shouted through the wind to Carra as she stood beneath the clothesline in an unkempt garden with her dreams in pieces at her feet. *Smithereen dreams,* she thought, as she turned her back on the mess of them. *Perhaps they'll help the grass grow.* This reminded her that the compost bin needed emptying and that time should not be wasted under the clothesline.

It was, after all, very precious time. Cherished and adored time. Nap time. Her twins, at almost ten months old, still blessedly slept for two hours (ideally) in the middle of the day and in the middle of this particular day, Carra needed that great swathe of silence more than ever.

The morning hadn't actually dealt anything singularly distressing, more an accumulation of frustrations: a dragging of bones from broken sleep at dawn's crack; multiple kettle boils without any actual cup of tea; the interrupted ablutions; the refused prunes; the crusts of something chewed stuck to her cardigan; the cardigan itself, shapeless and pilling. Nothing at all unusual for a new mother of twins.

Things had been slightly more fraught by the imposition of an eight o'clock appointment. This wasn't early by baby standards, but it did mean that by at least a quarter to eight, everyone had to be fully dressed, bundled out of the house and clipped into the car with clean bottoms, full tummies and something to rattle. Daisy's something to rattle wasn't found in time, which meant she was grizzling well before the end of the driveway and screaming by the time the car pulled up outside the medical centre. By then, Carra was the thing that was rattled. Also she'd had no time for breakfast.

She wasn't, owing to a forgotten nightdress under the cardigan, wholly out of her pyjamas either, but this had escaped her attention. She did at least have a clean bottom. *How did I end up here?* she thought, while summoning the energy to haul the pram from the car. *Thirty years old, white-knuckled and dreaming of cereal.*

The scheduled appointment was with the child-health nurse, Sister Julianne Poke. Sister Poke had alarming purple hair, don't-mess-with-me hips and flawless lip disdain.

'Strapping stock, those Finlays,' said Sister Poke as she deftly placed little denuded Daisy (now silent and staring fearfully at the purple hair) onto the scales. 'Your daddy' – she tapped Daisy's round belly – 'is made of good bones.' She handed Daisy to Carra, made some notes in the blue baby book and inspected Carra over her glasses.

'You're looking a bit washed out, though. Are you eating properly? You should be having plenty of steak if you're still breastfeeding.' Sister Poke jotted more things onto an official-looking piece of paper. Carra pondered what she might be writing. *Something funny about the mother? Not fit for purpose? NEEDS TO BE A BETTER WOMAN?*

'I'm vegetarian,' said Carra. 'But I eat very well.'

'Ah, of course, vego,' said Sister Poke's lips. There was more jotting. 'Plenty of eggs, then. Cheese. And get your hair done. There was a salon voucher in your mothercraft baggie. Use it, get out and about, see some actual people, join something. Surely you can get involved with one of Dr Finlay's things. Get a babysitter. What sort of support do you have around you? I know your mother-in-law would be a big help. She's a dynamo, that one.'

Carra thought of Lucie, her full-of-beans mother-in-law, and wilted a little more. 'Yes, she's great.'

'What about your own mother? She must want to see these beauties all the time.'

'She and Dad spend winters in the British Virgin Islands. Most of the year actually. They're really into sailing. We FaceTime.'

'La-di-da,' said Sister Poke. 'My sister's eldest daughter went there once.'

Carra tried and failed to raise the energy to reply.

'Now, tell me, are you looking forward to anything?'

'Pardon?'

'Standard postnatal depression screening question,' said Sister Poke. 'Is there anything you're looking forward to?'

'A glass of wine and some sleep,' Carra said without thinking.

The lips gathered themselves into a series of neat pintucks, then twitched in time with the note-taking.

'And,' added Carra hurriedly, 'I have a whole lot of dear friends coming to stay. After Christmas. Old uni friends.' Having read somewhere that a lie is often followed by a downwards glance to the left, she tried very hard not to look at the floor. 'They're, you know, my tribe. So much in common. One of them is quite famous now, she designs gardens for celebrities, writes books. Ursula Andreas?'

Sister Poke looked blank.

'Anyway, we studied together. She's a dear friend. We'll have a ball. So, yep, looking forward to that. Very much.'

Sister Poke engaged in some more writing, punctuated by several suspicious glances at Carra, who looked at her left shoe and felt a buzz of fury.

'Right.' Sister Poke lay down her pen and locked her hands. 'What questions do you have for me?'

Carra looked straight into Sister Poke's pale eyes and said, 'Is your hair a natural purple?'

Sister Poke's eyes stayed on Carra's face as she took the pen up again, pressed her signature into the bottom of the page and embellished it with a violent full stop. Then she examined the scratches on Ben's leg that he'd given himself with a rogue toenail and said, 'You poor little boy, what's going on in your head?'

This meant that Carra left with some baby nail clippers, a tub of ointment for the scratches, a new nagging concern for Ben's teeny state of mind and the dread that comes with offending the town's most conscientious gossip. She cursed Sister Poke, with her smarmy lips and her ointment, but mostly regretted her own runaway mouth.

'Out and about,' said Carra to herself when she got back to the car. She looked up and down the street. Out and about in Nowhere River's High Street meant either Pfaffs' Post and Groceries (where Mr or Mrs Pfaff were guaranteed to give you service with a grimace), the pub, the park, the library, the hairdresser, or the bit of lawn near the town hall with a seat and a rubbish bin. Carra had sometimes sat on that seat and gazed for a little too long at the back of the daily bus to Hobart as it drew away.

Mostly, she avoided the High Street in favour of a ramble in her garden. It wasn't large enough for actual ramblings, but adequate for Carra to lose herself among the weeds and let her mind cover quite long distances, designing borders, co-ordinating plantings and so on. She never did get past the planning stages. It was higgledy, the garden at Kinvarra, full of possum ravages, mysterious horticultural ailments and tumbledown walls. And despite her sophisticated planning, Carra had only managed to cull some woody daisies and remove the prickles from what was left of the lawn before twin pregnancy happened – with its cloy of all-day nausea and doctor's orders. This was followed by the slightly premature arrival of the babies, with their endless needs and their cycles of confining stymies. Carra wasn't quite prepared to be a mother when she went into labour at thirty-four weeks. The house wasn't ready and neither was she. Duncan's mother, Lucie, had done a beautiful job with the nursery but Carra's state of mind, even with two healthy babies sailing to their ten-month milestones, remained in a state of hobbled delirium.

Widespread drought in southern Tasmania had further stalled Carra's garden plans, along with a sort of stunned hesitation about putting down actual live roots. But still, she found solace in pouring bathwater onto the earth and watching the crickets run out of the cracked soil. She could let her babies crawl naked in the puddles without having to pack complicated bags, wrestle with car seats or run into any of the strange familiars who populated the town's High Street, the same ones who would regard and report upon her worn-out face, her cardigan and possibly now (since the purple-hair comment) her lack of respect. In the garden, Carra felt a semblance of belonging without any witherings of social anxiety.

Social anxiety. Carra wondered whether she should have just mentioned the words to Sister Poke. Perhaps the town could readily digest such a neat, clinical label and then stop looking at her as if she were a stray cat, startled and drab. But there was also the probability people would roll their eyes and mutter about woo-woo excuses, ungrateful whingers and getting on with things. Country people, Carra had noticed, seemed to do quite a lot of getting on with things. Also, she wasn't sure whether social anxiety was what she suffered from. *It could,* she mused, *have more to do with the gradual sinking of very high hopes.*

Carra looked across the street at a faded 'Life: Be in it' sign in the dusty window of an empty shop, just as Daisy began to whine.

'Right,' Carra said. 'Out and about.' With a deep breath, she turned away from the car and pushed the pram determinedly along the High Street. 'Let's just have a walk. Exercise is therapy.' She thought back to the days when it was nothing for her to run fifteen kilometres before work, or enjoy a really punishing spin class. She looked at the wheels of the pram, felt the race of her heart, and tried not to acknowledge the disparity.

Remembering a vague plan concerning fried rice for dinner, she steered towards Pfaffs' Post and Groceries, but decided she couldn't face the glooms of Mrs Pfaff. She turned instead down a side street towards the front door of the town's pub.

'How about some lunch?' she suggested. But the doors of the Fat Doe Inn were closed. It wasn't yet nine o'clock. 'Oh,' said Carra. 'Right. Most people's days are just beginning.'

A glimpse of the pub's vivid carpet through the window swept her back five years, to a time when its beery smell, mock Tudor beams and deep-fried camembert had seemed unabashedly charming. A time when everyone was abuzz with the news that Nowhere River's favourite son had brought home a girl. A time when Carra's life was shimmering with two-carat promise and glorious unknowing.

'Told you they'd love you as much as I do,' the gorgeous Duncan Finlay had whispered in her ear by the pub's fireplace.

Carra could see that huge fireplace from where she stood on the street. She saw herself too, five years younger, aflush with fire heat and wildest-dreams love.

She understood now why she had been so intriguing to Duncan's local friends. Nowhere River rarely saw newcomers, and certainly not young city girls. That was the same night she had met local farmer Josie Bradshaw and the two of them had drunk enough cider to see them dancing to Whitney Houston and pledging lifelong friendship.

It had been euphoric, that night. Carra turned away from the window and pushed the pram further along the High Street. She wondered how many moments of pure euphoria a person might experience in a lifetime.

The day was warming up. Carra removed her cardigan and pushed on until she caught sight of a familiar face in another window. She waved, and an instant later realised she was waving at herself. Herself was waving back, with an expression of flimsily veiled trepidation. Carra felt mildly disgusted. She dropped her hand and put the word 'stupid' into a scoffing, embarrassed laugh. Her eyes stayed on the face in the window, though, for a few moments more.

You're looking a bit washed out. Carra thought of stonewashed denim. *My fabric is threadbare, but I'm much more pliable.*

From the pram, Ben squeaked. Carra pushed on and wondered whether to brave the hairdressing salon. A sudden *toot-toot* from a car horn made her jump, then bristle with annoyance. The cheery sound grated against her morning. She turned to see a red ute pass, then pull into the kerb ahead of her. The driver's door opened and a tall woman in a blue work-shirt and a red cap jumped out.

Josie.

'Carra!'

Carra waved, then tried not to duck for cover.

'My God, a rare sighting,' called Josie. 'Are you real? Or just a mirage?'

'Haha,' Carra said, then realised that one shouldn't need to speak a laugh. 'Hi, Josie.' She scrabbled for her sunglasses and slid them on over her shadowed eyes.

Josie drew her into the kind of hug you could sleep in. Carra, particularly deprived in the sleep department, felt her limbs slacken.

'So good to see you,' said Josie. 'It's been, what? Months? Show me those divine babies!' She kept a hand on Carra's arm as she moved to inspect the contents of the pram. Daisy and Ben blinked up at her. 'Oh, look at you two, so grown up!' Ben smiled and held up his plastic set of keys as if to prove how grown up he was.

'Oh, the keys to my heart,' said Josie. 'Thank you, gorgeous godson.'

Carra's stomach muscles tightened into a cringe. *Social anxiety keeps your muscles toned,* she thought.

Daisy appeared spellbound by Josie. People were often spellbound by Josie, with her huge dark eyes and wide smile.

'Oh, Carra,' continued Josie, dropping to her knees before the twins. 'You've done so well, they're almost little people.' She pulled Ben's toes. 'Where did our tiny babies go?' She looked back up at Carra. 'You're not still breastfeeding, are you? Looking a bit pale.'

Carra gave a wry laugh. 'There's the slight problem of sleep. As in, not getting any.'

'God, it's hell, isn't it, the sleep deprivation.' Josie narrowed her eyes for a closer inspection of Carra, who looked at the sky and said, 'Gorgeous day.'

'Yes, I think it's going to get hot. Amazing for October. Do you want me to send Flo over? She'd love to babysit.'

'Yes, one day, that'd be great.'

'Even if it's just so you and I can go out for lunch or something. I'm sick of hearing about you from Duncan.'

'That sounds great.' Carra looked at her left shoe. *Stop saying 'great'.*

'So if I call, will you promise to answer?'

Carra nodded.

'We could even go away for a weekend.'

'Okay, great,' said Carra. 'Yes, please get me out of this baby-land.' She mimed strangling herself, showing the whites of her eyes, and laughed again.

Carra could feel Josie's big eyes searching her face. There was a knowing concern in their depths. Carra, grateful for the sunglasses, did her best not to look away.

'We could do the Overland Track. Or something. I've always wanted to do the Overland Track.'

Carra put her thoughts around some words but her mouth said, 'Yeah. But I am still breastfeeding so . . . maybe when that's finished.'

Daisy took Ben's plastic keys. Ben shouted. Carra shuffled under Josie's stare.

'Carra—'

'How's Jerry?'

'He's really well. Busy. I'll let you know when Flo is free. She's doing school by correspondence so—'

'She's left school?'

'Just for this year, I hope. Help her reset. She was having a bit of a hard time, and she's just not interested in curriculum stuff. She's not that interested in being a kid, actually. We should have babied her more, probably threw her on a horse too soon.' Josie glanced down at the twins.

Carra felt another prickle of self-consciousness and wished she hadn't dressed Daisy in pink. 'So no actual lessons?'

'Well, there are. They tick all the boxes, the correspondence teachers, but it's one on one so they get the stuff out of the way and then let her follow her nose. She's doing Nowhere River architecture at the moment. So boring, but she likes it. God, we've got so much to catch up on. Can I walk with you?'

'Oh, we're not really *walking* walking. Just, I don't know, loitering. We've come from an appointment.'

Daisy shrieked and rattled the keys into the air, in the direction of an approaching pedestrian. Ben began to cry.

'I'd better get them home . . .' Carra gestured towards where her car was parked and gave the pram a small push in the same direction, straight into the path of the incoming pedestrian, who shied to her left and said, 'Good gracious.'

'Gosh, I'm so sorry, Mrs Montgomery.' Carra felt herself curl up under the cool gaze of Mrs Patricia Montgomery, president of St Margery's Ladies' Club and matriarch of The Rises, the largest property in the entire Colleen Valley.

'What an enormous pushchair,' said Patricia, tweaking the sleeve of her perfectly ironed blouse. 'Positively titanic.'

'Sorry.' Carra watched Patricia's eyes as they travelled down to her feet and back up again.

'Hello, Patricia,' said Josie. 'Lovely day.'

'Hello, Josephine. Yes, glorious. If you like drought.'

'Ah well, if the sun insists on shining we might as well enjoy it.'

'I'm going in to close all the blinds so the St Margery's furniture doesn't fade. And to top up the flowers before our meeting. Bound to have been done in a slipshod manner. Phoebe Costas is on flower duty this week.' Patricia made another exaggerated step around the pram, casting a disdainful glance at the babies within. (Ben had stopped crying but had a very runny nose.) 'See you in' – Patricia looked at her watch – 'three and a half hours. Actually, three – you're setting up for this yoga business, aren't you?'

'Yes, very much looking forward to it,' said Josie.

Patricia frowned. 'Don't be late.' She sailed briskly on, across the road to a grand sandstone building that displayed perfect Georgian symmetry. There, she bent to pull a tiny but evidently offensive piece of errant Sweet Alice from the path, then disappeared through the large, navy-blue front door.

Carra waited for the door to close before she turned to Josie and said, 'Don't tell me you've—'

'Shut up,' said Josie, with a sheepish smile.

'You've joined St Margery's! Oh my God!' Carra was so tickled by the idea that she forgot to feel awkward.

Josie rubbed her brow. 'Well, the invitation arrived and I thought, you know, these dear old establishments will just die out if no one steps up.'

Carra, after a bit of being stuck on the word 'invitation', rallied and said, 'So you stepped up. With yoga!'

'I did. The yoga wasn't my idea, though. I haven't turned completely inside out.'

'Wow.' There was a pause before Carra added, 'God, she hates me. I can tell by her eyebrows.'

'You pander to her too much. "Gosh, I'm so sorry, Mrs Montgomery",' mimicked Josie. 'I think she prefers people who show her a bit of cheek.'

'What about your "very much looking forward to it"?' Carra laughed. A proper laugh. 'Not to mention you being a card-carrying St Margery's member.'

'Yeah, well, she breaks me sometimes.' Josie smiled broadly, enjoying the scatter of Carra's laughter as it filled the air. 'And she'd probably like you more if, you know, you didn't wear your nightie out in public.'

At this point, Carra stopped laughing and looked down at her nightdress, creased and faded and featuring a smudge from Daisy's rusk. Her lips returned from their grin and said, 'Fuck.'

Josie laughed. And then her phone rang. 'Dammit,' she said, after the brief call. 'Gotta fly. Walt's got two first-time mums calving. Poor buggers, they don't know what's hit them.' She kissed Carra's hot cheek and made for the ute. 'I'll phone to arrange a trial with Flo,' she called back. 'And you can call me too, you know. Anytime. Love you.'

Carra blew a little kiss (it spun through the air, propelled by relief), then hurried to her own car, shoving on her cardigan despite the incoming heat of the day.

Both babies wailed most of the way home, possibly protesting the sabotage of their outing, but more likely, decided Carra, crying out for easygoing Josie to return and liberate them from the washed-out weirdo in the nightie.

'I know what you mean,' said Carra. 'I need rescuing from the washed-out weirdo in the nightie too.' She felt a sudden yearning to be like Josie: strong and capable, pulling out calves just as easily as she could whip up a three-course meal. Or like Ursula Andreas, who was not actually a 'dear friend', as Carra had described her to Sister Poke, but a distant university contemporary. Carra was, however, in regular contact with Ursula via her Andreas Landscapes Instagram account and its arcadia of photographs. It was Carra's secret, self-flagellating indulgence, stealing moments to study images of Ursula in her designer overalls, snazzed up for awards evenings or laughing among impossibly glamorous park-estates from Cornwall to Copenhagen. Carra had never posted anything on her Instagram account (in truth it had been created purely to wallow among the idyllic episodes of Ursula Andreas). She couldn't remember ever throwing her head back in laughter among the hellebores and she hadn't actually spoken to Ursula Andreas since the day they graduated.

I should be more like Patricia Montgomery too, decided Carra, mentally adding Patricia to her list of Better People. Patricia, with her ladies' club dainties and all that flagrant, scorching front. A person's skin could blister under contempt like that. Such power. Against the backdrop of the cool, hushed and orderly interiors of St Margery's, Patricia seemed to Carra a flawless example of control.

Carra had been to St Margery's only once, for a ladies' cocktail party prior to her wedding day. It had been one of the many pre-wedding events organised by Lucie amid a whirligig of summer-scented, dreams-come-true, can't-believe-my-luck excitement. She'd been inspected and scrutinised, spoken to and questioned by the women of Nowhere River ('How many babies do you want?', 'When will you join St Margery's?', 'Where will you send your children to school?' and 'How did you snare our gorgeous Duncan?').

She'd been disarmed by it at the time, thought it quaint, the way a city girl would. She'd laughed with Duncan over the idea of belonging to a country ladies' club. But now the idea seemed quite attractive. *Any sort of belonging will do.* She pictured the St Margery's women with all their agency and purpose and committee-room productivity, and decided she probably wouldn't cope.

The babies' wails pitched higher until Carra wondered whether she might have a little wail herself. But Ben fell asleep just as Carra turned into the driveway and after a lot of complicated, hushed manoeuvring, he miraculously settled into his cot with barely a snuffle. Daisy went down only a few minutes later. So, with a sense of triumph, Carra had rushed to the clothesline. She calculated that if she hurried, she could get all her chores done *and* have an hour in the garden. *Just an hour's digging will make me feel better,* she thought, *or produce a hole big enough to hide in.*

It was inevitable, Carra supposed later, that just as she turned her back on the clothesline and all the soggy specks of lost ambition, a kookaburra would have landed on the fence outside the nursery window and hooted at the sky. The infant monitor in Carra's pocket crackled and bleated. Her heart dropped and her feet twitched.

'No,' she moaned, 'please no.'

But the bleat turned into a cry. She took the monitor from her pocket and said again, right into it, 'Please, please sleep. I can't do another endless day of tired baby. There are still so, so many hours. Please.' The bawling went on, eventually thickening with a second voice. The increased volume gave the sound a distorted, radio quality that Carra could almost imagine had nothing to do with her at all. She placed the plastic speaker on a garden seat and stared at it. Meanwhile, her twitchy feet agitated and pointed away from the house. And then, with a jaunty, almost joyful little skip to start them off, they ran.

▼▼▼

Sister Julianne Poke, 68

I was chatting to a bloke yesterday about mortgage rates when I realised I was his community health nurse when he was a baby. So I would have seen his donger when it was just a tiny cashew, and now he has a mortgage. Funny to think. That's how long I've been the community nurse up here in Nowhere Land. I love my job. You can keep abreast of things. I know when people aren't right. I saw Father John's depression coming before he did. And now he's as perky as all get-out. I came here because I married into the Poke family. They had the mill. They're all gone now, including my Bill. And the mill. I didn't see Bill's heart attack coming.

Chapter 2

'Shortbread,' announced Lucie Finlay to the newspaper, 'is a lot like us. Old-fashioned, crumbly and a bit boring.' The newspaper rustled in response, then dropped slightly to reveal the bespectacled eyes of Lucie's husband Len.

'Oh, I don't know about boring.'

'Often left sitting about to get stale.'

'You forgot sweet.'

'It's a shame no one likes caraway seeds in their shortbread these days. I do like a caraway.'

'Are we boring?' asked Len, still peering over the newspaper.

'Yes. Very.' Lucie sealed the lid on a plastic container of shortbread stars and thumped it for good measure. 'I mean, for goodness sake, I'm testing Christmas recipes in October.'

'Pop me in a tartan tin and give me away, then.' Len took a sip of coffee, raised his newspaper again and turned to the weather report. 'Still no rain on the horizon. My silver birches are in distress. It's meant to be spring. Spring my arsehole.'

Lucie gave a little tut, shuddered at the thought of Len's arsehole, and went to the bathroom to put her face on. Len lowered the paper again to watch her go. He spent a minute or two wondering whether he should look for a new, not-boring hobby. Lucie had so many – her music, St Margery's, her bridge playing, the theatre, the grandchildren and her most recent diversion, an oral history project in which she procured and transcribed odd little stories from townspeople (that one *was* mostly boring, Len secretly thought). He felt weary just listing all Lucie's hobbies and decided against seeking new pursuits. He had his garden, after all, and Lucie's hithering and thithering to withstand. He was never bored in the garden, and Len was of the firm opinion that only boring people get bored. Satisfied, he returned to the TV guide.

In the bathroom, Lucie tossed her head at her old reflected friend and sang a few lines of 'Defying Gravity'. She'd recently dragged Len along to the Theatre Royal to see *Wicked*, and that particular song had become her new anthem.

The phone rang. Lucie knew the newspaper wouldn't respond, so emerged from the bathroom with her make-up half done.

'Hellooo?' Lucie's telephone greetings often sounded like motifs from a hammy theatre production.

'Lucie? Patricia here. Look, can I rely on you to solve a flower problem? We have a bad case of wilt. This abhorrent northerly is scandalous, and Phoebe didn't put enough water in the vases, of course. I should bring back the floristry classes. I've had to put most of the arrangements in the rubbish bin – not that it mattered much, they were pretty hideous. Some sort of common waratah, I think. Why do Australian natives have to be so flamboyant? Look at the cockatoo – utterly raffish.'

Lucie dwelt for a moment on the fact that Patricia bothered to roll the 'r' in 'rubbish', then said, 'Oh dear, of course, I'll find something more subtle.' She bit her lip and wondered, not for the first time, why she was always so biddable when it came to Patricia. *She doesn't even ask nicely.*

'Excellent. Greens, silvers and whites are always nice. I know I can trust your taste, Lucie. And don't be long, I only have Abigail. Have you baked the shortbread samples for the fundraising meeting?'

'Yes.'

'See you directly.'

Lucie listened to the click as Patricia hung up, then said, 'Don't mention it, Patricia, and yes, I'm very well, thank you. See you soooooooon.' This last took the form of a perfectly executed high C with vibrato and an end flourish, and finished with the final clash of the phone on its cradle. She turned to see Len's eyes on her above the paper.

'She can't get enough of me,' said Lucie, heading back to the bathroom.

Twenty minutes later, after a hastily finished face and a rummage in the garden, Lucie had found only five flowers that would possibly pass the Patricia test – two white roses and three lissianthus. Plus some lamb's ears that were quite soggy from the sprinkler. *This cursed drought*, she thought. *And the bloody wind.* She considered finding an armload of silvery young gum leaves but decided they wouldn't do, either. She blustered back into the house and said, 'I'll have to go. Better see what blooms I can recover from the rrrrubbish bin.'

'Ah, Patricia, Duchess of Nowhere,' said Len, who was by now sipping tea over the crossword. '*She is bound by her o'erworked hands, to the queen of this old land.*' He was fond of misquoting poetry.

Lucie tutted and wished he might display a bit of supportive stress.

'Aha!' he shouted at the crossword. '"Bliss on a tape" is sonata! There's life in the old fool yet.' He wrote down his answer, then said, 'The elms are flowering at Kinvarra, don't forget.'

'The elms!' said Lucie, bumping a palm on her forehead. 'Of course!' She thought of the fluffs of pale green blossom. 'Perfect.' She kissed the top of his bald head and said, 'There's *a lot* of life in the old fool yet.'

He patted her knee. 'Phone and check that Carra is home, though. We can't have you climbing up a ladder. Elderlies are always falling off them.'

'Oh, do shut up,' said Lucie, gathering her things into a basket. 'You're the fuddy with the bockety leg.' A ping of something like regret sent her back to him with a kiss, on the lips this time. 'I won't need to climb a ladder. And of course Carra will be there, she always is.'

Lucie's pug, Beans, appeared at the doorway to see what he was missing out on, then smiled at Lucie.

Lucie Finlay made everyone smile without having to try very hard. Inborn, pink-cheeked, blue-eyed charm. It meant also that she could get away with most things, including wearing a mink hat to the Nowhere River High School quiz night, and suggesting to Patricia's husband that he might get his teeth whitened.

Len thought of hectored, dormousey Ambrose Montgomery (better known as 'Poor Old Rosie') and thanked his lucky stars for Lucie. Len's lucky stars had, over the years, received a lot of thanks, some of it the deliberate, desperate kind, given in the search for small mercies, but all of it genuine. Mercies, he discovered long ago, could always be found, no matter how small or how shadowed by life's general ruthlessness.

He looked over at his wife as she ransacked her handbag in search of keys. 'What's happening next with your history project? The one with Julianne Poke talking about dongers? That was a highlight.'

'My Nowhere People project,' Lucie said firmly, aware that Len's interest in her projects came with a modicum of derision.

'That's the one.'

Lucie sniffed. 'It's still going. Ish.'

'Hmm,' said Len with satisfaction.

'I'm just looking for a better platform to give it the exposure it deserves. I'm still gathering stories . . . occasionally.' She sighed. 'Penning little pieces to keep in some dank cupboard in the musty old Nowhere River town hall just sometimes seems a bit pointless. It doesn't . . . I don't know . . .'

'Tickle your glory bone?'

'No, that's not it.' Lucie grumpily took up her garden basket, then twiddled its handle. 'Actually I suppose that *is* it. But also because people's stories deserve more than a council cupboard, don't they?'

'Well, it depends how dull they are.'

'But it's the workaday things that ultimately end up being the most interesting in the end. They become sort of ordinary oddities. You know, how Vivvy Cox likes her trout, that sort of thing. Archaeologists go gaga over buttons and bits of plate.'

'Hmm,' says Len again. 'I think you should interview Alan Lamb. He'd add some colour. Don't know about his buttons, though.'

But Lucie had to pretend she wasn't listening, because Len's advice often made infuriatingly good sense. 'Anyway,' she said, 'I'll probably turn the whole Nowhere People thing into a musical one day – give it its rightful stage. You'll no doubt see me on Broadway with my second husband.' She bustled out, but was already wondering whether she might squeeze in an interview with Alan Lamb after the St Margery's meeting.

'Drive carefully, my Lucie,' Len called, returning to the crossword. 'No speed limit should be ignored, even for the Duchess.'

Beans looked worried, which mightn't have meant anything at all because by nature, pugs carry a perpetually worried expression. But mostly Beans *was* actually a worried pug. He kept his bulging eyes on the door through which Lucie had departed, then licked Len's ankle skin to see if it might make him feel better. It didn't.

Lucie didn't need to be told to drive carefully. She never went much above seventy. The whole of Nowhere River knew not to leave town on a Monday morning just after eight, which was when Lucie drove to Hobart for city chores, a saunter in the shops and her singing lesson.

'Get ahead of the '97 gold Merc,' Barry Fronda, the service station owner, would tell Monday morning motorists, 'or you'll be stuck all the way to the Rosegarland turn-out lane.'

Lucie's car, with its 'state of the art' ten-stacker CD player (located in the boot), was the best place to perform her vocal exercises and to practise belting a high D, a skill which eluded her even after a lifetime of singing and six years of formal lessons. Kinvarra, where her son Duncan and his wife Carra lived with their baby twins, was a good eleven kilometres along the Whistler's Road, plenty of time for Lucie to experiment with how the corrugations in the dirt road affected her vibrato.

Once satisfied with her resonance (and quite pleased with her upper register), she turned the stereo's volume up to its usual high setting and found that it had shuffled and clunked a CD of obscure Celtic ballads into play. A song rose up, one that Lucie hadn't heard for quite a while. She'd shuffled it away, too, into a dark recess of her memory, along with other stumbly things.

The haunting soprano vocal, at its considerable volume, would have been instantly affecting to anyone. For Lucie, it tore through a part of her that, caught unawares, offered no resistance. A wound dehisced again.

And she went her way homeward with one star awake
As the swans in the evening move over the lake

Through the searing of a familiar pain and the folds of misstepped time stood a little girl, tulled and twirling, on the verge of the road.

Lucie gasped, her right foot pressing instinctively and heavily on the brake. The Mercedes dragged to a long, crunching stop. Dust billowed around the car, clouding Lucie's vision and for a long moment she blinked into it, held her breath and listened to her heart fill her ears.

'Felicity?' she whispered.

In the far, far away, the little curly-headed blonde girl in her tutu and gumboots pranced out of the dust, across Lucie's view and into the distant past. Lucie's thoughts darted after her, fleeing into dreamscapes, ducking past truths and reaching into impossibles until the painful grip of her hands on the steering wheel brought her back. She gulped the air inside the car again, then took herself out to the empty road where the dust scudded off with the wind.

But one has a sorrow, that never was said
And that was the last that I saw of my dear

The serene voice floated out from the car speakers, towards the Whistler Hills on either side. Lucie wondered if it could be heard decades ago.

After several minutes of standing, pressing her fingertips to her lips, listening the song to its end and then closing the car on any more musical landslips, Lucie allowed herself a moment to slump heavily against the Mercedes. Her son Duncan (a GP) had told her once that people enter an altered state of consciousness immediately after a seizure: the postictal phase. She'd remembered that, and learned to apply it when she found herself struck by these episodes. It permitted a period of disorientation before it was time to hurry up and get on.

She was still there, resting her forehead on the car's long-suffering door, when the rhythmic crunch of gravel announced the approach of a person on foot. It took her pressed eyes a moment to readjust to the bright day, and the emergence of another figure on the road, this one tall and tangible and very, very old. A man, with skinny, rounded shoulders and a red beanie strode along towards Lucie from the direction of town. At his feet loped a ferret tethered by a lead and under his arm was tucked a gleeful-looking garden gnome. Lucie watched the way the beanie wobbled at its empty top and smiled.

'Good morning, Cliffity,' she called. The sound of her voice, steady and working, was calming somehow. Normal. As was the sight of Cliffity, for all his quirks.

Cliffity didn't slow his step, but doffed his beanie and said, 'That it is, Mrs Finlay. Good for the soul, good for the bees, good for the 'aystacks and good for me.'

'Where are you off to this morning?'

'Off 'ome,' called Cliffity, 'for me brekkie. Bit o' cluck'n'grunt with any luck.' Cliffity rubbed his stomach and smiled. His dentures shimmered in the sun.

'Nuyina's the other way, Cliffity!' Lucie had to shout; Cliffity's stride was long and fast.

He stopped. The ferret was jerked to a halt. 'Oh,' he said. 'Look at ol' Cliffity, pangle-wanglin' along in the ruddy wrong d'rection.' He turned on his heel. The ferret fidgeted and flipped on the end of its lead. 'Ah, Narelle,' he said fondly. 'She's as mad as 'ops for 'er walks.'

'Can I give you a lift?'

'No, thanking you very kindly. It will do me good, keep me bones limber and me morbs at bay.' He touched his beanie, adjusted his gnome and walked back the way he had come.

Lucie returned to the driver's seat, and smiled into the rear-vision mirror where Cliffity was already bobbling off into the middle distance. The stereo had shuffled on to 'Eleanor Rigby' by The Beatles.

▼▼▼

Vivvy Cox, 96

Well, I just love the river. My dad's family were all good fishers – taught me how to catch a brook trout. I love a brook trout. My maternal grandmother was Tasmanian Aboriginal, from a clan around here. She used to sit and watch the land a lot – they all did. My father and others said what a bunch of laggards they were, but they weren't doing nothing, they were being watchful and respectful and imagining. It's important to idle sometimes, to lay on one's oars. No one does anymore and because of that, the earth is suffering, isn't it. And the masterpieces aren't being made, because no one has the brain space to think 'em up. I'm idling all the time now, in my easy chair. I can't see so well so I think about things, let my mind wander all over. And I try to talk to people about our stories, that's the best I can do now. Brookies are best cooked in a pan, with butter and parsley.

Alan Lamb, 81

I was still playing footy for the Colleen Wombats when the country league got swallered up into the fucken southern Tasmanian Footy League. Nothing's ever been the same since. No one can think of nothing to do on a Sat'dy now, and there's people growing the fucken marry-juana up the creeks. They smoke the marry-juana and then never get off their holes again, end of story.

The world's had the chook as far as I can see . . . I was three games off me four hundredth game. Would've got a fucken plaque. So yeah, whatever drongo made that decision should be strung up by his arse-ropes.

Chapter 3

Carra had run almost halfway up the biggest of the Whistler Hills by the time her lungs registered considerable discomfort and her mind caught up with her body. She stopped running and turned into the wind, looking down at Kinvarra.

What if, she thought, *none of this is real? What if I hadn't fallen aboard the Duncan train and rearranged myself to fit into a life with him? What if there weren't two babies crying for me in that house? Where would I be?* She imagined a glossy, unrumpled version of herself as director of her own landscaping firm, designing gardens in Sydney, giving a lecture in a hall, running by a somewhere sea . . .

She realised with disgust that she was placing herself squarely into the life of Ursula Andreas. She shook herself and sniffed, then remembered the trill of her mother-in-law.

'Surrender, Carra, surrender. Give yourself time to adjust. It wasn't just two babies who were born, it was a mother too. The three of you need to navigate uncharted territory. And one day you will blink and your peeplings will be people who don't need you anymore. Your time is their time for now. Here's a coconut cake, Duncan's favourite. Don't thank me.'

Carra gritted her teeth.

Come on, called the nagging wind, *I can take you higher. Just a little walk it is, to the top. We won't be long.*

'Won't be long,' Carra called down the hill to the cottage. *I can still see the house; it's not on fire. They call it controlled crying, don't they? Do us all good.* And she let the wind take her up until she could see how the town nestled into the deep curve of the Nowhere River. She could see tiny cars moving along the High Street, one turning into the car park of St Margery's Ladies' Club. Carra imagined Patricia sharpening little gold pencils into pins for their meeting, talking about how to raise money to pay for more library books, making jam for the school, and other useful things. *Imagine having time to worry about how sharp your pencils are.*

She looked east, to Josie and Jerry's property, Everston, where Josie's horses dotted the white-fenced paddocks, and past that to the roof of the Everston farmhouse near the river. Carra knew that by now, Josie would have helped deliver Walt Wallace's calves and was probably out mending a fence while the slow cooker finished off the dinner and the vegetable garden grew.

Carra's thoughts returned to the awkward exchange on the footpath in the High Street, and she realised she should have asked more about Flo's school problems; about Alex, Josie's twenty-year-old son, who was away working on the mainland; and whether Josie had found her engagement ring, which she had lost somewhere in the stables ages ago. But such questions, after months of Carra deflecting any meaningful contact with Josie, seemed token and all too late.

Are you ghosting me Carra, FFS? said a text message, received three months ago, when they were still sisterly enough for relaxed incredulity.

Carra had replied with the tired face and poo emojis and the words, *Babies holding me hostage. See you in a few years when I'm liberated.*

Let me help! pinged Josie back to her.

You're too busy! Can't possibly.

I miss you!!

Josie had phoned the following day, but Carra had had her hands full and didn't answer. A week or so later, Josie dropped in, but the babies were asleep and Carra was hiding in the garden. She hadn't meant to hide, she had just heard Josie's call, thought about the state of the kitchen and found herself ducking behind the wisteria.

Beyond Josie's house, in the far distance, Carra could see a cloud of dust, which was probably Jerry on his tractor. *Poor Jerry,* she thought, *tending to the parch.* Carra was in awe of (and a little intimidated by) the bronzed resilience of these country people. Her eyes prickled. *I miss you too.* She blinked and turned away. The light surrounding Josie was bright and no-nonsense and a little too hard to bear.

Back towards town, Carra could see the school's oval, the only piece of true green, being freshly striped by a mower, and another tractor beetling along in Walt and Lurlene's home paddock. People doing things. But with no accompanying noise, just the sounds of wind and birds. It all seemed worlds and worlds away, perhaps not even real.

Her house at Kinvarra, when Carra turned back to it, was now in miniature. A doll's house. Make-believe. She could no longer see the wobbles in the hedge, nor the tattered state of the garden.

'It's a lovely house,' whispered Carra, imagining a tiny toy mother tending to things on a tiny toy stove while two doll babies gurgled and rolled on the dust-free carpet. 'I'm very, very lucky.' The toy mother was wearing an apron dress and had a tiny handkerchief, which was never needed. Her babies had clean noses and were pink and scented. They spent their waking hours chuckling at one another or eating their porridge. There was a little daddy doll present at all times.

Carra let herself search the town again, until she found the silvery roof of the medical centre, where Dr Finlay was busy being vital and life-saving. She wondered whether he had eaten the sandwiches she'd carefully prepared for him.

Thinking of the sandwiches tucked into their compartment, next to a shiny apple and an Anzac biscuit, Carra felt disgusted with how fraudulent it all seemed. *Put your lies in a lunchbox and whisper your truths to the wind,* she thought. The wind, on cue, pushed her in the back.

'I'll come back down soon,' said Carra to her cottage. 'I'll dust and make porridge and iron some hankies and clean the bath. I could invite Josie over. Just as soon as I've had a little more air.'

And because the gum trees were dancing with cheerful beckoning and a swallow twittered a welcome from somewhere unseen, Carra ran again.

Down in the valley, Lucie pulled into the driveway of Kinvarra and paused a moment to watch, with a sinking heart, as the wind blew elm blossoms across her windscreen.

'Buggeration,' she muttered. 'Silly old wind.' She thought about the way Patricia's left eyebrow would curve disapprovingly at her tardiness as well as the lack of flowers. 'Let's check the elms anyway,' she told the Mercedes. 'There might be one or two branches. And I'll pop in on Carra and the babes.'

As it turned out, Lucie was about a week too late for elm blossom. What had survived the wind was already turning brown. But Lucie didn't look anyway. She was, upon arrival at Carra and Duncan's house, instantly distracted by the sound of screaming babies in the garden.

'Oh my darlings,' she said as she hurried around to the back of the house. After a moment of eerie confusion in a garden filled with the sound of crying but empty of any actual babies, Lucie located the infant monitor on the garden seat, and rushed inside through the kitchen and into the nursery. There she found Daisy and Ben standing in their cots, their little mouths wide with outrage, their eyes crumpled with grief.

'Oh, oh,' said Lucie, lifting Daisy, the nearest, out of her cot and holding her close. 'My darlings, what's happened? Where's Mummy? Carra? Carra!?'

▼▼▼

High on the hillside, Carra spotted an aeroplane heading on the flightpath out of Tasmania and felt the inexorable pull of Away. She wondered what passengers might think if they were to look down upon the naked, dusty hills, distinct from the aloof, forested blue of much of Tasmania's distant landscape. Would they follow the turns of the broad Colleen River through the valley, find the Nowhere tributary, then the bend, and wonder about the cluster of buildings not large enough to qualify as a town? *Probably not.*

Few people went out of their way to visit Nowhere River. It wasn't on a main road, didn't have a nice bit of coast or a celebrated place in history. It was not featured in any shiny tourism brochures and no one of any fame (or infamy) had ever lived there. Once, Father John from the All Angels Church found himself in the newspaper for photographing a ghost in his vestry, but the flurry of attention soon simmered down to nothing when no further sightings were made and a sceptical photography expert went on the record about exposure anomalies. That was twelve years ago, well before Carra had met Duncan and been left breathless by the idea of being Mrs Duncan Finlay in a stone cottage with a gloriously disobedient garden.

'Over the hills and far away,' Carra sang to the disappearing plane. She sneezed two deeply satisfying sneezes, then miscalculated that she'd been gone perhaps fifteen minutes. *It'll take me five to run down again*, she thought, *No time at all. I'll just find the hill's trig point.* The trig (which she had reached almost weekly in her fitter pre-pregnancy days) was a little over the brow of the hill and up a small rocky knob. To reach it, she would need to walk out of sight of the house. *Just five minutes, no more.*

From further up, Carra gazed at the town's one sealed road that led in and out but mostly out. Beside it, a cluster of grey, slumbering buildings marked the old Nowhere River showgrounds. Carra had seen pictures of the showgrounds in its heyday – shining horses with plaited manes, fleeces and frocks, flowers, conserves and laughter. And pride. Such pride. The Nowhere River Show had been the social event of the year. But she'd never attended. Its one-hundred-and-tenth show, eight years ago, had been its last. By then, most people had taken jobs in town and were too busy to organise working bees or sponsorship doorknocks. Not enough doors. And not enough children. The local timber mill had closed down, families were forced to leave and no one from outside the district had any inclination to look at someone's best ram or their prize marrow. By the show's final years, no one bothered with marrows and Walt and Lurlene Wallace were the only ones with a ram.

'Everyone's just too interested in their own business for big community commitments,' Carra's father-in-law Len had told her when she asked about it. She'd been sorry to have asked because Len's sad eyes had taken on another layer of grief. She watched as he recalled distant visions of his show-president days: Lucie in her best hat, a steward rosette pinned to her jacket.

'Those were good times for us,' he said, 'Busy as blowflies in a dunny. Now everyone is just rushing to get out of Nowhere River. Or passing on by. Oh well, not much left *to* show, I suppose.'

Southeast of the showgrounds, and a little farther away, was an avenue of ghost gums – just pale wisps from where Carra stood on Whistler's Hill. They led to The Rises, the much-lauded Victorian mansion of Patricia Montgomery and her husband Ambrose. Lucie had once taken Carra along to the house for a fundraising event. Generations of Montgomerys stared down from their frames while Patricia, looking impeccable in cream, lectured about community engagement and used a lot of obscure words. Carra, having been brought up in a modern house in Hobart by her financial-planner father and lawyer mother, was awestruck. She had never seen such deep roots. The whole Patricia picture, with its pale carpets, its perfectly formed gardens, one-hundred-year-old mulberry tree, marble urns, its dovecotes and finials, was utterly daunting. (The carpets had been the most daunting of all; there was beetroot mint puree in the vol-au-vents.)

Back on the hillside, a woolly brown cow bellowed companionably at Carra from the neighbouring paddock. Carra looked at the cows, as they drowsily chewed. She felt suddenly, overwhelmingly relaxed, and changed her mind about a swift trot to the trig point. Instead, she climbed over the fence and, in a sort of half-lit state, sunk into a pile of straw and gazed sleepily at the sky. Listening to the warm huff of the cows, she felt pulled into the blissful dream of uninterrupted time. She thought of cats in the sun and let the wafting, analgesic air sing her into long-lost sleep.

Having settled both babies into relative contentment on the floor with some cushions and bottles of watered-down apple juice, Lucie made a breathless phone call.

'Nowhere River Police, Sergeant D,' said an efficient female voice after a single *ring-ring*.

'Sergeant D? It's Lucie Finlay.'

'Yes, Lucie, go ahead.'

'I'm at Kinvarra and Carra isn't here. Something terrible must have happened. The babies have been left alone, they're hysterical.

The car is still here, the baby monitor was in the garden, but she's not anywhere. Do you think someone's taken her? A mother would never, *never* leave her babies, Sergeant D. Oh my goodness . . .' Lucie clutched a hand to her heart for the second time that day.

'It's all right, Lucie,' said Sergeant D in the sort of soothing tones that Lucie imagined must have been taught at the police academy. 'I doubt very much that there is reason to panic.'

Lucie had heard those tones before. They sickened her. 'Something's very wrong,' she said, with a shake in her voice.

'Okay now, Lucie, I need to take you through some quick questions,' said Sergeant D in a more businesslike voice. Lucie heard the rustling of paper. *She's getting out her notebook.* She imagined the fresh, blank pages – Nowhere River was not known for its criminal activity, and detective work had not been in high demand for the last few decades.

'What is the condition of the infants?'

Lucie looked at the babies, who, having never before been introduced to the delights of apple juice, appeared more than happy. 'They're very distressed. Possibly dehydrated,' she said, then, remembering how Len frequently called her out on her exaggeration habit, added, 'but they're settling. They're not injured.'

'Do they require an ambulance?'

'Oh no, I don't think so.'

'Any signs of a struggle? No other persons present?'

'Not that I can see.' Lucie looked around in alarm for any stalky persons or a broken lamp, a bloodied knife . . . 'It just looks so normal, except for no Carra. There's something very wrong, Sergeant, I feel it in my waters. She's not in the garden or fallen over. Not impaled herself on the fence or caught up in the clothesline. She's just vanished.' Lucie's voice wobbled on the word 'vanish'. 'I think we need a search party.'

Sergeant D dropped her constabulary tone and said, 'Don't worry, Lucie, it'll be fine. I'll be there in fifteen minutes. Have you spoken to Duncan?'

'No, I'll phone him now. Oh God.'

▼▼▼

Carra was in the depths of an oddly delightful dream about teaching Josie and Ursula Andreas how to grow water lilies when she was startled back to the hilltop by the loud chatter of a very cross plover.

She sat up, gasped, rubbed her eyes and said to the plover, 'Jeepers, you gave me such a fright!' She watched as the plover fixed her with its combative, masked stare and spread its wings while three tiny babies (little balls with legs) sped away behind it.

'Hey, it's all right, I'm not going to hurt your little ones . . .' Carra stopped, gasped again, checked her watch (which wasn't on her wrist) and saw with alarm that the ambling cows had moved all the way to the other side of the paddock. She clambered to her feet, brushed the straw from her clothes and, with heart pounding, ran full tilt back down the hill.

▼▼▼

Lurlene and Walt Wallace, both 78

Lurlene: Walt and I met at the Bothwell Picnic races in 1964 and it was love at first sight. For Walt. I had a crush on his friend, Virgil Shapter. But it was Walt who got my heart in the end, with his bashful eyes, and the way he could run down a ewe.

Walt: They had a jackaroo competition at the picnic races. We had to catch a greasy pig.

Lurlene: They had to catch a greasy pig. I never thought I'd be a farmer's wife. I'm from New Norfolk, a baker's daughter. I had big dreams of becoming a cake artist. But I fell for Walt and then I had babies and that was that. Sometimes I used to feel real angry about being the one to stay home. But the anger was more tiring than the babies, so it was better to just shut up and put the porridge on. I went a bit sullen, I suppose. I thought there was something really wrong with me. It was Walt who suggested I should try cakes again, and now I decorate cakes for everyone's occasions. And I help Walt on the farm. He says he can't do without me, can you, Walt? I don't feel so angry anymore. Most of the time I'm glad I didn't marry Virgil Shapter.

Walt: He'd drink his own bathwater, Virgil Shapter would.

Chapter 4

Thankfully for Lucie, it was the secretary of St Margery's Ladies' Club, Abigail Snelson, who received her phoned-in apologies – one for not producing any flower replacements and another formal apology on behalf of her position as vice-president of St Margery's for having to miss the Management Committee meeting.

'It's an extreme family emergency,' Lucie stressed. 'I should probably talk to Patricia. Should I?'

'Oh, Lucie,' said Abigail, 'I hope no one's dead or anything.'

'No, no.'

'Or maimed,' Abigail added, then, with a cough, finished with, 'Don't worry about Patricia, I'll let her know.'

'Thank you, Abigail,' said Lucie with genuine relief. 'I'll be back in touch.'

Abigail took the news back into the committee room, where the Management Committee meeting was well underway. 'Lucie can't come. An extreme family emergency. Oh dear.' Her voice wavered.

'Hell's bells, what new suffering is sent the way of the Finlays?' asked Bunty.

Abigail burst into tears. 'I can't bear it.'

'It wouldn't be something to do with their little girl, would it?' said Elaine. 'Holy cows, imagine that.'

'What's happened to the cows?' Daphne asked Bunty.

'They're talking about Lucie's tragical mishappenstance,' shouted Bunty.

'Perhaps someone's solved the mystery,' suggested Phoebe.

'I doubt it,' said Bunty. 'Only the wind knows by now. The wind and the birds.'

'Did Lucie say what kind of emergency?' Josie asked Abigail.

'Lucie's personal concerns,' snapped Patricia before Abigail could reply, 'are surely outside the province of our committee meeting. Pull yourself together, Abigail. And let's not indulge in a panic of conjecture. It's most unbecoming.' She directed her fearsome gaze in Josie's direction. 'Well, Josie, as our newest member, this is a good opportunity for you to take an active role in the meeting. You can undertake Lucie's job of reading the correspondence.'

Josie, who hadn't had time for a shower after her morning of calf-wrangling, and had barely managed to throw on a (requisite) skirt and wash her hands, was sitting uncomfortably by the window trying to summon the courage to open it. She suspected the air around her was infused with the smell of cow. The news of a Finlay family emergency further unsettled her, particularly after her unexpected meeting with Carra, which had left her feeling queasy. For months, she had plotted and rehearsed her reaction to such an encounter (inevitable in a town with one shop) and had determined to deliver a swift greeting, followed by a courteous departure. *That'll show her I have no time for her ghost friendship.* In the old version of their friendship, which was built on hilarity, teasing and endless conversation, courtesy was akin to rebuff. But the sight of Carra (a woman reduced, like an actual ghost) had not conjured indifference, and certainly not courtesy. Josie had felt a rush of warm, worried affection, followed afterwards by the yawning hollow of missing a friend very, very much. The scene had replayed in her mind all morning, until she was angry again, with Carra, and with herself, for somehow letting a precious thing slip away. She looked down at her hands, dusky with ground-in dirt against the pure white tablecloth.

Abigail took the attendance for the minutes. A paltry seven of fourteen members were in attendance, only just quorum. The list of apologies contained the names of women (with the exception of Lucie) who were perennial apologies, without ever actually apologising.

'I think we can safely say that Joyce Farquhar will not be returning,' said Patricia. 'That God-awful son of hers says she can no longer get herself out of bed.'

'Oh dear,' said Abigail. 'Poor Joyce. A little too well upholstered.'

'She's not paying her membership fees either,' said Phoebe, 'Actually, very few people are. I've sent numerous reminders, but what do we do?'

'No fee, no membership,' said Elaine, who continued to pay hers because it came with access to the St Margery's wine cellar. This was just one snippet of intelligence among many afforded to Josie by Abigail upon her inauguration. (Another was: 'St Margery was a medieval mystic who suffered hallucinations, had fourteen children and wore a hair shirt.')

'Then there'll be no members,' said Phoebe. 'Just us and a couple of stragglers on the Garden Committee, plus the two upstairs getting ready for yoga.'

'How many *paid* members do we have in total then?' asked Patricia.

Phoebe did a quick calculation and said, 'Nine, now that Joyce is at large.'

Elaine snorted. 'At *very* large.'

'*Nine?*' Patricia's calm rippled. 'That's the lowest in our history.'

'Let's face it,' said Phoebe. 'I mean, sorry, but no one has time for ladies' clubs anymore.'

'So you're saying that no one has time for community,' said Patricia. 'Or tradition.'

'Well,' said Phoebe. 'Yes, actually.'

Patricia's expression turned thunderous.

'Not me, of course,' Phoebe added hurriedly. 'I'm all about community.'

'And your usual book-keeping rates,' said Elaine.

'Well, *you* get your little honorarium.' Phoebe looked pointedly at the whisky glass in Elaine's hand.

'Josie,' said Patricia. 'You can do the rounds of the St Margery's members, reel them back in. It'll be a good opportunity for you to meet them all.'

'I've already met them all,' said Josie.

'All the better,' said Patricia. 'You can rouse some new members, too.'

'A recruitment officer!' said Abigail. 'I can make you up some pamphlets.'

Josie was already regretting her own decision to sign up to St Margery's; spruiking the benefits to others seemed inconceivable. She was searching for a response and wishing she was back on the farm, feeding out with Jerry, when the St Margery's doorbell rang.

Patricia flicked her eyes in Abigail's direction, which sent the latter scuttling towards the front hall.

'That's the doorbell,' shouted Bunty to Daphne. 'Go now if you need the lav.'

Patricia performed another slow blink.

Abigail returned a moment later, followed by a young girl, who appeared to be hiding behind a curtain of dark hair.

'Flo!' said Josie. 'Everyone, I think you know my daughter, Florence. She's just coming in to observe, if you don't mind.'

'Members of the public always welcome!' said Abigail, waving the St Margery's constitution.

Patricia sniffed.

'She's doing a project about Nowhere River. I meant to ask you, Patricia, but . . .' Josie put an arm around Flo's hunched shoulder, 'I didn't think she'd actually come.'

'What sort of project?' asked Elaine.

'A history assignment,' said Josie. 'For e-school. Architecture.'

'E-school?' said Phoebe.

'It's correspondence school, it's online. Very good so far.'

'You're not going to the high school?' asked Abigail.

'No,' said Florence from beneath her fringe.

'Didn't you know, Abigail?' said Elaine lazily. 'She got the clappers bullied out of her, poor love. Kids can be cruel.'

'The blightery little scum-munging bastards,' said Bunty.

'That's enough!' said Patricia. It wasn't a shout, but the edge in her voice cut off any further comments. 'So you've come to study St Margery's. It's been very particularly maintained to the Georgian era, so a perfect subject.'

'She's really interested in heritage conservation,' said Josie.

'Can she speak?' asked Patricia.

'Um,' said Flo, peeking out at Josie from behind her fringe. 'I'm really interested in heritage conservation.'

'Well, heritage conservation is a practice that should not be peculiar or even interesting,' said Patricia, clearly gratified. 'But I concede the point – we do display a rare self-respect for our foundations.'

'Nuyina has wormy wood in its foundations,' said Bunty. 'It'll all fall away if it's not careful.'

'You could have a look at the bottom pub,' said Elaine. 'It's been abandoned since 1996. Crying shame.'

'I wouldn't risk going in there,' said Phoebe. 'George says it's full of enormous rats. Go to the showgrounds.'

'Snakes there,' said Bunty. She hissed out a snake impression. Flo shrank a little further behind her fringe.

'Anyway,' hurried Josie. 'I hope you don't mind, Patricia. She won't write about anyone or anything without permission and approval. And we should get on with the meeting.' She steered Flo towards a chair in the corner and took care not to see what Patricia's eyebrows were doing.

They had to wait (seven minutes) for Daphne to return from the lav before the meeting could amble into full swing. Josie read the correspondence (the electricity bill and an invitation to a flower show in Bothwell) and found that she felt unaccountably nervous with her teenage daughter present.

'Right,' said Patricia the moment Josie finished the correspondence. 'Business arising.'

'What?' shouted Daphne.

'Turn up your hearing aid, Daphne,' said Patricia with exaggerated enunciation. 'Or shall I fetch the ear trumpet?'

Daphne fiddled with her hearing aid until it shrieked.

'Business arising,' Patricia said again. 'I was going to further address the *starkly evident*' – she gestured balletically to her company – 'matter of memberships. But before I do, does anyone have any new business to present?'

'No,' said Phoebe immediately.

'Mmm,' said Daphne Partridge, who hadn't heard the question, but was trying to look engaged, clearly terrified that someone would produce an ear trumpet.

'I think I might,' said Josie, who had been scrabbling around for a way to exempt herself from canvassing the town for St Margery's recruits and thought she may have arrived at something. 'Maybe not actual new business, just an idea.' She paused and waited for encouragement. None was forthcoming, so she ploughed on. 'Well—' she said, just as the floorboards struck up a chorus from the upstairs sunroom.

'Goodness, those yoga ladies are having a good go,' said Abigail, glancing at Patricia, whose eyes were turned skywards.

The floorboards were nearing an impressive soprano, accompanied by some alarming percussion. Even Daphne heard it. She looked worriedly at the ceiling as though expecting someone to come crashing through.

Patricia tapped the table. 'Carry on, Josie.'

'My knees are very wrinkly,' said Daphne suddenly. 'They look at me from the mirror with very sad faces.'

'Oh, Daphne,' said Abigail. 'I'm sure you have lovely knees.'

'Lovely?' said Patricia. 'The definition of lovely is beautiful and attractive. No one's knees are *lovely*. I do despise the way people throw *lovely* around willy-nilly when actually not many things are truly, properly lovely. Everyone's a "lovely woman" these days, especially to you, Abigail. I haven't seen any *actual* lovely women in Nowhere River for years. YEARS. Just this morning, I saw Caroline Finlay in the High Street *in her nightdress*. Imagine! She was once verging on lovely and now, well, what a tabby she turned out to be. I do wish everyone would stop lowering their standards. No one has any shame these days.'

Hearing this offhand defilement of her friend, Josie's back straightened involuntarily and she felt suddenly hot. She felt Flo's eyes on her.

'That's a bit rough,' said Josie, more feebly than she'd have liked.

There was a bit of silence then, followed by another series of thuds from above.

'I hope no one does themselves an injury,' said Phoebe. 'There's no money for an increase in insurance premiums.'

'We have a record number of participants today,' said Abigail brightly. 'They're probably just jostling for space.'

'How many exactly?' asked Patricia.

'Two,' said Phoebe. 'I've checked the takings already. Ten dollars. Lurlene left an IOU. I wouldn't encourage IOUs here – so many forgetful brains.'

There was another creak, followed by a quiver of laughter and then silence.

'They're enjoying themselves, though,' said Abigail. 'And the instructor is amazing. She's come from Hobart and you should see how serene she is, she exudes calm. Her name's Alchemy.'

Patricia closed her eyes. 'You had something to say, Josie?'

The floorboards were silent then and the recess was long enough for Josie to say, 'So it's just a vague idea at this stage, but why wouldn't you run some sort of competition, with a prize, with the stipulation that all entrants must commit to a St Margery's membership? I remember how motivating the competitions were at the Nowhere River Show, just because there were prizes and accolade and things to be proud of. Everyone used to get involved. Maybe there's just not enough accolade these days. Not enough pride.'

'We are not a game show,' said Patricia tiredly.

'And we can't afford prizes,' said Phoebe.

'Well, we could get it sponsored, the way the show used to be,' said Josie. 'That way we could have some prize money, or other incentives, but money's usually best.' Josie could feel her idea taking shape, charging her confidence. *I should do this more often,* she thought.

'It would be a win–win situation for everyone,' she continued, looking around the room to see that the women were listening with apparent interest. The sight surprised her, then didn't, as she realised that at home on the farm, she had never really voiced any of her own ideas. Jerry and his stalwart belief system were the ideas in the family. Josie, bound up by devotion and conservative line-toeing, had always been the one listening. She looked up at Patricia, a woman who wore her opinions as comfortably as her well-cut blouse, who would never countenance the idea of losing her values among the washing, or to the surreptitious vacuum of love.

'Everston Pastoral will sign up as a sponsor,' Josie concluded, but her words were lost to an enormous thump from upstairs, followed by a clatter, a scream and an affronted peal from the chandeliers. Most of the Management Committee jumped to their feet in fright.

Josie was the first to arrive in the sunroom, followed shortly by Abigail, Elaine, Phoebe and Flo. They were (thoroughly) confronted by the image of Tabitha Gillies, the club's long-time bridge professional, flopped unconscious atop a screaming Lurlene Wallace.

Alchemy, whose state of serenity appeared wholly challenged, was scrambling to liberate Lurlene and place Tabitha in a more secure position. Patricia arrived coolly on the scene a number of paces behind the others, performed a brief survey, picked up the sunroom phone and dialled triple zero. 'Two ambulances, please. St Margery's Ladies' Club, Tiya Street. On the double.'

'Can anyone do CPR?' shouted Elaine, looking hopefully at Alchemy. Tabitha's face, now repositioned, was starting to match the bluish shade of her hair. Alchemy, by now in an apparent state of shock (or extreme meditation), said nothing and stared at the wall.

Patricia, her face now filled with a certain brand of disdain she reserved for hippies and overweight people, knelt beside Tabitha and put her ear to her mouth, then pushed two fingers into Tabitha's meaty neck, sighed deeply and said, 'First-aid box, Phoebe, now. The big one. You do the breaths, Abigail, I'll do compressions, thirty to two, though I'm not sure her encumbered heart will thank us.' Abigail looked fearfully at Tabitha's slack mouth.

Phoebe hurried in with the first-aid kit and without too much hurry at all, Patricia expertly dished out the necessary Tabitha-saving equipment. Josie gently stepped in for Abigail, who seemed more than grateful.

'You're a marvel, Patricia,' breathed Phoebe. 'Is there no end to your accomplishments?' Patricia gave a tiny sniff of pleasure as she expertly assembled some sort of breathing apparatus.

'Come on, everybody,' said Elaine. 'Let's go and have a sherry, much more relaxing than yoga any day. You'll have to reschedule the class,' she said to the catatonic Alchemy. 'It's lucky you yoga people are flexible.' She chuckled all the way down the stairs.

▼▼▼▼

Half an hour later, most of the St Margery's members (and a number of extraneous onlookers from Marceline Cash's hair salon across the road) were on the footpath of Tiya Street, watching two ambulances speed away.

'It's all happening today, then,' said Elaine, puffed up with news (and sherry). 'The ambos were saying that Sergeant D is out at Kinvarra, too. Must be something big going on down there. Lucie's family emergency.'

Josie's stomach lurched. 'Did they say what?'

'Nope. Probably Patricia phoned them to report Carra Finlay's fallen standards.' Elaine laughed again and wobbled tipsily on her feet. 'It's criminal behaviour around here, getting about in your foundation garments.'

'What?' said Daphne.

'Carra was in the street in her underwears,' shouted Bunty, loud enough for the hair salon clientele to hear.

'Lucie did sound in a flap,' said Abigail. 'I hope everything's all right out there.'

'That would explain why I couldn't get Dr Duncan here,' said Phoebe, who had been admonished by Patricia for not raising the doctor for some back-up support. No one had pointed out that a GP was perhaps superfluous to requirements in the face of two ambulances and Patricia's medical equipment. No, everyone always leaped upon an excuse to call Duncan.

'Come on, dear,' shouted Bunty to Daphne. 'Let's get you home.'

'I'll drive you both,' said Josie. 'Flo and I should head off too.'

'No, thank you,' said Bunty. 'We like a bit of a saunter, don't we, Daphne?'

Daphne shouted, 'We'll go and tell the river about poor Tabitha.'

Bunty linked her arm into Daphne's. 'And the river can tell the willow, the willow the bumble bee.'

As they tottered away, Josie heard them carol, 'And the bee can tell the grapevine, while the river tells the sea.'

▼▼▼

Patricia was still in the sunroom when Josie poked her head in to take her leave. She was sitting on a chair by the window staring at a framed photograph on the wall. Josie waited, admiring Patricia's impeccable posture, and then waited a bit more, until she wondered whether she should knock, or cough.

'Nineteen fifty-seven,' said Patricia, just as Josie was working up to a knock. 'That was the first ever meeting of St Margery's. Twenty-eight vibrant women. Most of them under forty. Energetic, willing.'

Josie, unsure whether Patricia was talking to her, said, 'Good women.'

Patricia turned and looked at Josie.

Why, thought Josie, *does this feel like the first time she has ever seen me?*

'Look at them,' Patricia said. 'Splendid women, all of them. Fresh-faced, lovely . . . properly lovely.'

Josie hid her fingernails and wondered what her hair was doing.

'Not a trace of osteoporosis or heart disease.' Patricia drew in a breath, stood up and brushed nothing from the front of her tailored pants. 'Something must be done,' she said. 'Yes, it *will* be done. Josephine, I think you've hit upon something with your idea. We *do* need a full-blown membership drive with incentives. Nine members is simply untenable. And now we're down to seven. I'm entirely certain that Tabitha will not be gracing us with her presence again, unless in spectral form.' Here, Patricia paused, and was struck by a visible shudder. 'So,' she continued, 'your idea of some sort of contest is a plausible one. A competition addressing everything that is lacking in the women of this town – physical fitness, emotional health, creative fulfilment, community engagement, feminine cohesion, philanthropy, gratitude, good presentation, productivity and, above all, pride.

The women of Nowhere River have been moodling around for long enough, and the town has suffered. It has lost its backbone. So, we will run a search, for an ambassador. An ambassa*dress*.'

Josie tried to think of something to say that didn't equate to moodling.

'We will have everyone enter our quest for Nowhere River's most exemplary woman between school-leaving age to one hundred,' Patricia continued. 'We'll have a crowning ceremony. What shall we name this inspirational personage?' Patricia looked up to the sky as though this divine creature had already materialised.

'Um,' said Josie. *God, what have I done?* 'I wonder if women might have enough on their plates?' She hardly recognised the timid voice stuttering from her mouth. *Speaking of backbone, what's happened to mine?*

'They have all the wrong things on their plates,' declared Patricia, 'This will be a mere change of diet. A fresh new outlook.'

'It might be tricky getting people to enter.'

'Oh no it won't. I will be offering up prize money of *one hundred thousand dollars*.'

Josie choked on nothing and burst into coughs.

'So,' Patricia went on, 'I'll call another meeting in the week or so, once I've fully thought it through. I'll write the conditions of entry. We will save St Margery's *and* Nowhere River from the scourge of entitlement.' She looked back at the photograph, as if summoning those splendid women's guidance. '*Ah!*' She held up her hands. 'I have it! She will be crowned "Miss Fresh and Lovely".'

Josie watched as Patricia threw a parting look towards the photograph on the wall before exiting the room, her backbone as rigid as a board.

'Fuck,' whispered Josie.

▼▼▼

Bunty Partridge, 88

My twin sister Daphne and I were born in Nowhere River, in the bedroom of the house we still own on Faulkner Street. It's empty now, because we've moved into Nuyina, which is the old people's home. We just got a bit too creaky for our house. It has a huge rambly garden and open fires to light. Daphne found it especially parlous. She is eleven minutes older and much creakier than me. We've tried to find tenants but no one's very interested.

We were beauties, people said. But we never found someone to marry. We worked as mothercraft nurses so we had our fair share of babies. Our mother wasn't good to us because she only liked dogs. So we were always good to the babies, in case their mothers weren't. We loved every single one of those babies. Some of them still visit us at Nuyina. We like it there. We couldn't be without the Noey. That river runs in our veins.

Chapter 5

Carra, still woozy from her doze in the grass, was still quite a way up the hill when she caught sight of both Lucie's Mercedes and Sergeant D's four-wheel drive. *Police!* yelled the letters on the side of the car. *Trouble!* Carra stopped running and felt her rushing heart skip.

What's happened to my babies? She steeled herself against a series of stinging snapshots, images and horrors that mothers learn to shy from or shake away. They brought her, for a moment, to her knees. She whispered an involuntary, desperate prayer. *'Please let them be okay, please, please, please . . .'*

The rhythm of the words brought her back to her feet, and those feet took her home, to two very well babies playing on the floor with Sergeant D, a frowning Duncan, some crashing relief and a lot of music to face – Lucie's music, in the first instance, which was shrill and shot through with unfamiliar rage.

'For goodness sake, Carra, where did you go?' she said, her blue eyes flashing.

Duncan's eyes were weary. *He's so sick of me,* thought Carra. He held her shoulders and inspected her face in genuine confusion. 'What happened, Carra?'

'Have you lost your senses?' trilled Lucie. 'Or is this some kind of joke? I thought you'd filled your pockets with pebbles and put yourself in that cursed river.'

Carra realised that Lucie wasn't just being dramatic. 'I'm sorry Lucie, I didn't mean . . . I'm fine. I just fell asleep up on the hill.'

'You left the babies to go up the hill?' said Duncan.

'I didn't mean to.'

Lucie snorted. 'What? So you slipped over and fell up the hill, did you? The babies were beside themselves, Carra, we all were.'

'I'm so sorry, my darlings.' Carra knelt on the floor beside Sergeant D and tried to bundle both babies into her arms. Daisy squeaked. 'I'm sorry. I don't know what I was thinking.'

'Carra,' said Sergeant D, taking a proffered woolly lamb toy from Ben. 'It is an offence to leave a child or children alone without reasonable provision for supervision and care.' She looked at Carra with genuine concern in her eyes. Carra noticed how clear they were, Sergeant D's eyes, so alert.

'Something terrible could have happened to them.' Lucie felt her theatrical impulses stir, then brought them into check. 'But we needn't get too book-throwy, Sergeant.'

'What I mean is,' Sergeant D explained, 'I know you wouldn't be one to break the law, Carra, or put your babies at risk, so there must be extenuating circumstances. You don't look well. Should you talk to someone? Are you postnatally depressed, for instance?'

'I don't think we can just come out and ask, can we?' said Lucie. 'Isn't there a sort of quiz?' She sat on the couch, leaned in towards Carra and said sagely, 'Do you love your babies?'

'Yes, of course,' said Carra.

'Have you contemplated suicide?'

'No!'

'She's not depressed,' said Duncan. 'I would have seen the signs.'

Would you, though? thought Carra.

'Look,' she said. 'Sister Poke grilled me about this just today.

I don't have postnatal depression. You can ask her, Sergeant D, she'll have the documents.'

'Oh good,' said Sergeant D. 'She's the one I was going to suggest you see for therapy. She's done a course, apparently.'

Carra felt sickened by the thought of having her innermosts poked by Sister Poke once a week. 'No, thank you.'

'I would strongly encourage it for your emotional wellbeing. And we can't risk you running away again,' said Sergeant D. 'I could enforce it.'

'But I didn't run away. I was getting some air. I was tired. I fell asleep on some straw, there were cows and a breeze and sleepy things up there. I just—'

'Carra,' said Lucie. 'This baby business is very, very hard. And you have two of the little blighters. Let's all of us have a think about some strategies for you.'

'There's a childcare centre in Bothwell,' offered Sergeant D.

'Can we maybe talk about this another day?' Carra looked beseechingly at Duncan, but Lucie was on one of her missions.

'The garden is looking poorly and the fridge smells.'

'Of course the garden is poorly,' said Carra. 'It hasn't rained for thousands of years and if I happen upon a spare minute, I have to use it to tidy up, or mush up pumpkin. I won't run away, the babies aren't at risk, I'll clean the fridge.'

'I'm only too happy to hang around for a bit,' said Sergeant D. 'I'll play with the babies, you have a sleep, Carra. Dunc can go back to work . . .' Sergeant D trailed off. 'Or is that a bit, you know, weird?'

'Thank you,' said Lucie. 'What a kind offer, but you're needed elsewhere, of course.'

'Mum, Sergeant D,' said Duncan, 'thank you for everything, but it's fine. You can go. I'll take the rest of the day off, Carra can have a sleep.'

'But you can't cancel a whole afternoon of patients!' said Lucie. 'The town will be in ruins, what with the sudden change in the weather and everyone so ancient or unhealthy. I'll stay, you hop into bed, Carra.'

'You know,' said Carra, feeling an unexpected surge of energy (*Oh look, anger reserves*), 'Lucie is right. This town will be *destroyed* without you, Dunc. Like, torn apart. So yes, you should go back to your rooms and see to your people. Really, Lucie, I don't know why you didn't call your son Jesus. Someone get this man some loaves and fishes, everything's going to be all right.'

There was a paperweight silence and from beneath it, something fluttered inside Carra. A gust of wind made the house creak, a draught puffed motes of dust into a beam of light. Carra watched them billow. She wanted to be one, a dust mote. Or something else with no expectations, something that other people could clean up and take responsibility for. A child, an old woman, a missing person, a drowned person. *How many pebbles would I need in my pockets?* The thought startled her. She looked at Duncan. *Oh, that beautiful Duncan face, set so perfectly into that gorgeous nature.* Guilt twisted in her chest. 'Oh God, I'm so sorry.'

'It's okay,' said Duncan. 'You're tired and overwhelmed.'

'That must be it,' sighed Carra. 'Lucie, I'd love it if you could stay. I'll have a really, really good sleep and be right as rain when I wake up.' She laughed weakly. 'Wait, what's rain again? I only know wind, which drives me crazy. Clearly.'

Some of the trouble disappeared from Duncan's brow. 'I'll send an apology for tonight's halls and parks meeting,' he said. 'I'll be home as soon as the last patient leaves. We'll talk more once you've had a good sleep.'

What are we going to talk about, thought Carra, *how baking soda absorbs fridge smells? Whether you want to be married to such a poor excuse of a wife?*

'Oh, you should go to the meeting. Really. I'm so used to tackling the witching hour alone, you'll only get in the way.' Carra had tried to make these words light, but they clunked.

'Nope, I'm coming home.'

'I'll be at that meeting,' said Sergeant D, with a dimpled smile for Duncan. 'I'll pass on anything important. It's a routine get-together so we'll just be going through the motions. Rising insurance premiums, decreased hall usage, you know. The usual.' Sergeant D gave a tinkling laugh.

Carra thought about how she had once planned to take garden-design classes in the Nowhere River Hall, and how no one had ever asked if she wanted to go to the halls and parks meeting so that she might know what 'the usual' was and be able to laugh prettily about it.

Sergeant D made some motions of departure. 'Right, well, I'll have to check in on you, Carra, see that there are suitable measures in place to ensure this sort of thing doesn't happen again. It'll be on my head if one of these infants gets themselves tangled up in the curtains or some bloody thing.'

'I'll keep you informed on how things are going,' said Duncan.

Wonderful, thought Carra. *You two highly evolved, ridiculously attractive humans can have a nice cosy chat about hapless Carra. The one not fit for purpose.* Carra noted Sergeant D's flattering uniform, her glowing skin and her authority. Like a small-town superhero.

'Well, I'll be writing a formal report and making regular checks,' said Sergeant D. 'And I'll need to see some evidence that you're getting some therapy, or you, know, engaging somehow. There's a mothers' group at Bothwell. You need to get out and about.'

Oh, for fuck's sake, thought Carra. *Next someone'll say I'm looking washed out.*

'And I'll check your iron levels,' said Duncan.

'A little piece of juicy steak once a week wouldn't hurt,' added Lucie, who refused to accept that her son had married a vegetarian.

Carra merely nodded.

'And,' said Sergeant D as she made for the door, 'I'd love to look after the babies anytime I'm not working. I really would. If that's, you know, anyway . . .' Sergeant D blushed, and she turned away as the air quivered.

'Thank you,' Carra said to Sergeant D's back.

'That's a really kind offer,' called Duncan as Sergeant D left.

Without turning back, she raised one hand and said, 'Sure thing.'

'Eek,' said Lucie, once Duncan had closed the door. 'Little taint of awkward in the room. Such a shame, isn't it, that she's never found a chap, had her own babies.'

Duncan grabbed an apple from the fruit bowl and bit into it. The crunch put a full stop on the topic. 'Right, you,' he said to Carra. 'Something to eat, then bed.'

▼▼▼

Later, Carra was deeply submerged in her bed, slipping in and out of a state that was half sleep, half I-should-be-up-reading-storybooks-and-singing-lullabies, when there was a soft knock on her door.

'Are you awake, Carra?' came Lucie's voice.

Carra considered the question.

'Carra?' The door opened a little.

Carra replied with a rustle of the doona.

'Sorry,' whispered Lucie. 'But I have some news and I just couldn't contain myself. I think it'll cheer you up.'

Carra rolled towards Lucie. 'What's the time?'

'Twenty to five.'

Carra gasped and raised herself, flapped about trying to untangle an arm from the sheets and then patted her tender, heavy breasts. 'God, they must be hungry.'

'They've had plenty of water,' said Lucie. 'And lots of fruit. We're having a lovely time out here. I made them some playdough. And some vegetable soup for you, with a beef-broth base for the iron, no actual meat. But listen, the happiest of happenstance has just happened!'

Carra decided that the sound of the doona's rumplings in her ear were far more appealing to her than whatever Lucie had to say.

Lucie piped on, regardless. 'Well, it's not all that happy for Tabitha Gillies. She died this morning at St Margery's, poor love. Though there wasn't much quality of life there, what with that goitre.' Lucie left a pause for Carra to fill with appropriate dismay, but it remained empty. 'Anyway, she fell on Lurlene Wallace, and her death – as well as the simultaneous breakage of both of Lurlene's hips – has prompted Patricia to go on a full-blown Margery membership drive.' Lucie paused mid-beam, for effect.

'Right,' said Carra.

'She's gone quite bananas, in fact,' Lucie continued, 'but it's an *incredible* opportunity to get all of us out of our ruts. It's a competition: a search for an ambassadress. One hundred thousand dollars to the best woman in town! Can you imagine? The place is abuzz! We have to come up with a community-improvement plan or some such. And prove ourselves to be presentable, effective citizens. And join St Margery's. There's a community meeting about it in a few weeks, apparently, once Patricia's documented the terms. You will come, we can take the babies. The sergeant will see you, she'll be appeased. Everyone will surely enter but you could have a real chance at being the winner. You were born to be a beauty queen. You just need to find your project idea and your mojo.'

Just the word 'mojo' seemed exhausting to Carra. Then, upon establishing that Lucie wasn't hallucinating, sleepwalking or dispossessed of her marbles, Carra looked at the hollow in her pillow and thought she'd gladly forgo $100,000 for a week in bed, followed by the long overdue achievement of the luminous life she'd always imagined for herself.

'Oh *and*,' continued Lucie, 'I think Daisy just said her first word. "Granny"! Isn't that perfect!'

Carra experienced a sensation in her heart that could well have been a tiny bit of competitive mojo.

▼▼▼

Having watched Daphne and Bunty's departure from St Margery's, Flo Bradshaw decided that she too would like 'a bit of a saunter' and a chat with the river. Citing her history project as reason enough, and agreeing to drop in to Pfaffs' for some necessary items, Flo was left to take the long way home.

There were a few gardens to inspect on her way. Flo had recently learned that Nowhere River was once, in a bygone, house-proud era before water quotas, a hotbed for green thumbs. Springtime had unearthed all sorts of floral history. She wafted a hand in the warm, pillowy air, saw a perfectly formed cloud and felt pleased that the sky was otherwise clear. *It's hard to know*, she sometimes thought, *how many nice little clouds are lost on an overcast day*. She quite often felt sad for things she couldn't help. Like a fresh sprig of leaves blown off by the wind before summer or a rooster with a wobbly call. Looking at all the daisies in a nature strip and deciding against a daisy chain, she instead tried unsuccessfully to identify the dull ache in her chest. Had she more experience, she might have understood that the feeling was nostalgia. Her encounters at St Margery's and the downfall of Tabitha Gillies had left her feeling wistful on behalf of all the people watching time fade their days and take their comforts away. The wallpaper in the sunroom at St Margery's, she'd noticed, featured a French toile farmyard scene, so bleached by the sun that it was hard to tell the ducks from the pigs, and the farmer from his wife. She thought of her own early childhood in the farmyard and wished herself there, back when the sound of the chooks amazed her and the tiny fluffball chicks seemed impossible.

From somewhere above, a cockatoo screeched. Its grating performance reminded her to put some thought towards how to bring Cosette Hamilton undone. Cosette had a Pomeranian pup, perfect blonde hair and an ego dripping with sickly mock humility ('I can't bel*ieve* I'm the only girl in southern Tasmania to be selected for the state eisteddfods, I feel sooo bad', et cetera). She called Flo 'Flo-poke' or 'Loser' or (more recently) 'Drop-out'. Flo's fantastical Cosette takedowns were her most creative and vibrant thought productions. This time she imagined the screeching bird swooping over Cosette in the schoolyard, carefully lining her up and splattering her smooth pink face with its white poo.

These sorts of thoughts took Flo all the way past Nuyina and onto the river flats on the northern side of the river. The Clyde Flats, named for Walt and Lurlene's sheep property, Clyde Farm, had once run all the way between Bothwell to Nowhere River. The Flats, onto which Flo's springy skips took her that day, boasted a walking track, three derelict fisher cottages and a convict-built granary known as the Abergavenny ruin. Abergavenny was a crumbling stone structure with a sagging roof, elevated on precarious-looking staddle stones. Next to it stood a lopsided brick chimney and a weather-beaten gum Flo had nicknamed 'the lonely tree'. It was all – cottages, ruins and tree – owned by the local council and heritage-listed. The whole town looked forward to the day it might collapse so it could be cleared away and cleaned up, the stone and bricks repurposed elsewhere.

'Makes us look like a ghost town,' Flo's father Jerry often said.

Everston farmhouse, Flo's home, was exactly a kilometre from the fisher cottages and not five hundred metres from Abergavenny. They, and the river, formed the landscape of home. Flo's bedroom looked out towards Abergavenny and she'd developed a strong affinity for the humble structures. Sometimes she'd whisper to the staddle stones, 'Hold on, old mates,' and to the lonely tree, 'I love you.' Often the tree, crooked and unassuming, waved back.

This day, she smiled at the fisher cottages, which winked at her, seemingly pleased to have the sun on their cracked windows. She felt another little fizz of spring gladness and performed a few more skips, then broke into a run. At the lonely tree, she stopped, placed a hand on its trunk and looked up into its gawky branches.

'Well, don't this day just razz your berries,' said a rough-hewn voice from close by.

Flo jumped and turned to see Cliffity Smith sitting on the edge of the brick chimney. He seemed to Flo to be as old as the Whistler Hills behind him. But wiry, like the lonely tree. His red beanie matched the chimney bricks and the sagging lower lids of his eyes.

'Hello,' said Flo. Then, remembering her manners, added, 'Mr Smith.'

'Cliffity to you, lass,' said Cliffity Smith. 'Mr Smith was my poppy and he met d'liverance moons and moons ago. So many moons.' Cliffity looked into the sky. 'Good riddance to another bogarty winter.'

'Yes,' said Flo, who wasn't quite sure what she was agreeing with.

'Thought I'd bring Bandit and the sprites here for a visit. They is plum sick of livin' in with the crumblies at Nuyina. Some of 'em are only eighty, and given up on ever skippin' stones on this river again.'

'Bandit and the sprites?' Flo wondered whether Cliffity was part of some sort of band. *Or maybe*, she thought, *he's an actual ghost, haunting the streets and riverbanks with his creepy friends.*

'They's me ferrets.'

'Oh, of course,' said Flo. Cliffity and his ferrets were so common a sight in Nowhere River that they had become part of the landscape.

'Rabbit 'oles a-plenty in this patch,' continued Cliffity. 'Reg'lar playpark for 'em now that the wombats have taken off.'

'They'll come back though, won't they? The wombats?' Flo felt a pang of worry. 'They've always been here.'

'Doan reckon, duck, them wombles are knowing as all get out, they'd have their reasons.' Cliffity pulled a rubber chicken out of his pocket and squeezed it. It startled Flo with a series of wheezy squeaks.

"ere she is,' he shouted suddenly. 'Dasher. She's the smartest by far. Knows the 'ometime bugle.' He squeaked the chicken a couple more times.

Flo had to search the vicinity before locating a slinking, leaping body and a neat, slightly disgruntled face with little shiny-bead eyes.

'Dash, me girl, where's the rest of 'em? Lost in the rabby wazza?'

'There they are,' said Flo, pointing at the side of the granary, where two more little faces were bounding towards them. 'Oh, they're so sweet.'

'Them's Barbara and Narelle. We'll have to wait a minute for Bandit. He's a tricksy rummin', that one.'

While they waited for Bandit, Cliffity let Flo hold Narelle. ('She's the neighbourly one.') Narelle chirped into one of Flo's ears while Cliffity nattered into the other. He told her tales from his life as a butcher, about his enormous collection of garden gnomes and the times he ran a trick display with his ferrets at the Nowhere River Show.

'Thems were the daysies.' He wiped a tear from his eye and reached into his pocket. "ere's a little mate for ya,' he said, placing a small gnome in her hand. Red hatted and ruddy cheeked, with an impish grin and a fishing rod, the gnome could have been a caricature of Cliffity himself.

'Thank you,' said Flo.

Cliffity smiled and clicked his dentures. "e'll keep ya laughin's up, remind ya that it's a good and lucky thing to live on the smile of a river.' He swept a long arm in the shape of the river bend. 'Now where's our Bandit, Narelle?' he said with a sniff. 'That wily rascal, 'e come back dead and I'll kill 'im.'

Cliffity spent the next twenty minutes or so pacing and muttering and squeaking his rubber chicken over various rabbit holes.

Flo had just begun to wonder whether she should call in for help, when Bandit, with his enigmatic masked face, appeared from a hole and eyed Flo suspiciously.

'Flamin' 'eck, Bandit,' shouted Cliffity. 'Where's you been? Set yerself up a camp down there, didja? Have a cuppacino and a bit o' cake? Or was ya snufflin' about one of them 'amilton moonshine cellars?' He winked at Flo. 'Swoozie 'amilton's always parrotin' on about them cellars.'

Flo smiled politely and watched Bandit as he weaved his way to Cliffity's boot, where he was scooped up and given a rough kiss on the top of the head.

'You silly old boob,' Cliffity muttered. It wasn't clear to Flo whether he was referring to himself or Bandit.

'That's us then,' said Cliffity. 'We'll be off to make a wigwam for a goose's bridle.'

But it was a few more minutes before he had his business of ferrets clipped into their walking harnesses and on their way with a 'Toodle-pip, lass'.

Flo watched after them in slight puzzlement and wondered again whether Cliffity was a ghost that everyone saw but never noticed. She looked at the gnome in her hand, at his little wonky hat and his white eyebrows. *I notice you, Cliffity.* She wished she could see his ferret trick show. To the twinkling, smiling river, she whispered, 'The Nowhere River Show.'

On the short walk from there to the Everston driveway, she pondered the day's bewilderments some more until she reached the battered, blackberry-tangled letterbox at the top of her drive, where she realised she was an hour later than expected, and that she'd forgotten to bring home a tub of butter, a loaf of bread and a tin of tuna. Josie's shopping list rustled in her pocket.

▼▼▼

Cosette Hamilton, 15

Yeah, well, I don't really have time to be interviewed because I've started online French classes and I have to learn my verbs. French helps me understand ballet. I'm probably going to go to a dedicated ballet school, like you know that film *Ballerina*? That was so unrealistic because, like, it takes for*ever* to learn those moves. I mean I wasn't *en pointe* until I was, like, seven. I'm definitely moving out of Nowhere River. I can't be a nobody, living up on the Nowhere.

Chapter 6

On the day of Patricia's Miss Fresh and Lovely community meeting a few weeks later, a large crowd of people gathered outside the Nowhere River town hall. Towards the bottom of the front steps were Len, Lucie, Carra, Daisy and Ben Finlay, alongside Phoebe and George Costas.

'She hasn't opened the doors yet,' Phoebe snipped.

'She loves her dramatic pauses, does Patricia,' said Lucie.

'We all look quite desperate, don't we,' said George. 'Is there anyone *not* here?'

'We shouldn't be surprised about all this interest,' said Lucie. 'We *are* talking about one hundred thousand dollars.'

'Yes,' said Len. 'People would dance naked through the streets for that.'

'That wouldn't win Patricia's approval,' Lucie said with a snort. 'Would it, babies? Nudie rudies everywhere.' She tweaked Ben's toes. He squealed with delight.

'Are we really sure there's that much prize money?' asked Carra. 'I mean, why would she give away so much?'

'Absolutely sure,' said Lucie sharply. 'I wasn't sensationalising.' She turned back to the twins. 'I think your mummy considers me quite the histrionic.'

A flush of irritation heated Carra's cheeks. *Please don't send out barbs via my children*, she thought, wishing she could be somewhere else. *Anywhere.*

Len, clocking the tension, cleared his throat and said, 'It's loose change to Patricia, I think.'

'Yes,' said Phoebe. 'All those money trees she planted with Ambrose's inheritance.'

Everyone wistfully wondered again (the whole town did, on occasion) how Patricia could have known that the purchase of four ten-dollar abalone licences in the 1960s would turn into a multi-million-dollar investment portfolio.

'A humble, muscly sea snail,' muttered Lucie.

Carra spotted Josie and Flo Bradshaw walking up the High Street towards them. Her heart sank a little further.

'Hi, Finlays,' said Josie. She looked at Carra, who was dressed in a smart linen dress that somehow dishevelled her more than a tracksuit might have. Something about the creases in the skirt and the way it hung from her thin shoulders. Josie felt a rush of compassion and forgot again what it felt like to be cross with her friend, who gave a wan smile and said, 'Here we all are, then.'

'Rattling our cups at Patricia,' said Len. To Flo he added, 'If Lucie wins, perhaps I could convince her to trip off somewhere very exotic that's not the coast of Tasmania.'

Lucie rolled her eyes and said, 'Everything we need is on this island.'

Flo smiled behind her hair and silently agreed.

'Will you put in a project, Josie?' asked Lucie.

'Of course! The way beef prices are going, I'd be silly not to. Won't everyone?'

'Poor Carra didn't want to until I insisted.' Lucie patted Carra's arm. 'Penance for running away.'

'I didn't run away,' said Carra.

'What's your project idea?' asked Josie, sensing the need for a change of subject. 'Will you revisit your landscaping business plans? Remember when we broke into the old post office and scoped it out as a potential shop?'

'Ha,' said Carra. 'My fairytale shop idea. Back when I was living in a love song.' Carra heard the bitterness in her words and felt instantly disloyal to her idealistic old self.

'I always loved that idea,' said Josie.

'She's going to get the town moving,' said Lucie. 'Improve fitness and health.'

'So *everyone* can run away,' said Len, with a wink.

'Fitness and health? Nothing too challenging then,' said Josie. They watched Mr Pfaff from the grocery shop waddle past eating a doughnut.

'What's your Miss Fresh and Lovely project?' asked Carra, discovering that they were tricky words to say without a certain level of sneer. 'Cloud seeding?' She gestured to the dazzling blue sky.

'There's an idea,' answered Josie. 'I'm not sure yet. I thought I'd wait until the briefing. What about you, Lucie? A theatre show?'

'Don't encourage her,' said Len.

'That was my first thought, of course,' said Lucie. 'A grassroots version of *Les Mis* or some-such. But I thought talent might be a bit, er . . . sketchy.'

'Sketchy at best,' said Len. 'Even the grassroots are suffering in this dry old town,'

Lucie ignored him. 'So, I'm thinking about upscaling my Nowhere People project. Perhaps get photos of everyone and turn it into a book or an exhibition.' She glanced over in the direction of Vivvy Cox, who was being helped up the steps alongside several other Nuyina residents. 'My participants deserve to see their stories properly documented and shared.'

'Carra?' called someone from the crowd. Sister Julianne Poke emerged, leading with her pursed, purple lips. 'I heard about you running away. When I said you should get out and about, I didn't mean you should do the bolt.' She gave a snorty laugh. 'You still look peaky.' She studied Carra for a moment and then said, 'Has anyone heard how Lurlene is doing? Or seen Walt? I've found a spare wheelchair for her.'

'I'm looking for him, too,' said Phoebe. 'They owe St Margery's ten dollars for the yoga class.'

'I heard about your, um . . . not-running-away business,' Josie said to Carra. 'I shouldn't have left you the other day without demanding a drink and a full mental health assessment. I'm sorry.'

'I wasn't *running away* running away. I was just . . . I don't know. And I'm fine. Just a bit . . . it wasn't such a drama.'

Unconvinced, Josie inspected Carra for damage. Carra inspected back. Strong, capable Josie, who described her body as the type that would have a lifetime warranty, was in her usual rude health, but her thick chestnut hair was newly streaked with grey.

'Josie, you look amazing,' said Carra, trying not to stare.

'Amazingly old. I know. I just couldn't live the hair-dye lie anymore. Also, can't afford it. That's why I'm usually in my hat. So, I've joined St Margery's *and* I'm turning grey. Which means I can say things like "get off my lawn" and "what say you". It's great.'

Carra laughed. 'What about "thanking you", "mustn't grumble" and "bloody council"?'

'Yep, those too.'

Carra felt the sudden, freewheeling joy of her friendship with Josie, followed by a sharp turn in her chest.

Josie must have sensed a key change because she said hurriedly, 'I'm not letting you scarper off today without making a date for a catch-up, okay? I have to tell you all about perimenopause. It'll be riveting.'

'Oh gosh,' said Carra. And then, because there was a noisy silence, she said, 'Have you found your engagement ring?'

'Shhh,' said Josie, looking around at Flo, who was a distance away, behind her fringe.

'Still haven't mentioned it?'

'I just can't.'

'It'll turn up.' Carra tried to add something more helpful, but couldn't think of anything.

Len brushed a flake of paint from the fence post beside him. 'I hope someone pledges to tart up this old hall,' he said. 'She's a sorry old pensioner these days.'

'Bloody council,' said Josie.

Carra laughed again.

'You can bet your mother *they're* not here,' said Sister Poke. 'When did any of us last see the mayor? Colleen–Lyell Council, my arse. It's all Lyell and no Colleen from where I stand. Couldn't I tell you some stories.'

'Excuse me, Mrs Finlay,' came a small voice. Lucie turned to see that it had come from beneath Flo's fringe. Josie turned too, in amazement. She'd rarely witnessed her daughter address an adult unprompted and so directly.

'Yes, Flo?'

'If you want stories, you should talk to Cliffity Smith. He has heaps of them.' Flo shook her head so that her fringe flopped back and out of her eyes. Lucie saw that they were an unusually bright hazel colour.

'Oh, I bet he does,' Lucie said. 'He'll be next on my list.'

'And I wondered,' continued Flo, with a glance to Len, 'whether it would be all right if I could see the Riverhouse? For a history assignment.'

'Of course you can. Our funny old house,' said Lucie. 'Come over whenever suits. Just phone first so I can make sure Len hasn't left his smalls lying about. We can have morning tea and a tour, can't we, Len.' She smiled up at him.

Len looked at the eager expression and felt the nudge of a small qualm. He wondered what a qualm would look like, should it be a thing you could touch. Perhaps something like a river-stone.

'Leonard?'

'Yes, yes, that would be fine. And if I don't remember the facts, I'll make something up.'

Just then the doors of the hall were flung open by Abigail Snelson, who shouted into a crackly loudspeaker, 'Patricia says you may enter, in a courteous and convivial manner, and to please keep rowdy chatter to a minimum.'

Except no one understood a word she was saying and the able-bodied population of Nowhere River streamed in willy-nilly, with not all that much courtesy and a great deal of chatter.

'What did she say about cheese platters?' Carra heard Daphne Partridge shout. 'Is there morning tea?'

There wasn't any morning tea. Patricia was all business.

Upon entering the hall, community members received a leaflet containing a map showing district boundaries and a long list of eligibility requirements. They were given 'eight minutes precisely' to read through the leaflet. Carra skimmed through it the same way she had read any printed material since having babies, then had to go back to the beginning again for the sake of retention, but was interrupted by Daisy throwing a shoe at Father John, the Anglican minister.

Lucie, on the other hand, used all her eight minutes to read every word.

All entrants must:

- *be female*
- *be a resident of the gazetted municipality of Nowhere River*
- *be aged between sixteen and one hundred, and must not be attending school, to which their attentions must remain directed*

- *be or become a paid, engaged and productive member of St Margery's Ladies' Club (fees may be paid monthly or as an annual lump sum)*
- *not have a criminal record or a questionable background*
- *not behave in a manner that is offensive, acerbral and likely to bring the title of Miss Fresh and Lovely into disrepute*
- *provide, by no later than the specified date, a written submission in the form of a pledge, detailing how $100,000 worth of prize money would be spent (the Prize Money Pledge). It is expected that 100 per cent of the monies be utilised for the preservation, enhancement, sustainability and/or improvement of the Nowhere River community.*

The crowned winner of the Miss Fresh and Lovely quest must:
- *remain an active and representative resident of and ambassador to Nowhere River for at least a decade after receiving the title, unless death intervenes*
- *remain an active and representative member of and ambassador to St Margery's Ladies' Club for at least a decade after receiving the title, unless death intervenes*
- *remain true to her Prize Money Pledge.*

Note that entrants will be disqualified for misbehaviour, slander, deception or sabotage.

If Mrs P. Montgomery determines that one or more of the above criteria have not been adhered to, the crowned winner may be required to return prize monies and other accoutrements associated with her title.

Please note that should the winning entrant decease or become severely incapacitated, the prize monies will be utilised for community works the nature of which will be determined by a committee.

All submissions and subsequent entrants will be critically judged upon:

- *propriety, etiquette and conduct*
- *community spirit*
- *benevolence, munificence and compassion*
- *commitment*
- *enterprise*
- *presentation (appearance and health)*
- *sincerity and honesty*
- *patriotism and pride*
- *talent*
- *courage*
- *positivity and enthusiasm.*

Successful entrants will be granted a judging period of up to twelve months in which they may implement their initiative, display genuine relevant attributes (listed above) and prove their worth in the competition.

All entries will be granted at the discretion of the Competition Patron, Mrs P. Montgomery. Entries will be judged at the discretion of a small panel, with the final decision made by Mrs P. Montgomery.

'And now,' said Patricia, after the prescribed eight minutes, 'I will spell out and elucidate the rules and conditions. Please save questions for afterwards.' She moved gracefully towards an overhead projector. Carra shuffled in her seat and smoothed a wrinkle in her dress. Patricia was wearing a knee-length camel-coloured skirt and a white linen shirt cinched in at the waist with a navy-blue belt, and matching navy-blue loafers. Her hair was shining obediently under the control of a tortoiseshell slide. Carra noticed a woman a few seats away hurry some lipstick on and another smooth her trouser fronts.

On the back of the chair in front of Lucie someone had scratched *woopdefuckingdoo.*

Patricia switched on the projector and the contents of her pamphlet appeared lit up, in perfect Marion Richardson cursive, on a large screen beside her, which she tapped with a long piece of bamboo, for emphasis.

Just as Carra's breasts throbbed to remind her that it was feeding time, Patricia brought her presentation to its conclusion, with a final transparency that elegantly declared, *Good luck to all applicants and entrants.*

Then the questions began.

'What's "munificence", please?' called Marceline Cash, the town's hairdresser.

'Exceptional generosity,' said Patricia, looking pleased to be asked.

'And how long do the successful candidates have to prove their magnificent munificence?' asked Phoebe. 'When will you make your final decision?'

'In twelve months' time,' said Patricia. 'As stated previously.'

'Whaddaya mean by "questionable background"?' asked Tameka Deakin, a raggedy woman with tobacco-stained teeth.

Patricia paused a Patricia Pause, involving a slight head incline and an eyebrow movement, which might be missed by the majority but not by Lucie, who after years of vice-presidency had grown hypersensitive to Patricia's minutiae.

'Any background of mischief, misdemeanour, *drug abuse* or other offensive behaviours will automatically render an entrant ineligible,' said Patricia.

'You're stuffed then, Tameka,' came a shout from the corner.

'Fuck off,' yelled Tameka.

Patricia executed a long, elegant blink.

The mayor, who had indeed fronted up from New Norfolk despite Sister Poke's predictions, grasped the opportunity to let everyone know he was accountable and relevant, and stood up and boomed, 'Patricia, congratulations on such innovation. I heard about it on the grapevine as there was no formal notification to council. Have you had this cleared with the gaming commission?'

Patricia looked down at the mayor (something she could have done even had she not been standing above him on a stage) and said, 'A *game of skill* does not fall under the governance of the gaming commission and requires no permit in any state of Australia, nor does it require the involvement of council. I'll thank you for raising your hand if you have a question.'

'Patricia for mayor,' shouted someone from the back rows.

People laughed for a short moment before Patricia barked, 'Hecklers will be ejected. Yes, Josephine?'

'God forbid we're among the ejected hecklers,' whispered Len.

Lucie held in a laugh.

'Would it be acceptable,' said Josie, 'if the nature of the winning project led to the winner giving a lot of their time – time during which they would otherwise be working and earning – would it be acceptable to use some of the prize money to live on? At least for a bit while the project gets up and running.'

'Yes, that would be acceptable,' said Patricia. 'Within reason, salary replacement to allow for protracted commitment is partly the point of the prize money.'

'Thank you,' said Josie, and Patricia gave her a brief smile.

Josie sat up straighter in her chair and then felt annoyed with herself for enjoying Patricia's approval. She slumped back a little and wondered whether a single-malt whisky fell *within reason*. A nice glass of whisky was one of the things Josie missed most since the bum had fallen out of the beef industry and the winters stayed dry.

'Isn't it a bit sexist to just offer this to the ladies?' came a man's voice from the back.

'Yeah,' came another male voice, this one followed by a slap and an 'Ow!'

'And isn't all this just a tad degrading to women?' yelled Tameka.

There was an uncomfortable, *uh-oh* sort of silence in the room as Patricia became very still. The smile returned, this time reaching her eyes and lighting up her face.

Gosh, thought Lucie above the jangling of her alarm bells, *Patricia's quite lovely to look at when she's enjoying herself.*

'Heavens above, you're absolutely right,' said Patricia through the smile. 'Forgive me, and please know that some of my best friends are straight white males. It's just that, what with tens of thousands of years of oppression, emotional, physical and sexual abuse, of thankless, endless, fettered, apron-strung labour, and of persistent, flippant, baseless and frankly ball-less belittling by jackanapes like you, I considered it the *women's* turn to be in receipt of some sort of *edification*. How thoughtless of me. I would explain further, but I have neither the time nor the finger paints, so we shall continue moving on with our *celebration*' – a lingering look at Tameka – 'of female potential.'

'Seddle down, fucken Jesus,' said Tameka.

'Yeah,' sneered the hollow-eyed man beside her. 'Who fucken died and made you the Queen of fucken Sheba? Want a bitta this, Madam President?' The man raised his fist.

Everyone gasped.

'What?' the man shouted. 'I'm a fucken feminist, all right? I treat 'em equal.'

Abigail sent up a small prayer to spare the weak in the face of Patricia being told to *settle down*. But the instant was lost in a slowly built but rousing applause.

'Patricia for mayor,' shouted someone again.

'Kick that fucker out,' thundered Elaine Thorold.

'Hear, hear,' yelled Julianne Poke.

'Oh dear,' said Len.

'Did she say "ball-less"?' asked Carra, feeling suddenly alive for the first time since the hillside.

'Kick him out, kick him out!' shouted the crowd. 'Kick the mongrel out!'

'Leave Cryton alone,' screeched Tameka.

'Hey, hey, hey,' tried the mayor.

'That's enough,' said Patricia into her microphone. 'Enough!'

But a few of the men's shed blokes were out of their seats and moving towards Cryton and Tameka.

'Just fucken try me,' boomed Cryton. His face was a ghastly mask of rage.

'Come on now, come on,' said Len. 'That'll do, this isn't Billingsgate.'

But only Lucie heard him. She put a hand on his arm and said, 'Surely Sergeant D is here somewhere.'

Sergeant D *was* there somewhere.

'Oi!' she bellowed from the back corner. 'Everybody shush, please. Just calm down. Come on.' She picked up a chair and slammed it back down again. 'SHUT YOUR FRIGGING CAKEHOLES.'

Everyone shut their frigging cakeholes, even Daisy and Ben, who'd begun to wail.

'You and you.' She gestured firmly in the directions of Cryton and Tameka. 'Out!' She threw a thumb over her shoulder towards the door.

'Whaddid I do?' sneered Tameka.

'And you lot,' Sergeant D said mildly to the looming men. 'Out of it or I'll bash your bloody heads together. Sorry, Patricia, you can get on with your presentation very soon.'

'Thank you, Sergeant D,' said Patricia.

'As you wish, Sergeant *Darling*,' sneered Tameka as she grabbed Cryton's wrist and stalked towards the door. Sergeant D's eyes narrowed.

Carra sat up in her seat and cast an involuntary smile at Josie. Josie mouthed 'whoa' and smiled back. Everyone knew how Sergeant D preferred not to use her surname. Too many cocksure academy peers, one of whom was in the habit of patting her bottom and calling her 'Darl'. She famously rounded him up during an end-of-academy paintball game, and shot him six times in the chest and once in the balls.

'Youse can all get fucked,' shouted Cryton before the door slammed behind him.

'And that,' said Patricia into the microphone, 'is precisely why I am actively working to raise the abhorrent standards of this town. Generally speaking, when it comes to decorum, cohesion and good citizenry, Nowhere River is *sadly lacking*.'

Later, once peace was restored and Patricia was able to field a few more questions ('Do we need to get about in hats to meet your appearance standards?', 'Can my aunty from Magra enter, she lived here years ago?' and so on), the meeting was called to an end with the final announcement that, 'Submissions are due one month from today, at close of business – five pm on Monday the twentieth of December.'

Abigail opened the doors and everyone began to shuffle out, many with a newly determined set to their jaws. The dismissed Cryton, having apparently loitered outside for another opportunity to display his lack of decorum, stalked back into the hall, took the loudspeaker from Abigail's hands and shouted into it, 'Youse are all a pack of fuck-knuckles.'

Thankfully the ancient loudspeaker did a wonderful job of censoring his words, so only those close enough, including Len and Lucie, heard them.

'Strewth,' said Len. 'What's his story?'

Lucie took his arm and said, 'I don't know but I think it's important we find out.'

Len, seeing that she was quite serious, experienced his second qualm for the day and thought, *God starve the lizards, what next?*

Cryton Plunkett, 37

No fucker's ever given a damn about me. Not one, not ever. So I don't neither.

Cliffity Smith, 96

I ain't afeared of dying but one thing that does havoc with me brain box is what's to come of me ferrets and me gnomes when I'm gone. I had me gnomes all over the town once, used to sneaky them into people's gardens, like they'd just nipped round for a visit. Cheer people up, you know. But then some gobby ol' hoity-toities cast a petition about, so the gnomes are snuggled in with me at Nuyina now. And me ferrets, they're here too. I've had them since me dad got ferreting. He started out fetching rabbit skins and ended up with the butchery. Me shop and me house are still up there on Tiya Street, all shut up. Can't sell them for chippies. But yeah, I mostly stay on this Earth for gnomes and ferrets. I thought I lost one the other day, didn't I? Bandit, he darn vanished down at Abergavenny. He was gone a real long time and I thought that was it. I had a darn cold feel about me, the way the wombats must have when they leave their holes to the rabbits. Them wombles know when to leave off a burra. Anyway, he come back after all, musta found 'imself a friggin' timeslip down there. Yeah, I love me little fezzles.

Chapter 7

Carra watched as Daisy released a determined grip on her rubber giraffe and finally fell into sleep. In the neighbouring cot, Ben had already laid his lashes down on his cheeks, and was sending out little sleep sighs to mingle with mild air breezing in through the window. The year had slipped into December, the days were heating up, and Carra was finding Daisy trickier to settle than usual.

She decided, while bracing herself to creep from the room, that there should be a word for the feeling of adoration you have when you watch your babies sleep. It was more than adoration, because it was love fortified by achievement: the sheer relief of getting them to that point in time where they are temporarily safe from mothering mistakes. Love bolstered by the resolution to be better when they wake.

She made it to the door without squeaking a floorboard, and once out in the hallway, she tried to sort through all the things she'd resolved to do during naptime, but couldn't think where to start. She felt the clunk of the same faulty mechanism that caused her thoughts to evaporate the minute she walked into the grocery shop. *Another phenomenon without a name. Motherhood needs an expanded vocabulary.*

Boil the kettle was the first instruction from her brain. Others followed: Tidy the toys, look in the fridge, check the calendar

(Duncan's myriad commitments needed bracing for), check the birthday calendar (Duncan had eight godchildren, *for God's sake*), look in the fridge again, boil the kettle again, do something about her Miss Fresh and Lovely submission . . . but Carra paused in the hallway, in front of a framed wedding photograph, and all The Things scuttled away.

In the photograph, Duncan and his exquisite smile beamed out of the muted colours, right at Carra. A smile that was very nearly a laugh. *Such joy.* Against his cheek was another smiling face. A luminous young bride, with a touch of girl still about her, her shining hair softly waving, skin as clear as bells. Carra could hear the bells. On her face was an expression of utter delight, the look of having been collected up and placed in the echelons of the extremely fortunate. It was a face that would never think to envy a soul, not even the likes of Ursula Andreas. One of the bride's hands was curled softly around Duncan's neck, its pearly, perfect nails peeking out. A gesture of carefree possession. *He's all mine.* Carra looked down at her present hands, nails no longer pearly but ridged and chipped.

Carra had never considered herself beautiful, but the bride in the picture seemed almost so. *I very nearly lived up to everyone's expectations.* She reached out and touched the cheek of the shiny new wife, with eyes wide enough to see every detail of the perfect life to come.

We will have picnics, she had told herself. *There will be laughter in the kitchen, jasmine and lemon-drizzle cake. I will show him every day how much I deserve his love.*

And she had shown him, every day. In the traditional, passionate ways and also with other little gestures – sometimes spontaneous, often measured and planned. A little note left in his car, a heart-shaped sandwich, a love letter on his computer screen. Occasionally, early on, Duncan would bashfully acknowledge them, but seemed to stop noticing after a while, until Carra began to feel ridiculous, and smaller, as if each act of love was a giving of herself that whittled her away. More recently, she had thought of those silly little offerings with scorn and laughter. *Soppy nonsense.* Self-deprecation seemed a noble way to save face. But the words left behind a sad pity for the bride and her simplistic ideas of love.

'And now,' Carra said to Duncan-in-the-photograph, 'my day is made up of a million little things. But none of them are for me.'

She'd never got around to lemon-drizzle cake and there was occasional laughter in the kitchen, but mostly mess. *What's wrong with me? Why can't I get anything done?*

Carra thought of Josie, and all the getting-things-done she managed. It was Josie who had told her that when ewes have their first lamb, some calmly deliver their offspring and wait for it to feed, while others seem unable to believe what horror has befallen them, and bolt away with barely a backwards glance. High-tailers, Josie called them. *Am I a high-tailer?*

Her thoughts turned to Ursula Andreas. That well-trodden path. Carra realised with a little masochistic thrill that she hadn't checked Ursula's Instagram page recently. There would be more images to discover, dwell on and ache over. She derived particularly brutal relish from the shots of Ursula with her family, in some garden or other, all of them dressed in linen and gumboots, smiling at one another on a lawn so lush there wouldn't be the slimmest chance they could be dreaming of greener pastures. The dun-dry paddocks sat unmoving in the wind outside as Carra remembered the viridescence of the pastures she'd found herself in when she first met Duncan. Up until then, she'd always felt unremarkable and beige. *Am I just meant to be a misfit?* she wondered.

In high school, Carra moved in and out of a circle of polished city girls – pink-lip-glossed, hockey-playing head tossers with loud *oh-my-god* voices. They wore low-riding skinny jeans, collected Beanie Babies and had a relative that belonged to the yacht club. Most of them shone at something: dance, netball, languages or charm. Their entitlement was thinly veiled by cultivated manners and an eagerness to babysit.

Carra never saw herself as a true member of that circle, but she was kind and funny and looked good in skinny jeans, so was accepted. She didn't have any Beanie Babies, though she lived in a big house on the water. She also had a pretty face, but her mother wouldn't allow her to wear make-up. Carra wasn't particularly talented at anything, but she quite liked drawing and detective novels. Her mother was not just a member of the yacht club but the commodore, a world-renowned sailor and a fearless activist for ocean health. Her father was a three-time Sydney to Hobart line-honours skipper and a passionate patron of the whale-saving vessel the *Sea Shepherd*. Neither of them had time for frivolities such as drawing or novels. They encouraged Carra to join them on the high seas but Carra, while she learned to sail at a very young age, did not have a natural flair for reading the winds and was reliably seasick.

Carra's view of herself, therefore, reflected her parents' slightly pat affections: humorously hopeless, funny frizzy hair, slim, tall, soft white skin prone to sunburn, not very brave. This left her in a state of constant yearning for the right things to say, the right things to wear, how to be, how to have better hair, how not to care. She clung to her familiars – compliance, humour, athleticism and an occasional flaring of contrary competitiveness – hoping they might be enough to get her to a place of acceptance and occasional admiration. And they did, to a degree. By the time she reached her late teens she'd had several boyfriends and had kept a few of the friends, the more ordinary ones, who didn't care how fast she could hoist a spinnaker or how accurately she could read a spindrift.

She even had a fairy godmother of sorts, an elderly neighbour who inadvertently stepped in on similarly wobbly sea legs and took Carra's self-esteem in hand. Carra's parents were busy people, Carra a latchkey child. Her mother, who worked full-time to stock up her 'running-away fund' and keep her philanthropic interests burning, issued a daily command as she departed the house each morning: 'Work hard, enjoy yourself and don't be a dick.' Everything else she left up to her daughter. Carra would make her own way to school, then make it home again.

Cybill from next door, who was alone and not partial to social activities, became Carra's afternoon companion. Cybill had endless patience with homework questions, a large jar of melting moments and a sprawling, enchanting garden. 'Everyone should know that all we really need for company is a garden, some birds and the sky,' Cybill was fond of saying. It was with Cybill (by way of thanks for the homework) that Carra learned how to prune things, how not to overwater box hedge or upset the roots of peonies. How to work hard and enjoy herself. How to breathe in a garden and let it bloom into her imagination. How not to be a dick.

When Cybill's heart stopped one glorious April day as she grubbed out her dahlia tubers, Carra, through her grief and the melting away of any more moments with Cybill, decided that in Cybill's honour she would learn how to truly keep company with a garden, the birds and the sky. And so, after leaving school, she shrugged off the indifference of her parents and enrolled in a Bachelor of Landscape Architecture at the University of Tasmania. That same year and on the same campus, Duncan began his medical degree and their paths entered similar terrain.

Prior to university, Carra had heard of Duncan Finlay, but never put his fabled face to the name. He had attended school in his hometown, somewhere beyond Carra's city-limited awareness, and then enrolled at an all-boys boarding school for Years Eleven and Twelve. This afforded Duncan a mysterious attraction even before anyone caught sight of him and reported upon his extraordinary good looks. Such reports came to Carra via fervid gossip from girls with brothers at his school, or from someone who made a rare sighting as he was transported back to his hometown every Friday afternoon. She'd heard he lived on a river, and assumed him to be one of those people, leagues above her, with a strong stomach and an affinity for boats.

By the time he moved into a college for university, Duncan's hallowed reputation had been replaced by genuine popularity. He was known to be kind and good at sport, hard-working and bright. He moved in college-lad circles – country boys, farming stock, the ones who got up early for rowing training, drank beer on Sundays, were named Hugh or Tommo and called people 'old mate'. The girls, meanwhile, flocked.

Duncan maintained an element of enigma by being mostly absent from social events. His weekends were spent in Nowhere River or studying in his college room. He only occasionally attended parties and didn't seem to harbour fears of missing out. Carra occasionally glimpsed him, marvelled at his tanned skin and perfect teeth, imagined a parallel universe in which she had the courage to talk to him, and then got on with her day.

Duncan's popularity peaked in his third year of university, by which time he'd casually taken up with several of the flocking girls. By Carra's final year, it had become quite uncool to be interested in him. Like Baby-G watches or Tom Cruise. People started inventing reasons not to like him, a sort of self-protection. They tried 'boring', 'reserved' or 'pretty boy'. And sometimes 'robot'. But the underlying intrigue of him remained.

Carra realised that she herself had arrived at an uninformed opinion of his character: unapproachable, standoffish – even cold. What she didn't know, but had come to see, was that Duncan quietly shouldered a huge, tremulous investment placed in him by his parents and an entire Central Highlands town. He was regularly teased about how focused he was on his schoolwork, how faithfully he returned home most weekends and every holiday, but he never mentioned why it was so imperative that he never go astray.

Carra turned her attention to the bride in the photograph. 'Look at you,' she whispered, pointing a stern finger at her own face in the picture. 'You have him. You're in that parallel universe with the greenest grass. Everything you ever wanted. Now hurry up and be the luckiest woman in the world.'

Carra directed her feet to the laundry, where the walls, painted white for its soothing effect, felt cold. Carra thought that she'd quite like to sing something heavy metal and screechy, something counter to the hush of white. Either that or scream. Both of those would, she knew, wake the babies and send the day into tired-toddler chaos. So she picked up a pot of finger paint from where it languished in the wash trough, scooped out a blob of yellow and wrote *Carra* carefully across the wall.

'There we are,' she said, before adding a few fingerprinted dots. 'I was here.'

Standing back to survey her handiwork, Carra accidentally thought, with a twitch in her toes and a flaring of her old competitiveness, *What a perfect boost $100,000 would make to a running-away fund.*

▼▼▼

'I think I'm going to start a movement,' announced Lucie to Len as he came in from his daily shuffle with Beans to find her furiously whisking cake batter.

'Right,' said Len. 'I hope that's not a statement about your bowels, my love. Some things must stay sacred despite the indignities of the ageing marriage.' He loomed over the mixing bowl with his little finger poised for a taste.

Lucie slapped him away. 'Esther Very from the library is working on a museum, and she has reserved a whole section for my Nowhere People project.' She banged the whisk on the side of the bowl and handed it to Len. 'I am going to actively seek all the participants I can find so the tales of this town won't be lost to the ethers. It's a crying shame how many priceless words just disappear because no one ever asked. Honestly, I can feel them, poor long-lost things. Look, the river is rippling with them.' She nodded at the window, with its watercolour picture of hawthorn trees and shimmering brown water.

Len did as he was told, he looked at the river. 'Good god,' he said in mock surprise, 'you're right. There they are, all the bygone stories twinkling their way to oceanic obliteration. I should get my landing net and fish them out at once.' He put the kettle on.

'So the stories I've captured so far,' Lucie continued, 'have been taken from random conversations. I haven't had a very clear plan on how to structure my questions to get the good stories, the life-lesson type ones, right from the heart. And I haven't taken any photographs. I'll need to do some sort of photography course. I'm very inspired, Len. Do you know that no one has ever loved Cryton Plunkett at all, not a soul? Imagine that. No wonder he's such a twat.' Lucie sighed, her eyes still on the river. 'We're lucky, after all, Len.'

Len watched the late afternoon shine through Lucie's pale hair and ceased his mocking. 'It sounds like a very noble undertaking,' he said. 'And a happy bit of mudlarking. Wait for the low tides and you'll find all sorts of treasure.'

'I've done the research. They're big on the internets apparently, these ground-level introspectives into humanity,' Lucie said to the window. 'So Esther tells me. She's going to show me how best to put it all together into a permanent exhibition that can be added to in perpetuity.'

Len nodded his approval. 'And is this renewed enthusiasm arising from your good and generous nature, or does it have just a little bit to do with Patricia's Miss Fresh and Lovely?'

Lucie looked at him. 'Don't be ridiculous, Len, it has *everything* to do with Miss Fresh and Lovely, of course it does. I mean, I would like to think I would have happened upon the museum idea regardless, but actually pulling it together and finishing it, with a tangible result of exhibition standard, well, that's for the win, my darling.'

'We don't need one hundred thousand dollars.'

'No, but wouldn't it be lovely? Fresh and lovely. And I do fancy the idea of being an ambassadress. You'd have to call me "Your Excellency".'

'She's as daft as a brush,' said Len to Beans. 'Living in the land of the broken biscuits.' But he patted Lucie's bottom before reaching above her for the teacups.

'We have an extra for afternoon tea. Flo phoned while you were out, she's coming over to see Riverhouse for her history project.'

'Ah, yes.'

'She's a shy little thing. Perhaps we can coax her out of her shell a bit.' She hummed a tune and went to the pantry for vanilla extract. 'I'm sure you'll do your best tomfool act, darling, bring out her laughs.'

Len paused for a moment, a scoopful of tea leaves hovering in his hand and his thoughts running off to a faraway elsewhere. After a moment, they returned, with a little wake-up cough, and he said, 'Is Josie coming too? Perhaps you could ask Carra along.' He watched Lucie's nose wrinkle.

'No,' she said. 'Flo will be almost here by now, she's walking over. And Carra seems a bit distant at the moment. I think she's gone off me since the running away incident. I don't think I over-reacted, did I?'

'You might start by not calling it "the running away incident" with that ever-so-slightly melodramatic undertone.' But Len caught a glint of real concern in Lucie's face and added, 'I'm sure a bit of melodrama was entirely warranted under the circumstances.' He watched her as she gazed into the cake-tin cupboard.

'It's so tricky to know,' Lucie said, twiddling the cupboard latch, 'how much help to offer one's daughter-in-law. I try not to overstep, but I adore those babies, and Carra's own mother is so reliably unavailable, I just assumed I'd be called upon all the time.' She picked up a large square tin. 'It would be far easier if she were our actual daughter . . .'

Len turned the teapot, apparently lost in its pattern – a pretty pastoral scene with sheep and an apple tree with tiny people standing beneath.

'I can't blame her for not really wanting my parenting help, I suppose,' Lucie went on, returning the square tin to the cupboard. 'I've hardly earned my stripes in that department, have I?'

'Lucie.' Len's voice was taut.

'Sorry.' It was more a sigh than a spoken word. Lucie selected a round tin with a hole in the centre and set it on the bench. 'Anyway,' she said, 'I could be imagining things. Carra's so distracted, under-standably so. And I expect she felt a bit uncomfortably caught out after the running away— after the hill thing. She'll recover. And in the meantime'—Lucie glanced at the kitchen clock—'Flo will be here soon. She's such a nice girl, Len. So in the moment, so . . .'

Len waited as Lucie's gaze went to the window with its cloudless sky.

'She's so *here*.'

▼▼▼

Leonard Finlay, 66

Once upon a time, I was floating up the Nowhere minding my own business, in a boat called *Little Toot*, or was it *Wind Passer*? I barely remember. Anyway, minding my own business, when I bumped into a pack of pirates who hijacked my boat and stole my dog, Beans. And they told me that they would return Beans to me safe and sound only if I agreed to stay in the town of Nowhere River and keep a watch for the mythical and terrifying bottywaddler. Every riverside town must have a bottywaddler watcher. So that's what I have done, all these years.

Sometimes I dabble in a bit of town planning, but that's just a wily ruse.

Chapter 8

Flo was on the pebbled Riverhouse driveway, beginning to feel burdened by the idea of entering an unfamiliar domain and trying to find the confidence to use manners, when she saw Lucie waving to her from a window. Flo felt her face break into a huge smile. It surprised her, the smile, and had something to do with Lucie's sparkling eyes and her pink-rubber-gloved hand waggling cheerily through the French-paned window.

'Yoohoo!' came Lucie's voice, bright with notes of welcome. 'Come in, Flo, darling!'

Len opened the front door before Flo could knock. 'Come in, come in, I've just been in the cellar feeding the sea kelpies, there's two nymphs and a siren in the garden shed – oh, and don't mind the bunyip.'

'Don't mind the resident loon either, Flo. And come and have some afternoon tea.'

Flo relaxed. 'Thank you,' she said, following Lucie into the kitchen.

After a large piece of cake, more of Len's stories and some sniffs and a nuzzle from Beans, Flo found that she was laughing readily, and quite enjoying herself.

'All right, Len, the boring old truth,' said Lucie. 'No fantastical water creatures, please.'

'Well,' said Len, 'this was the first house to be built actually on the bend, making it the keystone of the town, really, even though Patricia and Poor Rosie assume they are the presiding squires up there on their Rises . . .'

'Len,' scolded Lucie.

'Yes, m'lady?'

'Flo has an actual history assignment to do. Could you attempt a modicum of reverence?'

'*If not for reverence*,' quoted Len with the theatrical voice he reserved for impressing Lucie, '*if not for wonder, if not for love, why have we come here?*'

Flo laughed again, delighted to have stepped into this strange Riverhouse realm. 'What year was it built, Mr Finlay?' she asked.

'Please, call me Len. My actual title is Professor the Honourable, anyway.'

'No, it isn't,' said Lucie. 'Oh Len, that's quite enough.' She sent an exasperated glance in Flo's direction. 'Professor of nonsense.'

'Or "Mr President" will do,' added Len. 'I still hold the office of president of the – admittedly defunct – Nowhere River Show, did you know?'

'Mum is thinking of getting the show going again,' Flo found herself saying. Then she blushed, because she remembered that she wasn't meant to tell anyone about the idea.

Lucie's eyebrows jerked upwards. 'The Nowhere River Show?'

'Um . . .'

'Holy gobstoppers, surely not,' said Len. 'She'd have to be mad.'

'My hat!' said Lucie, clapping her hands together. 'Good on Josie! Is it her Miss Fresh and Lovely initiative? How brave.'

'If she were to succeed, she'd be a shoo-in for the crown. And she'd have to be canonised too, because that would be a proper miracle.'

'Oh dear,' said Lucie. 'She will have her work cut out for her. Len and I couldn't get anyone to help us in the end, other than the creaky old usuals, and they were more liability than help.'

'And no sponsorship.'

'Not a sausage.'

Lucie and Len turned wide-eyed towards Flo, who hid behind her fringe.

'But we mustn't discourage.' Lucie's hands flapped. 'It would be a wonderful salute to the heritage of Nowhere River. And of course, we will do what we can to help.'

'It's just an idea,' said Flo. 'At this stage. She'll probably think of something else.'

'If anyone can do it,' said Lucie, reaching out to pat Flo's hand, 'it's your mother.' She gave Len a hard stare. 'Josie came and got a family of rats out of our cellar once. Picked them all up with her bare hands, didn't she, Len?'

'It was actually the sea kelpies,' whispered Len. 'Pretending to be rats.'

The doorbell rang, and Len hurried to answer it, saving himself from Lucie's umbrage. It was Abigail Snelson, wearing a tweed blazer and a felt bucket hat embellished with a cluster of dusty silk flowers.

'Abigail,' said Len. 'Looking jaunty today.'

'Oh,' said Abigail, touching her hat. 'It's, er, it's a thing I'm trying . . .' She trailed off and giggled awkwardly, then blushed.

'Come in,' said Len, benevolently pretending not to have seen the blush. 'Lucie is in the kitchen.'

'Thank you, I won't keep you. I have something to run by— Oh!' Abigail had arrived at the kitchen and stopped in the doorway. 'Gosh, you've done things up! It looks lovely. Actually lovely, in the true Patricia sense of the word.'

'Hello, Abigail, what a nice surprise.' Lucie got up and kissed Abigail's cheek. Abigail tried not to giggle again, but failed.

'It's been a while since you've been here, then we had the kitchen done . . . what is it, Len, seven years ago? How terrible of me not to have had you sooner. All passing across one another's nature strips but never asked in, aren't we? Sad, really.'

'Not to worry,' said Abigail, turning a smile to Flo. 'Hello there, Florence.'

'Hello,' said Flo. And then, remembering manners, 'Mrs Snelson.'

'It's Miss,' said Abigail. 'But Abigail will do. Or Mrs. I could pretend, then, that someone loved me.' She laughed again, then stopped because Flo was looking mortified. 'Oh gosh, sorry. Stupid thing to say. Not funny. Don't mind me, I'm conscientiously stupid.' She coughed. 'Well, I haven't asked you to my house either, Lucie, so there we are.'

'Come and sit down,' said Lucie. 'We were giving Flo a potted history of Riverhouse.'

'For your project? Good idea. It's an enchanting house. Mine is classic mid-century cracker-barrel brick if that's ever of any interest to you. Ugly as can be.'

'Thank you,' said Flo.

'Cup of tea, Abigail?' asked Lucie.

'No, I won't trouble you, Lucie, thank you. I wanted to run something by your ears, if you don't mind. Just that I've set upon an endeavour for Patricia's great Miss Fresh and Lovely quest, and now I'm second-guessing things, as I do, and I'm not sure . . . well, Patricia always respects your views so perhaps you could endorse my idea – or disendorse it, that being the case, just so I can plough on with a jot more confidence than I can manage on my own.'

'Of course, Abigail,' said Lucie, patting Abigail's fidgety hand. 'I'm sure your judgement is perfect, though. I mean, you know Patricia as well as I do.'

'But I irritate Patricia to high heavens, I'm afraid, and the more I try not to, the more I do. It's a constant trial for both of us.'

'You might be overthinking things, Abigail. What's your project idea?'

'Josie Bradshaw is thinking about reviving the Nowhere River Show,' said Len. 'You can't get more harebrained than that.'

'She's not!' Abigail looked at Flo. 'What a thing that would be.'

'She probably won't,' tried Flo. 'I don't think I should have said—'

But Abigail's imagination was captured and she interrupted with, 'I won the egg-and-spoon race once. The only thing I've ever won in my life. She'll have to bring back the egg-and-spoon race.'

'And the pip spitting,' said Len.

'Yes! The pip spitting,' agreed Lucie.

'Now, the show really *is* Patricia's cup of tea,' said Abigail. 'Sponge cakes and horses and other wholesome things.'

'Community,' added Len.

'Actually,' Abigail said, jumping forward in her seat, causing her hat to jig about. 'The show would be the perfect complement to my own initiative, which is . . .' She paused, evidently to gather courage. 'The Nowhere River Old Folks' Treats Committee.'

'Well,' said Lucie, 'that sounds . . .' She scouted for words.

'Like a very good idea,' suggested Len. 'Splendid. Treats for our old folks, which is most of us in town. You'll be busy.'

'The very old, I mean,' said Abigail. 'The Nuyina residents mostly, in particular the ones who are living firmly in the past. I'm going to try and bring them some old-time treats – outings and singsongs and so on. Take them to eras they feel at home in.'

'I have a time machine in the attic,' said Len, with a wink at Flo. 'But if I give it to you, Abigail, you would certainly win, and then Lucie would be cross with me.'

'It's a wonderful idea, worthy of a win,' said Lucie firmly. 'And Patricia is sure to approve of it.'

'Ah!' said Len. 'Your hat and tweed is a time-travel thing.'

'Yes.' Abigail shook her head. 'As I said, enduringly stupid. But I can't bear to think of those old souls wasting away up there in Nuyina, not without a few last treats.' Abigail stared out the window and burst suddenly into tears.

'Oh no!' said Flo involuntarily.

'Please, oh please, just ignore,' sobbed Abigail, waving a hand in front of her face as if to scrub it all away. 'Just carry on and it'll pass.'

'If you spend a bit of time in the vicinity of Abigail,' said Lucie, 'you will come to know that she is quite prone to weeping.'

Beans licked Abigail's knee.

'Yes, I am,' agreed Abigail, giving Beans a pat. 'My tears spill out at frequent intervals. Such as when I think of the palliative patients in the top rooms of Nuyina. They won't know any more treats.'

Len pulled a neatly folded handkerchief from his pocket and offered it to Abigail.

'Thank you, Len, but it'll stop in a minute. And your lovely clean hanky . . . oh, but I am ridiculously leaky about the eyes. I can't even watch the news, and Lucie, for all your tragedy, you never seem to shed tears, do you?'

Lucie fixed her eyes on the window and said, 'Ah . . . well, tears are mostly useful for ridding the eyes of irritating things.'

Abigail was suddenly flustered. 'I mean, I'm not saying you should cry. I cry enough tears for your, ah, your little, you know, Felicity. When I think of her, you know, I think of a magical little water-colour fairy. I would want to paint her, if I could paint. I can't paint. But she was a picture. *Is* a picture. That's to say, she would be if she were, um, still . . . ahem. Oh. Sorry. I'm sorry.'

Abigail did appear very sorry. She looked down at Beans, as though willing him to erase her with his licks, or just gobble her up altogether. Beans shuffled uncomfortably.

Len cleared his throat and also shuffled uncomfortably.

Lucie's eyes remained fixed over the river, on something only she could see.

'I'm s-sorry Lucie, sorry Len,' Abigail stammered. 'There I go, mentioning the unmentionable. I didn't even know Felicity, so I don't know why I should be saying such things and digging it all up for you.'

Lucie squeezed her eyes shut. *Will these raggedy etchings in my heart ever stop stinging?* she thought. She opened the stubborn window, took a breath, and turned back to the agitated Abigail.

'Thank you, Abigail. Felicity *is* a treasure. And she is as pretty as a picture. Thank you for saying so. It means so much just to hear her name aloud, doesn't it, Len?'

Abigail opened her bleary eyes to see Lucie's clear ones aimed right at her. She managed to nod and smile through her sniffles.

Flo twiddled her teacup, stared at her hands and accidentally added her own sniff to the moment. Lucie and Abigail glanced her way in time to see a tear drop splash onto the tabletop. They all stared at it.

'Um,' said Flo, 'I cry for things sometimes, too.'

Lucie smiled at her. 'Oh, you silly-billies.' She attempted a laugh, then took a deep breath. 'Do you know about Felicity, Flo?'

Len ceased his shuffling and became very still.

'Felicity is our daughter,' Lucie said. 'We lost her in 1991.'

Flo nodded and tried to look up.

What followed was a bit of silence that seemed too tender to interfere with, so they let it hang for a bit, until the breeze came in through the open windows and ruffled it enough for Len to say, 'Ah, well then, Beans,' and get up to limp outside with the dog.

Lucie watched him go, then sighed and said, 'He'll be all right. It's good for him. He decided long ago to pop her away for the time being. Keep her in his pocket, he said, but not on his sleeve.'

Abigail let out a little squeak. Tears streamed down her face.

Lucie patted her. 'Anyone for a gin? It's five o'clock somewhere. Oh, sorry Flo, of course not . . .'

'I'll have one, Lucie,' said Abigail. 'Or two.'

Meanwhile, Len took himself into his garden shed, where he put some Debussy on his turntable and settled in to weather the unforeseen Felicity storm.

▼▼▼

A few days later, Flo picked her way through the blackberry vines that crept across the steps of the grandstand. When she got to the top, she perched herself on a section of wooden bench that was free of raised nails, splinters and bird droppings. From there, she could see the whole of the Nowhere River showgrounds, and most of the town.

Flo's memories of the show were both faded and enhanced by time. She was only seven when the Show Society closed the committee room door for the last time, so she'd forgotten her dad coming home from meetings grumbling about wasted hours and pernickety busybodies. She'd also forgotten the sad feeling that came with the showbag van, because she and her older brother, Alex, were always desperate for a showbag but Josie had always said, 'What a waste of money. And teeth.'

The Bradshaws had no money to spare for things like showbags. But Flo did remember the barbecue smell in the air and the whistles from the sheep-dog trials, the bagpipes in the grand parade and the excitement that started days before, with the arrival of the gee-whizzer ride and the colourful marquees. She could still summon the stomach butterflies that came before the horse competitions, the scratchiness of her too-small riding jacket. There wasn't enough money for a new one of those either.

Never any money, thought Flo, who mostly didn't mind but sometimes did. Sometimes they had to do without less luxurious things as well, like orthodontics and someone to fix the washing machine. And good cheese. She craved nice cheese almost as much as she craved the company of Alex. She adored her brother; he was the bravest person she knew. She believed he could do anything, and he believed in her right back. But her dad had sent Alex away to find work on a properly productive cattle farm. And now Alex and Jerry were barely on speaking terms.

Flo never did question why the show stopped. It was a few years before she realised it wasn't a thing anymore. But now, sitting among the ghosts of squealing, parading showgirls and prize-winning roosters, she felt that wistful ache again and thought of Abigail's old folks and their ended eras.

Josie walked out from behind the grandstand. Flo watched her scan the grounds, a hand shading her eyes from the sun.

'I'm up here, Mum.'

Josie turned and looked up. 'I don't know if it's safe up there, Flo,' she called.

'It's fine. Come up.'

Josie tested the bottom few steps. 'Jerry seemed to think it might need to be condemned.'

'It's fine.'

'It's rickety.'

'It has a good view.' Flo shuffled over to offer up part of the clean bench.

Josie braved the rest of the steps. 'It is a good view,' she said as she reached the top. 'I'd forgotten.' She sat and the two of them were silent for a moment. Above them, a skylark fluttered and sang. Trilling, glittering notes that seemed new and shiny. Flo imagined freshly minted coins falling from the sky, at odds with their ramshackle surroundings.

Josie looked up. 'Do you think that bird is yelling at us to leave?' She pitched her voice higher. '*Don't do it, don't open that can of worms! Leave the place alone.*'

'No,' said Flo. 'He's happy. I think he's welcoming us. I think he wants to go to the show.'

'I don't think he does.'

'He loves worms.'

Josie laughed, then tapped Flo's knee. 'Seriously though, we shouldn't be dumb about this. If we pledge to bring back the Nowhere River Show, we have to see it through. No half-arsed job.'

'I know that.'

'I've seen your maths homework.'

'This isn't maths.'

'It's harder than maths.'

'There's no algebra.'

'But there are people. People are harder than algebra.'

'No, they're not. You can talk to people.'

'Some people don't listen.'

They sat among the shimmering notes of the skylark.

'Well, I talked to Len Finlay and to Abigail Snelson,' said Flo, 'and they both mentioned how much Mrs Montgomery likes horses, and equestrian, and sponge cakes. And community. The show is all of those things. As well as being people's favourite memory. It's a winner. It's *the* winner.'

'I wouldn't feel right taking a hundred thousand dollars from Patricia.'

'We don't actually take it though, do we? The town gets it, really. We can just have a little bit of it. I could get a decent saddle.' Flo flipped her fringe out of her eyes.

'Would you please cut that bloody fringe?'

'If I cut my fringe, will you pitch for the show?'

'Maybe.'

'Alex can come home and help.'

'Dad won't let that happen. Come on, get what you need for this history assignment and let's go. This place is depressing me.' Josie got up and made her way down the wooden steps.

Flo searched the sky and after a moment found the distant lark.

'You'll get your can of worms,' she whispered. She hadn't let on that the history assignment was finished and submitted.

On the drive back home, Flo spotted Cosette Hamilton pushing the Finlay twins along Jones Street in their pram.

'And the evil Princess Grimhilde made off with the young children and they were never seen again.'

'What?' said Josie.

'Cosette Hamilton. She must be babysitting Daisy and Ben.'

Josie slowed the car. 'What? Are you sure it was Daisy and Ben?'

'Mum, don't slow down! She'll think we're spying on her. She already thinks I'm a creep.'

'Why wouldn't Carra ask *you* to babysit?' Josie sped up again, with a tiny, incredulous tyre squeal.

'I don't know. Maybe she didn't want to bother me. Maybe Cosette asked if she could. It's all good.'

'But I offered your services to Carra only last week.'

'Oh my God, she just flipped the bird.'

'What?'

'Cosette just gave me the rude finger.'

'In front of the babies? I'm telling Carra. You'd never do that.'

'I just did.'

'Flo!'

'She did it first.'

Flo watched the figure of Cosette Hamilton shrink in the rear-vision mirror and imagined a comprehensive scenario in which Cosette was in charge of a kissing booth at the Nowhere River Show and was obliged to kiss the residents of Nuyina, plus Mrs Pfaff.

Josie, meanwhile, tried to work out *again* where on earth she had gone wrong with Carra.

Abigail Snelson, 52

I'm a very shy person, and then when I'm talking to someone I don't know, I say too much. It's as though I have to say lots and lots of things, to increase the chances of saying something worthwhile. But there are always about ten idiotic remarks for every worthwhile one. It's rare now that I meet someone in Nowhere River who I don't know, so I try very hard to stay quiet. It's probably safer that way.

Chapter 9

Carra walked into the medical centre in what she hoped was a breezy fashion.

'Hello, Ruth!' she called to the receptionist.

'Morning, Mrs Finlay.'

Carra felt the familiar warm fuzz brought on by the idea of being Mrs Finlay. *Ooh,* she thought, *I'm more myself already.*

'Where are those babes?' Ruth asked.

'With a babysitter,' said Carra in a tone she hoped didn't betray any first-time-with-a-sitter anxiety. 'Just for an hour or so at the park to give me a break. Self-care is essential, apparently.' She cursed herself for feeling the need to explain herself to Ruth.

'Right,' said Ruth, in a tone that made Carra want to say other things about why she wasn't teaching her babies the piano or taking them on a nature walk.

'Dr Finlay is already behind, I'm sorry,' said Ruth. 'And he has back-to-back patients.'

'I thought he would be,' said Carra. 'That's why I'm one of them.'

'Oh,' said Ruth and peered at her appointment book.

'It's all right, I'm aware of what Hippocrates would say. It's only something very minor. Just a . . . funny toenail . . . thing.'

Ruth, who appeared not to know about Hippocrates, didn't respond, so Carra took her place in the waiting room and picked up an old copy of *Hello!* magazine. She opened to a feature on the royal family, leaned back in the cushioned chair and hoped that there were at least two appointments before hers.

There were three. Two of them were double appointments and the other was Alan Lamb with eye pain, arthritic ankles and an urgent need to talk to Dr Finlay about the River Committee's plans to tackle erosion. Duncan gave him the time he wanted, and fell further behind.

By then, Carra had stopped luxuriating among the magazines and started worrying about what pastimes Cosette Hamilton might be conjuring up for her babies. Lollipops? Television? She was confident it wouldn't have anything to do with storybooks. She was aware of an unfamiliar fluttering behind her sternum, and realised that she hadn't read a single magazine article, just flicked though the pages dismissively without taking anything in. *Everything is different with babies,* she thought. *It's as if something in me had to be disconnected in order for the mothering to be activated.*

Just as she'd decided to give up on waiting and scurry back to the park, Duncan emerged from the surgery door. 'Carra?'

She tugged her T-shirt down over her lycra leggings. She had felt good in them when she'd left the house. After the pyjamas and baggy tracksuits of early motherhood, proper activewear from her fitness days was akin to dressing up. She tried to embody the svelte woman who had previously occupied the leggings.

'Hello, Doctor,' she said. It came out a bit sleazy.

Duncan smiled in a puzzled way and showed her into the surgery. 'Are you all right? Where are the babies?'

'With Cosette Hamilton, across the road in the park.'

Duncan's eyebrows shot up. 'Really? Good idea. Have you been for a run or something?'

'Yes, self-care is essential. And I need to get in shape before I start getting the town in shape.'

'You made an appointment?'

'I feel like it's the only way I can see you.' She hadn't meant it to sound vinegary, but it did. She tried sweetening it up with, 'I need to see my doctor very badly.' *Eek, too much?*

'Do you?' He clearly wasn't understanding.

'You probably need to take all my clothes off and put me on that examination bed, so you can, you know, examine me.'

Duncan laughed.

'It's not a laughing matter, I really need you, Doctor.' She sat on his knee, wrapped her arms around him and whispered, 'I'm very lovesick.'

'I think I have something for that,' he whispered back.

'I think you do too.' She kissed him, lightly at first, detecting the shape of his smile, then more passionately. He gave a little moan, which Carra took as encouragement enough to place her hand on his crotch.

He laughed again. 'Carra . . .'

'We just have to be quite quick, if that's okay.' Carra unzipped his trousers. 'You kept me waiting quite a long time.'

'I can't— Hang on.' Duncan blocked her hands. 'We can't . . . in here.'

'Of course we can. I booked a long appointment. We'll close the curtains.' She pulled him towards the bed, peeling off her leggings. 'I'll be very quiet. And quick.'

'Carra, I really—'

'Why are there words coming out of your mouth?' said Carra. She smothered his next laugh with a full-tongue kiss. He cupped one of her breasts in his hand.

'Ow,' said Carra. 'Sorry. They're a bit full.' She looked down into the front of her T-shirt. 'Oh, and leaky. Maybe just . . .' She took his hand and slipped it inside her knickers.

'Carra, I can't.' He pulled his hand away. 'It just doesn't feel right.'

'What, my vagina?'

'No,' he laughed again.

'Well, good because, I know it did two babies and has been generally traumatised and a bit shy ever since, but I think it's bouncing back pretty well. What do you think, Doctor? Do you need a closer look?'

'Yes, I think I do.' He lowered Carra onto the bed, kissing her, then paused again. 'Wait. This . . . this whole scenario isn't right. No means no. I'll call security.'

'I can see the headline: "Country doctor raped by depraved patient". I wonder whether they'll ask how provocative your clothing was.'

But Duncan wasn't laughing now. 'Can we pick this up at home?'

'When? In the two seconds between you getting home from a meeting and me being yelled at by a tiny human or being bullied into sleep by extreme fatigue?'

'I don't have a meeting tonight. Just a phone call with Ambrose Montgomery about heritage listings.'

'That's a meeting.' Carra touched her tender chest. One breast pad had slipped and there was a spreading wet patch on her shirt. 'How do you like me now?' She tried to smile, but it turned into a sob.

'Hey.' Duncan drew her into him. 'There's no rush to get things back to normal. People say it could take years after babies to get back into the swing of things. Especially multiples.'

'What's normal?' Carra mumbled into his shoulder. 'I don't even know anymore.'

Duncan held her at arm's length and looked at her. 'You're doing a fantastic job, you know. Those babies are the healthiest, happiest little people I've ever seen.'

She sighed. 'I had such a perfect picture in my head. It had beautiful light and apple pies and flowerbeds with foxgloves. You know those pictures? With old-fashioned lampposts and cherry trees and smoke coming from the chimney. And me. I'm there too. *Me* me, not this me. You haven't had to change at all, not one single bit. I don't even recognise myself. I'm mostly too tired for the garden and I can't cook very well. And now look at me without the children, I'm even less myself. It's hard to be with them all the time but it's harder still to be without them. How did life get so . . . abstract?' She leaned on him and looked at the carpet.

He put his fingers into her hair, lifted her face, kissed her, then said, 'No one puts those perfect pictures on their walls. They're so twee. I much prefer abstract.' He pulled her into a hug.

'I wouldn't mind a bit of twee,' said Carra. She remembered she'd brought him some heart- shaped shortbread and that it was probably now squashed in her bag.

There was a knock on the door and a 'Dr Finlay?'

Carra, still lamenting lampposts and cherry trees, momentarily forgot her pantless state and was startled as Duncan suddenly pushed her back towards the bed and the pulled the curtain in front of her face.

'Yes, Ruth?' he said.

The door opened and Ruth said, 'Sorry, you know I'd never look in when you have a patient, but I knew you were only checking Mrs Finlay's toe.' There was a pause. 'I hope it's all right, Mrs Finlay. Your toe?'

'Yes, thank you, Ruth,' called Carra from behind the curtain. 'It ended up being a fungal infection, actually. Which has spread. So there's had to be a bit of an examination.' *Shut up*, Carra thought. *For the love of God.* But her mouth kept moving. 'Nothing that a bit of fungus powder can't fix, is that right, Duncan?'

Duncan cleared his throat. 'Is everything all right, Ruth?'

'I mean *anti*-fungus powder,' Carra continued. 'Obviously.'

'Oh, yes,' said Ruth. 'Sorry. I just wondered if you'd mind me taking an early three minutes for lunch, Doctor.'

'Of course, go ahead.'

'Just that I have a meeting to consolidate our Miss Fresh and Lovely application. It's called "The Shiny-town Project".'

'Great,' said Duncan. 'By all means.'

'I've partnered with Deidre Wagner. She's obsessive-compulsive, so I think I'm on to a good thing. This old town will be shining like shot silk in the sunshine when we're finished with it.' She gave the air a little scrub and emitted an excited squeak.

'Okay, I'll see you after lunch.'

'Thank you. Oh, and Mrs Finlay, if the fungal infection has reached your privacies, try putting a wet teabag up there dipped in oregano. Works a treat.'

'Thank you, Ruth,' said Duncan.

'Byeee.'

Duncan closed the door behind her.

Carra peeked through the curtains, smiling, and said, 'I think we've officially lost the moment.'

Duncan nodded tiredly. 'Yes, and I have a full waiting room.'

'And I have full boobs.'

'Okay.'

Duncan relaxed, picked up the lycra pants from the floor. 'Don't put a tea bag in your privacies.'

'Better than nothing,' said Carra, swiping him with the leggings. Before she left, she handed him his shortbread biscuits in a paper bag.

Back in the waiting room, on her way out, Carra found Alan Lamb settled in in front of the television.

'Meself, I use vinegar on me fungus,' he said, without moving his eyes from the telly.

'Right,' said Carra.

Duncan, a step behind Carra, said, 'Was there something else, Alan?'

'What? Nah. I just as soon as stay here in peace for a short while as me missus'll be on at me about her bloody project ideas. It's a rum deal, this Miss Lovely and Fresh business, Doctor. Got the ruddy town in loops. I mean, she's illusional if she thinks she's going to win. T'aint nothin' lovely nor fresh about my old cheese. She's had a proper beating from the ugly stick, poor old Myrtle.'

Carra thought of Myrtle Lamb's sparse teeth, her huge, pitted nose and her distinctive aroma, and felt it would be best to remain silent.

'See you soon, Carra,' said Duncan, evidently trying not to laugh.

'Yes,' said Carra. 'Thank you, Doctor.'

Duncan returned to his surgery and peeked into the paper bag. The shortbread was still miraculously intact, but he ate it without noticing the heart shapes.

▼▼▼▼

Carra headed back to Queen Mary Park, where she'd left Cosette and the twins, fifteen minutes later than she'd promised. She was barely out of the door of the medical centre when the sound of two babies screaming carried across the road and struck her like an adrenalin dart, sending her into an instant run. Images of horrific injuries flashed as she crossed the lawn to where she found both Cosette and Lucie respectively rocking Ben in the pram and jiggling Daisy on one hip.

'What's happened?' Carra said through her panic. 'What's wrong?' But even as she said it she could see that there were no protruding bones or lacerated faces. 'Oh, my babies!'

'They are staging a very rousing protest,' shouted Lucie above the din. 'Honestly, I could hear it from Riverhouse. I had to come and rescue poor Cosette.'

'They just, like, started each other off, I think,' said Cosette. 'For no reason. I don't know, I changed their nappies, gave them food . . .' She drummed at the handle of the pram with the tips of her fingers. Carra saw that she was sweating.

'Don't worry,' said Carra. 'I'm sorry, they do that.'

'My little sister never did.'

Carra saw that there was incredulity beneath Cosette's fluster and felt ashamed.

'It could be just a reaction to being left alone the other day,' suggested Lucie. 'Fear of abandonment.' She clucked at Daisy while Carra felt her shame surge, together with some anger. She gathered Ben up out of the pram and kissed his face until his cries dwindled.

'Holy crap,' said Cosette. 'That crying got, like, right into my brain, right here.' She thrust a finger into her ear.

'Yes, a baby's cry has been known to cause psychosis,' Carra remarked, then wished she hadn't. 'In some parts of the world.' She frowned. 'Ha, you should have seen me run. It was like my body registered the sound of my babies before my brain did. That maternal instinct is really amazing, isn't it?'

Lucie's eyes cast out over the river towards the fisher cottages. 'Yes,' she said, 'it's an animal thing. Wondrous and devastating.'

Carra's heart both sank and leaped for Lucie. 'Oh Lucie, I'm sorry, I wasn't—'

'Ew,' interrupted Cosette with an exaggerated shudder. 'I'm so glad I'm a dancer and I like, won't be having babies, like, ever.'

Ten minutes later Carra was back in the car listening to the odd, rather harrowing symphony of Daisy's screams in arrangement with 'Pop Goes the Weasel' on the car stereo. She took three deep breaths, then performed a series of shoulder movements and a few head bangs and said, 'I think I would have been an okay dancer.'

▼▼▼

Myrtle Lamb, 77

My name's not Myrtle, it's Belinda, which means 'beautiful', but my father said it didn't suit me, so he called me Myrtle. He called my sister Fatso and my mother Slutface so I reckon I got off lightly. He wasn't a nice man, my father. He killed my mother in the end, I mean he didn't murder her, but he gave her so many griefs that she didn't last as long as she should. He did, though. Lived right up until two years ago, he did. I had to look after him in his old age. Once I piddled in his tea and he drank it. That made me feel pretty good. I was tough by then. I had Alan and our family and I don't let people hurt me anymore. Sometimes you have to be treated rough to get tough. We've probably been too soft on our kids. I love 'em fierce, I mean I'd kill for 'em. We called our daughter Alanna, which means beautiful as well, and also daughter of Alan, so that worked out well. I hope she never needs to be too tough.

Chapter 10

The following week, Lucie approached St Margery's wearing pearls and a Liberty-print blouse and tried to convince herself that it wasn't to impress Patricia.

'Morning, Patricia,' she rehearsed while hurrying along Ashby Crescent towards Tiya Street. 'Oh yes, I just adore Liberty, have been wearing it all my life. There's nothing like the feel of a Liberty lawn in summertime.' She smoothed her blouse and hoped the Royal Peony print achieved refinement without being too much.

'I'm too much, aren't I?' she said to the grand St Margery's building when she reached it. Its half-blinded windows looked back at her. *Indifference or disapproval?* she wondered. On the front door hung an elegantly understated Christmas wreath fashioned from silvery blue spruce. Not a bauble in sight. 'I shouldn't have added the pearls,' said Lucie to the door.

Inside, Lucie found Patricia already in the meeting room, surrounded by papers, parcels and boxes.

'Goodness,' said Lucie. 'Are these all the submissions?'

'Yes,' said Patricia. 'You can see now why I need your help with sorting. We've received quite a flurry of entries in the final twenty-four hours. Typical Tasmanian haphazardry.' She looked up at Lucie and performed a long, frowny peer over her glasses. 'You look fetching. Trying to win Miss Fresh and Lovely points, Mrs Finlay?'

'Yes, Mrs Montgomery,' said Lucie, surrendering to Patricia's eagle eye. 'How am I going?' She smiled a good little schoolgirl smile.

Patricia peered on.

'Oh, come on, Patricia,' said Lucie. 'It's the Royal Peony print. So summery.'

'I've never been one to fall at the feet of peonies. Give me a scented cabbage rose instead. Peonies are perilously close to the common chrysanthemum. Anyway, we have a great deal to get through, so . . .' Patricia picked up a small box covered in plastic spangles and held it the way one might a pair of soiled underpants. 'Who knows what sort of hideous galootery we're dealing with.'

'Right,' said Lucie. 'I'll put the percolator on.'

By the time Lucie returned with coffee, Patricia had placed the contents of the sparkly box in front of her and was glaring at it.

'Oh dear,' said Lucie, taking in the flurry of dried rose petals and shimmery paper. The smell of rose oil drifted through the air. 'That bad?'

'Infinitely so.'

'Right.'

'It's a proposal to change the name of the town.'

'What?'

'See for yourself.' Patricia handed the glittered papers covered in flowery script to Lucie.

Dear Patricia Montgomery and any other esteemed personage this may concern,

The name 'Nowhere River' is widely known to sound like a town of no-hopers.

Unfortunate nicknames and catchphrases have arisen for years,
including 'The Town Going Nowhere' and 'No-fucking-where'.
We propose it be changed to something beautiful, exotic and/or
unusual that will attract tourists from far and wide. Examples
include: 'Everglade', 'Giverny' or 'Gloria'.

Accompanying this name-change will be our energetic
endeavours to clean up our streets. They are grubby and unsightly.

We would like to run a 'name-our-town' suggestion box, as well
as an enormous community-led clean-up day. A substantial portion
of the prize money will be spent on new town signage and upkeep of
very clean streets.

Tourism is the future for Tasmania – everybody says so, and
NOBODY WANTS TO GO NOWHERE.
Yours sincerely,
Deidre Wagner and Ruth Beaumont-Hudd
The Shiny-town Project

'It's been Nowhere River since settlement and Nowhere River it shall remain,' said Patricia with a sniff.

'Right,' said Lucie again. 'A clean-up is a good idea, though.'

Patricia picked up an unsuspecting blue and white striped envelope. 'This one is Sergeant D's proposal to get the Nowhere River football team back up and running. Preposterous. We don't even have eighteen able-bodied men in the district, do we?'

Lucie was considering her answer and then realised, as Patricia continued, that the question was rhetorical.

'Phoebe wants to paint the town hall high-visibility orange, for goodness sake, to harness the attention of air travellers. And this one'—she held a piece of lilac-coloured notepaper aloft—'is Fleury Salverson's notion to teach people how to yodel. Honestly, what is wrong with people?' She tossed the paper onto the table and a powdery scent puffed into the air.

Lucie began to feel uncomfortable about her Nowhere People idea. 'Yodelling is quite the lost art,' she said, 'and takes a lot of skill. Much like hedge-laying.'

'What on earth?' said Patricia, who had opened a fat, gold envelope filled with confetti, which spilled onto the desk and the floor. 'For mercy's sake.' She dropped the envelope in disgust.

Lucie fearfully picked up the offending document, opened it and read silently.

'Ah,' she said once she'd deciphered the calligraphy. 'It's Elaine's plan to transform Queen Mary Park into Tasmania's wedding capital, on account of it being the site of a rare seam of pinkish quartz known as the stone of love.'

Patricia turned her face away as though she'd smelled something foul.

Lucie grappled for positives. 'She's put significant effort into researching the heritage of Queen Mary Park, that's commendable. And those poor garden beds are in need of attention.'

'She'll fill them with gypsophila and carnations. And peonies.'

'It could be a site of sacred romantic significance, apparently.'

'Poppycock.'

'Well, even so, weddings are wonderful things. I haven't been to one since Carra and Duncan's. All that hope everywhere.' Her thoughts trailed off and her enthusiastic expression faded a little.

Patricia, watching Lucie, said, 'But hopes can be altogether exhausting, can't they. And so disorderly, always getting built up and then dashed all over the place.'

There was a fleeting hint of empathy in Patricia's eyes before she cast the wedding application, confetti and all, into the 'no' pile.

The next submission was a detailed plan (ostensibly submitted by the bedridden Joyce Farquhar but clearly drafted by her real estate agent son, David) to attract foreign investors into the town by offering up for sale at least six of Nowhere River's historic buildings. These included the old watermill, the boarded-up bottom pub, the abandoned Tiya Street workers' cottages, St Cuthbert's decommissioned church, the fisher cottages and, last but not least, St Margery's.

'The nerve of them,' said Patricia, looking as though she might spit on the offending documents. Lucie hurried them into the 'no' pile, despite thinking the idea worth further consideration on the grounds that much of Nowhere River was gazing blankly at the world through boarded-up windows, and going, well, nowhere. But she knew better than to say so.

Patricia placed Lucie's Nowhere People submission into the 'yes' pile, but said, 'Lucie, I admire your proposed commitment to our township's oral histories, and I do acknowledge the boost to *esprit de corps* that such an exhibit could deliver, but I would caution you against delving too enthusiastically into people's pasts. You may find yourself in some very dank places.'

'Or some very wondrous places,' suggested Lucie.

'And some places that are altogether made up, I wouldn't wonder.'

'*If not for wonder,*' said Lucie softly, '*why have we come here?*'

But Patricia had evidently moved on. 'Speaking of dank places,' she said as she opened another large envelope, 'Josephine Bradshaw thinks she can get the Nowhere River Show operational again by next spring.'

'Well, that *is* admirable,' said Lucie. 'You'd love that Patricia, wouldn't you? I mean an agricultural show is a sure sign of a healthy community.'

'Unless it's a dismal failure. I think that horse has rather bolted, don't you? She'll need an army.'

'With respect, Patricia,' said Lucie, her heart beating with nerves, 'do you think you might be viewing things in a slightly negative light? You invited all of this, after all.' Lucie waved theatrically at the jumble of submissions.

'I had hoped,' said Patricia, 'that someone might want to open a wonderful bookshop-café or plant an avenue of plane trees or something. Not go about flogging dead horses.'

'I think Josie shows considerable brio, and a rousing lack of lassitude and vainglory.' Lucie felt pleased. One of Patricia's favourite things were superior words and these ones appeared to work. With another scornful look at Josie's submission, Patricia slung it into the 'yes' pile. Lucie sent a silent thanks to Len for the vocabulary.

Marceline Cash's proposal to teach everyone about hair and beauty soon followed, but not without Patricia's uttered, 'Good grief, we'll be in the *Guinness Book of Records* for the most perms in one town.'

Patricia's spirits lifted considerably when they encountered Carra's fitness initiative. 'This is more like it,' she said. 'Finally.'

Both Lucie and Patricia were surprised by the level of detail in Carra's submission, and its impeccable presentation. And by the fact that her intended fitness program was to be combined with a 'sensitive renovation of the town's gardens and public spaces'. It quoted studies that showed the benefits of gardening on wellbeing and longevity and included a proposed dry-stone walling workshop. This sent Patricia into a misty-eyed homily about bucolic streets lined with cottage gardens and stone walls rambling across the Whistler Hills. The project's name, 'Sporticulture', was declared by Patricia as 'quite clever', which was high praise. Lucie felt a few telling pangs of envy, and had to give herself a stern, silent talking-to.

An hour later, Patricia had twelve submissions in the 'yes' tray, twenty-nine in the 'no' tray and three in the 'possible' tray. Among the no's were a zoo featuring gorillas, bears and lions; a graffiti street-art initiative; the world's longest flying fox; a vegan café ('*for heaven's sake*') and a medical-marijuana plantation. Esther Very's museum and Abigail's Nowhere River Old Folks' Treats Committee ('what a *terrible* mouthful') were other submissions that Patricia found 'adequate'. But overall, she looked significantly devitalised by the general standard of submissions.

'This would never happen in Deloraine,' she said, in a rare slump of her staunch allegiance to Nowhere River. 'They have an international craft fair and a mahjong club.'

'We should feel encouraged by the thought of all these new St Margery's members,' suggested Lucie. 'Every one of them will have to sign up.'

Patricia seemed irritated by Lucie's chirpiness. 'From what I've seen here, any new members are bound to be lacking in the required propriety.'

'I'm sure you can school them in propriety,' said Lucie, twiddling her pearls.

'I'm not sure I have the wherewithal, after this motley lot.' Patricia tapped the rhinestone box and added, 'At least the town isn't called Fannydene. Or Titwood.'

'There's a Granny's Bush somewhere in the northeast, I think,' Lucie added with a laugh.

Patricia gave the ghost of a laugh, then they sat in silence for a moment. A short moment, because it was soon filled with a loud, low groaning sound from somewhere in the walls.

'Ooh,' said Lucie.

The sound grew louder, pitched higher and then faded again, ending with a rude squeak.

'Just those old pipes,' said Patricia. 'They startle me every time.'

And then both women were startled again by another sound: water plopping heavily onto the carpet. They looked up to see the dark bloom of a water shadow on the ceiling.

'Oh dear God,' said Patricia. 'It was only a matter of time.' And she scurried away to turn off the water mains.

Lucie stood, momentarily stunned by what she had just seen – Patricia never *scurried* for anything – before scurrying after her, in case she needed any help.

'It's all right, old girl,' Patricia was saying to the walls when Lucie reached her. 'I'm going to make things better.'

And then there had to be more scurrying, back into the office to gather up the Miss Fresh and Lovely submissions, in case the water reached them and smothered all hope. Patricia piled up the yeses and the maybes and, after a moment's hesitation, all of the no's, declaring, '*Hope doth lie in unlikely places, oftentimes under thy nose.*'

Amid the kerfuffle, and with a little hum in precisely the same key as the water pipes, Lucie slid Elaine Thorold's Rose Quartz Weddings proposal in among the 'yes' pile.

▼▼▼▼

Once George Costas had been phoned to see to the St Margery's plumbing, and Lucie was satisfied that Patricia's ruffles had been smoothed, she set off for the walk home. Lucie felt exhausted from all the cheering-up and positivity she'd had to deploy. Her peony-printed shirt seemed sneery and ridiculous.

'My buoyancy has a slow leak,' she said to the river. 'Patricia's quite right about hope being wearisome. Essential, though.'

The river wrinkled in reply.

She perked up when she reached All Angels Church. Aided by the lofty romanticism of the Rose Quartz submission and gazing at the church's flagstone steps, she thought back to the excitement of Duncan and Carra's wedding day. The dressing up, the air kisses, the champagne, the theatre of it all.

She had been brimming with pride. And relief. The son she'd tiptoed along with for all his young life, hardly daring to hold his hand in case it might send him swerving off the rails, was unbelievably, wonderfully unscathed. And getting married. To a truly genuine, adorable girl who was going to move to Nowhere River and ask Lucie for recipes and advice, share the joys. There she was, Caroline Martin ('Carra of Kinvarra', Lucie was fond of saying) in her ivory silk with her beautiful manners. She was radiant that day, incandescent with love and promise. Lucie was enamoured with her, had put her hopes in her, secretly wished she might at least partially fill a long-empty void.

Lucie shifted her gaze from the church to the river. Felicity had been there that day, too. Felicity was there most days, sometimes everywhere. On Duncan and Carra's wedding day, she stood pressed gently against Lucie's legs in the church. She was in Duncan's speech and in Len's eyes. And she approved, Lucie thought. Felicity approved so much that during a certain part of the bridal waltz (when Len was whirling Carra around the dancefloor) she was, for a brief moment, not there at all.

'Life never has,' Lucie whispered to the oak trees at the entrance to the churchyard, 'as many flowers in its meadows as what you paint with your imagination.'

She turned for home and slowed her step, so that Felicity's little legs could keep up.

▼▼▼

Marceline Cash, 44

I never wanted to be anything but a hairdresser. And now my daughter is one, too. She works in Hobart and says she doesn't want a man. I'm okay with that. I love my husband but I don't think we need a man to be happy. Marriage seems like it could be the start of your life but it's actually the end of lots of things. He's often at sea, he takes supplies to the oil rigs and ships. He flies home every three months. I'm very happy with my clientele and their perms and rinses and sets. I must be the most experienced permist in the country, I reckon, and they're coming back in fashion apparently. I could be in high demand.

Joyce Farquhar, 63
When my children all left me with an empty nest and my husband passed on, there was only me to bake for. Baking and feeding and caring and picking-up-after is all I've ever done, really. Three boisterous children, gone on their own ways. And too much cake for me. I'm grumpy a lot of the time now. With myself for getting so fat and foundered, and with poxy old time, for slipping by like it does without asking. I'm beset with nostalgia too – pains something fearful sometimes. Just the smell of the river air through the window or the inside of the cutlery drawer will set me off. Those glass swans, that old lamp . . . I suppose nostalgia keeps us roped to who we are and what matters most.

Chapter 11

Jerry Bradshaw had seen the whites of the steer's eyes enough times to know that this one was a nutjob. He'd even told Josie about it.

'He's branded JJB88. Prick's got the mongrel in him. Keeps jumping fences, doesn't want to be with the herd. And he's worse with all this wind lately. Flighty as hell. I don't think I'll wait for the sales, even. He can go in our freezer.'

Josie felt the weight of guilt brought on by the slaughter of an unsuspecting animal. It was a weight that had increased over the years, particularly since she'd become a mother. She'd made some attempts to reduce her family's meat consumption, and even suggested once or twice that they veer the business away from beef farming to something with more conscience, but Jerry was so dismissive of these ideas that Josie came to see them through his eyes: ridiculous fancies. And a freezer full of homegrown beef meant they could eat well on a budget, so she continued to ignore her twinges of shame.

But, as is the way of farmers like Jerry, things other than wayward beasts took priority, and JJB88 lived on. Fences needed mending and there were feed-outs and accounts and tractor parts to fetch in. Jerry realised too late that the removal of JJB88 should have been at the top of his list.

Around the same time Lucie and Patricia were flustering over the pipes at St Margery's, Jerry was manoeuvring his own pipe – an armload of irrigation hard hose onto the back of his truck. He was listening vaguely to the blare of the radio and thinking about whether or not to invest time and money into a quarry-planning submission to the *bloody council,* when he was hit from behind by a great force and thrown violently against the tray of the truck. His immediate, contorted thought, just before the pain seared through his right side, was that he had been struck by lightning. But then he saw to the left of him the bucking and kicking of a crazed beast, thundering away over the crest of the hill.

Got the devil in him, Jerry thought. *Christ almighty.* And then he wished he believed in the Christ Almighty, because he felt himself slipping to the ground and decided that this sort of pain was the pain of death. He closed his eyes, fell, struck the back of his head on a sharp edge of the truck and no longer thought anything at all.

Back at the house, Josie and Flo were slicing up peaches, packing them into sugar syrup and chatting on the phone to Alex, who couldn't get away from his mainland jackaroo job to come home for Christmas. They had a horse ride planned after that and then the usual afternoon jobs. It was hours before they began to wonder why Jerry hadn't come home.

▼▼▼

Lucie was helping Len soak the root ball of a hydrangea when she heard the rapid-fire sound of a low-flying helicopter. It brought a rush of cold fear to her surfaces. She and Len both searched the sky, and could see without seeing the telltale red of the rescue helicopter.

Search and rescue, thought Lucie. *Search and search and search.*

Len appeared equally stricken. He looked at Lucie and squeezed her hand. She held her breath and found herself fascinated by the quickening of things around her, and the sensation of being thrown brutally back through the years. *Coming, ready or not. Felicity?* She took another breath and found the scent of jasmine, clasped onto it and hung there, feeling the skip of her heart begin to ease. Len curled up the garden hose and rubbed the top of his left thigh.

▼▼▼

Carra was home flipping through the *Women's Weekly* children's birthday cake book when she noticed the helicopter flying low over the Whistler Hills. Seconds later, the phone rang.

'Hello?'

'Carra, I'm on my way to Everston,' said Duncan. 'Jerry's had an accident. It's bad. The ambos called me. They think he got charged by a bull.'

'Oh God,' said Carra, immediately standing up, poised for something. She looked for her bag.

'Don't do anything,' he said. 'But I won't be home anytime soon.'

'I'll come. Josie—'

'She'll go in the chopper. You need to stay there.' This was Dr Finlay, businesslike and firm. 'I'll sort out Flo and keep you posted. Call Mum if you need her.'

Carra knew he was right. The scene of an accident was no place for two tired babies. *I hate being the women and children,* she thought. *Look at me: some kind of gormless action hero, searching for her bag.*

'Okay,' she said.

'Talk soon.' He hung up.

'Okay,' said Carra again, to the phone. 'But how bad is bad?'

She felt an overwhelming regret for being so neglectful of Josie and their friendship. Ever since her catch-up promises at the community meeting, she'd avoided any actual engagement by sending light-hearted little text messages, thinly veiled dismissives like: *Thanks for your message. Sorry for the delay. A catch-up soon would be great.*

Except a catch-up wouldn't have been great. It would, to Carra, have been an exercise in avoiding the elephantine truths about her vast inadequacies as a wife and mother and a friend. Josie's last message (*Don't make me come over there, I'm a grumpy grey-haired old lady*) had gone unreplied. Carra had been at a loss for a quick-witted, friendly but equivocal response.

'Mum-mum-mum,' shouted Daisy from her highchair.

'What do I do?' Carra asked her.

Daisy seemed startled by being addressed so directly and said nothing.

'Where have I positioned myself in this scenario?'

Ben banged the tabletop with his spoon and then dropped it deliberately onto the floor.

'Yes, should we be dropping everything?'

Daisy grizzled and squirmed.

'No, we should give them space. Everyone wants to be the best friend of the trauma victim. And why am I making this about me?' Carra spooned some mush into Daisy's mouth. 'Maybe we should say a prayer.'

▼▼▼

Flo was praying too. A barely whispered 'I'll do whatever you want, God' kind of praying.

'I'll try harder to concentrate, I'll save on water, I'll be better with manners, I'll be good, I'll be good, oh God, I'll be really good. Just let him be okay.' She stood as still as she could, in case a wrong move might weaken her promises. She tried not to look at the limp movements of her dad's booted feet as the brightly dressed people from the helicopter did things to his body.

That's not a body, she told herself, *that's Dad. He's right there.* But when she'd first seen him like this, all those terrible, long minutes before, it wasn't her dad she saw.

'Can you run out past the Sugarloaf and see what's keeping Dad?' Josie had said grouchily. 'Dinner's been ready for ages.'

And Flo had gone. She didn't protest or huff about it (Josie's grouches were increasingly fearsome) but she didn't hurry either. She meandered along the creek bed, enjoying the saved daylight and the warm evening, wondering what the crickets were saying with their chirps and whether the magpies could tell she'd had her fringe cut. When she drew nearer to her dad's truck, she saw him lying on the ground and thought that he must have been fixing something, that a breakdown was the reason he hadn't come in. Jerry was always lying at odd angles under machinery or on roadsides, leaning into culverts. She did a little spontaneous dance routine in the paddock and wondered whether she might catch her dad's attention and make him laugh. As she got closer, she saw that he didn't seem to be fixing anything, nor did he appear to be moving.

'Dad?' she called. He didn't respond. That's when she ran.

His face wasn't his face, but a grey, ill-fitting mask. On his blue work-shirt, over the right side of his abdomen, bloomed a dark patch of blood.

'Dad?' she whimpered, hoping he might be hiding under the mask, ready to pop out with his big laugh. She touched him, ever so gently because she remembered that injured people shouldn't be moved. Other things lurched into her memory. Urgent things like listen for breathing (*there, very quiet but there*), feel for a pulse (*not sure*) and get help. *Get help.* She ran, fast this time, so fast that before she'd rounded the Sugarloaf – the tree-topped, lone hill that rose out of the middle Everston paddock – her own breaths were ragged and painful. She jumped over a fence and launched herself at Bruny, Josie's horse, a young quarter horse with a big ego and no patience for fearful riders. With the sun setting before her and Jerry dwindling on the dirt behind, Flo gave Bruny not a moment's grace to show his distemper. With his mane firmly in her hands and her legs speaking to him about haste and urgency and no nonsense, the two were back at the house in five minutes.

'Mum!' Flo had screamed. 'Mum! Get an ambulance!'

She couldn't see her dad's face now. Dr Finlay had arrived and moved her a short distance away. And besides, she couldn't bear to look. Her mum had refused to be moved, instead slotting herself in as part of the team, helping to remove Jerry's clothes, holding bits of medical equipment and apparently being more useful than the volunteer ambulance officer, who was shuffling notes on the sidelines and trying not to appear dazed. Sergeant D was there too. She looked different. Serious. All business and practised calm, like a police-woman from the telly. Flo took this as an ominous sign. Terrible things happened on the telly, which is why she so rarely watched it.

They were saying that Jerry must have been charged and hit by an animal. Flo knew about steer number JJB88, her mum had told her to watch out for him, but she'd barely given him another thought. She heard Josie shouting about him to Sergeant D.

'Could you have that prick shot?' Josie had yelled. 'I never want to see him again.'

'Flo?' came a soft voice beside her. It was Father John, from the midnight mass at Christmas and from school services. Flo looked at his beard and wondered whether Christmas would be ruined. And whether her prayers had brought him here. She gazed up into the dusky pink sky.

'Doctor Finlay phoned me,' he said, which made Flo feel silly, because he must have known she had been looking to see if God was watching.

'Why?'

'Sometimes people just like a bit of extra support at hard times.'

'If it's because he thinks Dad's going to die, well, he's not. Going to die.' She firmed up her stance. 'I know what last rites are. I've read it in books. But we don't need you. You can leave now.'

'I would just like to stand with you, Flo,' said Father John after a moment. 'I don't feel you should be standing here alone. Is that okay with you?'

'Yes,' she said.

And a short time later, when Flo had kissed her mother's face and her father's hand, when Jerry was loaded into the helicopter with Josie climbing in behind, and Dr Finlay was busy talking to Sergeant D, Flo leaned into Father John and let the tears finally come.

▼▼▼

Carra was in the kitchen at Kinvarra when Duncan arrived with Flo and an air of faux optimism. It was well after dark and the babies were asleep. Carra had made a loaf of banana bread into which she'd mixed her sorrow and sense of powerlessness. An 'I don't know what else to do' loaf. It was rising in the oven, sending out what seemed to Carra a pervasive aroma of tokenism. She wished she hadn't bothered with it, but Lucie had arrived with soup in preparation for Duncan's return, and banana bread seemed to Carra like a complementary, wifely response to terrible news.

The news was indeed terrible. Carra and Lucie had both received a text message from Duncan that said, *Not good. Head injury. Internal bleeding. He's critical. Bringing Flo home.* Carra knew just enough to feel sickened by the word 'critical'. It was what officials said when preparing people for the worst.

'Oh my darling . . .' said Lucie to Flo in a much softer voice than usual, as if any sort of vibration might shatter her. Flo looked at her with exhausted eyes, and Lucie drew her into a long embrace.

'Flo, I want you to know that if there's anything you need to ask us, anything at all, we will try to answer it. Or you might want to eat something, have some hot chocolate. We could put a film on, anything you'd like.'

Flo simply nodded, and then after a moment said, 'Could I see the babies, please?'

'Of course,' said Carra. 'Come into the nursery.'

Carra and Flo crept into the nursery. The babies were facing one another, Daisy with one arm stretched towards her brother's cot, as though she had fallen asleep just before inflicting some sort of mischief.

'Ohhh,' whispered Flo. 'They're so big.'

Carra realised with a twinge of guilt that Flo hadn't played with the babies for months. Not since they were tiny, inert little mewing creatures.

'It's their birthday in two days. They'll be one! You should see how noisy they've got. And they can crawl.' Carra gazed at her babies with new, adoring eyes. 'I'd love you to help me plan their birthday cake, too. I'm thinking about making a train.' She watched Flo smile and nod politely, wondered if birthday talk was too celebratory at such a time, and stopped talking.

They stayed in the nursery a little longer, silent until Daisy stirred and gave a perfect sigh. Flo smiled and then didn't. Carra put an arm around her.

'Can I go to bed too?' asked Flo.

It wasn't a cold night but Lucie tucked a hot water bottle in with Flo anyway. She gave her a kiss, stroked her hair for a moment and then settled in a big squashy armchair in the corner of the room until sleep levelled Flo's breaths. Later, Lucie returned to the chair with an eiderdown and remained there for the entire night, sometimes dozing, sometimes allowing herself to dream that the girl in the bed – this safe, warm and watched child – was her own. At no time did the prolonged discomfort of a night in a chair convince her to leave.

▼▼▼▼

It was Duncan who woke both Lucie and Flo the next morning.

'Flo?' he said.

Lucie stirred, drew in a breath and opened her eyes.

'Flo?' Duncan repeated, touching her shoulder. Flo put the covers over her head and whimpered. 'No, please don't tell me.'

'Oh,' said Lucie, sitting up.

'He's still with us,' said Duncan quickly.

Flo drew back the covers enough for Lucie and Duncan to see her terrified eyes.

'He has a machine breathing for him, a ventilator. They want to keep him unconscious for a while, to give his brain a rest. He banged his head. And he broke some ribs and lacerated his liver. So he had to have an operation on that. We have to wait a bit now.'

Flo suddenly leaped out of bed and moved to the window. She pressed both hands to the glass and craned to look out past the hills, as if searching for something to affirm Duncan's words.

'Dad,' she whispered.

The elm trees waved at her.

'He's very, very lucky you found him when you did, Flo,' said Duncan.

'I should have got there sooner though,' said Flo, still facing the window. 'I was talking to the creek and finding bears in the clouds. And now he won't be able to run the farm. And what if he can't wake up without the ventilator?'

'One day at a time,' said Duncan. 'Your job for now is to look after yourself. Ask questions, talk to us.'

'Don't bottle things up,' said Lucie. 'And know that we're here to help. You can stay with me at Riverhouse anytime.' Lucie caught a certain zeal in her voice and stopped herself from saying more.

'Thank you,' said Flo, remembering that she'd promised in her prayer to improve her manners.

'Flo, would you mind helping me make some breakfast pikelets for the babies?' Lucie asked gently, raising herself from the chair.

Flo nodded. She could hear little squawks already in the kitchen. She envied their limited infant awareness. 'And afterwards,' she said, 'I would like your help with something, and Carra's, if you don't mind.'

'Of course,' said Lucie. 'Whatever you like.'

Flo swallowed her shy forebodings and said, 'I think there's a way I could really help Mum and Dad.'

▼▼▼▼

Josie sat quietly in a tiny hospital room, matched her breathing to the heaving ventilator in the corner and wondered how to behave. With the wide, double-glass window and the watchful eyes of intensive care nurses, she felt as though she should put on a performance. *Tears are probably appropriate,* she thought, but her mind didn't seem interested in tears. Instead it kept sifting through the reports from the emergency staff: *brain injury, lacerated liver, grade-three tear.*

'He's in a bit of trouble, love,' said one nurse gently, and Josie had appreciated her plain-speaking words.

When her mind could no longer make sense of medical detail, it took to leaping too far ahead, in flashes and glimpses, to a place without Jerry. His chair by the fire, with its Jerry-shaped sag; the pile of sports magazines by the bed; his boots at the door, spider-webbed and curling at the toes; the baby-faced wedding photo on the mantelpiece . . . all these would have to be dealt with, disarmed.

Josie tried to coax her thoughts into optimism, but she tripped on an image of Alex and Flo wondering what to do with Jerry's motorbike, trying to start the temperamental mower that always behaved under Jerry's hand. How to hold themselves in a shattered household with a brutal, obstinate drought at its door.

It all seemed utterly insurmountable.

This must be grief, thought Josie, looking at her callused hands sitting feebly in her lap. *It's so draining.* She shifted in her seat and braved a glance at Jerry, then wished she hadn't. His neatly positioned arms and his face obscured by apparatus turned the figure in the bed into a mannequin. She looked again and made herself see the freckled skin of the arms. Jerry's freckles. Alex had them too.

Alex. The thought made her gasp. She recalled the phone call she'd made to Alex in New South Wales. How her voice hadn't sounded like her own, how she could have almost imagined his wheezy sobs into laughter. Turned it all into a horrible joke.

'Oh no,' he'd said. 'Oh my God, Mum.'

'Get yourself home,' she'd said. 'We'll be all right. It'll be all right.' But the words didn't feel quite true.

'Alex'll have a battle, Jerry,' she said. 'He'd be lost without you.' She squeezed her limp hands into fists and wondered again where the tears were. 'So you can't go, and that's that. You have to stay, okay?' She tried a smile. 'I've ordered the Christmas turkey, and I've pledged to get the goddamn show up and running again, ha.' Her smile disappeared. It seemed trivial and pointless to put an agricultural show into a world without Jerry in it.

Later, Josie was ushered from Jerry's side and into a small, curtained room with a table, two chairs, a box of tissues and a middle-aged woman in a huge muu-muu.

'Hello there, my dear,' she said in a breathy, high-pitched voice that belied her size. 'I'm Sue. Trauma counsellor. They tell me you're having a terrible day.'

Sue ushered Josie towards a seat and sank into the chair opposite; it issued a pacifying 'shhh'.

'Now, I want you to ask me as many questions as you like, and if you don't have any questions, that's fine too. Sometimes shock can just knock all the questions right out of you and you just feel numb.'

Josie looked at Sue's cushiony bosom and had an urge to snuggle into it. She searched her mind for appropriate questions, gave up and said, 'I keep thinking he's dead already. I'm already planning his funeral. Aren't I meant to be sending him positive vibes?'

Sue studied Josie for a moment. 'You're a practical woman, aren't you, Josie? A fixer? I think you're just doing what you do: being practical. It could be what your little body needs to do to get through this. Don't fight it too much, but remember as well that maybe you could have a break from fixing things, and planning, and just sit here in the dark hole with yourself, and Jerry. You're both allowed a day or two to feel really bloody pissed off, I reckon.'

'Okay,' said Josie. 'I'll try that.'

Sue left some standard-issue silence during which Josie found another question.

'Do you think,' she said, 'that the symptoms of incoming menopause will be kind of neutralised by the worry of all this, or made worse?'

Sue looked momentarily surprised, and Josie regretted the question. 'I mean,' she added, 'just that sometimes lately, if I let myself get cross about things, then I find myself as angry as all hell. It made me break a plate the other day, menopause did. Should I lock up the crockery?'

'I think,' said Sue carefully, 'that either is possible. And whichever way it goes will be the right way.'

Josie was beginning to feel let down by this response, when Sue leaned in towards her and added, 'You know, it is thought that only three species on Earth experience menopause: humans, orcas and the Japanese aphid. There is a very specific reason why these three live on past their reproductive years.' She lowered her voice conspiratorially, 'Because their experience and wisdom is crucial to collective wellbeing. Our vital processes are rewired from our woo-woos' – Sue pointed a manicured finger towards her nether regions – 'to our noodles.' She tapped her head. 'And if you're angry, you're angry for a reason. Don't let any blithering idiot with a willy and a dominant mindset tell you otherwise. They're intimidated, and like any threatened species, they will seek out all sorts of creative oppressions.'

Sue nodded a full stop and flumped back into the chair. 'I have a whole other speech about the benefits of widowhood, but I'll hold off on that one. There's still a chance you won't be getting off that lightly.'

Josie found herself unable to hold in a loud, guffawing laugh.

▼▼▼

Father John O'Sullivan, 61

I know that faith doesn't explain everything, I know there are inconsistencies, but I do believe that there is enormous comfort in, you know, the Great Man Above. And I'm very privileged to be able to deliver that comfort. I'm at ease with death, and I've given a few people their leave, which always feels like an important thing, you know, just letting people know that it's all right to go. And very often they do, just pop off pretty much then and there. It happens all the time. Except for Cliffity Smith. I gave him leave when he had his first stroke at age seventy-five or so. He's almost hundred now. He has great fun reminding me of that.

Chapter 12

Carra and Flo stood at the front door of St Margery's and wondered whether to try the knocker, having waited some long moments since pressing the buzzer.

'It's a big building,' said Carra. 'Maybe she's coming from the attics or something. We'll wait a minute.' So they waited a minute, and then another minute, and then Carra knocked three times, loudly.

She was just finishing the third when Patricia opened the door. 'Yes, yes, I'm here, goodness, we don't have a butler, you know.'

'Sorry,' said Carra. In her peripheral vision she saw Flo deflate and cursed Patricia's heedless contempt.

'Oh, hello,' Patricia said when she registered their faces. She gave Flo a smile that was possibly meant to be sympathetic. 'I am very sorry to hear the news about your father, Florence. Please do send my very best to your mother. And you mustn't hesitate to tell me what you need. St Margery's can pull together a hamper, or manpower for stock feeds and farm things . . .' She turned her attention to Carra. 'Ah, our resident Sporticulturalist. Good to see you got out of your nightshirt for your town outing.'

God, she's truly awful, thought Carra, but smiled and said, 'Well actually, Flo was wondering something, weren't you, Flo?'

Flo received a little nudge from Carra, stared hard at the flagstones at her feet, swallowed what might have been some words and said nothing.

'Flo?' said Carra. 'What's wrong with Nowhere River?'

'Goodness,' said Patricia. 'This could take a while.'

Carra laughed a nervous laugh and then wished she hadn't. 'Deep breath,' she whispered to Flo.

Flo took Carra's suggested deep breath and, without looking up from the flagstones, blurted, 'If there's nothing to be proud of then there's nothing . . .?' She left the sentence hanging on an upward inflection.

Patricia's eyebrows requested more.

'Then there's nothing,' said Flo, giving the sentence its correct end point, but also rendering it a bit meaningless. 'If there's nothing to be proud of then there's nothing. Full stop. Said a very wise woman once.'

'You,' said Carra, pointing at Patricia and then remembering that it's rude to point. 'You're the very wise woman. I heard you say that once, at your house when you were hosting a fundraising thing.'

'What?' said Patricia. (She wasn't one for 'Pardon me?' or 'Sorry?') Then, perhaps remembering that Jerry was in a coma, she added, 'Go on.'

'Healthy communities . . .' prompted Carra.

'Healthy communities,' repeated Flo in a raised voice that gave everyone a start, including herself. She tried again, quietly this time, and slightly robotic. 'Healthy communities need an outlet for their achievements. A platform for their skills, and the space and permission to take a moment to pat themselves on the back, be together and celebrate their community. They need to be able to cultivate pride. A traditional agricultural show can boost morale, inform, delight, educate and highlight. It can tell our forgotten stories and celebrate our achievements. Nowhere River needs a show. I can make the show happen again. I am sixteen. I am not in school. I am interested in all the many and varied things around me. I can take over the submission of my mother, Josie Bradshaw. I am very excited to join the proud tradition and emeris . . .' Here she paused, and looked up at the windows of St Margery's. 'The e-mer-it-us – emeritus – ranks of St Margery's. Thank you.' At this point, she thrust out a fold of paper. 'This is my Miss Fresh and Lovely submission, what a generous initiative, thank you. Again.'

Patricia took the proffered paper. 'That was a very well memorised speech. You could perhaps do better for some instruction in drama and nuance. Lucie could help you with that.'

'Yes,' said Flo, hoping that Carra wouldn't let on about Lucie spending the last two hours trying to instil Flo's oration with drama and nuance.

'I will give it some thought,' said Patricia, making moves to close the conversation, but she noticed that Flo was looking quite directly at her now, with something desperate in her wide eyes. 'Is there something you'd like to add?' Patricia offered.

'Um,' said Flo, then winced. Lucie had told her about Patricia's intense dislike for 'um'. 'Um,' she said again, then hurried on from it. 'I don't think we can keep our farm. When Dad wakes up he will take ages and ages to work again, and things were very bad anyway, with the drought. Mum's been feeding us chicken pie but I know it's rabbits. The horses will have to go.'

'All submissions are judged in accordance with the guidelines,' said Patricia firmly. 'I won't be making special allowances.' But, she added (because Flo looked close to tears), 'St Margery's has an emergency fund from which we can purchase horse pellets. They'll be delivered directly. I must get on. Goodbye.' She moved to close the door, then paused and added, 'Emeritus might be overdoing it.'

By Christmas Day, six days after Jerry's accident, Josie decided that it was time to bring Flo to the hospital. Alex had arrived home from the mainland, having been given compassionate leave to oversee things on the farm and take care of Flo. He, being twenty-two and outside the jurisdiction of his mother, was already visiting the hospital every other day despite Josie's protests. Alex and his earnest, guilty brand of grief would bowl in and pace about, trying to find palatable farm news for his mother and the terrible, tubed and wired unfamiliar on the bed. Josie could hardly bear to look at this confused man-child with the dear, freckled nose and the bit of hair on the crown of his head that never behaved. It was easier, in fact, to look at Jerry, whose altered state was so pronounced she'd begun to imagine him into a stranger.

'Can I bring her in, Mum?' Alex had asked quite a few times. 'She's been keeping herself amused, hardly see her during the day, but she asks all the time. Maybe she'll be better than me at talking to Dad.'

Josie had encouraged Alex to talk to Jerry as much as possible, but she could tell he felt silly. He blushed and shuffled and talked about the weather until Josie spared him the stage fright and just let him flick through doctor's notes and stare at the machines.

'Yes, bring her in,' Josie said finally, after Alex had asked yet again. She couldn't find any more resolve and she missed her daughter so much it was making her bones ache.

So Alex drove Flo to Hobart. They made a trip of it, stopping in New Norfolk to eat toasted cheese fingers at a mock Tudor café with wagon wheels in the garden. Over a plate of brandy snaps, Alex listened in amazement as his timid sister talked and talked about her ideas for the show.

'I've set a date,' she said, 'the twenty-second of October, when the trees look fresh and new. Carra said she'll help me plant things that'll flower at that time of year. There's a woman from Hamilton who trains corgis to round up sheep. And a family of nine from Lawitta who throw one another around doing acrobatics.'

'Cool,' said Alex.

'And there's this boy who grows huge pumpkins, and Fleury Salverson knows how to yodel. She's going to give a demonstration.'

'You're serious about this show idea, aren't you?' Alex inspected his sister as if checking it was actually her.

'Yes, Patricia's accepted the submission with me in charge. I really want to win. The back fences out between us and Clyde Farm have had the dick. And I heard the stock agent talk about sale prices.'

Alex said, 'Right, well, I think you should let me worry about that, and you get on with your education. And being a kid. It's all over pretty quickly.'

'And if we can get the farm back on its feet, maybe buy a bit more land, then we'll need you here and you won't have to leave again.'

He looked at her for a long moment, then shook his head and pushed the last of the brandy snaps over to Flo. 'Shove that in your gob and let's get going.'

Flo leaned towards him. 'You'll help me, Alex?' she asked. 'If the submission gets chosen, I really want to make this work, and I can't do it on my own.'

'Yeah, of course,' said Alex, and, because he was twenty-two and an actual man, added, 'Don't get overly ambitious, though. I mean, it's a big ask. You need to think about marketing, logistics, scheduling, parking, entries, ticketing, rubbish . . . and don't forget the place is fair falling down.'

'Len and Lucie Finlay are going to give me some tips,' said Flo. 'Len was the president for, like, ten years or something.'

'Okay, well, don't try to be a hero, Florence Nightingale.'

Back in the car, to prepare her for what she was about to see, Alex described the hospital room and the machines. When Flo's hazel eyes began to appear too big for her face, he turned up the radio but that didn't stop her from trying to work out how best she could say *I'm so sorry* to someone in a coma.

Eventually, as they were passing through the outermost suburbs of Hobart, she tried it out on Alex.

'Hey, Alex, it's my fault Dad's in hospital. I should have found him sooner. I'm sorry for that.'

Alex slowed the car without meaning to. 'Don't be a dick, that's bullshit, Flo. You know that, don't you?' When Flo didn't reply, he continued, 'If we're going to blame someone, we can blame me. I should have been here working, not swanning around on the mainland. I would have had that bastard steer off the farm.'

'But Dad said you had to go away. For the experience.'

'Yeah, and I was too pussy to say no.'

They drove in silence for a while before Alex said, 'I didn't talk to him for months before his accident. Do you think he knows I love him?'

Flo swung around to stare at him. 'And you said I was being a dick. That's peak dickhead, that question.' But the pain in his face made her pat his shoulder. 'Of course he knows. I know he knows.' Her throat felt swollen and she had to stop talking then.

When they reached Jerry's hospital room, Flo made a run for her mother's arms. They held one another for a long time, each breathing the other in. Alex watched them until he had to tilt his face to stop his eyes spilling over. The only window in the room looked inwards to the nurse's station, where he could see a mug sitting on the desk with 'World's Best Dad' written on it.

'Flo,' Josie said softly, drawing her daughter away and looking into her face. 'Do you want to hold Dad's hand? The doctor's say there's a chance he might feel it. He might hear you too, if you want to talk to him.' Flo turned to the bed, stared for a bit and then tiptoed forward until she was standing beside Jerry, looking down at him. Alex and Josie held their breath.

'Merry Christmas, Dad,' said Flo softly, just as Josie was wondering whether she'd gone into a sort of traumatised trance. 'I'm going to make things better. When you wake up you can just relax and recover, because I'm going to win a hundred thousand dollars. And we can put it into the farm because if Everston does well then the town does well, doesn't it? I've got it all worked out.'

'Floey,' said Josie, 'You don't have to—'

'Mum, you need to save your energy too. For Dad. Alex's doing a great job. He hasn't even needed Walt, really. And Lucie and her St Margery's ladies are keeping us fed. Everything will be okay.' Her tone was moderate and matter-of-fact, no distress, no drama.

Josie looked at the bossy, unfamiliar girl before her and felt wholly comforted.

▼▼▼

Carra, despite protests on all fronts, had determined to host the Finlay Christmas at Kinvarra. It was her chance, she'd decided, to prove to everyone (including herself), that she was a worthy and actively contributing member of the Finlay family.

So resilient, those Finlays, she'd heard people say more than once. *How they've endured. Such an asset to this community, so amazing. Lesser people would just give up.*

Carra waved the turkey baster at the babies and shouted, 'So your birthday got a bit put off, and I never got around to your train cake. I'm sorry, darlings. And this is your first Christmas as actual born people, so I'm going to make it as jolly as heck.' She looked at the lopsided, Christmas-cum-birthday cake on the bench and sighed. 'Shoving your birthday into Christmas is the sort of thing my mother would do. She thought both were a waste of time. I promise never to do it again.'

That reminded Carra that she mustn't forget to phone in thanks for the Christmas present from her parents, the annually scheduled arrival of a decent sum into Carra's savings account. She wondered if the clinical nature of their generosity was the reason she invested so much in silly little gestures, like the babies' handprints she'd had framed for Duncan's Christmas present.

'Dada. Dada,' Ben said, smiling at Carra.

'Mumma. Mumma,' countered Carra.

'DADA.'

On cue, Duncan walked in.

Dammit, he's back early, thought Carra, surveying the remains of turkey stuffing and birthday cake that littered the island bench and floor.

'Right,' he said. 'I've done my Christmas house calls in record time. Now tell me what to do, how to help. Where do you want me, I'm all yours.'

'How many GPs that you know do Christmas Day house calls?' Carra waggled the turkey baster at him in mock disapproval, but there was an edge to her voice that meant business.

'I'm a country GP, it's what I do.'

'I'm not criticising. I'm commending. Your compassion knows no bounds, Dr Finlay.'

'It's my job.'

'Let me guess, you popped in on Joyce Farquhar to check on her bedsores, you reminded Alan Lamb about rich food and gout, and you sang "Good King Wenceslas" at Nuyina.'

'You're wrong. Joyce Farquhar doesn't have any bedsores because I haven't let it get to that, and Alan Lamb doesn't have gout, you're thinking of Stanton Godfrey. And we sang "The Little Drummer Boy" at Nuyina.' Duncan hovered in the kitchen and looked at the mess. 'So what can I do? Oh wait, I have presents.'

'Ooh,' said Carra. She was hoping for a gift voucher for the plant nursery. She had her eye on a double hydrangea and a highly scented rose. Or a weekend away. *Either will do.*

But it wasn't plants or mini-breaks. It was three piglets for the twins, to be delivered to a town in Africa. For Carra, a donation to a Pakistani women's rights foundation and a pile of pig manure so someone in Lesotho could grow food.

'That's perfect!' said Carra too loudly. She lowered her voice. 'See, such compassion.' She tried her best not to feel miffed, but from somewhere in her mind's weary eye, a quiet hotel room for two (or was it for one?) faded away. *You spoiled brat.* She hurried away to find her gift for Duncan (and hide her downcast expression), returning a moment later with the framed handprints and an envelope. 'Now I feel really selfish, because it's not a pig or a goat or anything.'

Duncan opened the envelope. 'Dinner for two at the Drunken Admiral. Wow.'

'It doesn't have to be the Drunken Admiral. Anywhere you like in Hobart. I've forgotten what's good and this was Mum and Dad's favourite . . .' Carra wondered vaguely why she was babbling. *Embarrassment?* 'I haven't actually booked it yet, because I needed to check when you'd be available, and it'll be a while away because we can't take the babies.'

'Sounds amazing.'

'So think of it as a sort of voucher, I guess. A promise. We can find where we were before these little monsters came along.' Carra laughed. '*If* we can remember. Can you believe they're one?'

'No, where did that year go?'

'It's a blur,' said Carra, and realised she meant it. She watched as he opened the parcel containing the picture frame.

'Awesome,' he said. 'I'll take it to work.' He kissed her. 'Thanks for the dinner voucher, too. Great idea.'

But Carra could see that her dinner idea was already falling flat. Getting organised for one evening in Hobart would be such an effort. And Duncan would be just as happy at the Fat Doe Inn.

'Oh, we got the babies a Jolly Jumper each for their birthday, by the way. And scooters for Christmas, to go with their piglets.'

'Okay, great. I'm not sure about those Jolly Jumpers, though. They can cause developmental delays, and the babies still aren't walking.'

Carra felt deflated. The Jolly Jumpers represented a few moments of hands-free time. She looked at the turkey baster on the bench and imagined hitting him with it.

At exactly twelve, Len and Lucie arrived. They brought Abigail Snelson and Father John with them, who Lucie had thought to ask and Carra wished she had.

Father John was wearing a lairy green-and-red knitted jumper, patterned with white snowflakes and reindeer. On his head was a matching beanie with a gold pom-pom.

'Sorry,' he said. 'The Nuyina knitting group have been rampaging again. I had no choice. I'll take them off later when it warms up.'

'He's having a phase of "radical acceptance",' added Len, 'whereby he says "yes" to life, instead of sitting about in his vestments worrying about climate change and trying not to drink too much whisky.'

'I've told him that sounds a risky business in light of the Miss Fresh and Lovely commotions,' said Lucie. 'We could put him up to anything. Abigail's already lining him up to join her Old Folks' Treats Committee.'

'Ballroom dancing is on the agenda, isn't it, Abigail?' said Len.

Abigail giggled.

'And karaoke,' said Duncan.

Carra tried to think of something to add.

'And online dating,' offered Lucie. 'Such fun.'

'Oh gawd,' said Father John.

Len laughed. 'You just broke the third commandment.'

'What?' said Father John. 'No, I didn't.'

'You said "gawd".'

'Did I? Perhaps it was "Lord".'

'It was definitely "gawd". On the birthday of the Baby Jesus, no less.'

'Oh.' Father John looked perplexed. 'I've always been a bit sketchy on that one.'

'Come in everyone,' said Carra. 'Duncan will get some drinks.'

'A double martini for the good vicar,' said Len.

'No, thank you, Leonard.'

'I thought you were radically accepting?'

'Shut up or I'll have the Lord send a small flood to break the Nowhere's banks just enough to wash out your lettuces.'

'There is no Lord, my friend, I've told you many times.'

'That's quite enough,' said Lucie, thinking of Abigail's Christian convictions. 'How can I help, Carra? Goodness, the house looks amazing.' She carried a basket of presents towards the kitchen. 'Look at those beautiful roses.' She briefly cupped the bloom of a white rose peeking out from its vase on a pot stand in the corner of the room. 'So fresh.'

'Fresh and lovely,' Abigail said, following behind.

'It really is a gorgeous cottage, isn't it,' said Lucie, looking around. 'When it's been given some attention.'

Carra winced inwardly.

Abigail, perhaps sensing something tense in the air, began to chatter. 'It's a sure sign of old age that I quite look forward to my big spring clean nowadays. I find myself trying not to get stuck into it in September, the minute spring comes along. This year I waited until October and had a proper declutter.'

Father John, carrying a small grocery bag filled with presents, stepped on a toy truck and stumbled into the pot stand, knocking the vase of roses to the floor.

'God dammit,' he said just loud enough for all to hear.

Len snorted.

'Terribly sorry, Carra,' said Father John. 'Always have been a bumbling fool.'

'Oh, Father,' said Abigail. 'So have I.' She gazed at Father John long enough for her cheeks to turn pink, then retreated into the safety of the spring-cleaning story, which came tumbling out in awkward spurts. 'I had a great pile of hard waste for the collection. It felt so good to clear it all. *And* I found a pot of cinnamon with a use-by date of 1991!' Abigail let out a hoot. 'Just think, I was only twenty-three in 1991.'

'I was just a baby!' said Carra, seeing to the mess of roses on the floor.

'That makes me ancient,' Abigail continued. 'I kept it! It just seemed wrong to throw it away, such a relic.'

Carra laughed. 'Careful. If that's a relic, where does that leave Len?'

Carra turned a teasing eye to her father-in-law. But Len, for once, remained silent. So did Lucie. Duncan looked pained. The three of them had sort of frozen into an awkward tableau. Abigail stared at them for a moment and then clapped a hand over her mouth.

'Oh my gosh,' she said, this time in a whisper. 'Nineteen ninety-one. Lucie . . . Len, I'm sorry.' She looked at Lucie. 'That's the year that Felicity . . . I'm so sorry.' She swallowed hard. Her eyes swam with tears.

Carra felt ill. She glanced at the roses in her hands, then up at Duncan. 'God, I should have realised . . .' She looked into her husband's eyes; they had clouded briefly but quickly composed into clarity. It was the first time Carra could remember hearing Felicity's name said aloud.

She remembered a time, years earlier, when Duncan had turned away from her and said, 'We don't really talk about my sister.' She had glimpsed a rigidity in his beautiful face, noticed the sudden slouch in his shoulders and the quick correction back to their usual, neutral repose. She had rested a hand on his back and put her lips to his cheek, but he had brushed her gently away. 'It's fine. I don't even remember her. Just easier for Mum and Dad not to talk . . .' He had left the sentence unfinished. Carra thought of the little curly-haired girl whose eyes watched, unblinking, from two framed photographs in the Riverhouse hallway. Everything about her was unfinished. Unfinished, unmentioned, undone. *Felicity Finlay.*

Abigail was babbling again. 'I'm so sorry, Lucie. On Christmas Day, too, of all times. I promise to be quiet now, because everything that comes out of my mouth is stupid, isn't it? I could change the subject to something banal – I'm very good at that, at least. Unless – oh dear – unless of course you *want* to talk about Felicity. I'm never very sure and I don't want to be disrespectful. Would you? Like to talk about . . . ?'

'Thank you for asking that, Abigail,' said Len hurriedly, as if to stem the flow of runaway words. 'I think we can just change the subject.' He looked at Lucie, whose face was pale, her eyes feverishly bright. She nodded. Duncan looked away.

'All right,' said Abigail. There was a stretch of silence as she scrabbled for a new conversation topic. 'I can also probably just leave you to your day if that would help. The Nuyina residents won't remember that I've already been there this morning. I could lunch with them. Honestly, just tell me to get lost if you like, I won't mind.'

Carra and Duncan froze. Len patted his bald head agitatedly. Lucie gasped, put a hand on his arm, another on Abigail's shoulder and burst into a peal of laughter. Everyone stared at her. Len looked alarmed. Abigail burst into fresh tears.

'Oh Abigail,' Lucie said, still laughing. 'You poor love. I know this isn't at all funny, but your face!' She reached over and patted Abigail's face as if to make it better. 'Shall we get you a shovel and you can dig your hole a little deeper? Dig, dig, dig, you might even actually find Felicity in your hole, given that I *lost* her so thoroughly.' Lucie laughed again. 'Twenty-nine years. Think of that. Twenty-nine years lost and not a single trace.'

Lucie's wild eyes met Carra's. Carra gripped her apron and tried to think of something to say.

'Lucie,' said Len, his face awash with distress.

But Lucie put a hand on his arm and continued. 'I think, after all this time, we can at the very least offer our missing daughter the small dignity of mentioning her name. At Christmas. Without a whimper or a sob, but with a laugh. She was so fond of laughing, if you remember.'

Carra gulped and watched Duncan's face for signs of trouble. It remained carefully fixed. She wondered whether he'd learned such composure at medical school, and then realised he'd probably been practising it far longer than that. Since 1991.

'Look,' Lucie said, with more equanimity, 'if we can't laugh just at this one moment then it proves that we're dead inside and I'm not – dead inside. We refuse to be, don't we, Len? I think of her every day and I'm still desperately, desperately sad, but today, I give everyone permission to laugh. Felicity does, too, I know it.'

Abigail, with her face in her hands, could not oblige. Len's laughter didn't emerge either.

Carra glanced at Duncan but he'd resorted to looking at the floor.

'Ha,' Carra tried softly. 'Haha.'

Lucie looked at her gratefully and joined in. Carra found that laughing came more easily then; Lucie's laugh had always been infectious. Duncan managed a smile and Len, with the aid of a hug from Lucie, performed a small, short nose-breath, which might have been the beginnings of a chortle. It swirled into the tempering Kinvarra air.

Later, once everyone had recovered and Abigail had been jollied out of her mortification (mostly by Len's special Christmas sparkling burgundy), Lucie took her aside and asked if she could perhaps have the cinnamon.

'I can't say why,' she said. 'It's something about holding a thing that's been lost for just as long as Felicity.'

'Of course,' Abigail said. 'It's yours, Lucie. Of course.' She shut her mouth in case something idiotic came out.

Lucie watched the purse of Abigail's lips. 'And another thing, Abigail,' she said. 'Thank you.'

Abigail nodded, surprised.

'Len decided quite early on that we shouldn't turn Felicity into a sort of occupation, or hobby. I agreed, of course, and the community is very respectful of that. Consequently, it's become a very silent thing, this loss of ours. Well, it hasn't really. Sometimes it's so intrusive I can hear it in the tick of my clocks and in the creak of my bones. But we don't speak it, as a matter of course. And sometimes I'm just bursting to shout her name. *Bursting*. And now, I don't feel quite so full with it, and I can resume Len's quiet sorrow.'

'For some,' said Abigail, '*Grief is a mouse, and chooses Wainscot in the Breast for his shy house*.' She laughed self-consciously. 'Emily Dickinson said that.'

Lucie squeezed her arm. 'There you are, see, not everything that comes out of your mouth is stupid.'

▼▼▼▼

Alexander Bradshaw, 20

When I was in primary school we all did a test to see who was gifted and who wasn't. I was told I was. Gifted. Ever since then, people said I should think about professions other than farming. But I only ever wanted to be a farmer. I don't think there's anything more important, except maybe teaching. Now, Dad keeps telling me how vital it is that I see the big, wide world, broaden my horizons. I don't think he wants me to be a farmer. He knows how hard it is. But I can't imagine anything else. And I think it's okay to just want to be in one place. I've been away from Nowhere River for seventeen months now, and that'll be a broad enough horizon to satisfy everyone. I wish I never did that gifted test. I think they messed up the results anyway.

Chapter 13

On 30 December, just as the townspeople of Nowhere River were thinking they might have a gin and tonic with lunch, a bit of a lie-down in the afternoon and bring the year to a gentle end, Patricia pinned her

SUCCESSFUL MISS FRESH AND LOVELY ENTRANTS
(FIRST AND FINAL LIST, in order of merit)

onto the front door of St Margery's Ladies' Club.

Lucie, from over the road in Marceline's hairdressing salon, was the first to see the unfamiliar white sign.

'Ooh, Marceline,' she said, 'it looks as though the Duchess hath spoke.'

Marceline paused mid-roller. 'Oh my God, I think you're right. Look, Bunty, Patricia's put up a sign. Have you got a project in?'

'No,' said Bunty. 'We're going to take part in all of Abigail's Old Folks' Treats. If we're helping Nuyina, we're helping ourselves.'

'Good plan,' said Lucie.

'I'm dying to know who got through,' said Marceline. 'Mind if I pop over and have a quick look?'

'Let's all go,' said Lucie. 'I don't mind going like this.' She touched her rollers. 'Shows I care about Patricia's precious appearances.'

So the three of them crossed the road, and joined a growing throng, which included the Pfaffs, Cosette Hamilton, Ruth Beaumont-Hudd, Phoebe Costas and the real estate agent, David Farquhar. This is what they read:

1. *Mrs Caroline Finlay: 'Sporticulture' – fitness and garden-improvement initiative*

2. *Miss Abigail Snelson: The Nowhere River Old Folks' Treats Committee*

3. *Miss Esther Very: Nowhere River Historical Society – museum addition to the Nowhere River Library, complete with new, minor excavations (with permission) and metal detecting at local sites*

4. *Mrs Marceline Cash: 'Get up and Glow' – improving self-esteem in Nowhere River*

5. *Mrs Deidre Wagner & Mrs Ruth Beaumont-Hudd: 'The Shiny-town Project' – clean-up (with possible town name change subject to strict guidelines, please see Mrs P. Montgomery)*

6. *Mrs Lucie Finlay: 'Nowhere People' – oral histories project*

7. *Miss Florence Bradshaw: The Nowhere River Show – revival*

8. *Mrs Lurlene Wallace: 'Sweet Lurlene Confections and Cakes'*

9. *Mrs G. Pfaff: Pfaffs' Post and Groceries improvement and innovation initiative*

10. *Miss Fleury Salverson: 'Miss Salverson's School of Yodelling'*

11. *Mrs Lucinda Price and Sr Julianne Poke: 'Save the Fat Doe Inn' – pub revitalisation*

12. *Mrs Elaine Thorold: 'Rose Quartz Weddings' and Queen Mary Park promotions*

13. *Mrs Rachael Hamilton: 'Nowhere River Ghost Tours'*

'Well,' said Phoebe. 'That just takes the egg. Of course I was over-looked.' Her fingers clenched and unclenched around the straps of her handbag, a hint of the effort it took to maintain composure. But her voice wavered when she added, 'I put a lot of work into that high-vis hall plan.'

'Oh, Phoebe,' whispered Lucie. 'I'm afraid it may have been just too unique for Patricia's hard-wired conservatism.'

Phoebe put her chin out and sniffed, but let Lucie put an arm around her.

'Mum, you're number thirteen!' said Cosette to her approaching mother, Rachael. 'You should be number one.'

'This is typical,' said David Farquhar, who had gone quite red in the face, 'of the near-sightedness of this town. Not a commer-cially viable project to be seen. Does anyone actually want this town to survive? Nowhere River will be a laughing stock. The *only way* this town will ever survive is to invite investment. You'll all be sorry.' And he marched off, his shiny suit flashing indignantly in the sun.

'Doesn't hurt to keep a town removed from the malaise of commercialism, though, does it,' Lucie muttered.

'Oh dear,' said Ruth, who'd forgotten her glasses and had had to find the correct reading distance. 'Does that say Florence Bradshaw and the Nowhere River Show?'

'Yes,' said Lucie. 'Brave girl.'

'Or silly.'

'Mum,' Cosette Hamilton huffed. 'You said kids aren't allowed to apply. How come Flo-poke Bradshaw gets a go?'

'It's children in school who aren't eligible,' said Lucie. 'Flo is not strictly in school.'

'Well, that's against the law,' said Cosette. 'Isn't it, Mum?'

'So is bullying, I'm told,' Lucie said casually. 'Well done, Lurlene, you're in.'

Lurlene, who had wheeled up to join the onlookers, raised a hand and gave a little cheer.

By then, there were more people congregating to inspect the St Margery's front door, and a hail of other remarks.

'I'm definitely joining that Sporticulture bit.'

'That's a heap more members for St Marg. The old girl won't know herself.'

'I'll tell you a few stories, Lucie.'

'Ooh, I adore your jelly cakes, Lurlene.'

'This'll get Nowhere River going somewhere, surely.'

▼▼▼

It was New Year's Day, thirteen days after Jerry's accident, before Carra summoned the courage to contact Josie.

'Josie,' she rehearsed as she mopped the floor after breakfast (and vowed not to dish up baked beans again), 'I just want to say I'm so, so sorry I haven't phoned earlier. I didn't want to interfere, and to be honest I just didn't know what to say. I'm hopeless with tragedy, you know that.' She paused and leaned on the mop. 'Shit. Don't say tragedy, he's not dead.'

She began her mopping again, quite vigorously. 'Josie, hi. Happy New Year! Jerry isn't dead! Yay! Hey, Josie, sorry I haven't been in touch since Jerry went into a coma. It's just that I've been so caught up in myself, as usual. It's funny, you know, I always thought I was a good friend, until I wasn't.' She mopped faster. 'And I can't face you because we used to tell each other everything and everything. But I can't seem to tell you that I'm horrified by the idea that I have to do *this*'—she banged the mop on the floor—'and *that*'—she kicked a piece of Duplo—'and *this*'—she forced an exaggerated, blissful smile—'for the next, I don't know, lifetime.' She squeezed out the mop with extra force and added a loud sound effect that was somewhere between a growl and a screech.

Ben began to cry.

'Oh, darling, sorry.' Carra set the mop down and collected him up. 'Did I scare you?' She jiggled him about. He wailed. She pulled out a breast.

Once she had Ben appeased and the mopping done, Carra opted for a text message. It took six-and-a-half drafts before she settled on, *Dear Josie, I just wanted to say I'm thinking of you as the new year dawns. I hope it's a better one for you. I've been keeping a good eye on Flo and Alex. They are both working hard, keeping busy. Lucie has a food roster going and Walt is helping Alex when he needs it. He's a great kid, Josie. They both are. I am thinking of you all, all the time. Just let me know if there is anything else I can do. Lots of love C XOX.*

She wrote and deleted *PS I miss you* only once. It would be a silly thing to say, given that Carra had brought the missing on herself.

Three hours and much pacing about later, her phone dinged with a reply. Carra hurried towards it, stubbing her toe on the way. The message was indeed from Josie. It said *Thanks.* Nothing more. No funny emoji, no kiss, no hug, no elaborations. Josie, who usually sent essay-long text messages, with multiple postscripts, had nothing left for Carra. At least that's how it seemed to Carra, as she stood in her kitchen, ignoring the pleas of her children.

I've blown it, she thought. And then she had to admonish herself for being so utterly self-absorbed. *She's in a hospital room, next to her critically ill husband. She's traumatised. She'd have nothing left for anything. And anyway,* Carra sank into a chair and let Daisy climb on her, *I deserve precisely nothing.*

▼▼▼

Josie had been watching an episode of *The Goodies* on a laptop in Jerry's hospital room and trying to keep her eyes off the waveforms on the life support machines when Carra's text arrived.

It had made Josie sit up in her chair. 'Hey, Jerry, listen to this. It's a Happy New Year text from Carra. She says that the kids are being looked after and keeping busy. And that Walt is helping Alex. Then she says I should let her know if there's anything else she can do. She sends kisses and hugs.' Josie was aware that her voice had taken on a nasty, bitter note, but she didn't care. 'Why is it,' she continued, 'that people say "let me know what I can do" and think that's enough? I just don't have the brainpower to start delegating my life to people. What if I text her back and say, "Oh hey, thanks for the offer, here's what I need: Jerry back, right now, please. And someone to take on Flo's riding lessons, you could help her with her flying changes and her engagement, couldn't you? And what do you know about peri-menopause, because once we could have laughed about it, but you know, it's not that funny on your own. And oh, PS, I need a friend. A goddamn proper friend, with laughs and tears and all the trimmings. No, not even the trimmings, just to be here."'

Josie put a hand to her chest as if to pat down her emotion, then put her head on Jerry's shoulder and closed her eyes for long enough to feel the wobble of incoming sleep. She sat up again with a sharp intake of breath, threw her phone into her bag and went back to watching Bill Oddie playing trombone in a superman suit. Later, she sent Carra a simple *Thanks* and wondered whether she'd ever laugh again.

It was almost noon that same day when Carra had just completed the elaborate set-up required for a morning shower (twins in the bathroom with a pile of pots of pans; clothes, hairdryer, towels all in position) that there was a knock at the door.

'Shit,' said Carra, looking down at her pyjamas and wondering whether to hide.

'Shit,' said Daisy. 'Shit.'

The knock came again. Carra peeped out a window and saw Sergeant D's LandCruiser in the driveway.

'It's the police,' she told the babies. 'Coming to check on my absconding-risk status and to arrest us all for obscene language.' She grabbed a coat from the hook in the hallway and called, 'Coming!'

'Hi, Carra,' said Sergeant D at the door. 'Happy New Year!' She looked at Carra's coat, which happened to be an old raincoat of Duncan's. 'Is there rain forecast?'

'No. The babies and I are trying a new drought-breaking strategy, in which you have to wear wet-weather clothing at all times.'

'Oh, I should have brought my umbrella.'

'Come in and join us anyway.' Carra led Sergeant D to the kitchen. 'Actually, I'm still in my jarmies. About to have a shower. It's taken me this long to get around to it.'

'Nothing like a jarmie morning,' said Sergeant D.

'Every morning is jarmie morning. And often it's jarmie day. Helps with not running away, though. I mean, I wouldn't want to run away in my pyjamas, would I?'

'I'm not here to check up on whether you're running away, Carra. I told you I'm comfortable that you won't.'

'Right.'

'Well, it is a little bit of a check-up.'

'Right. Well, good to know you're thorough.'

'And I wanted to say congratulations to you for the Sporticulture thing. So, congratulations!'

'You know about the Sporticulture thing?'

'Oh yeah, Patricia posted the finalists two days ago. I guess you and Duncan have been too busy to know. New Year's Eve parties and all that.'

'Yeah, I'm such a party animal these days.' Carra touched a hand to her unkempt hair. 'So, two days ago? I had no idea. Lucie's probably been trying to call.'

'She has.'

'And when I didn't answer, she called you?'

'Um . . .'

'Right.' Carra closed her eyes for a moment. *People are only interested in me when I'm not doing the 'right thing'.*

'But I'm glad she did, because I don't mind an excuse to see my little mates again.' Sergeant D looked around for the twins. For a long moment, Carra did too.

'Um,' she said, rummaging through her flustered thoughts for where she'd put the babies. 'Oh, they're in the bathroom. Haha, just a small moment of forget – we were about to have a shower. I mean, *I* was, and they have to come too . . .' Carra hurried to retrieve the twins.

She was bringing Daisy into the kitchen, with Ben crawling behind, when Sergeant D said, 'You're number one on Patricia's list, by the way. Order of merit.'

'I am? God, that's amazing. I thought Patricia sees me as an insult to her gender.'

'I didn't even make the cut. Not a bad thing, I was mad to think I could pull a footy team together.'

'We have to have big dreams,' said Carra.

Sergeant D looked at the floor.

Then Carra said, without thinking, 'You're really, really beautiful, aren't you.'

Sergeant D half laughed, half choked. 'What?'

'God, sorry.' Carra banged a palm to her head. 'Did I think that aloud? Must tell my brain to use its inside voice. But really, you have the clearest skin I've ever seen. And your hair is like, the perfect colour.'

'Righto, now I *am* worried about you,' said Sergeant D. 'How about I hang with these two while you shower. It mustn't be easy.'

'Would you?' Carra gaped. She couldn't believe there was a real live person before her, showing actual empathy. It was like Sergeant D had superpowers. *Maybe empathy is a superpower,* she thought.

'Go for it. Take your time.'

'Oh, my God, I can't tell you how nice those three words are. Take. Your. Time.' Carra breathed the words in, and closed her eyes on them for a moment, then skipped off towards the bathroom. 'Just call the police if anything untoward happens, they'll be here in the blink of an eye.'

Sergeant D looked at the babies and said, 'Okay, you mongrels, what have you got for me?'

'Shit,' said Ben, which made Sergeant D laugh and clap her hands.

When Carra padded back in from the bathroom with some freshly scrubbed rose in her cheeks and the scent of shampoo about her, she said, 'Sorry Sergeant. It's just occurred to me that I didn't offer you a coffee or anything. Or a lifesaving trophy, which you deserve. That bit of alone time was seriously lifesaving.' She filled up the kettle.

'It's so fine,' said Sergeant D. 'I don't drink coffee.'

'I probably shouldn't be spouting on about alone time. You'll think I'm headed for the hills.'

'Well, I have made note of the fact that you wear banana pyjamas.'

'Yes. Always under a raincoat.' Carra looked at Sergeant D's uniform. 'Are you ever not on duty? It's holidays.'

'Not really. Much like Dunc. And things always hot up over Christmas. Health problems, grog and crime rates.'

'Yep, the two of you are keeping us all together.' Carra coughed. 'Shit, sorry. That sounded kind of . . . I didn't mean . . .'

'Ah, I know.' Sergeant D smiled, but her green eyes were suddenly sad. Something fluttered in Carra's chest. She cleared her throat. 'What sort of criminal activity should I be aware of in the greater Colleen Valley?'

'You'd be surprised. Last New Year's Eve, someone drew an ar . . . sorry, a *bottom*hole on the Thorolds' fence.'

'Really?' Carra said. 'How do you even draw a bottomhole?'

'It was sort of just a big round bottom, with the crack and then what looked like a little sun.'

'A little sun?'

'Yep, that was the hole part. You know, with the wrinkles. Quite effective, actually.' Sergeant D gave a shy laugh.

Carra laughed with her, and felt a rush of pleasure to be doing so. She thought of Josie, and all their laughs over the years; the warm release of a great big, genuine bellow with a dear friend was like a safe haven. Josie had a wonderful laugh, unabashed and generous. She would screech with laughter to know that Carra was talking bottomholes with Sergeant D.

'So, anyway . . .' Sergeant D stood. 'I should go before there are bottomholes graffitied all over the place.' She waved at the babies and headed for the door, then stopped. 'And you should make sure your husband gets along to the Sporticulture meets. In his shorts. Everyone is bound to come along then. Hope you don't mind me saying.' Her cheeks bloomed with pink.

Carra laughed. 'I'll do my best.' She opened the door for Sergeant D. 'Is everyone in the whole town attracted to Duncan, do you think?'

'Yep. Without a doubt. Even Mr Pfaff.'

'Even you?' asked Carra.

'No way. He's like a brother to me these days.' The shy laughter came again, but this time it didn't seem quite so genuine.

As Carra watched the LandCruiser drive away, she felt again that same indeterminate flutter in her chest. It mingled with and fortified Carra's growing unease.

Phoebe Costas, 57

Nowhere River has been good to me on the whole, thank you for asking. I can't imagine what life in a big city would be like. Probably, for someone like me, a bit invisible. People see you here, mostly. It's important to be seen. And if you don't know what you're doing, someone else will tell you.

Chapter 14

Three days later, Flo stood with Lucie and Len at the Nowhere River showgrounds and tried not to feel overwhelmed.

'Well, this is exciting,' said Lucie. 'Who's excited?' She led the way onto the mangy-looking main arena, which was cracked and pock-marked with cattle holes.

'Um,' said Flo.

'Exciting in a sort of "what the jingoes are you thinking?" way, I suppose,' said Len.

Lucie tried to give him one of her looks, but he was busy survey-ing the sorry state of the showgrounds. 'It's all weed and splinter, really, isn't it?'

Lucie saw the slump of Flo's shoulders. 'Flo has great faith in you, Len,' she said. 'With your superior presidential knowledge of the plumbing valves and switchboards, et cetera. And where there's a will there's a way.'

'Where there's a will there's a row, in my experience,' said Len. 'Especially when it comes to the Show Society.'

Lucie sighed. Len was in one of his down moods, in which his limp got worse and he had trouble seeing any bright sides. Lucie felt pre-emptively exhausted at the prospect of lifting his spirits. She'd managed much heavier lifting in the past, but found that with age comes muscle fatigue. And there was the additional consideration of Flo's brittle spirits.

'But isn't it wonderful that Flo is willing to give the old show a crack,' she said. 'Dear old thing that it is.' She watched him sift through his memories and finally smile.

Amid the disarranged darkness of a child gone missing, Len had found himself trapped and pacing in a place he and Lucie could neither love nor leave. They were urban people, the Finlays, restaurant and theatre people. They'd been happily raising their children in central Hobart. Len had an influential job, Lucie had social connections. Neither of them had ever dreamed of leaving it all behind.

But the very worst had happened, and just like that, it was leaving Nowhere River that seemed inconceivable. Eventually they sold their house in Hobart, and bought Riverhouse. From there, Lucie could see the footbridge, the riverbank path, the fisher cottages, and very often a little curly-headed girl in tutu and gumboots, pointing at the river. Lucie was never sure what Len could see, but he appeared to gather strength from the country air, from the river and the rambling Riverhouse garden. And he didn't seem to be too often directing his view to the past.

Len had stumbled upon a Show Society meeting a few years after they settled into Riverhouse, back when there was an actual council in the hall's council chambers. He'd gone to enquire about reclaiming some land and putting in a jetty, and found all the staff gathered together in their lunch hour to discuss coming attractions and ground-space concerns. The clumsy handling of committee procedures and the lengthy debate over how best to peel hard-boiled eggs had made him laugh. And Len hadn't, for a good while before that, laughed very much at all. By the conclusion of the meeting, Len (an experienced town planner) had rearranged ground space to allow for all the stalls and attractions. In return, he received his jetty approvals, and a spot on the committee.

'Yes,' said Len, as he followed Lucie and Flo towards a side door at the base of the old grandstand. 'She was a good old girl, our show. But I'm not sure how cooperative she'll be with a grand revival.' He swung the door open with a flourish, only to have it thud against something, about a third of the way open. 'There we are, you see,' he said. 'She's seized up like a bad knee.'

'It can't be all that bad,' said Lucie, pedalling madly to keep Len on the bright side. 'Nothing a team of willing helpers can't sort out.'

'I can fix this on the spot,' said Len, who stood back, took a deep breath and gave the door an almighty shove with his foot. It burst off its hinges and clattered to the floor, falling onto whatever had been in its way.

'Jesus,' said Flo's shock, then, 'Sorry.'

'Well, that'll scare the snakes away,' said Lucie.

The three of them collected up the door and leaned it against the wall. Underneath it, on the dusty floor, was a large piece of chipboard, which must have been sitting atop an easel (now broken to pieces).

'Ah,' said Len, picking up the board and turning it towards the light. It was covered in grime and bird droppings, with letters painted in bright orange that still clearly read:

Welcome to the Nowhere River Show
Come along now, one and all, you'll have a country good time.

'There was a bit of a row over the tagline, if I remember rightly,' Len said.

'Yes,' said Lucie. 'Cliffity Smith was very set on "Come and drive yourself round the river bend" or something like that. Patricia said we shouldn't have anything at all, just a simple welcome, in a tasteful bottle green. She was probably right.'

But Flo wasn't listening. The enormity of the task ahead was becoming clear. All her colourful plans were shrouded in dust and cobwebs.

Len, observing Flo's downcast face, said, 'Well, if the town ends up with a new name, we can make a whole new sign.'

'Oh don't,' said Lucie. 'That can't possibly happen. They suggested "Gloria", for goodness sake.'

'Well, I wouldn't trust the nomenclature board,' said Len. 'They recently approved "Twinkly Valley" for a new locality in the northwest. And in the Huon Valley they named a marshy region "Hooper's Slop".'

'They're running a suggestion box at Nuyina,' said Flo. 'And another one in town. Elaine Thorold wants "Serendipity".'

'She does not,' said Lucie. 'That's so bad it's almost good.'

'"Wafty Valley" would be my suggestion,' said Len. 'That or "Grumbly Swallet".'

Flo laughed. 'Cliffity Smith suggested "Dinkumville".'

'Dinkumville, that's the dizzy limit,' said Lucie. She squeezed Flo's arm and the three of them laughed together.

'All right,' bossed Len, 'let's focus on what must be done. Flo is meant to be making a detailed list of things to be addressed.'

Flo looked at her blank paper, stopped laughing and wondered where on earth to begin.

▼▼▼

By day forty-eight of Jerry's hospitalisation, Josie had learned to distract her doomsaying mind by throwing herself into his care. She had seen Sue the counsellor again, several times, but had not managed to master the art of sitting with her thoughts. Her pragmatism, declared Sue, was Josie's coping mechanism, and she was therefore granted permission to assist with many of the simpler aspects of care. Having read all she could about the comatose patient,

Josie had determined not to let sensory deprivation play any part in Jerry's decline, and stayed on guard for moments when she could step in and keep him stimulated. 'Keeping him skippy,' she called it, echoing Jerry's vernacular. But he was far from skippy.

Jerry's doctors had told her weeks ago that by now he should be conscious. The swelling on his brain had settled, his liver surgery had gone well, when he was removed from the ventilator he breathed on his own, but their predictions were proving wrong. Still none of his neurological responses indicated consciousness. 'It can take some time,' the doctors had told her, but 'some time' had long passed, and the consultations began to include chilling words like 'cytoxic' and 'occult'. Josie became aware of a sheen of mystified alarm that blurred the requisite composure of the hospital staff. It put her on the breathless edge of panic. Her fists clenched against it, their words became muffled and dull. *Don't look at him, don't touch his skin, don't make me cry, do nothing in the manner of goodbye.* The refrain came to her every time a doctor entered the room.

And through it all came the horrible flashes of a life devoid of Jerry – an empty bed, a bereft cattle dog, a dusty hat. They were so pervasive, the visions, so vivid, that they seemed to change the light in the room, bringing a sinister suggestion of premonition that distorted Josie's vulnerable sensibilities and kept her working at his bedside. She moved parts of him like bits of machinery, stroked his hair, massaged his calves, whispered banal words to him and did anything but hold his hand. Holding his hand seemed too much like a scene from a bad film, too much like giving up. She stepped aside gratefully when the nurses saw to his hygiene. She had helped once with a hot wash but was crestfallen by the sight of his shrunken, cathetered penis. Josie could fix a broken fence, rebuild an engine and whack a heartbeat into a calf, but the shock of that glimpse made everything seem impossible.

She was relieved that Alex was visiting less frequently, clearly overcome by the intense waiting but blaming farm work. Flo asked regularly and bluntly why Jerry wasn't waking up, but also filled her phone calls with chat about show developments. Josie kept her panic in check, played down the mystery of Jerry's condition. She listened to them, offered up bright affirmations and held their voices to Jerry's ear. She said goodbye before the static on the line gave way to more probing questions, or betrayed Josie's fear.

After the calls, Josie related every scrap of news to Jerry. 'Flo says she's got a list of showground jobs a mile long. The men's shed blokes are practising their carpentry skills at the showgrounds, she's called Mick the snake man in to clear out the tiger snakes, and she's hooked in a Hobart rubbish-collection company as a sponsor. Crazy child. I've never known her to be so focused.'

And: 'Alex said he's grateful for Walt's help but wishes he'd leave him alone a bit more and that he knows how to work an irrigator. Lurlene's still in her wheelchair.'

Josie didn't want to add any more farm details in case it sent Jerry into a panic. There still hadn't been any rain. (Though even a decent rainfall without Jerry seemed unthinkable.) So she played music, put movies on, told him jokes.

Eventually she remembered that someone had given her an assortment of books. She dug them out and assessed them for suitability. Two classics, one romance, one thriller and a book on Tasmanian history. The thriller was the only one that would appeal to Jerry but Josie worried about the effects of manufactured suspense, so she opened the history text. She read it monotonously, filling the silence, for hours, and when her throat began to hurt, she read on.

She only stopped when the nurse entered the room to attend to a beeping intravenous pump, and said, 'Jeepers, that sounds intense.'

'Yeah,' said Josie. 'Van Diemen's Land was a brutal place, wasn't it? It's pretty interesting too, though.'

'Are you up to the bit where White Australia realises it's made a terrible mistake in thinking our Indigenous people were brainless savages, oh, but, oops, too late – we buggered the planet?'

Josie looked at the nurse, a man with long, red hair tied back in a ponytail, maybe around thirty. She'd seen him a few times. Jerry would call him a 'smartarse hipster millennial'.

She glanced at Jerry, his mouth slack, his indelible, cattleman values now silent. Part of her hoped he could hear. 'Yes, I think I am. I've been reading about how Traditional Owners on the mainland managed the land. They sowed crops for food, harvested them . . . they were farmers.'

The nurse jotted something on a medical chart. 'Yep, I reckon we could learn a lot from them.'

'Yeah,' said Josie, looking down at her hands and noticing how oddly clean they were after so long off the farm.

Later, seeking other forms of stimulation, Josie accidentally considered playing with Jerry's penis. *If anything could bring a man around . . .* she thought, but quickly dismissed the idea, on the grounds of it being non-consensual and entirely inappropriate. And because she didn't feel like it. She hadn't, she realised, thought about sex for months and months. She imagined her vagina as a dry, shrivelled place. *More drought.*

'Sensory stimulation,' she whispered to herself. She waved a piece of bread roll under Jerry's nostril, the one not blocked by a feeding tube. Then she ran a fingernail along his arm from his hand to his shoulder, in the light-touch way he loved at the end of a long physical day. She whispered into his ear, 'It would be very nice to see you again. To touch you again. To feel you inside me.' But that felt a bit like a bad movie too, and Jerry would be embarrassed by such talk. So she sat back into her chair. *I've run out of senses*, she thought.

She decided against opening up one of his eyes in the hopes it might focus on something, and instead wondered about resorting to the sixth sense. If those pervasive visions were causing a dark future to materialise, perhaps she could turn her mind against them.

She sat back in her chair, closed her eyes and imagined her thoughts into light waves, bridging the space between herself and Jerry. She sent out an image of the two of them, first in the sunshine, but rejigged to include rain. Proper driving rain, like none they had seen in decades. The sort of rain you couldn't turn your face upwards into because it would sting your eyes and hit the back of your throat. They were laughing, Josie and Jerry, laughing and drinking the rain, splashing and running towards the stables.

Inside, the noise above them, thunderous on the iron roof, drowned out their laughter and their words. So they didn't speak. They just fell into the pile of horse blankets and kissed one another's smiles, pulled away their soaking clothes and clung to each other, wet skin to wet skin.

Josie no longer felt the sticky vinyl of the hospital chair, she couldn't taste the disappointment of a hospital lunch, smell the chemical air or hear the systematic rhythms of machines. There were no ominous visions. She just had the rain, the stables and the wondrous, searing relief of doing life with another person. She sent it all through the close hospital air, to her husband.

And it found him there.

Less than a minute later, the nurse burst into the room and sounded an alarm, and Josie was quickly ushered away.

Josie Bradshaw, 45

I guess everyone has to go through bad times at some stage. You can't just expect to doodle along having everything happen the way you planned. Jerry and I always had a plan. Everston has been in his family for generations and his dreams became my dreams. We knew we'd get married. There wasn't even a proper proposal, we didn't say, 'Should we?' We said, 'When should we?' And then we had a perfect boy baby, then a perfect girl baby. And our kids are growing into good people. I guess that could be pretty boring. Maybe it's the bad times that wake us up.

Chapter 15

Flo, having spent the morning at Nuyina to assist with Lucie's Nowhere People interviews and collect everyone's favourite memories of the Nowhere River Show, had a head so full of stories and thoughts that her bike-riding went wobbly on the way home and she had to dismount by the river and offload everything from her brain onto paper. *Cliffity's gnomes*, she wrote, among other things. *Damper and billy tea, luncheon plates, guess the weight of the bull, dog jumping, prize-giving . . .*

If she wanted to have the show organised by October, she was going to be busier than a mozzie at a nudist colony (according to Fleury Salverson). Already, she'd been informed by George Costas that the showground plumbing was 'jiggered' and the toilets likely to overflow. And she'd had nightmares about the grandstand falling.

The stories from Nuyina, positive as they were, felt somehow more unsettling than the plumbing problems. Flo realised that the townspeople had invested a lot of hope in the show's revival, that it meant more to them than a mere day of entertainment.

'I used to stitch and bottle all year for the show,' Swoozie Hamilton had said. 'It helped us all get up out of bed.'

Flo wondered whether they should trust her with their tradition. *Have I really thought this through properly? No*, she decided, *but*

lots of things never happen because people think about them too much.
Nonetheless, Flo knew she must be very careful not to dishonour the
show by making a hash of it.

'Doan let nobody be shittin' on our show,' Cliffity Smith had
warned her.

She added *Cliffity's ferret performance?* to her notes and then
Revive, don't reinvent.

She zipped the notebook into her backpack and hopped onto her
bike. Then, not far from home, as she approached the Abergavenny
ruins, where the light was late-afternoon gold, she stopped again,
staying still and silent, in case a wombat was snuffling about. There
were only two rabbits, at which Flo wrinkled her nose. She felt a
sudden sting of tears. Looking up into the craggy branches of the
lonely tree, the tears pooled against her eyelashes as she sent the tree
a silent plea to grow taller, to be constant, to stay. She sat beneath it,
remembering what she'd learned about eucalypts preferring company.
They usually died if they stood alone, exposed to the elements for too
long. She rested her head back against the trunk and placed a hand
on a knobbly root that brought to mind the old, old hands of the
people at Nuyina. She mourned the spry, vibrant things those hands
had left behind. From somewhere in the upwards, a skylark sang.

'You have me,' she whispered to the tree. 'And the birds.'

One of the rabbits loped into her view and she threw a twig at it.
It bounded into a wombat hole just near the ruined chimney, leaving
Flo with a dull thud of something like homesickness. The wombats
felt like another piece of her childhood ambling away.

'Flo?' came a voice from the distance.

Flo jerked her gaze to the sky. 'Dad?'

'Flo!' It was closer now, and at ground level. She turned to see Alex
running towards her across the home paddock. She froze. *Oh no.* Flo
closed her eyes and tried desperately to hear the skylark again. *Please,
please, please.*

Alex jumped the boundary fence and slowed to a stop, panting. 'He woke up, Floey. He's breathing on his own, he's talking. Mum said he sort of sighed and coughed, then his heart rate went up a bit and he just opened his eyes!' Alex crouched, took her by the shoulders and gave her a gentle shake. 'She said it looks like he might be okay.'

Flo searched her brother's face for reasons to disbelieve him. She found none, so looked up into the celebratory flutters of the lonely tree's leaves and whispered her thanks.

It was February by then. The dry inland heat quilted the valley, bringing snakes to the riverbanks and smoke haze to the horizons. People put their bathers on, dove into the sun-blazed water and laughed bitterly about the scant blessings of a drought in Tasmanian bushfire season. 'Nothing to burn, not a cracker.' The river, with its unusual warmth, seemed kinder, but weakened.

February was also the month in which Daisy and Ben Finlay discovered the joyous occupation of walking. Ben spent his early toddling days pacing in large circles, slowly with his head down, watching in amazement as the earth moved beneath him. Daisy, on the other hand, darted about at acute angles with the ground, using the pick-up-speed method to balance herself, which made everyone gasp and run after her with hands at the ready. She would writhe and yell if said hands held her for any longer than a few seconds, then career off to the next thing: a plover or the coffee table, and quite often her brother, whom she'd fall onto so the two of them were a bawling mess of chubby limbs.

Up until then, Carra's Sporticulture sessions with her baby attachments had been operating tolerably well. The group, which met up to three times a week to spruce up the town's neglected gardens, had been very popular. There were always people willing to keep an eye on the twins, pick them up or play with them, adorable as they were – especially when crawling about on lawns and covered in bits of nature. Carra began to see glimpses of the village that might raise them.

But the walking business turned the chaos up a notch, and Daisy had begun to shriek 'Noooooo' to anyone who approached, which was deflating to a would-be minder. Then there was the matter of a rose thorn in Ben's hand and a wallop on his head from Daisy's trowel (she received a sting from a fair-minded bee shortly afterwards). Twice Carra had had to cut the sessions short.

'Now I'll have one toned arm and one tuck-shop flapper,' said a disgruntled Elaine Thorold after the second aborted session. 'And I've only half trimmed my box.'

On three occasions, Carra had left the babies in the care of Lucie and discovered the pleasures of a full and productive, wonderfully uninterrupted workday. Without impediment, Carra could transform an ugly garden or plan an entire month's Sporticulture timetable. The euphoria she felt at the start of these days, and her delighted amazement when she whipped through task after task, was akin to some sort of drug-induced high. She had trouble not singing and skipping away from Riverhouse, and even more trouble dragging her feet back there at the end of the day. These visceral reactions to her freedom came with an underscore of dull shame. *I really am a high-tailer.* Her evenings were spent guilt-baking and trying not to plot her next escape. Duncan would emerge for breakfast to find cooling racks filled with biscuits and slices, and the babies eating freshly made carrot-and-apple pikelets.

After the third day, during which Carra had lost track of time and collected the babies from Riverhouse an hour late, she decided that the pull of career and the resulting guilt (and all the baked goods) formed a dangerous and slippery slope. She stopped leaving the twins with Lucie and reverted to her usual chaotic juggle.

The streets of Nowhere River showed some tangible garden progress. The town hall's box-hedge trim was completed and the neglected plants watered and limed. The roundabout off the Pearce Highway – the one that housed the proud (peeling) 'Welcome to Nowhere River' sign – now boasted an assemblage of bright pink roses and yellow daisies. The Queen Mary Park stonework was repaired, weeded and cleaned, its edges sharpened. Plants battered by drought were replaced with sturdy, waterwise greenery.

Carra, while invigorated by the work, felt her edges continue to fray. One Saturday, when she was due to lead a small group through a mulching workshop at the church, she looked at her fractious children and wondered whether to give up on the Miss Fresh and Lovely idea and just surrender to everything, then emerge from the trenches in eighteen years to survey the damage and reassess her position.

'There are worse things,' she said to her reflection in the oven door, 'than being a maidservant.'

'Dadadada,' shouted Ben.

Daisy began to cry.

Ben threw a slimy piece of apple across the room. It hit the oven door. Carra closed her eyes for a moment, then opened them again to examine her reflection through the smear of apple. She wiped the oven door with a dishcloth, then picked up the phone.

'Ruth,' she shouted over the din. 'Hi, it's Carra. Can I speak to Duncan just briefly, please?'

'He's with a patient, Carra. I'll get him to phone you back?'

'Actually, could you put me through? I promise to be really quick.'

Carra listened to a small huff from Ruth, and then a series of clicks, followed by Duncan saying, 'Carra?'

'Sorry, I know you're busy, but I was wondering whether I could whizz the babies into you and Ruth for an hour or so. They're so unsettled and I have a quick mulching commitment to get to.'

'Can't you go after lunch?' said Duncan. 'I'll be home by half past twelve.'

'It's booked in for this morning. Normally I'd take them, but they're a mile a minute and I think they're turning people off. My numbers are dropping. And anyway, you never close up at midday on a Saturday. Never. You'll do house calls. And then you have that meeting with Sergeant D about the show attractions.' She paused. There were some muffled noises on Duncan's end. 'Duncan?'

'I'm with a patient, Carra. And maybe they're unsettled because they're coming down with something. Ruth'll have a fit if they bring germs in.'

'But there are germs everywhere in there. Everyone has them. And you're a doctor, germs are your thing.'

'Carra, I have to go. Let's work something out this afternoon. See you then, bye.' He hung up.

Carra threw the phone down. 'See you in eleventy years when you've finished saving everyone else's lives. I was told to ask for help, and I'm asking for help, and why is it even called "help" when it's your responsibility too? You're their father.' The word 'father' fluted upwards and threatened to turn into a scream.

Carra put a hand over her mouth, then looked at the babies. 'Sorry, he's at work, he's a good man. Okay, who wants to go for an exciting outing to the churchyard? Yay, woohoo, yippee!' She clapped her hands. Daisy wailed. Carra stopped clapping. 'Okay. You win. I'll cancel. We'll stay home and make something nourishing for dinner.'

She phoned her Sporticulturalists to cancel, then opened the fridge and surveyed its innards for inspiration. She pulled out a droopy carrot and an empty milk bottle.

'Or how about a drive to the shop? Ooh, the shop, it's so fun there.'

Half an hour later, Carra was blankly wandering the aisles of Pfaffs' Post and Groceries, when she encountered Elaine Thorold in the frozen meals section.

'Hello, Carra,' Elaine said gravely. 'Oh, I just can't believe it, can you? Statistically they say farmers are more likely to die on the job than firemen, did you know that?' She held up an onion. 'I'm making Josie two extra casseroles. They'll be able to freeze them. Julianne's doing quiche but I said I didn't think it's everyone's favourite. Quiche. Not at a time of high stress like this. It's more of a take-to-a-party thing. All that cream. There's talk that the family will stay in Hobart for good, to forget the trauma, have you heard that? The men's shed blokes are going to be feeding the stock for the time being. It's too much for Walt. I saw Alex and Flo heading out yesterday afternoon. I blew them kisses. The whole town is blowing them kisses, aren't they?'

But Carra had stopped listening. 'That's nice of you, Mrs Thorold,' she said mechanically. 'I just have to . . .' And then, just as mechanically, she paid Mr Pfaff for her groceries and wheeled the twins back to the car. Out on the High Street, everything began to blur through her tears. She fumbled the protesting babies into their car seats and shut herself into the driver's seat, where she wiped her eyes. *Just get home, just get home . . .*

Duncan arrived back at Kinvarra just after four that afternoon. He found Daisy sitting gleefully in a pile of flour, while Ben was pulling tissues from a box, *pfft, pfft, pfft*. There were pots and pans, plastic containers and wooden spoons everywhere.

'Carra?' Duncan called. 'CARRA?'

'I'm here,' said Carra, from the couch. She emerged from beneath a throw rug and a pile of cushions.

'What's happened? Are you all right?'

Carra touched her face – puffy eyes, runny nose. 'No, I'm not really. I know about Jerry.'

'Oh shit, yeah, I just totally forgot to tell you. I heard yesterday and then I was home so late and—'

'Yesterday? You knew yesterday?'

'I didn't see you this morning.'

'I spoke to you on the phone.'

'Yeah, but I was with a patient, and you were all pissed off.'

'I wasn't pissed off! Wait—' Carra extricated herself from the couch cushions and held up her hand in a furious stop sign. 'Wait, my friend just lost her husband and you *forgot to tell me?* Oh my God, Duncan. And now you're saying this is *my fault* that I don't know?'

'I'm not saying . . . Carra, she hasn't *lost* him—'

'Oh, sorry, right, I forget that the fucking Finlay family are the only people in the world who can rightfully lay claim to the word "loss".'

'Excuse me?'

'Let me correct myself. So my friend's husband falls from his medically induced coma into *death* and it just *slips* your mind?' Carra felt fury rushing up from her depths. 'Am I really so forgettable? Am I invisible?'

Duncan clasped her shoulder. 'Carra. Wait, he didn't die. Jerry isn't dead.'

Carra began to cry. 'Yes, he is, Duncan. Mrs Thorold said so, in the shop. She's made casseroles—'

'No, no, no,' Duncan grasped Carra's wrists, 'Stop. Listen, he came out of the coma. He brought himself out. His brain is okay. He's moving out of ICU later this week.'

Carra stared at him through her streams of tears. 'What?'

'I'm so sorry I forgot to tell you. That was terrible of me. And I'm sorry you thought—'

'Oh my God, that stupid Elaine Thorold.'

'Well, she would have assumed you already knew. I would have thought you'd have heard from Josie. Have you missed a call from her?'

'No,' Carra whispered. 'Maybe. I don't know.' She fell onto Duncan and sobbed. With relief, with regret, with sorrow – in equal parts they fed into her wellspring of tears. In the kitchen, Daisy banged a measuring cup on to an oven dish in perfect time with Carra's pounding heart.

Josie looked up as Alex appeared, his eyes wide with overwhelm, at the door of the hospital room.

'Alex,' she whispered, and felt a shimmer of tears. The little boy in him, the one who used to twirl her hair around his fingers when he was worried, was suddenly so present, she could almost feel the tug on her ponytail.

'Hi.' He looked at Jerry on the bed.

'He's sleeping, but come in, he asked me to wake him. Where's Flo?'

'She stopped at the gift ship.' Alex inched forward into the room.

'It's okay,' said Josie. 'He has some pain so he's pretty sleepy, but he's all here.' *I think,* she added silently.

'Don't wake him yet,' Alex whispered. 'Wait for Flo.' He continued to stare at the pale figure on the bed. The face, without all its tubes, seemed even less like Jerry's face.

'He's finding the pain quite a challenge,' Josie said, to give Alex's mind some purchase. 'He keeps saying he doesn't need the drugs, but then he moves and goes all white. He's trying to be tough.'

'Right.' Alex looked around, as if searching for conversational cues.

'Alex, sit down, mate.' Josie patted chair next to her. 'Come here. This is a happy time. We're celebrating.'

Both of them were relieved when Flo galloped in from the hallway, a sparkly bag in her hands and an enormous grin across her face. Josie felt a twinge in her heart. *And there's my other baby, still as much a little girl as she is a young woman.*

'Dad!' Flo waltzed up to the bed.

'Shhh,' said Alex.

'It's okay,' Josie said. 'Wake him, Floey.'

Flo leaned in and touched Jerry gently on his shoulder. 'Dad? We're here. Happy birthday.'

Jerry stirred. His eyes slowly opened, searched the ceiling then came to rest on Flo. For a long, heart-stopping moment, Flo thought he was going to ask who she was. But then, 'Hey,' he croaked. 'Flo.'

'Dad,' Flo whispered carefully, as if the word was a thing you could give. 'You missed your birthday.'

'Did I? Oh well, plenty more to come.'

'Yep, you're going to live to be a hundred now.'

Jerry gave a half-grimace, half-chuckle. 'That's a lot of calvings.'

'Alex and I will help you with those.'

'Will you?'

'He's here.' Flo beckoned to her brother. 'Alex?'

'Hey, Dad.'

'Zander,' said Jerry. The sound of the old nickname brought a flood of relief to Josie. 'I hear you've been at the helm, mate.'

Alex licked his lips and took a breath. Josie rubbed his arm. 'Ah well,' Alex managed. 'Keeping things going. Walt's been a help. And the men's shed fellas.'

Jerry frowned. 'They have enough to do.'

'They wanted to help,' said Josie. 'You'd do the same.'

Jerry remained silent.

'What's it like, Dad?' asked Flo. 'Being in a coma?'

'I don't know. Sort of nothing, I guess. Weird. I don't know.'

'So, you didn't hear us talking to you?' asked Flo. 'Mum read to you heaps.'

'Maybe it'll come back to me.' Jerry shifted painfully. 'My brain's going to take some time to return to normal. It shouldn't have far to go, though. I was never the brightest sparkler in the box.'

'Yeah, but you light up my world,' said Josie.

Flo groaned. 'Oh, please,' she said. 'So, Dad, I got you a present. It's partly to say happy birthday and partly to say sorry.'

'Flo . . .' warned Josie.

Flo ignored her and took a deep breath. 'I should have got to you sooner. I should have known something was wrong. I wasn't focused. I'm so sorry.'

'No,' said Alex. 'I should have been here.'

'Stop,' said Jerry. 'No more. I'm the only dickhead here. I knew about that feral steer. Now that's enough.' His eyes were cold with anger. He shut them away.

'Dad . . .' Flo put her hand on his.

'It's okay,' he whispered, opening his eyes again and fixing them on the ceiling. 'I'm all good. Off you go, you two. I'll be home before you know it. Don't do any more growing up, okay?'

It wasn't until Alex and Flo had long gone and the dinner tray was delivered that Josie remembered Flo's sparkly bag. Inside was a small, striped album filled with photographs taken around Nowhere River: the river itself, Pocket Island from the footbridge, the fisher cottages, the Abergavenny ruins, the bald dust of the Whistler Hills, the Goodbye Bridge. Alex and Jerry standing together in the stables. And the Everston horses, with the tree-sprinkled bulk of the Sugarloaf rising up behind them.

Josie leaned over to Jerry. 'From Flo,' she said, and turned the pages for him until he shifted agitatedly and she saw that his eyes had filled with tears.

Elaine Thorold, 67

I helped get the men's shed going so I could get my hubby out from under my feet. They fixed my lawnmower the other day. And they make wire-winders and things like that. God knows what they talk about, but they keep an eye on each other. It's important to keep an eye on people, especially in the droughts. Once, Ticker Wilson didn't show up to the men's shed, and so they sent some blokes over to rustle him up. They found him in his car, windows up, with a hose and that. He'd been getting in and out, trying to work out whether to turn the ignition on or not. He runs the community vegetable garden now. The men's shed is a good thing. But it took a woman to suggest it.

Chapter 16

Being theatrical and quite enamoured with scenes and events, Lucie persuaded Patricia to make an occasion of the St Margery's annual general meeting.

'A Fresh and Lovely affair,' she declared. 'To herald and welcome the new members. We can get out the good tablecloths that have been languishing in the linen cupboard getting musty.'

'The St Margery's linens never get musty,' said Patricia. 'I implement seasonal inventories, as you know. The autumn inventory is already done.'

'Perfect!' said Lucie, 'Let's use them, then, for a proper luncheon after the meeting. With champagne.'

'Very well,' said Patricia with a sigh. 'But one glass each. Elaine Thorold will be in attendance and I shall not tempt fate.'

Lucie hurried to send out the meeting notification and luncheon invitation before Patricia could change her mind.

The meeting fell on a Thursday, which meant a number of members were obliged to send their apologies due to work commitments. But even so, the remaining number would still be the largest to sit in the meeting room in almost a decade.

'St Margery won't know herself,' Lucie said, still trying to justify her luncheon idea. 'An actual gathering of people, planning and clinking the crystal and things. She'll be transported to her good old days.'

'No clinking the crystal,' Patricia said firmly, but appeared placated. Until Carra arrived with her babies.

'Ah,' said Lucie, watching Daisy wriggle free of Carra and tear along the hallway. 'This is my fault, Patricia, I insisted Carra bring them, otherwise she would miss out altogether. We are obliged to have wheelchair access; surely this should extend to prams.'

Patricia said, 'Hmm,' and sent a worried glance to the pieces of fine china on the mahogany sideboard.

'I've brought a playpen, just in case,' said Carra. 'It's in the car. And a portacot.'

'We'll pop them off to sleep upstairs when they get ratty,' said Lucie.

'It'll only take a moment to set up,' said Carra, mostly to herself.

'A playpen?' said Patricia. 'Is that one of those inhumane-looking cage things?'

'Um, yes,' said Carra.

'Good, yes, fetch it in.'

So Carra set up the playpen in the corner of the meeting room. This took longer than expected, mostly owing to Carra's voluminous dress. Carra hadn't known how to attend to the 'day attire' instruction on the luncheon invitation and had settled upon a dress she'd bought back when she thought that country life meant welcoming guests in through the front hall wearing a radiant (smug) smile and a flowery frock. The dress didn't fit very well, but none of her pre-babies clothes did. They weren't necessarily the wrong size, but they just didn't hang properly anymore, as though they'd been purchased for someone else.

The rest of the available members arrived in their various interpretations of day attire – none as frilly as Carra's, she noted with an inward cringe – but at least she wasn't wearing a diamanté fascinator like Elaine Thorold.

Abigail (in her felt hat) began the minutes by taking attendance.

St Margery's Ladies' Club
Minutes of Annual General Meeting in St Margery's Ladies' Club
Meeting Room
Thursday 26th March

Present:
Mrs Patricia Montgomery (President), Mrs Lucie Finlay (Vice-President), Miss Abigail Snelson (Secretary), Mrs Phoebe Costas (Treasurer), Miss Bunty Partridge, Miss Daphne Partridge, Mrs Marceline Cash, Mrs Caroline Finlay, Mrs Rachael Hamilton, Mrs Georgina Pfaff, Mrs Lucinda Price, Mrs Elaine Thorold, Mrs Deidre Wagner, Miss Daisy Finlay (observer), Master Ben Finlay (observer)

Apologies:
Mrs Ruth Beaumont-Hudd, Mrs Josephine Bradshaw, Miss Florence Bradshaw, Ms Esther Very, Mrs Lurlene Wallace

'Ooh,' said Rachael Hamilton, who was dressed in a pink bouclé suit. 'This is just as la-di-da as I imagined.' She gave a little excited squeak. 'Look, even the cutlery is all tarted up.' She raised a small fork. 'What do you call this, then?'

'It's a melon fork, Rachael,' said Lucie.

'No, it's not,' shouted Daphne. 'It's a melon fork.'

'That's what she said. A melon fork.'

'How many times do you think we can say "melon fork" before lunch?' said Phoebe, who was still crotchety about having her high-vis-hall idea rejected.

'May we move on?' said Patricia, raising her hand. 'And I'll thank everyone not to interrupt unless it is especially incumbent on them to do so. We have much to get through, not the least of which is my formal welcome.'

'Melon fork,' peeped Elaine.

Rachael snorted.

Carra sniggered.

Patricia froze for a long moment and stared straight ahead, waiting. The temperature in the room seemed to drop. Even the twins, in their caged corner, fell silent. Carra looked at the floor.

'I would like to say,' Patricia said finally, when the pause seemed ready to explode, 'how propitious it is to see the meeting room so abundantly attended. It is testament to the unanimity and cohesion of our community, and I am wholeheartedly encouraged by this display of allegiance. The Nowhere River community has sat around being nugatory for long enough. A new era begins today.'

There was a silence then, and a bit of shuffling while everyone wondered whether they were the only person not entirely under-standing Patricia's words.

'Raaar,' said Daisy, who had recently learnt what lions say.

'Phoebe, your financial report?' said Patricia.

'All right,' said Phoebe. 'Well, for a start, you new members have to pay your membership fees. So far, fifteen out of twenty-one of us are freeloading. Most of you paid one monthly instalment and then haven't followed up.'

'Oh, but I thought that one payment *was* our annual membership fee,' said Deidre.

'Yeah,' said Rachael. 'So did I.'

'No,' said Patricia. 'It's very clearly stated in the Miss Fresh and Lovely entry requirements that all entrants must be *paid members* of St Margery's Ladies' Club. And that payments may be made monthly or annually. The total annual fee is $770. We will give you another fortnight to meet your payments.'

'Whoa,' said Mrs Pfaff.

'What are we actually paying for, though?' asked Rachael.

'You are contributing to the upkeep of this gracious building,' said Patricia, with her head tilted at what Lucie recognised as a dangerous angle. 'You are given the opportunity to assist with charitable works. You are keeping alive an honoured tradition of womanhood and community and—'

'You get a sitting room. And off-street parking,' said Abigail. 'And there are overnight stays at very reasonable rates for your friends and family visiting from the city.'

'You get to stay in the running for Miss Fresh and Lovely,' said Elaine. 'No dosh, no crown.'

'And it's a platform,' said Lucie, only just resisting the urge to get to her feet. 'If you want it to be. For whatever you choose — sportsmanship, scholarship, mentorship, pastorship, leadership, and most importantly, friendship. Which is the most important ship there is, really, isn't it?'

'Well, trust me,' said Phoebe, 'It'll be *receiver*ship if you lot don't cough up.'

'And there's a bit of one-upmanship going on, too,' said Deidre with a glare at Carra. 'Ruth and I had very considered Shiny-town plans for the hall landscape and the Pearce Highway roundabout. But Carra's gone and stymied them by barging about, reshaping everything willy-nilly.'

Carra swallowed and tried to think of a response.

'They look lovely, though,' offered Marceline.

'The roundabout roses are a tawdry pantomime,' said Patricia. 'Like a warning beacon to visitors. I just can't understand why the basic notions of good taste are so difficult to grasp.'

'I agree,' said Deidre. 'There was no colour consultation with the community. I would never have voted for that shade of pink.' She nodded with a smug satisfaction that reverberated into her jellied jowls.

'Well, you might have come along and contributed,' said Carra. 'You could do with some exercise.'

Deidre turned red. 'That was a personal attack. She is attacking me, Patricia. She hasn't come along to help with any Shiny-town projects—'

'Because you haven't *done* any.' Carra was beginning to understand what it means to see red. She was seeing some. It was crimson. 'You are—'

'*Friend*ship,' Lucie said, interrupting. 'Don't forget the importance of friendship, ladies.'

'And propiety,' said Inda Price.

'Pro*pri*ety,' corrected Patricia firmly. 'Which means, for those who don't know, decorum, probity, decency, rectitude.'

At that moment, there was a loud fart from the direction of the playpen. Ben looked startled. Daisy laughed.

'Ha,' said Lucie. 'A small issue from Daisy's rectitude.' She laughed gleefully, but observed the purse of Patricia's lips. 'Carra, shall we get the babies settled in their cot? It's about naptime, I think.'

It wasn't quite naptime, which meant Carra and Lucie missed the next part of the meeting, because Ben and Daisy weren't tired and kept standing up to look at their unfamiliar surroundings. The meeting had entered into Business Arising when finally Carra and Lucie returned. The mood in the room had grown considerably darker.

'You speak so much shit that your arse is jealous of your mouth,' Inda was shouting at Elaine Thorold. 'This is sabotage. She *knew* that I had a working bee at the pub that Saturday. And now she's gone and organised her dumb mock wedding. SABOTAGE! She's a conniving little mongrel, I tell you.'

'Inda!' said Lucie. She was feeling almost equal amounts of exhilaration and alarm. (Slightly more exhilaration. *Oh, the theatre of it all.*)

Inda railed on, getting up out of her chair. 'My working bee was locked in long before this stupid wedding thing came up.' She flapped a mock wedding flyer in the air. 'You said it yourself, Patricia, entrants will be disqualified for deception or sabotage. It's written in the manifesto! It's very clear that Elaine "Fulloshit" Thorold has brazenly stolen my thunder. And everyone knows there's not a sniff of that stupid rose quartz in the park. Rose quartz comes from Madagascar – I looked it up. And sometimes India, but mostly Madagascar, and never, *ever* Tasmania. Did you know that? Look it up! She's a fucking fraudy cunt.'

There was a series of gasps around the room, and a stifled laugh, followed by an icy silence. Inda evidently knew she'd gone too far, and apparently tried to induce some sort of turn. She drooped towards a nearby chair.

'I think you'll see,' said Patricia, without a speck of give, 'that the clause includes deception, sabotage *and* slander. What do you think, Vice-President Finlay, does "fucking fraudy cunt" qualify as slander to you?'

'Um,' whispered Lucie. 'Possibly.'

'What's everyone saying?' shouted Daphne to Bunty.

'Inda called Elaine a fucking fraudy cunt,' Bunty replied.

'Enough!' Patricia clapped her hands. The action produced an inordinately loud sound for such delicate hands. 'I will look into your allegations of deception et al.,' she continued, aiming her icy eyes at the shrinking Inda. 'But in the meantime, you and your Save the Fat Doe Inn campaign are disqualified from the Miss Fresh and Lovely competition, as of now. I have seen nothing fresh or lovely about you today. Abigail, see Mrs Price out, please, and then come and witness the official report. I'll draw it up immediately, while we're all here.' Patricia turned to a fresh sheet of paper.

Abigail was compelled to jostle Inda out the door, which she did gently, with the offer of a glass of water.

'I will take nothing from this stuck-up establishment,' said Inda. 'And I won't be crossing its doorstep again.'

'Good,' said Patricia, and Lucie realised that Patricia was rather enjoying herself. 'Well, that should reveal to the ill-informed,' Patricia announced, with a pointed look towards Carra and her temper, 'that those sort of lubberly, lewd demonstrations will get you precisely nowhere. Right then, any more business arising?'

The remainder of the meeting ambled on in a far less thrilling fashion. Lucie tried to remember Inda's insults to relay them accurately back to Len and struggled to remain present for Patricia's review of non-negotiable traditions (including the no-trousers rule and the mandatory-celery-and-olives-on-the-table rule).

Carra began to experience the (not unpleasant) sensation that she had fallen into some sort of parallel dimension. *No trousers? Celery and olives? What on earth?* But the meeting finished at its prescribed hour, the flowers were sending just the right amount of scent into their allotted spaces, and by the time the members were given their allocated glass of champagne (consumed quite rapidly by Carra), she was beginning to feel as though she might quite like the orderly logic of St Margery's. Everything seemed to fit to a carefully crafted structure, and if it didn't (such as Inda and the swearing), it was swiftly handled with eviscerating efficiency. What's more, the St Margery's trappings of correctness seemed to have an effect on even the greenest of members. Mrs Pfaff didn't grunt or belch, Rachael stopped talking about money and no one mentioned melon forks again. It seemed that Patricia could command order without issuing any actual commands. She had only to walk into the room. Even the furniture, with all its little curved feet turned out, its proud cushions bulging and its surfaces shining, seemed to defer to Patricia. Carra tipped her glass at an elegant side table and thought, *Maybe I can do this.*

The luncheon, scheduled to finish at three o'clock to allow time for the caterers to clear up and the cleaner to clean, finished at three

minutes past three, with a curt, 'Thank you, all. Abigail will send out
the minutes. I will see you all very soon. I am sure you have things
to get on with.' She cast a sober eye towards Carra. 'It's been an
enlightening day. I'll be in the office if anyone needs me. I'll stay to
lock the doors. Lucie, if you could ensure the upstairs is free of baby
clutter. And Abigail, please check the water levels for the flowers.
Thank you.'

Carra watched Patricia's smooth departure and decided that when
she grew up, she wanted to be Patricia Montgomery. With Ursula
Andreas's landscaping career. And personal stylist.

'Do you think,' said Lucie, as she and Abigail wrestled the
playpen into Carra's car, 'that we might continue our *enlightenment*
at my house? I rather fancy another bubble or two. Patricia's measly
one glass is a terrible tease. And we should be celebrating Carra's
St Margery's induction, shouldn't we?'

'Well . . .' said Abigail, 'I should probably pop into Nuyina—'

'Oh, you've done enough for them until tomorrow, surely. Come
on, Abbie.'

Abigail seemed to enjoy being called Abbie. She blushed and said,
'Well, if Carra is keen . . .'

Carra, still buoyant in her frills (and bolstered by a cheeky second
glass of sparkling given to her in error by the waitress), agreed that
further enlightenment was necessary. 'If you don't mind my two
items of excess baggage.' She hoisted Daisy into her seat. 'They're
noisy, smelly and their wheels are always falling off.'

But Daisy settled into her seat with unusual acceptance and calm.
Gosh, thought Carra, *the St Margery's effect.*

At Riverhouse, Len was muttering obscenities at his computer
screen when Lucie yoo-hooed from the hallway and clattered in with
Abigail, Carra and the babies.

'Ah,' said Len. 'One of you will know what the buzzards is wrong
with this wretched computer machine.'

'No idea, darling, but Carra's bound to know. And then you can pop over to Father John, if you like. We're having a girls' afternoon.'

Len, noticing a particular trill in Lucie's voice and knowing what it spelled (social excitement; showboat-y behaviour, given to protracted singalongs), offered no protest.

'Yes, I'm well overdue for a decent Jesus fulmination.'

'Don't be too hard on the poor Baby Jesus, darling,' said Lucie, with a tiny head-tilt towards Abigail, 'He had a terrible life.'

'Of course he did,' said Len. 'All fictional characters have terrible lives, it's their cross to bear.' He chuckled at his own joke and said to Daisy and Ben, 'Your grandfather is one of the last true wits.'

'The last true twit, more like,' said Lucie. 'Off you go, Leonard. Take your ruminations over to the rectory, Father John has far more patience with you. I'm sorry, Abigail.'

'Abigail doesn't mind. She's not going to be swayed from her Lord Saviour by an old coot like me, are you?'

'Ah . . .' said Abigail, apparently wondering how to reply without agreeing with the old coot bit.

Ben shouted, 'Pa!' and clapped his hands.

'Ah,' said Len, his smile lines fully engaged. 'Ben appreciates my witticisms.'

Carra, meanwhile, had a look at Len's computer screen but Abigail, to everyone's surprise, was the one to fix it. Len was delighted.

'Have a lovely afternoon then,' he called, but Lucie, having already dismissed him, was already distracted, detailing her next move in her How-to-save-the-Bradshaws scheme.

'When they're home, they'll need more support than ever. Particularly dear Flo with her show. She has so many ideas, and I've never seen a teenager so curious – they're usually only interested in themselves. And even after Len and I introduced her to the showgrounds' many foibles, onwards she goes, bless her.'

Len hovered on the doorstep and felt a wave of concern over Lucie's devotion to Flo. *She's not our girl,* he thought, and then murmured, 'Go carefully, my Lucie, it's slippery on the patio.'

Lucinda Price, 72

I had eight kids – my first baby when I was seventeen. His father didn't stick around. Then I had four to my first husband – two sets of twins. One of the twins, little Jessamy, didn't get to a week old. After that husband died of the cancer I married Hedley and dropped three more of the little blighters. Two more of the kids have since passed, and Hedley's lost his marbles. I get a bit of help caring for him, but I only have one of the kids living nearby. I get jack-shit help from the government. I've mostly been a cleaner to get by, mucking out pigsties and stuff. Some people around here probably think I'm a proper piece of work, and they'd be right. I just can't abide very much more.

Chapter 17

Ben and Daisy were enjoying their third *Play School* DVD in the Riverhouse sitting room while Carra, Lucie and Abigail continued their extension of the St Margery's luncheon. Their conversation had started out as a sort of sisterly rallying of the spirits and, three bottles of rosé later, was turning into a full-blown exercise in mutual admiration.

'Oh, Abigail,' said Carra in response to something self-deprecating that Abigail had said. 'I adore your hat and your box-pleated skirts.'

'You don't think I'm frumpy?'

'No! What's frumpy again?'

'I think I could take a leaf out of your pretty-frocked book.'

They all looked at Carra's dress.

'Well, you have great hair,' offered Carra, in deflection.

'If you need some steel wool to plug up your mouse holes,' said Abigail, taking another sip of wine.

'You have gorgeous hair too, Carra,' said Lucie, which gave Carra more pleasure than she would have liked to admit.

'And Carra,' said Abigail, 'I simply must say it, I mean it's the elephant in the town, but you and Duncan make *the* most beautiful couple, as in, number one for beauty. Do you not know that? You could be film stars. Someone would definitely cast you in something if you just turned up in Hollywood.'

Carra laughed. 'Duncan maybe. People would think I was his plain assistant.'

'Nonsense,' said Abigail. 'I mean it. I heard someone in Bothwell say that our GP is a cross between Brad Pitt and Harry Styles. I don't know Harry Styles, but . . . what must it be like to kiss Duncan, Carra?' She clapped a hand over her mouth and turned scarlet. 'You don't have to answer that. Oh, what a grubby old woman I am.'

'That's okay, Abigail,' said Carra, with a shy look at Lucie, who was laughing. 'Kissing him is . . . you know, nice.'

Abigail forgot to be embarrassed and leaned forward on her elbows. 'How did the two of you meet?'

'Ooh, I'll tell,' said Lucie. 'It's a classic.'

Carra took a deep breath and poured herself some more wine.

'So,' Lucie said, quite pink with delight, 'I don't think it's boastful of me to say that Duncan was very popular among the girls. There was usually a bevy of fluttering beauties loitering about nearby, poor little ninnies. He was nice to them, but he didn't encourage them. He was more interested in his work, our Duncan, and is naturally very shy, much like his father. You wouldn't know that about Len – he does a very good job of hiding behind his humour.

'Anyway, Carra and Duncan were in the same year at uni, but different fields of study, different friends. And Duncan was so busy with his head in books. He never complained about his looks, of course, but it wasn't easy for him to get to know girls. Just too much idolatry. Occasionally there'd be a particular girl that would display more persistence than the others. You know, call here asking what his favourite food was or sending him letters to receive when he was home, that sort of thing. One of them rode her bike the whole eighty-eight kilometres from Hobart and then felt ill and needed a bed to sleep in.'

Carra swallowed a large mouthful of wine.

'But of course there was always the most devoted one of all. Her persistence was astounding and, honestly, this young woman had more front than Myer. She just kept turning up wherever he was and insisting that she was his girlfriend. And she wasn't a complete clinker, don't get me wrong. I mean, absolutely, stunningly beautiful and very nice. I mean, we'd known her since they were in playgroup together.'

'Is she local, then?' asked Abigail.

'No,' said Carra quickly.

Lucie threw Carra a look. 'She had a lovely sense of humour, too. But she just wasn't quite . . .' Lucie sent her eyes to the ceiling in a thinking expression. 'Not quite *Finlay*. Her Christian name was Harmony, for goodness sake. Oops!' Lucie clapped a hand over her mouth.

'Harmony?' Abigail said. 'You mean—'

'It's a very common name, really,' said Carra. 'I mean, not *common*, just, you know . . . it's quite pretty.'

Abigail gaped at them.

'Forget everything I tell you today,' said Lucie firmly.

Abigail performed a delicate lip-buttoning charade.

'She – Harmony – would phone me up about elaborate plans for Duncan's birthday or turn up at his work with presents and so on. Once, he arrived back to his flat to find that she'd washed his sheets and made him a supply of frozen dinners.'

'Golly,' said Abigail. 'I don't suppose there were stalking laws back then.'

'She wasn't very threatening,' said Carra. 'Just lovesick.'

She pictured the earnest, shining-eyed woman with her beautiful dimpled smile and her heart on her sleeve. *Harmony*. Harmony had fallen for Duncan somewhere around the time when hormones and heartstrings tangle and trip up adolescents. And that fall – from friendship into love – had been headlong and hard. She had possibly never fully recovered from the resulting injuries.

'And then one day,' Lucie continued, 'she followed him to the pub when he was out with his friends, and was on about booking an overseas holiday for the two of them.'

'So bold,' said Abigail. 'Surely she really believed he loved her.'

'And on a desperate whim, Duncan took her aside and blurted out that he was very sorry but he was in love with someone else.'

'Gosh, the poor girl,' said Abigail.

'No, she needed to be put right,' explained Lucie. 'He couldn't have given her false hope if he didn't feel anything for her. Anyway, this mad girl—'

'Harmony,' said Carra.

'*Harmony* just wouldn't have it. She wouldn't believe him.'

Carra thought of Harmony's stricken face.

'And Carra just happened to be sitting on the other side of the bar at a party. Correct me if I'm wrong, Carra – you were at a party?'

Carra said, 'Mmm,' because correcting the story seemed too complicated. Her thoughts cast back to that August evening in Hobart, six years ago.

She hadn't been at a party, but had ventured to the pub with a friend in a shameless effort to be invited into the Ursula Andreas crowd. They had finished their bachelor degrees and Ursula had been immediately employed by a mainland company. She was already winning awards, had an edgy new Melbourne haircut and a distinguished older man. Carra, who was spraying weeds for the council and had a weekend job in a pub to avoid her parents' yachting events, had an envy-fuelled crush. Everyone, regardless of whether they wanted to bed Ursula or become her best friend, found themselves fascinated, if not mesmerised, by her effortless charisma. That night, Carra and two of her similarly afflicted friends (wearing their best I'm-not-a-fashion-victim classic black with earrings that they hoped made cool-but-not-wacky statements about their identities) rocked in and spent all their money on two bottles of the second-cheapest wine for Ursula and her friends. Ursula said Carra's earrings were 'zany' and called her 'Cathy'. Twice. And then asked her what course she had studied. (They'd been in the same tutorial group for a year.) Carra was experiencing a potent blend of inferiority and self-loathing when a truly gorgeous young man approached her with a shy smile and the words, 'Hi. Sorry, I know this is weird but can you do me a huge favour, please? I need your help.'

Carra blinked at the incredible face, tugged at a heavy earring and tried to think of something coherent to say.

'Please?' Duncan continued. 'I'll explain ASAP, but for now, can you just . . . go with me? What's your name? I'm Duncan.'

'Um,' said Carra as she found herself swept from her seat at the bar by Duncan's arm, which was incredibly, wonderfully around her. Firm and warm. 'Carra. And you're . . . you're Duncan Finlay.' It was a simple statement, made quietly among the drop of pennies. *My God, no wonder everyone at uni raved about you.*

'Harmony,' said Duncan as he steered Carra over into the beer garden and stopped before a beautiful, solemn-faced woman. 'This is Carra. My girlfriend.'

'Wait, what?' said Harmony, her eyes wide.

Wait, what? thought Carra.

'I've been trying to tell you—'

'But that can't be right.' Harmony's angelic face was febrile with panic. 'You said—'

'I mean, we haven't known one another long, have we, Carra? But it sort of just hit us out of the blue.'

'Ahh . . .' Carra turned to him and accidentally looked him straight in the eyes. *What amazing eyes. What planet are these two from?* 'No, we didn't plan it. It was totally unexpected, but it just crept up on us and . . .' The words fell so easily from her mouth, spurred on by the encouragement in Duncan's face. 'It was like, you know, that magical thing.' Carra locked eyes with Duncan again.

God, he's even more beautiful in extreme close-up, she thought. Her eyes moved to his lips.

'Yeah, it was sort of, you know, crackers,' said Duncan, adding some firework explosion noises. He glanced at Carra and then glanced back again. The second one lingered. 'Firecrackers.'

'But I thought . . .' said Harmony, her voice wavering. 'We were always . . .' She cupped her hands in front of her, as if attempting to stop it draining away, the precious always.

'Always really great friends,' said Duncan. 'Best friends, from way back. I mean, you know that, you'll always be . . . but I don't think I ever said I wanted anything more than, you know, a friendship. Did I?'

'You kissed me!' Harmony cried. 'You told me—'

'Wait, *you* kissed *me.*'

'But you kissed back. I know you did.'

Carra's discomfort made her cough. 'I should let you two—'

'No, wait, Carra,' said Duncan, reaching for her hand. 'Look, this is my fault. I kind of knew how you were feeling, Harmony, and I did try to discourage you, lots of times. But I probably wasn't clear enough. So I'm being clear now. I'm in love with Carra, and I think you're a great girl and a true friend, but I'm not the one for you.'

'I'm sorry too, Harmony,' said Carra, who was feeling slightly buoyed by the feeling of his hand clenching hers ever so slightly each time he emphasised a word. 'I didn't know about the two of you.'

'Well, apparently there wasn't . . .' said Harmony, angry now, and flushed with humiliation, 'there wasn't any two of us. But there *was.*' Her eyes fixed on Duncan. 'You know there was. Duncan?'

His name came out suffused with pain. It hovered in the air between them and quivered as Duncan looked at the floor. Carra felt his clasp on her hand tighten determinedly.

Harmony waited, holding her breath for his reply. When it didn't come, she turned her eyes to the floor, exhaled and walked quickly, quietly away.

Duncan watched her go, then apologised for dragging Carra into his drama, and expressed a pallid regard for Harmony's feelings. 'Gosh, I've really hurt her.' He seemed smaller to Carra somehow, and more adorable.

She laughed and made some comical firework explosions until he laughed too. And when he stopped laughing, but stared, shame-faced, at the beer garden gate and then the pebbled ground, she was the one to take his hand. Inside the pub, laughing at the bar with her sophisticated friends while they asked about career progression and being a woman in a man's world, was Ursula. But Carra had forgotten she was there.

While Lucie recounted her version of the Carra and Duncan story, Carra remembered all of this. In particular, she recalled with breathless precision, the quiet grace of Harmony as she, with her face all crumpled with humiliation and grief, carried her broken heart away.

'How incredible,' said Abigail dreamily. 'That's straight out of the cinema.'

'Yes!' said Lucie. 'So perfect. And wasn't Carra a picture on her wedding day.'

'Oh, a picture,' agreed Abigail. 'I cried all the way through, of course.'

'She had no idea how beautiful she was.' Lucie placed a proud hand on Carra's arm. 'Remember how the whole town came out to catch a glimpse? It was like Windsor.'

Lucie's account was taking on a decidedly squiffy brand of aggran-disement. *Rosé-coloured glasses,* thought Carra.

'Was, er, Harmony there?' asked Abigail. 'At the wedding? I don't remember.'

'Oh Lord no,' said Lucie. 'She's over it, though, isn't she, Carra?'

Carra bit her lip. 'Shall we have some cheese?'

'No, thank you,' said Lucie. 'I ate far too much at lunch. Anyone for another glass?'

An hour later, the mood descended somewhat, because Lucie's performative state of mind and the rosé decided to grasp the moment and thrust Felicity into it.

'Do you think,' she said in mysterious, low and slightly slurry tones, 'that the river took my Felicity?'

There was, predicably, silence. Lucie swayed in it for a bit. 'That's what I've chosen to think. I mean, it's the lesser of many evils, isn't it. Unless it turns out she was raised in Rosebery by a loving family of teachers and paediatricians.'

Abigail attempted a titter, but it turned quite quickly into tears. 'Perhaps she was stolen by a pair of prodigious musicians who have taught her to sing like an angel and now she's on the stage somewhere completely unaware of her roots, but happy and adored.'

'Drowning is meant to be a very pleasant way to die,' said Carra without thinking.

Abigail gasped.

'Sorry,' said Carra. 'Lucie, oh my God.' She covered her face.

There had to be some silence and some more sipping of wine. Carra gulped hers.

'I never used to think,' said Lucie presently, 'that it was the river, you know. It just seemed too full of wisdom and promise. Like an old friend, winking at me all the time.' She sighed. 'But a promise isn't a promise if it comes with a wink, is it? Now the bloody thing just looks cold and uncaring, and I think it must have taken her, tucked her away into some swallet somewhere, the little Nowhere girl.'

There was some more bulging silence, after which Lucie asked, 'May I tell you? What happened that day?'

Carra had the vague impression that she ought to intervene, but couldn't quite work out how.

So Lucie spoke. 'It was autumn 1991, the eighth of May. Felicity was five, Duncan was one. Len was a town planner then, and he'd been asked to consult on a sewerage upgrade for Nowhere River. He'd arranged a meeting with the mayor. It was a kindergarten day for Felicity, but she had a mild head cold and I had kept her home from school, so Len suggested we come along for a day out. I jumped at the chance to get out of the house. Felicity wasn't all that sick and a bit of a handful when bored, and Duncan always slept in the car, so an outing meant a bit of peace. Also, I'd never been to this part of the state. Generally, people don't make unsolicited trips to Nowhere River, unless you've taken a wrong turn.' Lucie smiled at Carra. 'Or fallen in love.'

Carra smiled back, and saw that Lucie's blue eyes had turned a swimming aquamarine.

'Yes, so, anyway, we came up here,' said Lucie, after a little throat clear. 'The roads were dreadful then, even worse than they are now. Felicity was carsick, all that business. We had to stop a number of times. But I remember, when we eventually got here, we were quite charmed by the place. The poplars and the willows were in their yellow best and the river seemed so protective, keeping the town all tucked in. And the crystalline air revived Felicity very quickly from her motion sickness.

'We parked the car in the High Street and Len went on to the council chambers, which used to be annexed to the town hall. I got Felicity an apple cake and a fruit box, and the children and I had a wander about. With Duncan in his pram and Felicity tripping along with us, we went up the High Street to the park, then across to the tennis court and over to the Goodbye Bridge. On the bridge, we threw sticks into the water and watched the leaves floating along. I told her that fairies used the leaves for boats. We followed the walking path up along past Nuyina and the fisher cottages to the

Abergavenny ruins, where we found a wombat. She loved that. She went perfectly still and just watched and watched. I told her about how it has a pouch and hairy nose and oh, she laughed! She loved the idea of a hairy nose. Just imagine if she could see her father's now!'

Lucie chuckled, releasing some of the tension in the air just enough for Carra to take another sip of wine and for Abigail to sniffle.

'I could see the footbridge from there, and was tempted to go over it, but I was unsure about how to find my way back to Len and so I retraced our steps instead. Back at the fisher cottages, Felicity begged me for a game of hide-and-seek. Duncan was wriggly in his pram so I agreed to the game, got him out to let him play in the grass, and started counting. Felicity ran around the back of the second cottage, away from the river, and when I got to fifty, I picked up Duncan and trotted in the same direction, shouting, "Coming, ready or not!"'

Lucie took a moment and swallowed it down, for fortitude. Abigail squeezed her arm. 'And we looked, and then we searched, and I kept shouting her name and asking Duncan, "Where's our Felicity?", searching and searching and . . . she wasn't anywhere. I couldn't find her anywhere.'

Lucie's gleaming eyes darted. 'I kept thinking, *we're on the River Nowhere and she's nowhere*. And I'm still asking that same question, in this same town, on this same river that I can never leave. *Where's our Felicity?* And I hear, "Coming, ready or not" over and over and over again.' Lucie put her shaking hands to her ears then, and left them there for a long moment before reaching out to brush a tear from Carra's cheek.

Carra tried to smile, tried not to think about the little boy in the pram, laughing along with a game that would change his world forever, but the words echoed in her head too. *Coming, ready or not.*

Abigail let out an enormous, almost comical sob and put her arm awkwardly around Lucie's shoulders.

Lucie took a deep breath. 'They checked the cottages, under the cottages, they dredged the river, they searched the hills and the watermill and every possible hiding place within a bull's roar of the town. Nothing. Sometimes I think she just got swallowed up. Or taken. But I can't think about taken.' The hand returned to her mouth. 'Other times I wonder whether I just imagined her, that all along she wasn't real.'

'You didn't imagine her, Lucie,' said Abigail. 'I've seen her dear little photograph.'

Carra thought of the collage of Felicity pictures on the wall of the Riverhouse hallway and realised she possibly wasn't behaving the way a daughter-in-law ought to in such a moment.

'She was a dear little girl. *Is.*' She winced. 'Sorry. You know what I mean.'

'She is,' said Lucie, staring right through Carra. 'She's beautiful. And if I'd just counted to twenty instead of fifty. If I'd taken the footbridge . . .'

'Oh, Lucie, don't,' said Abigail.

'If I'd shut up about fairy boats . . . do you think she went in looking for leaves?' Lucie didn't wait for an answer before continuing. It seemed as though she was addressing something not in the room. 'If I'd not felt the need to have a bit of space from her five-year-old chatter.' She got to her feet. 'That's what it was, you know, that's why I said yes to hide-and-seek in the first place, so that I could have a little break. Just think . . .'

Carra watched Lucie's face fold up into its well-worn lines of agony and tried to decide what to do. Abigail stood immediately, drawing Lucie into a hug and murmuring soothing words to her. Carra looked at her hands and silently asked them why they were so useless, and why they couldn't seem to do anything to make anyone feel better.

'God, Lucie,' she said loudly. 'Needing a little break is nothing. Most of the time I feel as though marriage and children have left me disabled.' She laughed. 'And that the rest of my life is ruined.' Carra observed the shocked faces around her, but ploughed on. 'You needed some alone time, Lucie. Sometimes I think it would be far easier to know yourself if you could just be alone. Other people's perceptions of me get all muddled with my own until I'm just a fuzzy blur. Ha. A fuzzy old blur.'

Daisy yelled something cross from the sitting room.

'And now,' Carra said loftily, 'my breast milk is alcoholic, and I have to get those relentless little fuckers home.' She stood, swayed only slightly and went to her babies.

'I don't know,' said Abigail quietly. 'Alone can turn rather quickly into lonely. And then you reach fifty and you go from blurry to invisible.'

Lucie nodded. 'And altogether empty.' She replenished Abigail's glass.

Len arrived back at Riverhouse, whistling and jolly after two strong whiskies and a very satisfying debate with Father John, to find his tear-stained wife asleep on the couch, Carra wrangling two very tetchy babies and Abigail looking ominously pale at the kitchen table.

He surveyed the scene for a long moment, muttered some mutterings, and phoned Duncan. 'We have the wreck of the Hesperus here. There's been a severe wine attack, probable gin involvement too. Three casualties, two helpless children. Your mother looks like two penneth of Lord help us on a workhouse doorstep, your wife is wobbly, your babies are wailing and Abigail's about to chunder. Send reinforcements immediately. Over.'

Duncan Finlay, 31

One of my earliest memories of Nowhere River is jumping off the footbridge with my friend, Harmony. She dared me. Mum was frantic because she didn't think I could swim, but Dad had been secretly teaching me. It's the perfect place to grow up. When I was sixteen I had to go to boarding school in Hobart to do my final years. It was pretty hard leaving all my friends, and Mum was beside herself. Dad had to get stroppy with her to get me into the car. University was really difficult for me. I mean work-wise. I had to study really hard. So I was a bit of a nerd, I suppose, always keen not to disappoint anyone. I'm glad I chose medicine. It means I can raise my own family here and give my children the life I've been given. And I just really like making people feel better. Do I sound like a boring wanker?

Chapter 18

Just over a month after Jerry opened his eyes, re-entered the land of the living and sent his family into a spin of joy and relief, Josie found herself hiding in the shearing shed and sobbing tears of frustration into an old Driza-Bone.

She hadn't expected miracles; the doctors had warned her his rehabilitation would be slow. Even while they were giving her hope for a full recovery, they had cautioned her against dreams of skipping joyously off into the future.

'You'll need to keep all the extra help if possible,' Duncan had told her before she brought Jerry home from hospital. 'He's going to monopolise your time for a while.'

Josie had been ready and willing to step out of her workboots and into the quiet, soft shoes of a nurse. But she had not been prepared for her patient's extreme aversion to being cared for, his apparent distaste for her in a caring role and a blatant repugnance for himself.

He wasn't able to move about unassisted, wash himself or even stay awake for long periods. He couldn't be left alone, but didn't seem to want company, so Josie had taken to busying herself in the kitchen to cover her constant surveillance. The kitchen was the one place in which Josie had always felt mildly incompetent.

Compounding these issues was the fact that autumn had well and truly arrived, with its usual dewy mornings and earthy, cider smells, but no rain. For the third year running, there had been no autumn break. Alex had agisted half their stock to Broadmarsh, and sold the rest at market, for what Jerry called 'small potatoes'.

Before she fled to the shearing shed, Josie had carried with her all morning a sort of leaden gloom. It had variously weighted her movements, made her sigh and several times sprung up to sting her eyes. A daggy old country and western song on the radio had put a lump in her throat, a burned piece of toast had made her stamp her feet, and the sound of Flo's youthful intonations as she chattered to Jerry about the Nowhere River Show had made Josie inexplicably furious.

'Everyone has so many ideas,' Flo had said. 'I think people are really excited. Carra's offered to help make the showgrounds entrance look fancy. She's going to take her Sporticulture group along. You should see what she's done on Faulkner Street . . .'

Josie had taken her anger to the freezer in search of dinner options: casseroles, lasagnes, pies and endless containers of soup. Much of it had come from Lucie, who had been constant with her care packages and her attentiveness to Flo. None of it had come from Carra.

'And she knows everything about what grows well in a drought,' Flo had continued, 'and what we can put in pots and tubs to decorate the showgrounds. She's amazing.'

Josie had willed Flo to stop talking about Carra, wished terribly that she could hear all this from Carra herself, dreaming and laughing and teasing the way they used to do.

But I don't think I have any laughs left in me, Josie had thought, angrily shutting the lid of the freezer. *And I can't remember how to tease. I'm not friendship material at the moment, anyway.* She had opened the freezer and slammed it a second time, in disgust for such simpering self-pity.

An hour or so later, while she was delving into the hat stand
for a long-lost apron, Josie had come across a yellow knitted scarf.
Untangling it from a skipping rope and a string bag, she pulled the
scarf out from under the layers of coats and instinctively pressed
it to her face.

The wool was soft and cheerful, in buttercup yellow. Josie held it
aloft, inspecting its dropped-stitch holes and smiling at its comical,
irregular shape. It had been the result of a misguided effort by Carra
to 'become a country woman'. Josie had bellowed with laughter over
it and made Carra wear it as a vivid reminder to never try to be something she's not. And then Carra had gifted the scarf to Josie on her
fortieth birthday, using it as wrapping for a box containing a silver
necklace and a card with the words 'My dear friend'.

Josie had touched the silver necklace at her throat, worn there
always, thrust the scarf back into the depths of the hat stand, then
run from the house in a hot, overflowing rage.

▼▼▼

In the shearing shed, she inhaled the soapy-dusty scent of the
Driza-Bone and thought of Jerry. She wallowed in his pain and
his frustrations, then let her mind wander to other concerns: Flo's
schooling, the farm, Alex's future, her increasingly irregular, heavy
periods, these bouts of melancholy and then, because self-pity still
seemed wrong, Jerry again. *Will he ever be the same?*

Jerry had never – even after the deaths of his parents, failed crops,
crippling feed costs and low beef prices – been a negative person. 'It
is what it is' was his favourite expression. He'd always been fighting
fit and strong. He was once voted, in the pub after the Anzac service,
the bloke you'd most prefer to go to war with. He cruised through
life with the stubborn belief that he would always be okay. But after
three weeks of what didn't seem at all like recovery, he was not okay.

Josie and Jerry had never lived in one another's pockets before. They worked together, but with plenty of space between. The hours and hours of housebound proximity had left them with nothing to talk about. Josie was doing her best to be loving and kind, but her usual brand of love was much more rough and tumble than this. And Jerry was an appalling patient.

'I can do it,' he kept saying to her through clenched teeth as he pulled his trousers on or tried to get himself breakfast. 'You should be with your horses.'

'Fuck off then,' Josie said once, with a tight laugh. 'Go on, fuck off and do it yourself.'

Teasing had always been their default mechanism. But Jerry hadn't laughed. He'd just stared at the floor from his chair in the sunroom, unable to speak. Unable to fuck off. There was a pale, angry man where her husband used to be.

'Things will get better,' Josie told the cat, who had wandered into the shearing shed and stopped to fix Josie with a long stare, as if to cast some sort of hex. 'It's early days.'

The cat, who hadn't been blessed with a name, owing to her insolent demeanour, blinked lazily, then trotted back out the door. Josie followed, wiping her face with a sleeve and giving the Driza-Bone a last pat. She hurried back across the paddock towards the house, thinking of Flo, who must by now be wondering where her mother had got to.

The cat raced on ahead, then darted off to the trees by the house. Josie wished she could go darting off into trees. She wished she could bike about with a notebook and a job to do, like Flo, or climb the windmill in the far paddock, like Alex. She thought suddenly of Carra, holed up in the Kinvarra kitchen at the mercy of two toddlers with the same needs and different needs all at slightly incongruent times. She made a third wish: for Carra to join her, the two of them searching only for another laugh and the next errant idea.

Josie took an extra few minutes to gaze at her horses, but the sparse home paddock, de-stocked and yielding nothing much more than a smattering of nodding dandelions, took her spirits back to their lowly position.

She was almost at the garden gate when she abruptly stopped, paused and turned back. She crouched over a cluster of dandelions, inspected a flower closely, then began to gently dig one from the soil. It took a minute or two, the ground being hard and dry, but before long she had a full dandelion plant in her hand, roots and all. She rubbed the dirt from the roots and exposed a fat, pale tuber, about four centimetres in length.

'Hello, sweetheart,' she said with a smile.

▼▼▼▼

Inside the Everston farmhouse, Flo was still chatting, telling Jerry about the eureka moment she'd had upon hearing that the school could apply for a large state government grant for community service.

'Lucie told me about it,' she said. 'And I went and pitched it to the principal. The school gets fifteen thousand dollars in exchange for getting their students into community service. So now the whole school is going to help with the Nowhere River Show!'

Jerry looked at her until she shuffled uncomfortably. 'What?'

'Are you different?' asked Jerry, 'Or is it me?'

'Huh?'

'You're, I don't know, louder or something.'

Flo shrugged. 'I had my fringe trimmed again?'

'Maybe that's it. But it's probably me. Everything seems kind of louder.' He went back to staring out the window.

'You were on the show committee once, weren't you, Dad?'

'Yep.'

Flo waited for him to elaborate. He didn't. 'You should go back on it. I need experienced committee members.' She waited.

Jerry cleared his throat but no words followed.

'What were you in charge of at the show?'

'The rodeo,' said Jerry, tipping his head back and closing his eyes.

He's sleepy again, thought Flo. 'Maybe we can find you something to be in charge of. Not a rodeo. Apparently we can't organise anything that might hurt animals.'

Josie came in then. 'Right,' she said. 'That's done. What will hurt animals?'

'A rodeo.' Flo glanced at her mother, glanced again at the shine of something unfamiliar in her eyes. 'Mum?'

'Mmm,' said Josie, averting her face and moving to the kitchen. 'The animal activists would be all over it.' She pulled the little tuber from her pocket and ran it under the tap, gently rubbing the dirt from its pale skin.

'Bloody vegans,' muttered Jerry.

'Well, they have a point,' Josie said.

Jerry made a soft scoffing noise that Josie chose to ignore.

'Speaking of animal cruelty,' she said quickly, taking a paper bag from a drawer and dropping the tuber into it. 'Flo, can you feed the cat, please, before it finds a bird? And then maths. Half an hour at least.'

'Nooooo.'

'Yes,' said Josie, throwing her daughter a warning look. 'You can do maths *and* be here for Dad for a minute. I have to duck to Fronda's for a tractor part.'

'I'll be right,' said Jerry gruffly. 'I don't need full-time supervision.'

Except you do, thought Josie, glancing under his chair at the green plastic bottle, shaped perfectly for an invalid man to wee into.

Flo was about to further protest the maths point, but there was something edgy about Josie that made her think twice. 'Okay, I'll feed the chooks and get the eggs too.' She planted a little kiss on her mother's face as she got the chook bucket and called, 'Time me, Dad?' as she went out the door.

'Am I expecting too much of her?' Josie asked.

Jerry didn't reply.

'I feel like her motivation is due to burn out at any moment and she'll go back to counting clouds by the river. And then the show will be a disaster.' Josie wiped her hands and said to the wall, 'I wish I hadn't ever suggested the idea of a show revival. We'll never get enough people to justify the effort.' Josie caught the whining tone in her voice and cleared her throat. 'She's learning a lot, though. Yesterday she told me that red capsicums are actually green capsicums, but riper. Did you know that, Jerry?'

'Nope,' said Jerry.

'And maybe she'll win a handy hundred k.'

'Yep,' said Jerry. 'That *would* be handy. Handier than a famer with a buggered spleen and no bloody insurance.'

Josie's smile disappeared. 'The decision to stop the income-protection insurance was made by both of us, Jerry.'

'We'd have been better to have made use of the life insurance.'

It took Josie a moment to catch his meaning. She readjusted the tea towel on its rail until it was perfectly straight. 'Swoozie Hamilton from Nuyina told Lucie and Flo that loneliness is just as deadly as smoking.'

Jerry didn't reply.

A few minutes later, Josie was listening to the tappety rattle of the ute's engine and giving it extra, angry revs.

'You might as well bugger up, too,' she said as she shoved it up a gear and watched the dust billow into the rear-vision mirror. 'Fucking rain, where are you, dammit?' she said between gritted teeth to the cloudless sky.

On the straight approach to the Everston gate, Josie spotted a station wagon pulled in to the verge. It was Carra's car. Josie felt her heart rate increase.

'What are you drumming about?' she asked her heart.

She slowed the ute and brought it to a stop just level with the letterbox, which had been newly painted a vivid, beaming white. It had also been straightened up and realigned, so that it smiled eagerly at Josie from the roadside. Standing beside it, with a garden fork in her hands and a slightly more cautious smile, was Carra.

'Hi, Josie.'

'What's going on?' Josie craned to look towards the ground. At the base of the letterbox was an oval-shaped flowerbed, trimmed with edging bricks and filled with cheerful-looking flowers. Beside it was a pile of cleared blackberries.

'It's a Sporticulture–Shiny-town team effort,' said Carra. 'Deidre and Ruth painted. I'm just doing the flowerbed.'

Josie stared. She felt strangely disassociated from herself as the general distemper of the day came swelling back. *Ah, here comes the rage again.*

Carra tapped the handle of her fork. 'I'm almost done. I hope you don't mind. They're daisies, so they won't need much water. And daisies mean new beginnings. Or something.'

'Another introduced species,' said Josie.

'Well, I was—'

'Fuck. Off.' Josie felt the words rise from her boots and emerge, barely audible.

Carra stared at her.

'I said, fuck off.'

'Josie—'

With sudden, fitful movements, Josie had her seatbelt off and was out of the car. She steamed around to the letterbox, kicking up her own dust.

'I *do* mind,' she shouted. 'I mind a whole bloody lot. I liked it how it was. All this does is make everything else look crappier. And trust me, everything else doesn't need to get any crappier. I don't need your too-late friendship gestures or your cryptic daisy messages. I need actual real stuff and none of this is real. *You're* not real.' She snatched the garden fork out of Carra's hands, flung it over the fence into the border paddock and stood, breathless with rage, staring into Carra's face. Josie saw crushed, raw hurt and thought, *Good.* Then she kicked at the brick border, stomped back into the driver's seat, slammed the door as hard as she could and roared off.

Carra watched the ute drive away. When it was gone, she stood long enough for the road dust to settle around her. Then, with shaking hands, she reset the kicked bricks back into their places, packed her tools and pots into the back of the car and scaled the fence to retrieve the garden fork. In the paddock, she sank to her knees and pressed her hands to the hard earth.

'I'm sorry, Josie,' she whispered. 'I think I've forgotten how to be real. Or maybe I never knew.'

From somewhere above her, a bird sang. She looked up, but couldn't see for the sun and pressed her hands to her eyes. She got to her feet, picked up the fork and its broken-off handle, then returned to the car. From the boot, she lugged a large water container and filled a watering can.

You're not real, you're not real. The words reverberated through her with each heartbeat. The daisies shook their heads at her from beneath their gentle shower.

▼▼▼

Swoozie Hamilton, 88

I used to try to enter something in every category of the Hall of Industries at the Show. Crochet, tatting, jams, sponge cakes, pavs, cordials – oh, everyone loved my lemon cordial. And for the most part I'd win the aggregate prize. One year I even entered the poetry competition. That was a turn-up. No one took me for a poet. It was just a little ditty. It went:

> *My old pop had a cellar full of bottles,*
> *He'd a cellar full of bottles, on the sly.*
> *My old pop hid his bottles from the coppers,*
> *Good and proper from the coppers he would hide.*
> *Then one night, my pop's bottles they went poppin'*
> *Pop and bang and fizz went all them lids.*
> *Now my pop, with his popped and popping bottles,*
> *And his cellar full of nothing's in the clink.*

Haha, just a bit o' fun, but it's true – my family is riddled with bootleggers, dastards and wastrels.

Chapter 19

Carra perched a packet of Easter buns at the top of a veritable sculpture of groceries installed on the hood of the twins' pram. It wobbled, so she put the packet under her arm and pushed on. Just as she reached the end of the aisle, Mr Pfaff rounded the corner at pace and bumped straight into the pram. The delicate balance of groceries fell, scattering cans, squashing bread, breaking eggs and sending rolls of toilet paper coasting gracefully back along the length of the aisle.

'Oh God, sorry,' said Carra, then laughed, because it had been Mr Pfaff's unheeded march around the corner that had caused the accident. She waited for him to cover her apology with his own.

He didn't. 'There are trolleys at the front of the shop,' he said instead. 'Trolleys. They are for putting the groceries in. You are a hazard.'

'Oh, come on,' said Carra. 'That wasn't my fault. If I had a trolley, you would have run into that, and we all know the pain of a trolley to the shin. My padded pram saved your shin.'

'There are broken eggs on my floor. They are also a hazard. I will have to clean them up. You will have to pay for them.'

'Are you a robot, Mr Pfaff?'

'The trolleys are by the door.'

'God, there's nothing like a bit of good old-fashioned country service, is there?' Carra said, with particular emphasis on the first syllable of 'country'. 'Where do you think I'd put my babies if I got a trolley?'

'Leave them at home.' Mr Pfaff continued on his way.

'Oh, what, leave them with my myriad helpers? Sing out to the birdies and the trees and get them to keep an eye on things? You think I'm goddamn Cinderella?' Carra found herself yelling. She looked at the babies, breathing deeply. 'He called me a hazard.'

Ben held out a block of butter with a bite in it.

Carra smiled weakly. 'You're the hazards.'

Daisy reached for the butter and let out a wail. Carra watched, impressed by the perfect upper-case 'O' Daisy could form with her lips. She wondered what people would do if she just opened her mouth like that and wailed.

At that moment, Josie appeared at the end of the aisle. Carra's heart dipped. Only two days had passed since the scene at the letterbox and she was still smarting, still working out what to do with her shame. *Of course*, she thought. *Of course I have to see Josie.*

'Hi,' Carra said with what immediately seemed an embarrassing amount of eagerness. She dropped her eyes to the floor. 'We're wreaking havoc, as usual.'

Josie surveyed the scattered groceries and said, 'Life without havoc is no life at all.' She bent to pick up a few of the items.

'Josie, I'm so sorry about the letterbox.'

Josie said nothing, just stared down at a tin of potatoes in her hand.

'They're surprisingly waxy and delicious,' said Carra, taking the potato tin from Josie and wishing it would disappear.

'Right.' Josie busied herself picking up the remaining fallen groceries.

'I didn't think it through, I know that now.'

Josie remained silent.

'Mr Pfaff is really crabby about the eggs,' said Carra with a small laugh. She knelt to retrieve the bread and a pot of cheap 'miracle' wrinkle cream from under the shelf.

'Mr Pfaff is crabby about the world.' Josie put a pile of Carra's groceries into her own shopping basket. 'These'll be at the counter for you.' She headed back out of the aisle, passing Phoebe Costas, who was staring intently at the teabag selection.

'Thanks, Josie.' Carra felt the air swirl with all the things she wanted to say.

But Josie didn't answer. And she didn't look back.

Carra suddenly thought she might cry. Instead, she looked down at the wrinkle cream and muttered, 'Send me a miracle.' She thrust the tin of potatoes onto the nearest shelf and pushed on, with a nod to Phoebe, who said, 'It was Snow White who sang with the birds, not Cinderella.'

By the time Carra had constructed another grocery pile, Mrs Pfaff had tallied up the items deposited by Josie, packed them into boxes and was drumming her fingers on the countertop.

'Sorry,' mumbled Carra, and then wished she hadn't.

'We have a new line of health food, if you're interested.' Mrs Pfaff jerked her thumb at a rack of sesame bars, low-fat chocolate and diet drinks. 'You with your fitness caper.' She grinned a grin that could also have been an expression of extreme discomfort. 'It'll give your Sporticulture people a leg up, won't it? I'll hit you up for a percentage if you win Fresh and Lovely.' She rubbed her thumb and fingers together. 'We can form a partnership.'

Carra felt alarmed. 'Um . . .' She imagined, in snapshots, Mrs Pfaff and her becoming best friends. Going shooting together, hitting up the pokies. She remembered that she hadn't checked Ursula Andreas's Instagram page lately. *What would Ursula think of me now?*

'But just quietly,' Mrs Pfaff went on, 'I reckon I'm a favourite. Poor Rosie Montgomery was in for his foot powder and he bought a protein bar and a packet of pumpernickel, so he's on board with my health foods.' Mrs Pfaff eyed Carra's proffered card. 'EFTPOS is down, can't you read?' She pointed at a greasy sign on the corner of the counter that said *Cash only, bloody EFTPOS is down again. Don't blame us.*

Carra wondered whether to laugh or scream, but decided against both.

'Typical bloody nowhere town,' Mrs Pfaff said. 'You know why this shithole is called Nowhere, don't you? Because the river bends back on itself, so it's going nowhere. No matter how much spondoola Her Arseholiness up there on her rises throws at it.' She emitted a wheezy cackle. 'We're going no-fucking-where.'

Carra paid hastily with what cash she had, then left with half the groceries, no wrinkle cream and a vague sense of unease about the state of the world.

As she approached her car, Carra came across Abigail Snelson pinning a sign to the High Street noticeboard.

'Ah, Carra, I know you and Duncan will help with this.' Abigail flapped a hand at her sign, then put it over her mouth. 'Oh gosh, what I should say is this: hello, Carra; hello, baby Daisy; hello, baby Ben! How rude of me.'

Abigail had got the twins confused but Carra didn't have the heart to correct her. 'Hi, Abigail.'

'And I've been wanting to say how sorry I am about my behaviour at Riverhouse the other week with the rosé. I was three sheets to the wind! The last time I got like that was in 1988 for a Bicentenary barn dance. So naughty.'

'Please don't worry, Abigail. I was quite drunk myself. So was Lucie.'

'I'll never drink again – I'm only just over it, you know. Could only manage Bovril and dry toast for two days.' Abigail leaned down to the babies. 'Say no to alcohol, children.'

'What would you like help with?' Carra looked at the sign. It featured a large picture of a garden gnome under the words 'Adopt a Gnome'.

'Ah, well,' said Abigail. 'My Treats Committee has concocted a plan to give Cliffity Smith's gnomes a bit of a lift. It's called Adopt a Gnome, but really it's just asking people to give money towards paints and bits and bobs for the craft class to work on the Nuyina gnomes. There are hundreds of them, did you know? Cliffity's been quite the collector.' Abigail handed Carra a flyer.

'He's had a long life to collect them, I suppose,' said Carra, reading the flyer. 'Thirty dollars per gnome. Put me down for three.'

'There's absolutely no obligation,' said Abigail. 'That seems too generous, and it's an odd thing to do, I know. Patricia will hate it, but the residents are so enamoured with the idea and Cliffity's been getting very agitated about his gnomes. He really is becoming quite the contrarian in his old age. He's taken exception to poor Swoozie Hamilton, on account of his ferret getting lost or something. He told her the Hamiltons are a pack of "gimcrack scobberlotchers".' Abigail chuckled. 'Swoozie didn't seem to care, just called him a silly old loon and Stanton Godfrey got shouty. Although Stanton's always quite shouty. It's been really quite quarrelsome at Nuyina lately. But they have the courage of their convictions, which is admirable.' Abigail paused and went pink. 'Gosh, listen to me! I should "get a life", as they say.'

'You're very passionate,' said Carra. 'It's wonderful to see.'

'I love them so.' Abigail sighed, her eyes shining. 'Anyway, I thought the gnomes might be a good distraction.'

'I'll have four, actually,' said Carra, mostly to curb Abigail's tears. 'One for each of us in my family. Don't tell Patricia, though. I need her to think my garden tastes are way above a common garden gnome.'

'I do understand,' said Abigail. 'They're quite sweet really. And some of them are very scruffy. I've adopted ten, God help me. But you will remain anonymous, I give you my word.'

Carra found herself quite struck by Abigail's kind heart, worn so prominently on her sleeve. Her gloom began to shift.

'Gnome!' shouted Daisy. 'Gnome!' She grabbed the flyer from Carra's hands and crumpled it gleefully. 'Gnome, gnome, gnome!'

Abigail smiled at Daisy. 'Well, it looks like Ben is keen to adopt. Thank you, Carra. And I do have one other favour to ask. Sorry to be so demanding, but I've been roped into doing Rachael Hamilton's ghost tour. I wish I knew how to say no to things. You wouldn't consider coming along, would you? I'm not sure exactly when yet, but, you know, safety in numbers and all that.'

Carra felt wary again. 'Gosh, I'm not great with ghost things.'

'Oh, never mind, of course you shouldn't spook yourself—'

Carra regretted her instinctive selfishness. 'But if we were to get a group of us together, maybe, if Duncan can be home with the twins . . .'

Abigail's face lit up. 'Lucie might come along, too. And some of the other St Margery's ladies. I thought it best not to present it to the Old Folks' Treats Committee. Too many weak hearts. Oh, thank you, for both gnomes and ghosts. Now let me help you all into the car.'

Carra drove home thinking of Josie, and of gnomes and ghosts, then pondered the abundant peculiarities of a place going nowhere.

She looked at her babies in the rear-vision mirror. 'Right. Great. Today is a new day. I think it's time I found the courage of my convictions.' She considered this and added, 'Well, first I'll sort out my convictions, and then I'll find their courage. Maybe the ghost tour will help – get me out of my comfort zone.' But all the way home, Carra tried to work out whether she'd actually ever had a comfort zone.

▼▼▼

Several weeks later, five women (including Flo, who was beginning to forget that she was still a child) were bundled up against the chilly night air and clustered together in the picnic area near the old post office.

'It's so dark. Where on earth is the moon?' said Lucie, blowing on her hands. She'd forgotten her gloves.

'Where on earth are the street lights?' said Phoebe Costas. 'This isn't safe.'

'We should be getting the Shiny-town crew onto some extra street lights,' said Lucie. 'That would be much more shiny and helpful than painting all our rubbish bins gold.'

'I like the gold rubbish bins,' said Phoebe.

'We can't have a street-lit ghost tour,' said Carra. 'That wouldn't work. A creepy lantern or two, maybe.'

'Boo!'

'Fuck!' screeched Lucie.

'Lucie!' said Carra, but she couldn't help laughing.

'Sorry, Flo, darling,' said Lucie. 'But that's not funny, Phoebe.'

'It wasn't me,' said Phoebe.

'Who was it, then?'

'I don't know, I can't see. Esther?'

'Not me,' whispered Esther Very, the town librarian (who rarely spoke above a whisper, ghost tour or not).

'It wasn't me either,' said Abigail. (Lucie didn't suspect her anyway, Abigail not really being the 'boo' type.)

'Is it eight o'clock yet?' asked Lucie. 'Perhaps that's how the ghost tour starts, with a "boo".'

'That'd be a bit lame.'

'BOO!'

They all screamed. Someone laughed. 'Sergeant D?'

'Ha,' said Sergeant D, revealing herself by shining a torch under her chin. 'Just getting you all in a ghost tour sort of mood.'

'Isn't there some sort of rule against the constabulary frightening the socks off the people they're meant to protect?' said Lucie.

'Good turnout,' said Sergeant D, flicking off her torch. 'Rachael will be pleased.'

'We're only here because she's promised to bring her family along to volunteer for our projects,' said Phoebe. 'Everyone's a bit working-bee weary.'

'I know,' said Carra. 'My Sporticulture numbers are dwindling.'

'I want to get a photograph of a ghost,' said Flo. 'It would make a good show attraction.'

'Wonderful idea,' said Lucie.

Esther agreed. 'People would flock from all over to see that. I could use it in the museum, too. I'm not exactly run off my feet with visitors.'

'Early doors,' said Abigail.

'God, it's cold,' said Lucie. 'How did you talk me into this, Abigail? I'm homesick for my fireside chair. And Beans.'

'Ghosts can turn the warmest of places cold,' said Sergeant D.

Carra shivered.

'It's April in the Tasmanian high country, Sergeant,' said Phoebe. 'We don't need ghosts to keep things cool.'

'Yoohoo!' came Rachael Hamilton's voice from the darkness. 'Happy April Fools' Day!'

If Carra had tried to think of a less effective way to kick off a ghost tour than shouting 'boo', then a cheery 'yoohoo' would be it.

'Oh gosh, I forgot about April Fools' Day,' said Flo. 'How creepy.'

Carra thought about the complicated April Fools' Day pranks Josie had always been fond of playing. (She had once glued goggly eyes on every single item in Carra and Duncan's fridge.) Carra worried about the day passing unheeded at Everston.

'This is more like it,' Rachael said. 'I've so far only had Mr Fronda on a tour, and he spent the whole time debunking my stories. I need to get some practice in for when the tourists come.'

'Tourists?' asked Phoebe. 'Nowhere River isn't exactly on the tourist map.'

'Well, Miss Fresh and Lovely might change all that,' said Lucie. 'Carra's gardens, Esther's historical society, Flo's show.' She tucked an arm into Flo's.

'And your Nowhere People,' added Carra, feeling a rush of fondness for her mother-in-law.

'Next they'll be raving about the supernatural presence here,' said Rachael. 'We have hotspots everywhere, you know.'

'That's a dubious claim to fame,' said Lucie with a shudder.

Esther rubbed her hands together. 'I've been reading up on the hotspots. Are we starting with the All Angels Humming Stones, or the headless horseman on the Goodbye Bridge?'

Rachael forced a little laugh. 'No, we'll begin here. The picnic ground has its own sceptre, actually. If you have a torch, please keep it off. Let's begin.'

The ghost tour was a mixture of stories they'd heard before – the face at the St Margery's attic window, the sound of crying in the post office, the light in the watermill, the horseman on the bridge, the humming stones – and an array of colourful new ones: a dead lifeguard at the old swimming pool, a horse and carriage in Zephyr Lane, screams from Pocket Island, and a poltergeist at the bottom pub.

'Golly,' said Esther as they were leaving the old pub, 'there aren't this many ghosts in the whole of England and some of their buildings have been there since the Common Era.'

'Can you show us an *actual* ghost, though?' asked Lucie, who was tired and cold and didn't fancy peering into any more dusty windows. 'Fleury Salverson bet me five dollars we wouldn't see an actual ghost.'

'Well, our most common sighting is over by the cemetery at All Angels Church,' said Rachael.

'Funny that,' said Phoebe.

'It's the hottest of our hotspots, along with the humming stones, of course. Sometimes there's an old woman dressed in mourning clothes. We'll go there now, it's our last stop.'

'Oh good, close to home,' said Lucie, as they set off along Church Street.

A few minutes later, Rachael gasped and put out a hand. Everyone stopped.

'There,' she whispered. 'On the Ashby Crescent corner. I thought I saw something.'

'That's a tree,' whispered Phoebe.

'No, no,' whispered Rachael. 'It was a figure, I'm sure of it.'

Someone sniggered. Lucie wondered whether she might just slip off home. She'd had enough. Rachael led the group further down the street towards the cemetery. 'Is anyone getting a sense of something? A change in the atmosphere?'

'Yes, I farted, sorry,' said Sergeant D. 'That'll bugger up your hotspot detector.'

Everyone laughed, except Phoebe, who said, 'I'm taking you seriously, Rachael.'

'So am I,' said Abigail, despite her laughter. 'I promise. My hairs are standing on end.'

'Yes,' said Rachael sombrely. 'That's what I'm talking about. Our bodies know things before our minds. It's called horripilation.'

'Or goosebumps,' added Carra.

They walked on a bit further before Rachael hissed, 'There!' and pointed towards the circle of dim light cast by a lamppost above the cemetery gate.

'I saw something too,' said Esther. 'There, by the hedge.'

'Oh my Lord,' whispered Abigail. Even Sergeant D fell silent. There was a rustling sound from somewhere in the dark space beyond the lamppost, where the hedge loomed over the path. They waited.

Across the silence came the call of a boobook. Flo gasped and tried
not to drop her camera. Carra clutched Abigail's coat.

'Okay,' whispered Rachael. 'I have sage in my hands, which
creates a healthy boundary between the spirit realm and ours.' She
raised her voice. 'You may show yourself, spirit. There is nothing to
fear.' The hedge rustled again, as if to respond. From somewhere on
the other side of the graveyard came a faint humming sound. It rose
and fell on the night-time air, forming patterns that could have been
a melody.

'The h-humming s-stones,' said Rachael. She whimpered and
tucked in behind Abigail, holding out her sage with a shaking hand.

Carra shivered. 'I think we should probably just—'

But before she could finish, a figure burst from the hedge and
darted across the light of the lamppost. It was just a flash, a fleeting
glimpse of two little running gumboots, one pink tutu and a head of
bouncing, blonde curls, but it was enough – and far, far too much –
for Lucie to see all her dreams come into vivid, stunning focus.

'Coming, ready or not,' called a child's voice from the cemetery.

Lucie staggered forward, whispered, 'Felicity? Felicity?' then
barrelled into the darkness.

'Lucie,' said Carra, moving fast. But Sergeant D was ahead of her;
she flicked on her torch and scanned the area.

Lucie hadn't got far. She was gripping the rails of the cemetery
fence and searching blindly, frantically into the unyielding dark.
'I can't see her. I can't see.'

'Oh my God,' Rachael was babbling. 'Oh no. No, no . . .'

The torchlight cast a feeble silver wash over the gravestones, which
seemed huddled against the cold, or the night. Or around a precious,
abiding secret.

Lucie's eyes darted around the scene, desperate to fill it with
movement. But there was none. The river mist hung, undisturbed.
She crumpled to the ground, releasing a scream of such unfettered,

lacerating anguish it had Carra searching for a jagged tear in the black velvet of the sky.

Mrs Georgina Pfaff, 64

We're in Nowhere River because it's the least likely place to be taken over by the Russians. They've been investing in their Western assets since 1987, and they're closer than you think. They have communist China on board, even. We have a shop, with mostly tinned food, candles. And we're informed that there are bunkers from pioneer survivalists somewhere. The best thing about this town is that there aren't too many humans. Humanity is mostly a sinister force. There are only a few of us who are normal. I know because I've been working in retail for over thirty years and pretty much everyone's a fuckwit.

Stanton Godfrey, 86

I was one of the first to wash out tins and reuse them. And way back I did some research into recycling the oil from old tyres. It's called pyrolysis oil and there's about seven gallons of it in each tyre. But no one asks me about that anymore, they all buy their children plastic toys and nylon clothing that before long just go on the tip. And I just sit in my chair and think, *Oh well, I won't have to worry about any of this soon, I won't need the moon colonies and I won't have to watch the planet die. And at least I can say I tried.*

Chapter 20

Len was at home, just across the avenue from the church, watching a re-run of *Rumpole of the Bailey* with Beans and nibbling on a sneaky bowl of chocolate raspberries when he heard Lucie's scream. He was out the door and across to the churchyard in his slippers in a matter of seconds.

'What on God's earth?' he said, marching aslant towards the women gathered around the torchlight. Father John had also emerged from his house, and was scuttling across the lawn saying, 'Oh my goddy, goddy God.'

'Oh my God, I'm sorry, I'm so sorry,' wailed Rachael Hamilton. 'So sorry.'

Flo looked up at the steeple of the church with a beating heart and thought, *Are you even there, God?*

Sergeant D was doing her best to keep everyone calm. 'Okay, come on Lucie, just take a moment, you've had a shock.'

'Oh Father,' sobbed Rachael when she saw Father John. 'Forgive me, please forgive me. This is all my fault. That wasn't Felicity Finlay, it was my youngest, Ruby. It's just that no one wanted a ghost tour and we thought we could spice things up a bit with some play-acting. I didn't mean for Lucie—'

'Let me get this straight,' said Len, 'You had your daughter dress up as our Felicity to *spice things up* for your *ghost* tours?'

'It was meant to be Cosette as the old lady tonight. She must have skived off and sent Ruby. She's impossible, that Cosette – you know teenagers. Oh God, I'm sorry. I thought—'

But no one got to hear what she thought because Carra surprised everyone (including herself) by smacking Rachael smartly across the face.

▼▼▼

'Everyone was just seething with rage,' Carra told Duncan the next morning at breakfast. 'You should have seen your dad. I mean, we could almost see sparks coming off him. Incandescent. And so horribly silent, you know how he gets.'

Duncan sipped his water. 'Mmm.'

'It's pretty certain that Rachael will be disqualified from the Miss Fresh and Lovely contest. I thought Sergeant D should have arrested her, frankly.'

'I reckon she's genuinely sorry,' said Duncan. 'Don't be too hard on her.'

'What?' Carra thumped down her cup harder than she meant to. 'This is your family, Duncan. I'm furious on all your behalves. Lucie was just, like, struck down. She might never be quite the same again.'

Duncan turned towards the sink. Carra wondered whether she'd gone too far.

'She's been through worse,' he said, putting down his glass and washing his hands. 'I'll pop in and see her on the way to work. But maybe this is a good thing. A bit of release. Lately she's been kind of, I don't know . . . simmering.'

'Oh my God, Duncan, can you ever just say something slightly negative? Ever?'

He turned towards her and smiled. 'We have no muesli?'

Carra sighed. 'You could have toast. We have bread.'

'No worries, I'll steal some of Ruth's. She gets the good kind from Hobart.'

'Coffee?'

He shook his head. 'Brushed my teeth, see?' He gave her a kiss. 'I'll let you know how Mum is. Stop worrying.' He paused before reaching the door. 'You gardening today?'

'Yep, up at the fire station, cutting deadwood from the buddleias. The men's shed blokes are coming.'

'Great. You're doing a really good job. The streets look amazing.' He smiled at her, flashing his Colgate-commercial teeth.

Don't brush your teeth, thought Carra. *Just once. I dare you.*

'And if you're popping in for muesli, could you grab some milk, too?'

'Maybe,' said Carra, 'because you *never* have two babies in tow, *you* could *pop in* and grab some milk. My days of *popping in* to anywhere are long gone. You could do a full grocery shop by the time I get around to doing a wee.' She swabbed the sink edges with the dishcloth, leaving a smear of rice-bubble residue.

'Okay,' said Duncan. 'Of course. I can do that.' He massaged Carra's shoulders and said, 'You only need to ask.'

'Do I, though?' she said, shrugging him off. 'Do I really need to ask? Isn't it obvious? The shop is two minutes from your work and you have a personal assistant.'

'Office manager. And I've always said, I'll help whenever I can.'

'Mmm, do we really call it "'help"? Or is it "parenting"? I struggle to brush my hair. And I haven't changed the bedsheets for three weeks. I don't even know how people get time to change bedsheets.'

'Look, why don't we go to the Bothwell childcare centre together? I'll book out some time. Just to have a look. It might be just for a day a week. Or maybe think about doing less of this garden stuff. You don't need the Miss Fresh and Lovely title, Carra, or the money.'

Oh, but I think I really do, thought Carra. She tried to hold her tongue but it ran away from her. 'Maybe *you* should think about doing less of this doctoring stuff. Less of your community work, less of that thing you do when you just walk out of the house with nothing but your wallet and your thoughts of the day ahead and your freedom. Look at all your freedom, it's everywhere, it's so beautiful.' Carra waved her hands around, aware that she must appear insane. 'Who even eats muesli every single day, including weekends?'

'Um, you?'

'And I don't even like it that much!'

Dr Duncan, with his perfect bedside manner, gave the tension a few silent beats, then simply took Carra into his arms. She tried to wriggle free but his grip tightened around her, until they both felt the sag of her surrender.

'Sorry,' she whispered, then wished she hadn't. 'Sorry,' she said again, louder, because there was a strong sense that overriding her own wishes was the thing she was meant to do.

'It's okay. It's normal to behave irrationally when you're tired.'

He held her for a few more beats, then moved his hands down her back. Instantly Carra detected a change in his touch, a slowing of his movements and a shift in his breathing. And instantly her heart knocked out a warning. *Oh, and now he wants sex.* As he leaned in for another kiss – this time a lingering one, with lips softened by desire and a caressing hand in her hair – Carra reprimanded her heart. *It's closeness you crave, you idiot,* she thought. *Don't push it away.* But closeness in this sensual form, with its requirements of motion and time and focus, seemed like just another demand. She coerced her body into moving with him; tried to block out anything but his touch, but it was no use. She wished he'd simply let her go and make a cup of tea. Talk to her, listen to her, see.

As it happened, because Duncan took a moment to set the babies up on a rug with a *Play School* DVD, and because it wasn't yet 8 o'clock, there was just time for Carra's desires to hush her racing thoughts, take control of her head and allow for actual, covert love making in the laundry. There was time for Carra to reinforce her devotions with her hands, to reconnect her wayward mind with Duncan's needs. There was time for Duncan's triumphant shuddering climax and Carra's (embellished) very-nearly-an-orgasm. There was time for a short, breathless lean against one another, a 'Wow' and a smattering of laughter. And then Duncan smoothed his suit and his hair, and rushed out the door to get to work before his first patient.

Carra was left to ponder why she hadn't yet washed the painted yellow 'Carra' off the laundry wall, and to try to gather any newly made love from the rumpled atmosphere before she un-paused the day.

It wasn't until later (once Daisy had vomited on the fire station driveway after eating four biscuits from Snowy Thorold's packet of assorted creams, and had to be taken home before any dead wood had even been trimmed) that Carra ruminated on the word 'irrational'. She said it aloud, then mentally spat it through her teeth and out the window of the car into the fresh peppermint breeze.

Daisy fell asleep with that same breeze on her face, well before home, which meant Carra had to keep driving so as not to wake her. Ben fell asleep too, so Carra drove the full hour and a half to Hobart, where she was able to bulk-buy Duncan's favourite muesli and a coconut cake. With nursery rhymes blaring from the car speakers on the way home, she drove past an enormous hardware store and wondered whether they might have a supply of sackcloth and ashes she could stock up on as well.

▼▼▼

For almost four days after the traumas of the ghost tour, Lucie couldn't get herself out of bed. She slept on and off, rousing occasionally to encounter the waking world with its terrible, galumphing grief. It trampled and sneered and wore her down her until she had to close her eyes on it again. Even when she half-dreamed a tug at the bedclothes from a small blonde child in a tutu, she turned aside and whispered, 'No more, darling-heart. I've had enough.'

Beans, who was also poorly (having found himself alone with Len's chocolate raspberries the night of the ghost tour) lay beside her all the while. Len paced in and out of the bedroom and around the house, fiddling with teapots, worrying the roses and waiting for Lucie to revive. She had always revived before.

At the end of day four, she finally got out of bed and moved herself to the sitting room, where the chair smiled at her with its comforting creases, and the coffee table offered up toast and butter. She sat facing the window for less than a minute before asking Len to close the curtains.

'I can't look out these windows,' she said. 'I'm done with looking. I'm done with that river. And I think I'm done with this town. When I'm not so tired, Len, it might be time we packed up and went home.'

'What do you mean, Lucie, love? We *are* home.'

'I don't know that we are. I thought we might have been, once, but I'm so haunted here, Len. She doesn't leave me alone.'

'That wasn't a ghost, Lucie, by the church. It was the Hamiltons playing cruel foolery.'

'Yes, yes, I know that,' Lucie said. 'But before that, well before that, I'd been seeing Felicity everywhere.'

'What do you mean, Lucie?' Len looked suddenly like an agitated old man, not at all like her handsome husband.

'I don't quite know what I mean,' she said. 'But I see her sometimes. I mean, not the other night, I know that was a silly prank.

But odd times. Sometimes she's in the garden, or walking beside me. Sometimes she leans into my skirt the way she used to.' She paused, her blue eyes fixed. 'And this is how I know she must be gone, Len. It's how I know she's not alive, or ever coming back. And how I know it must be time for us to leave.'

Len winced. His joints throbbed. Lucie's words seemed to grate and clash against his bones.

They presented the matter of Lucie's affliction and her thoughts of leaving Nowhere River to Father John, who had always been a voice of calm and reason beneath the blusters of the cloth, and was visiting daily.

'Grief has many manifestations,' he told them. 'And you must not expect it to ever go away, especially when it is so unresolved. It will send up the occasional walloping blow. Give it time to recede.'

'I know those wallops,' said Lucie. 'This one is different. This time I'm skewed, my thinking is different. I don't want to see her anymore.'

'I've grown so fond of this house,' Len said, when it was his turn to speak. 'And the river. This funny old town and its motley crew. I'm more surprised than anyone to find that I don't want to be anywhere else. I thought I was trapped here, on the River Nowhere, but it turns out I'm not trapped at all.'

Father John, who'd learned that Len's truths best emerged when there was no banter to distract him, just nodded and sipped his tea.

Sure enough, the clock on the wall ticked thirty or so seconds into the silence before Len added, 'I know we won't find Felicity. I know that in my brain. But there's a bone in here' – he pointed to his chest – 'and another one here' – a hand on his hip – 'that still feels her in the Nowhere air.'

'She's still in my prayers,' said Father John.

Len chortled. 'It'd be more useful if you'd help me prune the plum trees.'

'I can't tell anymore,' said Lucie, 'whether I sense her or whether it's my hope that puts her here. And sometimes I'm scared to see her, other times I'm scared I *won't* see her. Sometimes I don't, for days and days, and I wonder, does that mean all hope is gone, or *she* is gone?' She slipped a foot under Beans, who was curled into a chubby knot on the hearth rug. 'Either way, we might as well be anyplace, mightn't we? I mean, what are we waiting for, Len? For Felicity to knock on the door, or float in on the tide?'

'I didn't think,' said Len after a long moment, 'that we were waiting for anything. I thought we were just getting on with things, with Felicity alongside. Had hoped we might have reached a sort of sunlit uplands.'

'Perhaps I'm waiting for death,' said Lucie. 'So that I might see her face again.'

'Well, that's a silly thing to wait for,' said Len. 'When we have no guarantees there is anything but nothing in the great afterlife. And you can please shut up, Very Reverend Rector Man.'

But Father John said gently, 'I don't think, Len, that it is up to you to let your beliefs impose on the comforts of others.' He turned pointedly towards Lucie. 'A wise man once said, *When you are used to this horrible thing that will forever be cast into the past, then you will gently feel her revive, returning to take her place, her entire place, beside you.*'

Lucie blinked at him, and asked him to repeat the words, which he did.

'Her entire place,' said Lucie. Something shifted in her chest.

'Bible blunderbuss,' said Len.

'Proust, actually,' said Father John.

'You've read Proust?' Lucie watched Len try not to be impressed.

'Bits of him. That part I know well. *At the present time . . . let yourself be inert, wait until the incomprehensible power that has broken you restores you a little, I say a little, for henceforth you will always keep something broken about you . . .*' He trailed off. 'Something like that.'

'That's very true,' said Lucie. 'Thank you, Father John.' She patted her chest, as if to cherish the part of her that was broken. To keep it. She looked at Len. 'That's what I've been doing, then, isn't it, being necessarily inert?'

'I've also heard it said,' added Father John, 'that one may not be depressed, just in need of a deep rest. Get it? Deep rest . . . depressed.'

Len gave a disapproving snort. 'If I'm going to subscribe to any philosophy, it'll be that of the Stoics. We are in charge of our own responses. We get on with things.'

'Well then,' said Lucie. 'When I'm up to getting on with things again, we can get on with them back in Hobart, can't we?'

'There is plenty to get on with here,' said Len. 'Such as your Nowhere People project. I'm enjoying the little narratives you've been gathering. It's a noble and important venture.'

Lucie was silent, suddenly exhausted again. 'Shhh,' she said. 'Enough now. I'm being inert. Having my deep rest.' She closed her eyes and slipped the other foot under Beans.

Father John cleared his throat. 'I will leave you to it. A final thought. Proust also said that one should always keep a patch of blue sky above one's life. So perhaps you should consider a bit of a holiday. Somewhere other than the chilly old Central Highlands. We're headlong into winter. I can keep on gathering your Nowhere stories, Lucie. It's what I do anyway, really. I quite like interviewing people.'

Lucie imagined her carefully curated project in the hands of the dear, clumsy priest, and decided that a holiday would be a very bad idea.

▼▼▼

Rachael Hamilton, 39

My husband is fourth-generation Nowhere River stock, and I'm third. I was a Plunkett, of the greyhound-racing Plunketts. My brother still races greyhounds. He has a current champion called 'Nice Try Tracy'. He is recently divorced. His ex-wife's name is Tracy. I'm the last Plunkett in Nowhere River. Well, apart from my other brother, Cryton, but we don't count him.

The Hamilton family were one of the first in the district. We've always owned Pocket Island. Our girls love to tell people we own an island. They're so hilarious.

Chapter 21

'Someone's graffitied a penis and balls onto the Hamiltons' garage.' Sergeant D stood at the Everston front door and watched Josie's reaction.

'Good,' said Josie. 'You can't get away with her kind of fuckwit behaviour without copping the old cock-and-balls treatment. Come in, you're making the verandah look untidy.'

'Thanks, but I don't want to intrude.'

'Oh, for God's sake, why does everyone keep saying that? Maybe I want someone to intrude. Maybe I don't want a series of pussy-footing chats about lasagne at my front door.'

'Jeez, rightio then,' said Sergeant D, stepping into the house with a little salute.

'Jerry's asleep. Come and have a cuppa with me, and tell me all about this inspired penis-and-balls mural. Rachael deserves a bit of what-for.'

'Well, I think Rachael's almost had enough what-for. Patricia disqualified her from Miss Fresh and Lovely, everyone's dishing her up either hot tongue or cold shoulder. She was beside herself when she phoned in with this. And wait, is this really Josie Bradshaw talking? Or some normal person who is able to apply ruthless judgements without empathy?'

'This is the new me. I'm hitting menopause. No one is safe. And besides, I've struggled to like Rachael since she crashed into my Datsun and lied about it in 1999. Now my dislike can sail free. Anyway, did you bring me this news to cheer me up, or what?'

'Not exactly. I found this at the scene.' Sergeant D pulled a plastic bag from her pocket, containing a tin of green spray paint.

'Okay, well, generally graffiti artists need paint. Or so I've heard.'

'It was purchased by one Florence Bradshaw yesterday from Pfaffs'. Mrs Pfaff confirmed that this morning.'

'Oh,' said Josie. 'Shit.'

'Is she here?'

'She's somewhere.' Josie ran her hands through her hair. 'God, it's no wonder I'm grey. She's gone all, you know, Flo again. Dreamy and silent. I think she's losing interest. She's not one to finish things, our Flo, school being one of them, and now, apparently, the show.'

'The penis and balls was pretty well complete.'

'Ah, well, that's something. Bloody hell, she should know better, this isn't like her.'

'There are a lot of people behaving strangely. I blame this Miss Fresh and Lovely business.'

'You're just pissed off that your footy idea didn't get up.'

'Probably.' Sergeant D sniffed. 'Anyway, I don't think there needs to be a song and dance over this graffiti offence. She left the evidence there, she's not going to become a career criminal.'

'She needs to apologise, though, and paint it out or something.'

'Mind if I have a chat to her, in the first instance?'

'Please do. She's probably out grooming the horses, far side of the stables. Don't be soft on her.'

▼▼▼▼

Flo wasn't grooming the horses, nor was she on the far side of the stables. She was inside the stables, lying on her back in the straw, striped by sunbeams that had gleefully found their way through the cracks in the old weatherboards. She had one hand in the air, with index finger raised, and was sending dust motes flailing off their trajectories.

'Hey,' said Sergeant D softly.

Flo sat up, startled. 'Hi.'

'What you doing?'

'Not much. Nothing.'

'Ah. I remember doing that once.' Sergeant D sat beside her.

'I was thinking that I really like those sunbeams. But I shouldn't too much because what we actually need is a huge big rain. Rain's the only thing that will save our farm.'

'I thought you were going to save the day with the show and your Miss Fresh crown.'

Flo wrinkled her nose. 'I don't think it's going to work. The showgrounds are a wreck. Carra's snazzed up every garden in town and Mrs Montgomery loves Abigail's old folks thingo. And Lucie's stories. Have you given Lucie your story?'

'Yep. She's pretty much got around to everyone. No one can say no to Lucie.'

'She's showed me some of the stories. They're great. She deserves to win.'

'So you'll give up?'

'I think I might.'

'Well, that's good. Because you're probably going to get disqualified anyway. Due to a certain piece of artwork on the Hamiltons' garage door.'

Flo widened her eyes before she lowered them to the floor. 'Oh.'

'Nice job, you should take up life drawing.' Sergeant D produced the plastic bag containing the paint can. 'But probably not a life of crime. You'd need to cover your tracks better than that.'

Flo looked from the can to Sergeant D. 'Right.'

'Or we could keep this on the down-low if you agree to keep going with the show.'

'What?'

'All you need to do is knuckle down, work hard, keep up with your schoolwork, and I won't tell a soul. I'll get Ruth and Deidre to repaint the garage as part of their Shiny-town project. Job done.'

Flo gaped at her. 'Am I being blackmailed?'

'Looks that way.'

'Right.' Flo slumped back into the straw.

Sergeant D lay down next to her and watched the dust wheel about. 'Don't worry, everyone I know loved the Nowhere River Show, so you're in for a great chance.'

Flo thought for a moment. 'There's so much to do.'

'I'll help you; everyone will. I'll enter stuff in the Hall of Industries, judge the mangelwurzels, whatever. And let's ask Father John to help coordinate the working bees – he has a new rule about saying yes to everything, and he's worried about you.'

'Is he?'

'Yep. We all are, Flo.' Sergeant D gave her a friendly shove. 'You Bradshaws are the backbone of this old town.'

'Are we?'

'What industry do we have without our farms? Without Everston Pastoral especially? A retirement home and a shop. That's not going to sustain a town. But a good operational farm and an agricultural show can.'

Flo was silent.

'You should get your dad to judge the animals, and the wool. Get him involved.'

'He doesn't want to be involved in anything much.'

'He will.'

Flo put a hand back into the sunbeams.

'Come on,' said Sergeant D. 'Where there's a willy there's a way.'

Flo laughed. The cat came in, eyed them suspiciously and tried to decide whether she was hungry or sleepy. She noticed the sunbeams and opted for a snooze.

'What do you think happened to Felicity Finlay?' asked Flo.

Sergeant D sighed deeply. 'I don't know. I think about it all the time but I just don't know. Some days I think the river – I mean, that's the obvious explanation, but other days I wonder . . . I really wish we could find something.'

'There were no clues, not even one?'

'Nope, not a trace.'

'Wow.' Flo swallowed a lump in her throat. 'Poor Lucie.'

'It always amazes me,' said Sergeant D, 'how there are no secrets in this town, but so many mysteries.'

'Everyone knows everyone, but no one knows anyone at all.'

Sergeant D nodded. 'Most of us don't even know ourselves.' They were silent for a moment, breathing in their words, before Sergeant D added, 'Except Swoozie Hamilton. She knows herself very well.'

'Yeah, so does Vivvy Cox. And Bunty.'

'And Daphne. Especially Daphne.'

'Oh yeah, Daphne *really* does. And Cliffity.' Flo reached into the pocket of her jeans and pulled out the tiny, rosy-cheeked gnome. 'Cliffity gave me a gnome.'

Sergeant D smiled. 'Of course he did.' She took the little figurine from Flo's hand. 'Would you like to go to the show, Mr Gnome?'

'Yes indeedy-do,' replied the gnome in a squeaky voice.

Flo laughed again.

'That settles it, then,' Sergeant D said, handing back the gnome and sitting up. 'A disappointed gnome is very bad luck.'

Flo touched the gnome's cap. 'But what if the show's a failure and I disappoint the whole town?'

Sergeant D shrugged. 'I think everyone in this town is pretty at home with disappointment. I have dinner with mine every night.' She laughed softly. 'And wouldn't it be worse if you never tried? If there was no expectation in the first place? There'd just be a whole town saying, *Ah there we go again, just another thing that didn't happen.* That's when people just drop their bundles and wait to die.'

Flo's eyes widened.

'So, do we have a deal?'

Flo observed that the gnome's expression had apparently altered from simple happiness to hopeful anticipation. She took a deep breath. 'So, if I give the show my best shot, you won't tell Patricia about the penis and balls?'

'Brownie's honour.'

'Okay, deal.'

▼▼▼

Sunday the ninth of May of that year was Mother's Day. It was also the thirtieth anniversary of Felicity Finlay's disappearance.

Lucie, who'd committed herself to a good month of 'deep rest', had been slow to rouse. Even when she felt strong enough to get dressed, open the curtains and resume an element of normality, the ninth of May and its brutal truths sent Lucie back to her bed.

Len had made an anxious, pre-emptive overstep by inviting Duncan and Carra for lunch and putting a leg of lamb on to roast. He tried in vain to coax Lucie out, and by eleven o'clock gave up and phoned Kinvarra.

'Oh dear, Carra,' he said when she picked up the phone, 'I think we'll need to pull the pin on lunch, I'm afraid. I don't think Lucie can bear it.'

'Of course,' said Carra. 'Are you all right, Len? What can we do?'

'It's very hard to know,' said Len. 'I've done a lot of tiptoeing about with tea, some hand-wringing and a bit of tearing hair out, but none of that has worked. I broke a teacup, which wasn't ideal. There are enough broken things in this house.' His words were whispery and hoarse on the ends.

Carra's heart ached for him. 'Oh, Len,' she said. 'Wait, I'll get Duncan.'

Duncan took the call into another room, and emerged a few minutes later wearing his coat. 'Carra? I think I'll take the babies over. At least we can be with Dad, and if Mum needs distraction . . .' He smiled apologetically at Carra. 'Do you mind? It's your day.'

'Of course not, go! You must. I'll pack a bag.' She busied herself with face cloths, toys and snacks, trying not to think in case there were selfish, *what-about-me?* thoughts to contend with. 'Just call me if you want me to collect the twins, or bring something, or whatever. I'll be on standby.'

She helped them into the car and waved them away, then returned to the kitchen, where she was halfway through decorating a Mother's Day cake. *'Happy Moth,'* said the wonky letters. Carra waited to feel miffed about the loss of her second Mother's Day, but the utter silence that descended interrupted her train of thought and brought to light a whole new, uplifting awareness.

An empty house, she thought, *with me in it.* She listened, for a long and blissful moment, then whispered, 'I'm truly sorry, Lucie. And Len and Felicity. But happy Mother's Day to me!' She stretched her arms into the silent air, then cut herself a large piece of cake.

At Riverhouse, Len sat himself down on the edge of the bed and whispered to Lucie's back, 'Duncan will be popping in shortly, just briefly with the feral monsters, no lunch, no fanfare, and if you don't feel up to it I will entertain them in the garden.'

Lucie stirred just faintly. Beans, who was curled up against her, snorted softly.

'I do like the garden in late autumn,' Len continued, 'The stories all told and so much good to come.'

'Spare me your thinly veiled allegories,' said Lucie. 'And your effortful optimism.' She reached behind her, found his shoulder and gave it a pat. 'Just hop into the darkness for a bit. Sit with me.'

Len swung his legs onto the bed (wincing a little with his left), settled against the bedstead and put a hand on Lucie's shoulder. 'Of course,' he agreed, but after a while, he cleared his throat. 'I wonder . . .'

'No, no,' said Lucie. 'No wondering.'

Len drew out his next pause a little longer before saying, 'You may at any time tell me to clear off to Coventry, but I was vaguely thinking, a bit, about Esther's historical society.'

Lucie remained silent, so he continued. 'She – Esther Very – asked me the other day, gently, about putting together a sort of story memorial . . . for Felicity. When she was researching, she said she kept finding newspaper reports and references to us, and she wondered whether it might be a healing thing, at this thirty-year juncture, to help her put together a sort of tribute.' Len gave Lucie pause to offer up her thoughts, but none were forthcoming. 'So she's not just a lot of hushed whispers and speculation. What do you think? I thought it was rather brave of Esther to ask. She's clearly been gearing up for it for a while.'

'I think,' said Lucie slowly, 'that Felicity is not a museum exhibit.'

'That's not what she—'

'She is not ancient history.'

'No, but I think it was more about us—'

Lucie turned to face him, her eyes flashing. 'And I think that it's a bit rich of you to ask me to get all showy about Felicity's story when all this time you've been telling me to move forward and not dwell. My God, for years we've sat by this nowhere river with this enormous nothing and we didn't even say her name.'

'I thought that was the right thing . . . you were so consumed—'

'She's my daughter! I lost her! Of course I was consumed.' Lucie lowered her voice again, sank back into the pillows. 'And of course she's been reduced to speculation. She's a missing person. A mystery. A whisper. Our daughter is a whisper.'

Len looked at his hands. Beans trotted into the silence, whimpered and furrowed his brow at Len.

Lucie leaned over and put a hand on Len's cheek. 'We're just starting to talk about her a bit. Let's keep it at that for now, shall we? Not leap into an illustrated memoir.'

Len cupped her hand and nodded. 'Sorry.'

A silence surrounded his sorry. Beans touched his nose to Len's knee, then tucked it back into his paws. A Len apology was a rare and weighty thing, and probably shouldn't be sniffed at.

▼▼▼

By the first week of June, Flo had appointed her committee, drafted a mud map, listed maintenance needs and firmly re-asserted her focus. The first community-service day at the showgrounds for Nowhere River High saw her instructing her former schoolmates to scrub bird-poo, shovel cowpats and prise old staples out of walls. They were far from thrilled (students and showgrounds both appeared unwilling) and after the initial thrill of Cosette Hamilton being obliged to follow her orders, Flo felt entirely out of her depth. Cosette, at any rate, chose quickly to eschew obligation in favour of hiding under the grandstand with her BFF Kirrily and throwing insults out to Flo at any opportunity.

'Basic bitch,' she hissed. And, 'Up-yourself loser dropout.'

Anticipating this sort of behaviour, Sergeant D had sent Father John along to help, but she would have done better to send Beans the pug.

'I have a renewed enthusiasm for writing sermons,' said Father John, gazing enviously at Walt Wallace, who was expertly carting bits of scrap metal and wood with a front-end loader to a giant skip bin, being properly useful.

'I think Sergeant D can take over next time,' said Flo. 'But she's busy organising my permits and things.'

They watched a group of young girls galloping around on brooms. 'A police-issue baton would be helpful,' said Father John. 'Or a taser. Otherwise I fear I'm not very useful to you, Flo.'

Flo kept on with her scrubbing and said casually, 'You could enter something in the Hall of Industries. That would be very useful. It needs filling up. Just a drawing or a bit of knitting?'

'Um,' said Father John. 'I don't think . . .'

Flo smiled up at him and said, 'Yes to life, Father John!'

'Jesus H. Christ,' he said. 'Are there no secrets in this town? I'm sorry, Flo, but in this case it is kinder to refuse. My craft offerings, I fear, would only serve to smite your Hall of Industries with their terrible mediocrity. I may be able to stretch to a small, very badly done painting, at best.'

He looked at Flo with genuine anguish, so she said, 'That's okay. A painting is perfect. And maybe you could try convincing Lucie to keep up with her Nowhere People exhibit? Everyone's looking forward to it, seeing themselves and others.'

'I'm doing my utmost,' said Father John. 'Poor Lucie.'

'I'm not going in any exhibition at your sketchy show,' yelled Cosette, suddenly popping her head out from under the grandstand.

'Well, there probably won't be an exhibition anymore,' shouted Flo. 'Thanks to your family and your stupid haunting. You could have stopped Lucie's heart.'

Cosette rolled her eyes. 'I've prayed for forgiveness, haven't I, Father?'

'You, um, do have to, well, *earn* forgiveness, Cosette . . . somewhat.' Father John cleared his throat. 'Flo, I would be honoured to be included in the Hall of Industries. I'll attempt two paintings, large ones, and I'll try my hand at some baking as well. Abigail will lend me a recipe book, I'm sure. And some hints. Yes . . .' He took a deep breath. 'I'll have a go.' He appeared to be feeling quite woozy from all the radical acceptance and had to excuse himself to go to the luncheon room for tea and a biscuit.

Once he'd gone, Cosette and Kirrily emerged from the grand-stand, laughing.

'You need to do some work or you won't get a community service grading,' said Flo.

'*You need to do some work or you won't get a community service grading,*' repeated Kirrily in a sneer.

'You're a thirsty bitch, Flo Bradshaw,' said Cosette. 'Look at you, firing shots at everyone and dick-teasing with the priest.'

Flo stopped dead. 'What did you say?'

'I'd be careful if I were you, Flo-poke, you know what those dirty old priests do to little girls.'

Kirrily laughed.

'Say that again, I dare you,' yelled Flo, marching towards Cosette.

'Ooh, look at poor little Flo Bradshaw, with the fucked-up dad. Leaving off her adulting for one second to throw a little tanty.'

'Your family are bootleggers, dastards and wastrels,' Flo shouted.

'What are you on about?' Cosette laughed. 'God, you're a nerd. No wonder the priest—'

But Cosette's acid words were jolted to a stop, because Flo pushed her into the side of the storage shed with such force that a crack echoed around the arena, followed by a bloodcurdling scream.

Sergeant [Christian name redacted upon request] D, 31

I've been in Nowhere River all my life. Well, except for when I went to the police academy in Hobart and then on to a posting in Scottsdale. Midway through the academy I had my heart broken pretty badly and I just wanted to start again, as someone else really. And the police force did change me. It helped me move on, stay confident. I'm still not sure I'm really me.

Anyway, this is my heartland, I guess. I couldn't stay away. I love the people. They're like, 'Here's my shoulder, you can lean on it for a moment and then we're going to go and catch a fish for dinner.' And now I'm thirty-something and I'm still here. Far out! I don't have a bloke. I'm too busy. And my heart healed up all hard, I think.

Chapter 22

The nicely rounded shape of the Everston Sugarloaf had long served as a landmark for Josie; a point of reference. Someone was always 'out beyond the Sugarloaf' or 'this side of the Sugarloaf' and from a distance, it was the most visible part of home. On this day, Josie was *on* the Sugarloaf, clearing a section of earth on the northern side. The sunny morning had chased threads of mist from the trees, the air was soft, warm for June, and Josie found herself peeling off layers of clothing as she worked. For once, though, she didn't begrudge the sky its lack of clouds, but allowed herself to enjoy the sun on her arms. She touched the warmth it left on her dark trousers and said, 'Go on then, sun. Shine on.'

From up on the Sugarloaf she could see the whole northern aspect of Everston. *Sparse* was the word that came to mind. *Battling.* But Josie, now that Jerry was able to move around more, see to his own basic needs, and be left alone for short periods, was up for the battle.

'Bring it on, you dry old bastard,' she said to the wind. She turned back to the slope, the growing pile of rocks and the bare patch of earth she had cleared.

It was a while before Josie lifted her gaze back to the bigger picture, and another few moments before she registered a distant figure walking from the house to the stables.

Alex, she thought, but then she couldn't see his car, and knew he was at the showgrounds helping Flo. *Walt? But why would he be in the stables?* She sighed. Probably just another farm drop-in. A stock agent or a rep or a Jehovah's Witness. Or someone with another lasagne. Josie toyed with the idea of pretending she hadn't seen the unexpected visitor, but sighed again and jumped into the ute. She knew that if someone was heading for the stables, they'd be looking specifically for her. And, since Jerry's accident, Josie had been on constant high alert for worst possible scenarios.

It was only a few minutes before she entered the stables, calling, 'Hello?'

There was no reply.

'Hello?' she called again.

She walked towards the stalls, all empty save one, which housed Alex's old pony, Biscuit. Biscuit, being twenty-seven and a bit on the wheezy side, much preferred a stable and a daily fix of chaff to the tiresome outdoors. Josie gave Biscuit's nose a rub, listened to the clicks and creaks of the heating iron roof and tried to decipher the difference in the stable air.

Keeping a casual eye over her shoulder, she took up a nearby shovel. 'Whoever you are, and whatever it is you're doing, I suggest you stop it right now and show yourself.'

'Okay,' came a voice from the stall beside Biscuit. There was a clatter and a 'shit', then another 'okay'.

'Carra?' said Josie.

Carra appeared from the stall. 'Yes, it's me. Sorry. Hi.'

'What are you . . .' Josie looked from Carra's face to the implement in her hands. 'Is that a metal detector?'

'Yes. I borrowed it from Esther Very. She's been using it to find relics for her museum.'

'Right. Well, are you going to tell me why you're hiding in my stables with a metal detector?'

'Yes, okay, sorry. I was, um, I thought you were at the show-grounds with Flo.'

'Nope. I still can't be too far from my sick husband.'

'Oh. Yep. I was looking, um, for your ring. I thought I could, you know, do something real.'

Josie lowered the shovel. 'Well that's a waste of time, I found it yonks ago. In the thing by the sink with the dish brush in it.'

'Oh.' Carra switched off the metal detector.

'Weird. I'd searched for hours in the stables and in the barn and it was right under my nose the whole time.'

'That's great. Great news.' Carra looked at Josie's left hand. 'You're not wearing it, though?'

'Nah. Sold it.'

'What?'

'I'd already fessed up to Jerry about losing it. And I had vet bills I couldn't afford, so I sold it to the pawn shop in New Norfolk.'

'Oh, Josie.'

'It's okay. My animals are far more important to me than diamonds.'

Carra looked at the floor.

'What were you going to do with my ring if you found it? Put it in the tarted-up letterbox?'

'I don't—'

'Look, I understand the gesture, but I don't need a fancy letter-box, Carra. What I need is a real-life, here-for-me friend.'

'I know. I'm sorry. I've been a shit friend.'

'A really, *really* shit friend.'

'And I know you told me to fuck off and then I didn't, but if you could just let me—'

'It's a bit late.'

'I just . . . it's just that our friendship was so much about laughter. We just laughed *all the time*. And since the babies, I don't know,

I haven't been finding many laughs. I tried to, I really did, but it felt forced and, I don't know, fraudulent. I was trying to think of something else to offer you.'

'So you're saying our friendship was a fraud?'

'No. Sort of. On my part, anyway.'

Josie looked at Carra for a long time, shook her head and sat herself down on a railing. 'So who was that brilliant woman I got to know?'

'I don't know,' said Carra. 'I don't know. I'm so tired and . . . disillusioned, I guess. It feels as though sometimes I have to save every positive part of me for my family. And I just didn't think someone so well put together could be friends with someone so fallen apart.'

Josie snorted. 'We're all pretty fallen apart, aren't we?'

Carra tried to think. 'Are we? It feels as though I'm the only one in the whole world not coping very well with being a wife and mother.'

Josie stared. 'You think I'm coping?'

'But that's the thing, you are. Things have been terrible for you and you're *still* coping. You're out there in your rolled-up sleeves being a farmer. I don't have an excuse, apparently. I'm struggling with the Sporticulture thing and motherhood. I can't even get my own garden in order. I have healthy babies, an *incredible* husband – a brilliant life, everyone's always telling me. I'm meant to be the embodiment of happily-ever-after.' Carra heard her voice wobble.

'So what *is* your excuse?'

'I don't feel happily-ever-after. Why is that?'

Josie sighed. 'I don't know. Postnatal depression?'

'Everyone says that too, but postnatal depression supposedly makes you feel nothing. I feel *everything* about my babies, with a sort of magnified intensity. I left them with Lucie a few times while I worked and I missed them until it hurt, but then I loved the freedom so much, that I hated it again. I'm all over the place. I'm guilty, I'm questioning myself, I'm washing, I'm cleaning, I'm wistful, I'm bored *all the time*. I don't know what's happening in the world, I don't know any music except nursery rhymes. I felt a bit better when I started the Sporticulture project, but then I get home and there's stuff everywhere and no one's done anything because I'm the one. *I'm* the one. Doing all the things. And I have to do a sort of late shift, or a second shift. And then if we don't have sex I don't seem to get noticed in any meaningful way and I'm just someone who has to produce breastmilk and stock the cupboards and wash the socks.'

'Yeah,' said Josie. 'They need to have sex to feel close and we need to feel close to have sex. The old paradox.'

'That's a thing?'

'Hell yeah.'

'Then why don't I know that? Why doesn't anyone tell you that *before* you put on the white dress? And why didn't I know that – even after sex and sometimes even a blowjob – I'm still the one who has to get up for the crying baby while Duncan rolls over to sleep because he's the important doctor who holds the whole town together with his perfect care and attention? Why didn't I know that? Did I somehow miss all the warnings while I was busy being in love? My own mother lives and breathes independence – she has a family and a fulfilling career *and* an elite-level hobby.'

'And she barely speaks to her daughter.'

Carra was silent for a moment, then lowered her voice to say, 'But she raised me to know better, to be outraged by gender inequality, and somehow I don't know anything.'

'She raised you,' said Josie, 'to know better than to be like her, didn't she, Carra?' Josie ignored the edge of cruelty in her own voice. 'She raised you to never remove yourself from your children's lives to chase the goddamn wind.'

'Except I did, didn't I?' Carra said. 'I ran away.'

'Only momentarily.' Josie sighed, irritated. 'Look, Carra, we all think it's going to be different for us, but then in one way or another we meet all the stereotypes.'

'Would it be stereotypical of me to say I don't think I can remain resigned to this institution of relentless chore and expectation and disappointment anymore?' Carra's words echoed around the stalls.

'You're not saying you want to leave Duncan?'

'Yes!' Carra shouted the word. 'Yes, I am.' She covered her eyes with her hands for a moment, as if to protect the moment of clarity from contamination, then sat herself down on a nearby oil drum. She spent a moment trying to catch her breath, and her thoughts, then took her hand from her eyes and braved a glance at Josie's disbelieving expression.

'Josie, I'm sorry. I didn't come here to talk about myself. I have no right to be here at all—'

'Are you serious about leaving your marriage?'

Carra couldn't bear the outrage in Josie's face, so spoke her next words to the floor. 'The thing is,' she said, 'it's been wonderful, of course. Love, passion, and then a beautiful wedding and two babies who we both adore. But why can't we say, "Well, wasn't that a great success – look what we did! I think I'll be off now, thank you. I didn't bank on having so little freedom, and having to do so much fucking cleaning."' She peeked again at Josie. The outrage remained. 'Those stereotypes you speak of, Josie, I just had no idea that I'd fall into them. Soon I'll be like every other mother – domesticated and conditioned and trapped.'

'What the fuck?' said Josie, her voice rising. 'You could get a job and a nanny if you hate it that much.'

'Or,' said Carra, 'maybe some regular rostered days off, paid annual leave, a room of my own and an occasional assistant?'

Josie's face was a mask of disgust.

'See!' said Carra, 'Look at your face! You're brainwashed too. Have you never felt suspicious about how well our devotions suit society?'

'No, Carra, I'm just really grateful to have a family to love.'

Carra looked Josie right in the eye. 'Then you are the perfect selfless woman. And anyone listening in on this conversation would send me straight to the ungrateful, selfish corner too, where all the poor choices go. I put myself there all the time.'

Josie ran her fingers through her hair in exasperation. 'You know what I think, Carra Finlay? I think it's a bit rich of you to blank me completely, ignore me at the darkest possible time and then ask for my support as you break your unbelievably beautiful, kind husband's heart.'

'I'm not asking for your support! I was actively *not* involving you.'

'And you know what else I think? I think you're a mental case.'

'And *that* is exactly why I knew I couldn't talk to anyone. Don't worry, every day I tell myself, *Come on Carra, for fuck's sake, where's your mind? Get over yourself, feel the joy, everyone else is managing.* But every day I've felt unaccountably furious, until I took time to think about it more, and hold myself accountable for being so thoroughly *dependent.* And you don't need to gaslight me – I do a lot of that, too.'

'You're not thinking straight. I mean, you're probably still hormonal from pregnancy. Give it time.'

'There you go again.' Carra groaned. 'Maybe hormones don't create problems, maybe they just expose them. Maybe marriage is a conspiracy. Who were you before you were the other half of Jerry? Where's *your* mind, Josie?'

'Don't turn this around onto me,' said Josie icily. But for a moment, her thoughts wrestled with a ringing of truth. *Where is my mind?*

'But come on, seriously Carra, even *I've* had moments of being in love with Duncan and he's like a brother to me. Every straight female just dies for him. Even some of the gay ones. Wait.' Josie gasped, then froze, her eyes wide. 'Maybe you're gay. Is that it?'

'Oh, come on, now *you* can fuck off.' Carra picked up the metal detector and stomped away. At the stable door, she turned back. 'This is the precisely sort of response I'd expect: "How can Mrs Duncan

Finlay ever be unhappy? How very dare she? He's so perfect." Believe me, I live with him and I know he's perfect. His shit doesn't even stink – it really, literally, doesn't! He never loses his temper, he looks amazing all the time. And I'm asking myself those very questions and at the same time feeling not one bit worthy, ever. I wish I *was* gay – at least then there'd be a reason that might satisfy everyone.' Her words thickened with tears. 'Anyway, I came here because I wanted you to know that I'm sorry. I buggererd up our friendship. It was always my problem and you suffered for it.'

'You know what?' said Josie, kicking at a clod of chaff on the cement floor. 'I think maybe we're both a bit overwrought. I'm just going to put aside what you've said today, so you can have some time. Neither of us has the energy for this at the moment. You've been good to Flo, so, you know, let's just skip to the bit where we become civil acquaintances. Do you think we could do that?'

Carra drew in a long, quivering breath. Tears spilled from her eyes. 'We'll see each other around, as happens in a town like this. We don't have to cry. And we sure as hell don't have to laugh, God forbid.'

But Carra, despite every effort to choke it down, continued to cry.

'Or you can keep carrying on like that and I can call the police to report a trespasser.'

In an effort to pull herself together, Carra sniffed and wiped her face. 'Jerry is doing better, thank you.'

'Great.'

'Nice weather we're having.'

Carra only managed to nod. Her eyes rested on Josie's silver necklace and her mind flashed back to Josie's fortieth birthday party, when they'd both had enough champagne to link little fingers and swear eternal friendship, like schoolgirls.

'Anyway,' said Josie. 'I should get on. Stuff to do. And you should get home.'

'Okay,' said Carra. She walked quickly out of the stables, her chest bursting to sob. As she rounded the corner towards her car, she came face to face with Jerry. Pale, diminished, different, but definitely him.

'Jerry!'

My God, you barely look human, she thought.

'Carra!' He was puffing slightly, and clearly in some distress.

'Jerry?' Josie appeared from behind them and hurried to his side. 'What's the matter?'

'It's Flo, she's been in a fight. She's okay, but Sergeant D has her at the station.'

'Oh, fucking hell, what next?' Josie took his elbow. 'Come on, I'll get you inside.'

'I'll help Jerry,' said Carra. 'You go, Josie.'

'No, thanks. I'll call Alex over the two-way.'

'Nope,' said Jerry. 'Leave Alex, I'm coming too. I'll be fine. She needs her dad.'

Carra watched the two of them swing into action, Josie's hand moving automatically to Jerry's shoulder, their heads in close as they turned away. Carra, firmly excluded from the confederacy of family and shared crisis and teamwork, watched on helplessly until they were in the car and driving away.

She was about to get into her own car when she realised she'd forgotten the metal detector, so had to return to the barn, where Biscuit was still snuffling into his chaff. Carra surveyed Josie's realm: the perfectly organised bridles and helmets, the nametags tacked lovingly above each stall, featuring Josie's spidery handwriting. Carra put a shaky hand on the old horse's neck, watched his left ear move towards her in mild interest, and envied his uncomplicated place in Josie's world.

'Should I phone my mother?' she asked Biscuit. 'Tell her I want a pony, please, and a party dress and maybe a bit of her time? And oh, I could tell her all about how I seem to be turning myself inside out trying not to be like her, and how I actually am a mental case, haha, miss you, Mum, wish you were here.'

Biscuit's ear moved away from Carra, in the direction of a forest raven's laconic heckle. Carra sighed, collected up the metal detector and marched herself out into the harsh winter light of day.

▼▼▼

Josie and Jerry entered Sergeant D's office to find Flo hunched in a chair, staring at the floor. Father John stood at her side.

'Jerry!' said Sergeant D.

'Dad!' Flo jumped up. 'Dad, you should be at home. I'm sorry. Are you all right?' She put her arms very gently around him.

'I'm all good,' Jerry said. 'You?'

'Fine.'

'What happened?' Josie looked from Sergeant D to Flo to Father John.

'I dislocated Cosette Hamilton's shoulder,' said Flo before anyone else could speak. 'It was my fault. She's a horrible cow and I lost my temper.'

'Oh, Florence.' Josie closed her eyes.

'Cosette and her friend Kirrily both say it was an unprovoked attack,' said Sergeant D.

'I wouldn't say it was entirely unprovoked,' said Father John. 'I did witness Cosette Hamilton in particular being a bit unpleasant towards Flo. I overheard the words "basic bitch" at one point, I believe.'

'Is this true, Flo?' asked Josie.

'Yes.'

'Is that all?' asked Jerry.

'Pretty much.'

'This isn't like you, Flo,' said Josie. 'What else did they say?'

'I don't know, just stuff.' Flo glanced at Father John. 'I didn't mean for her to get hurt like that, but I'm glad she did. *She's* the bitch.'

'Okay, that's enough,' Josie snapped. She looked at Sergeant D. 'Where's Cosette now?'

'She's been transported to Hobart for X-rays. The ambos put the shoulder back in no problem, she'll be fine. Rachael Hamilton may be a problem, though; she was screaming about pressing charges.'

'I can talk to Rachael,' said Father John. 'She's been under a lot of strain lately. After her, ah, error of judgement.' He sighed. 'I have found it rather trying, I must say, to remain sympathetic to her woes. Lucie is not at all well. And Len hasn't clipped any of his irises or exposed the rhizomes. So unlike him.'

'They're moving away,' said Sergeant D.

'Oh, there's no confirmation of that,' said Father John. 'Len is dead against leaving Nowhere River.'

'What?' said Josie.

'What?' said Sergeant D. 'I meant the Hamiltons. They're selling up.'

'What?' said Father John. 'Oh.'

'Does Lucie want to leave?' Josie asked. At the same time Sergeant D said, 'Are Len and Lucie thinking about leaving?'

'What?' said Father John, in a fluster. 'No. No, they're not.' He blinked at the stricken faces of the two women. 'Sorry.'

'The Hamiltons are moving away?' said Flo, sitting straighter in her chair.

'Well, Rachael screeched that at me at some point today,' said Sergeant D. 'She says they've sold their house and land to some development company. For millions. They're going to build some sort of retreat on Pocket Island.'

'Christ on a cracker,' said Jerry, revealing a delightful glimmer of his old self. 'I'm sorry, Father.'

'Don't be,' said Father John. 'I quite agree.'

'No way,' said Josie. 'They won't get the approvals.'

'Don't bet on it,' said Sergeant D. 'Colleen–Lyell Council haven't given two hoots about what's good for Nowhere River since the council amalgamation.'

'I can't get them to even look at the potholes in Church Street,' added Father John.

'Anyway,' said Josie, 'what next for this raging brawler?' She tapped Flo on the knee.

'Well, if she doesn't have anything to add . . .' said Sergeant D, leaving a pause for Flo's use.

Flo remained silent.

'I think you can take her home. Consider yourself reprimanded, Flo. Again.' She gave Flo a hard look. 'And if you remember anything about the incident – any inciting factors, for instance, don't hesitate to let me know.'

'Okay,' said Flo to her shoes.

On the way home in the car, Flo said, 'I really am sorry, Mum and Dad. Not for pushing Cosette, but for worrying you.'

'She had it coming, I reckon,' said Jerry. 'Nasty piece of work.'

'Oi,' said Josie. 'Violence is not the answer. A cock and balls was quite enough.'

Jerry sniggered. It was the closest thing to a laugh since his accident. 'Well, none of us has to worry about the Hamiltons anymore. Rummins, the lot of them.'

'I like Swoozie Hamilton,' said Flo. 'I was with Lucie when she interviewed her at Nuyina and she told us about her grandfather's illegal brewery. And that he poached trout.'

'That'd be right,' said Jerry.

When they reached the Everston driveway, Jerry said, 'What happened to the letterbox?'

'It got a Miss Fresh and Lovely upgrade,' said Josie dryly.

'Carra did it,' said Flo. 'I like it. Mum thinks it makes everything else look worse.'

Jerry turned to the window. A moment later he thumped the dashboard and said, 'Fuck it, maybe we should just sell up too.'

Josie snorted.

Jerry said nothing.

'Jerry?' said Josie. 'You can't be serious.'

'Well,' said Jerry. 'We might get a squillion for it.'

'But it's our life. Our home.'

'What would Alex and I do?' Flo could feel panic rising.

'You'd be right. Alex could work his way up on the stations. There's big money in those manager roles. He wouldn't want to work with his grumpy old dad anyhow. You could go to uni.'

'I want to live here,' said Josie. 'We all do. The horses . . .'

'We could agist the horses, or buy a house with one paddock.'

'I want to *farm* here,' said Flo as the car pulled up in its place alongside the Everston farmhouse.

Jerry looked out the window at the parched landscape. 'I don't know if I want that for you.'

'It's not your choice.' Flo was close to tears.

'It won't be anyone's choice if we keep going the way we're going. No rain, supermarkets dropping beef prices. It'll all be up to the banks. And it won't be pretty.'

'Wait,' said Josie. 'Stop. This is madness. If they're building a resort on Pocket Island, imagine what they could do to Everston.' Her voice cracked.

'Whoa,' said Jerry, startled by his wife's rare show of emotion. 'Look, I'm not jumping into anything. Just throwing out suggestions. Sensible ones.'

'Okay,' said Josie. 'Well, here's another sensible suggestion: let's forget you even brought it up.'

'I might win a hundred thousand dollars if I really try,' said Flo.

'Hmm,' said Jerry. 'I'm not sure Patricia will think much of your recent criminal behaviour.'

'She doesn't know.'

'Oh, she'll know. Everyone knows everything in this town. Any other bright ideas?'

'Actually, yes.' Josie took a breath. 'Not just an idea. I have a whole rescue plan.'

Kirrily Kalbfell, 16

My parents have always taught me how to be self-confident. They make it clear how special I am. My mum gets me to dance classes and eisteddfods and stuff, and she never makes me wear second-hand dance costumes. She's already bought me a car. It's a blue Mazda. I'm going to be a dancer and an actress. I'll get out of this town, for sure. I'll go to NIDA probably. Dad says my drama mono-logues are amazing. He even cried in assembly last year when I did a Shakespeare piece. I did Rosemary from *As You Like It*.

Chapter 23

Len rifled around in the back of Lucie's Mercedes and extracted some of her favourite albums from the CD stacker. He took them inside, chose one to play on the sitting room stereo, then set one of the speakers at the open window. 'Memory' from *Cats* soon flowed out onto the garden terrace. Lucie appeared almost instantly at the sitting room door, pulling on her dressing gown and looking puzzled.

'What's this?' she asked cautiously.

'This is Monday. We're going to have a refreshing breakfast on the terrace and then I'm going to drive you into Hobart for your singing lesson.'

'No, you're not.'

'Yes, I am. And I have pineapple juice. Very good for the vocal cords, they say.'

'So I hear.' Lucie walked tentatively to the terrace door and looked out at the breakfast table. 'I don't like that sort of bread.'

Len showed her to a chair. 'We can get whatever bread you like in Hobart later.'

She sat for a moment, facing the garden. '*Winter was come indeed*,' she whispered to the naked branches of the birch tree. She took her gaze to the Abergavenny ruins. 'Have the wombats come back to the ruins?'

'No,' said Len. 'The rabbits have well and truly taken up residence.'

Lucie sighed, picked up a piece of toast and forgot to not look at the river. The sun, playing merrily on the surface of the water, sparkled at her through the trees. She jerked her gaze away, her feathers ruffling.

'All right then, Leonard,' she said. 'Let's have a day out. I do think I need to get away. And I think we should take Flo.'

Len sighed.

'She mentioned that she had some show sponsors to visit. She was going to catch the bus.'

'Right. All right.' Len felt outwitted. And weary.

'I'll get dressed, she mustn't see me like this.' She rose from the table again. 'But I'm not going to singing.'

'As you wish.'

'And I'd like a new winter cardigan.'

'A new winter cardigan you shall have.'

Lucie tried to think of something else she could request while Len was being so agreeable, but couldn't think of anything and so braved a proper look at the river instead. The expanse of deep-brown water she could see through the break in the hawthorns didn't seem at all fussed about her recent rebukes. It just flowed on into its smiling bend, danced with the daylight and ignored her altogether.

'You don't need me here, do you,' she whispered to the river. 'You don't need me here at all.'

She closed her eyes and tried not to let her mind go where it had been so, so many times before: downstream.

▼▼▼▼

Carra's day, meanwhile, went downstream before she'd even got her oars in. She had planned to shape and dig two feature beds on either side of the showgrounds gate, but had only got as far as marking out the edges when Ben fell over, banged his head and put a deep cut through the middle of his left eyebrow. He screamed immediately, which was something of a relief to Carra (silence is the scariest thing for a mother of an injured child). Then Daisy, who'd been busily trundling her cart full of blocks over to Ben, screamed louder. And then Carra, with her gardening tools everywhere, her thwarted plans and her distressed babies, wondered whether she might scream as well.

However, she remained strangely calm, and sort of detached. *Here it is,* she thought. *Today's bad thing.* She collected up her writhing toddlers, bundled them back into the car and drove to the medical centre.

'Ah,' said Duncan when he entered his small procedure room to find his forlorn family within. 'Not to worry. Just a bit of skin glue will do it, poor old Benjie-boy.'

Ben said a sad little 'Ow' and reached out to touch Duncan's face. 'Ow, Daddy.'

'Ow!' shouted Daisy.

Carra watched how tenderly Duncan lay Ben down on the treatment bed, how skilfully he prepared his dressing trolley and washed the wound. She held Daisy close and wondered why there were tears pricking her eyes.

'Maybe,' said Duncan, once Ben's eyebrow was glued back together and both babies were sucking on a jelly snake, 'you could have another think about the Bothwell childcare centre, for your gardening days. Daisy and Ben are a full-time job.'

'Yes,' said Carra numbly. 'Yes, you're probably right. They're my job.'

'And you're great at it. I could never do what you do.'

'You could actually. You just haven't.'

Duncan looked confused.

'I'm not saying you're to blame. I've been led to believe that women are better at changing the nappies and sorting the washing, too.'

Duncan rubbed her shoulder. 'I think you've had a shock this morning, and you should get home.'

Carra felt her heart begin to pound. *Shut up,* she told it silently. *You've caused enough trouble.* She gathered up her things.

'Hey, I keep forgetting to ask you,' said Duncan with his even, white-toothed smile. 'Will you marry me?'

'What?'

Duncan laughed. 'Elaine's asked whether I would mind being the pretend groom for her mock wedding. She's doing it to get some marketing material for her Rose Quartz Wedding business, I think. I said I would, but only if my lovely wife could be my bride.'

'Oh God, I can't! My hair hasn't seen a salon in years. They should call in a model.'

'Bugger that,' said Duncan. 'We're locked in. It's in three weeks. Book yourself into Marceline. I have to run. Full waiting room.'

Carra made her way back to the car, wishing she could feel excited about the idea of a mock wedding. Her younger self would have jumped at the chance to dress up and have a bit of fun with it. She clipped Ben into his seat. His face was jelly-snake sticky and there was a smell about him.

'I have to run,' Carra said to herself. 'Full nappies.'

▼▼▼

In the end, Lucie, Len and Flo spent the entire day in Hobart. They visited Flo's show sponsors, then strolled around Battery Point and the waterfront, ate cake in Hunter Street and visited the museum, where Flo laughed at Len in the interactive dinosaur exhibition, read all about the Gordon Dam protests and went quiet amid the displays of beautiful shell necklaces made by Tasmanian Aboriginal women.

After the museum, they went to the shops, where Len was able to witness the reappearance of some spring in Lucie's step.

'I do love shopping,' she said with a little squeak.

She bought a cashmere cardigan while Len chose a navy woollen jumper to match all his other navy woollen jumpers. And for Flo, despite her protests, Lucie bought an Akubra Cattleman.

'Every country show president needs a good hat, isn't that right, Len?'

'Most certainly,' said Len. He felt funny about the bewitched expression on Lucie's face, but when Flo put the hat on and smiled shyly at them from under its brim, he felt a little bit bewitched too.

Later, Len and Lucie took Flo to the Botanical Gardens, where she stood beneath a one-hundred-and-thirty-year-old spotted gum and said, 'This is a lucky tree, being looked after here. It has friends all around.' She felt a wave of homesickness for her lonely tree, trying its scraggy best, and an aversion to the great big Hobart river-mouth, sending her Nowhere River out to the sea.

'Thank you for today,' she said loudly to Lucie and Len, because the homesickness made her feel childish and ungrateful.

'It's a dear old place, Hobart,' said Lucie, looking upwards into the tree's blemished branches. 'My heart's here, I think. Waiting for me to come back to it.' The tree peered down at her from beneath its wrinkled brow. She gave it a pat. 'Before we head back to Nowhere River, Len, why don't we swing back past Red Chapel Avenue? Just for old time's sake.' She looked at Flo. 'Where we used to live. We still have friends in that street.'

Len rubbed his head. 'I think we'd be best to beat the dusk, wouldn't we? That flat light can be treacherous, particularly around the bends at Hayes . . .' His words mumbled away to nothing because Lucie wasn't listening, then he wondered why he'd suggested the Hobart outing in the first place.

'I had a life here,' Lucie said, as she put an arm around Flo and they turned away from the tree. 'Used to think I might join the repertory theatre once, then maybe break into professional work. Other fanciful notions . . .'

Len sighed, followed them up the path towards the car park, and surrendered again.

In Red Chapel Avenue, as Len's Volvo puffed up the steep incline, past well-cared-for, well-to-do houses and gardens, Lucie let herself imagine how they might fit back into their former life, before Felicity. *Yoohoo, we're home! What a time we've had. What did we miss?* Would Mrs French on the corner still throw tennis parties? Would Tom Raspin at number twenty still throw tantrums about rubbish bins? But when they reached number twenty-three, she saw that her pale-blue house was now an austere grey, with a regimented garden of standard roses and sharp hedges. Someone had removed the weeping birch from the front lawn.

'Goodness,' said Lucie with forced generosity. 'Hasn't someone pulled dear old twenty-three into line.'

The side view of the house revealed a large, boxy extension.

'It looks very uncomfortable in its new get-up,' said Len. 'And without our silver birch.'

'It's a really nice house,' offered Flo. 'I did an architecture assignment last year and I learned that new extensions shouldn't try to reproduce past eras.' Her words were meant to cheer, but they matched the air of melancholy in the car, so she added, 'And without the tree there's an amazing view.'

They turned to look. The view was amazing. It showed the water, blue like the sea but hemmed with land like a huge river. Flo thought of Josie, up by the Nowhere River. At the same time, Lucie wondered, *When is a river not a river anymore?* And then, *That great expanse of pretty blue is likely where Felicity was swept in the end.* She coughed then, in an effort to terminate the terrible, grisly images that haunted her from time to time. They dissipated quite quickly (she was an expert), leaving the water to throw her its best afternoon azure.

'All right, off we go, Len. Must get Florence home.' Lucie fixed her eyes on the road ahead, asked Flo about school and forgot to look in on Mrs French's house.

On the trip back to Nowhere River, with the fading city lights in the rear-vision mirror, Lucie watched the sun setting ahead of them and she felt the old hurry-hurry feeling of twilight – a remnant of early motherhood. A heaviness rested against her breast; the weight of a small child. She swallowed nothing, looked back at the glowing western sky and thought, *Ocean blue is a much nicer colour than river brown.*

Ruth Beaumont-Hudd, 59

I've only been up on the Nowhere for fifteen years, so I still see it with fresh eyes, but to me this is paradise. We have a river, fishing, we have hills, we have a close-knit neighbourhood, country values, a hall. And a pretty poor internet connection. That's the best thing, because it won't be the global warming that will get us, it'll be those dastardly computers, mark my words. I have a good job, managing the medical centre. Dr Finlay is a treasure. He says he can't do without me. I'm very good with files. I moved here because the rent was affordable, and it's a long way from my ex. My ex hates water, so phooey to him.

Chapter 24

When Patricia Montgomery wore her black velvet Alice band, Lucie knew to be careful. When Patricia wore the Alice band *and* dusty pink nail polish to a St Margery's meeting, there was good reason to brace for calamity. Lucie glanced across the meeting table at Abigail who, in a similar state of wariness, was chewing her bottom lip and gazing intently into her water glass. The other women, all thirteen of them, appeared slightly awestruck by Patricia and her polished domain but otherwise relatively relaxed. Phoebe Costas was shuffling papers, Deidre Wagner chatted to Marceline Cash, and Lurlene Wallace opened a packet of Fruit Tingles. Patricia, in her navy woollen gilet with the leather piping (possibly another ominous sign), stood at the head of the table and seemed to grow taller.

My eye and Peggy Martin, thought Lucie, deploying a Len expression. *Patricia means business today.* She wished, with a rush of fondness, that Len were beside her, offering up a hand squeeze and a chortle. She had a strange sense of being only half there.

'I thank you all for coming,' said Patricia. 'It is gratifying to make use of the meeting table's drop leaves. That hasn't happened since the early nineties. However' – she paused for a skyward glance and a small huff of Lady-Grey-scented breath – 'I will not waste anyone's precious time with quibbles and equivocations, and you should know that today's meeting will not be entirely gratifying to some of you. It is a review meeting, designed to track the progress of our Miss Fresh and Lovely initiatives, and there will be no mincing of words.' She peered over her glasses at the St Margery's cohort, who were beginning to look fearful. Lurlene stopped crunching her Fruit Tingle.

We're away in the gloomy ranges, at the foot of the ironbark, thought Lucie, realising that she'd have to work extra hard at keeping things cheery. She thought of her chair, with Beans at its foot.

'You're taking the minutes, Abigail?' Patricia said loudly.

This caused Abigail to jump, rustle her papers and shout, 'Yes!' She coughed. 'Yes,' she said again, quietly this time. She held up the book of minutes and nodded obediently.

St Margery's Ladies' Club
Minutes of 'Miss Fresh and Lovely' Review Meeting in St Margery's Ladies' Club Meeting Room
Thursday 30th June

Present:
Mrs Patricia Montgomery (President), Mrs Lucie Finlay (Vice-President), Miss Abigail Snelson (Secretary), Mrs Phoebe Costas (Treasurer), Mrs Josephine Bradshaw, Miss Florence Bradshaw, Ms Marceline Cash, Mrs Georgina Pfaff, Mrs Elaine Thorold, Mrs Deidre Wagner, Mrs Lurlene Wallace, Mrs Ruth Beaumont-Hudd, Ms Esther Very, Sr Julianne Poke, Mrs Fleury Salverson

Apologies:
Mrs Caroline Finlay

Absences:
Miss Bunty Partridge, Miss Daphne Partridge

'We are very pleased to have our vice-president, Lucie Finlay, here and looking well,' Patricia continued.

'Thank you, Patricia,' said Lucie. But she didn't feel entirely well. It occurred to her that grief is a terminal illness. *It'll get me in the end.*

'And welcome back also to Josephine Bradshaw. We are encouraged to hear that Jeremy is convalescing well.'

'Thank you,' said Josie. 'Yes, he's getting there. A bit better every day.'

'Did anyone remind Daphne and Bunty of today's meeting?' asked Patricia.

No one could confirm.

'Well, they'll have forgotten, then.' Patricia frowned. 'And where is Caroline? Do you know, Lucie?'

Josie's polite smile tensed, faded, then forced itself back to position.

'She wanted to be here,' Lucie replied. 'But Daisy has a slight cold and she didn't feel she should bring her in. And she's working, I think.'

'She's finishing the garden beds at the entrance to the showgrounds,' said Flo. 'I'm going there to help her with the twins after this.'

'The town is starting to look like the bloody Chelsea Flower Show,' said Elaine Thorold.

'It's lovely,' said Marceline.

'She's working very hard,' added Lucie.

'It's like she's on a Sporticulture frenzy,' said Deidre. 'Not a day goes by without her tizzying up some street corner.'

'Her determination is admirable,' said Patricia. 'She clearly has a goal, and is achieving it.'

Josie lost the battle with her facial muscles and frowned.

So did Patricia. 'However,' she continued, 'she ought to have availed herself to this meeting. This establishment expects commitment, engagement and good, old-fashioned reliability.'

As if in response to this statement, from somewhere in the bowels of the building came a loud clunk, followed by a protracted, baritone groan.

Patricia jumped and placed a hand over her heart.

'Ooh,' said Elaine with a snigger. 'Was that the resident poltergeist?'

'Enough of this schoolgirl foolery,' Patricia snapped, then added three exclamatory raps on the table.

Lucie looked into Patricia's darting, pale eyes and began to wonder whether she might be poorly. *Len would say she looks a bit off her kadoova.*

'Business arising,' Patricia said, her eyes narrowed and fixed on Mrs Pfaff. 'Georgina Pfaff.'

'Yeah, what?' said Mrs Pfaff.

Patricia didn't respond, merely picked up her mobile phone and, with her little finger curled, swiped and clicked until it emitted a crackling sound. After a moment, there came Mrs Pfaff's singular drawl. *'You know why this shithole is called Nowhere, don't you? Because the river bends back on itself, so it's going nowhere. No matter how much spondoola Her Arseholiness up there on her rises throws at it . . . we're going no-fucking-where.'*

Patricia quietly placed the phone on the table and smiled at Mrs Pfaff. The hairs on Josie's arms stood on end.

'Would you, Mrs Pfaff,' said Patricia, 'consider that ambassadorial material? I am very interested to know.'

Mrs Pfaff offered up a small pony noise and a scowl.

'By all means, continue with your shop improvement initiative, Mrs Pfaff – with your token array of supposed health products and other feeble efforts – but you are hereby disqualified from the Miss Fresh and Lovely quest. You are welcome to keep your St Margery's membership, of course, provided you pay your levies.'

'You can't—' began Mrs Pfaff.

'Indeed I can.'

'You can shove your fucking membership right up your posh old jaxie, Patricia Montgomery. If I stay one more minute in this place, someone'll shove a stick up my arse.'

'Oh no,' said Patricia. 'The stick-up-the-arse initiation doesn't happen until your second year of membership, just after the bit where we teach you about manners, honesty and community spirit.'

Lucie looked at her hands. They were itching to clap.

'Rightcha are,' said Mrs Pfaff, rising from her chair. 'Means I don't have to come back to these stupid meetings.' She reached for a cake on the sideboard but Lurlene, her arm reflexes lightning-quick since her confinement to a wheelchair, slapped her hand away.

Mrs Pfaff angrily shrugged her bag onto her shoulder. 'I'll leave all you arse-licking, suck-up fuckwits to it, then.'

'That's the best idea you've had all day,' said Patricia. 'Thank you and goodbye.'

She performed a flourishy tick on her agenda and flicked to her next page of notes. 'Right, so if we were to take stock of the current Miss Fresh and Lovely situation, that's three disqualifications. The general store and the ghost tours are out, the Fat Doe Inn plan is out, and . . .' Patricia ran a finger down her list. 'Ah, yes. I would like to issue a formal caution to Deidre and Ruth with their Shiny-town schemes.' She put down her papers and directed her gaze at Deidre Wagner. 'It is important that you align your manoeuvres with the principled aspirations that we at St Margery's hold for our town. Gold rubbish bins, for instance, are not oriented to traditional St Margery's standards. It was clearly stated in the original rules that entrants were not to behave in a manner that is offensive, acerebral and likely to undermine the integrity of Miss Fresh and Lovely. Is that clear?'

'Nope,' said Deidre.

'What I mean is, gold rubbish bins and changing the name of our town to Serendipity is brainless and indecorous. We already have one hideous eco-tourism development in the works, set to defile our delightful Pocket Island and no doubt bring with it a stream of sanctimonious, pungent vegetarians. We do not need any internal incursions upon our faultless *comme il faut*. Our self-respect depends on it.'

Deidre, confused by everything but 'brainless', and mindful that the gold rubbish bins had been her idea, burst into tears.

'Um, Patricia,' said Ruth, putting a hand in the air. 'I think everyone wants what's right for Nowhere River. I think those gold rubbish bins add a bit of class to the place. They're very Versace, if you ask me.'

'I didn't,' said Patricia.

'I'm just saying,' Ruth continued. 'We can't all be doing things your way.'

'Gawd, imagine that,' said Elaine. 'The whole place would be draped in chintz.'

'The gold rubbish bins are a violation,' said Patricia. 'Nothing less.'

Fleury Salverson suddenly huffed, shuffled about with her chair and after quite a struggle and a lot of vexed grunting, eventually got herself to her feet. 'I can't stay here anymore, thank you very much. I'm obliged to you, Patricia, for bringing me back to my yodelling, but I will not be party to this unkindness. You inherited the St Margery's presidency, but your status as lady of the manor *and* your personal investment portfolio does *not* entitle you to make people feel awful. I remember how you led the petition to rid the town of Cliffity Smith's gnomes. He's still heartbroken over that. Oh, I know all about you and your gentrification plans. And I refuse to listen to your pin-tucked preaching any longer.'

'I beg your—'

Fleury raised her voice over Patricia's. 'I am very old, Mrs Montgomery, with a very long memory.' She looked confusedly about her for a moment, as if she'd been remembering the past so much that she'd forgotten the present. But she reoriented herself, collected up her handbag and walking stick and shuffled towards the door. 'I don't need any prize money. And I don't need this club. I will send an official withdrawal from this whole idiotic Miss Lovely fiasco. A crown's no cure for a headache. Good day.'

She attempted a dignified march from the room, but it took quite a long time, so there was a considerable wait while Fleury ambled towards the door, during which Patricia's eyebrows performed a poignant accompaniment.

'Right,' Patricia said, once Fleury's departure was complete. 'Where does that leave us?' She sank down into her chair, performed a long blink and then stared at her papers. There was a small toot from the water pipes. Lucie heard her whisper, 'For heaven's sake,' under her breath.

'Well,' said Lucie, pitching her voice into its best vice-president tone. 'We have some marvellous projects in the pipeline. Abigail's Old Folks are loving their treats, I'm told, and Nowhere River is shining under the capable and very clean hands of Deidre and Ruth—'

'There's my Rose Quartz Weddings,' said Elaine loudly.

Lucie raised her voice a little. 'There's Esther's museum and Marceline's hair-dos and Carra's gardening, of course, and then, *dum-di-dum*, Flo's much anticipated reinvention of the Nowhere River Show.'

Josie reached over and gave Flo's knee a squeeze.

Patricia raised an eyebrow. 'There is considerable expectation surrounding the show,' she said. 'I hope you can shoulder it, Florence, without any further reports of rough-housing or scrimmagery.'

Flo blushed.

'She's staying out of trouble,' said Josie. 'And has plenty of support.'

'And there's your lovely story project, Lucie,' said Marceline. 'That'll give everyone a boost.'

'Ah, well, that's a thing.' Lucie looked at the floor and brushed nothing from the table. 'I think I have . . . I *definitely* have . . .

decided to withdraw my Miss Fresh and Lovely entry.' Her hands clapped together in a gesture of decision. She looked from Abigail to Patricia and back again. 'I have a great pile of stories from everyone in town. I've put them all together and I'll be handing them over to Esther for her museum.'

Esther gasped. 'Really, Lucie? But all that work . . .'

'It's been a pleasure. I just don't think I have the energy to pull it all into a full photographic exhibition, the platform it so deserves. I don't want to make a complete bobble of it.' She wondered what would happen if she added, 'And I don't think I'll be staying in Nowhere River.'

'We can help you, though,' said Flo.

'Yes, of course we can,' agreed Abigail. 'My old folks have loved talking to you, Lucie. Some of them haven't been asked about themselves for as long as they can remember.'

'Thank you, all,' said Lucie, feeling suddenly a bit sniffly. 'You still can help, by giving Esther a hand. But I can't take any credit and I definitely wouldn't be accepting an ambassadorial role. I'm too . . . I don't know, hither and thither.'

'Well, I certainly won't accept any Miss Fresh consideration for Lucie's work, either,' said Esther, glancing timidly at Patricia. 'I will simply act as an advocate for the Nowhere People.'

'This is your fault, Patricia,' said Lurlene, with a sudden thump on the table. 'You know that, don't you?'

'Mind the furniture please, Mrs Wallace,' said Patricia.

'Mind yourself, Mrs Montgomery,' said Lurlene. 'If I wasn't in this wheelchair, I'd march over there and shove a mirror up in front of you so you can have a good old look at yourself, you toplofty old bag.'

'Lurlene . . .' said Lucie.

'No, Lucie, I won't have it. It's her fault you dropped your bundle. You talk about self-respect, Patricia and then you start up this three-ring circus, everyone clambering over one another to get to the prize, doing awful things like giving Lucie that terrible scare at the ghost tour. Rachael Hamilton isn't a bad woman, neither's Inda Price. They were just blinded by ambition, like the rest of us.'

'You're moving dangerously close to—'

'Oh, look,' interrupted Lurlene. 'You'll sack me out of the running before long, anyhow. Everyone knows my sweets don't meet your precious *standards*. I know marshmallow slice doesn't go well with cucumber sandwiches. I'm with Fleury. I quit too.' She wheeled herself away from the table.

'I love your coconut ice, Lurlene,' said Marceline. 'And your caramels.'

'Of course you do,' called Lurlene, as she manoeuvred herself towards the door. 'Everyone does. Everyone liked Cliffity's gnomes being about town, too.' She swivelled menacingly back to Patricia. 'If you want to be the bellwether, you have to know your flock.' She propelled the wheelchair towards the doorway and whizzed triumphantly out of sight.

There was a moment of silence before Abigail muttered, 'She'll need help with the front door,' and scuttled after Lurlene.

Patricia drew in a shuddery breath. 'I think I might simply declare this meeting closed.' She studied her watch. 'Twelve thirty-six. So we'll just . . . I'll, um . . . ' She got to her feet and began to sort through her papers, but wavered, grasped the back of the chair and executed a graceful descent to the floor followed by a delicate sideways slump, coming to rest with her pale cheek on the Persian rug, her Alice band skewed to one side.

'Sweet baby geewhilikins,' yelled Elaine. 'We've fucking killed her.'

Fleury Salverson, 77

I never married. People used to say to me, 'Fleury, when will you be getting yourself a husband? You must have a lot of clobber in your glory box by now.' First I was a free spirit, then on the shelf, then a maiden aunt, then a spinster, then an old maid, and now, in this day and age, I'm ahead of my time. More and more women are waking up to the idea that they can be alone. I've loved my life. It's been very much mine. No one could probably put up with all my yodelling, anyway. I love it so, it soothes my heart, but I know I make some sounds not typical of usual listening. I've never been afraid of dying alone, but I was very afraid of giving myself to a one and only. Penises are very funny looking things if you ask me, dangling away down there. Not to mention scrotums. Men have no idea how much those things make us laugh.

Chapter 25

Carra buttoned the twins into their tiny pea coats, adjusted Daisy's stockings and felt a sudden, potent squeeze of love. She pulled her babies close and held on until they wriggled and yelled.

'Oh, no, don't push me away,' said Carra. 'Don't grow.'

She sat in the feeling and let it wash over her until it pricked her eyes. The moment was, amid the routine chaos of life with small twins, a precious find. It was brought on by the act of dressing Daisy and Ben in their (slightly twee) outfits for the Rose Quartz promotional wedding, brushing their hair (Daisy's went up into tiny pigtails), putting them into new shoes and standing back to watch them peer suspiciously at one another.

Duncan walked into the moment and seemed similarly struck by it.

'Well, look at the perfect page boy and flower girl,' he said, placing a hand on Carra's back and a kiss on her lips. 'You look stunning too. I wish you were in a wedding dress, though.'

'Ah,' said Carra. 'But you wait till you see your incredible bride. I mean it; she's breathtaking. And *everyone* will be swooning over you.' She looked at him – utterly gorgeous in full morning suit with his dark-blonde, neatly parted hair sitting up off his scalp in a perfect wave. 'The quintessential dishy groom.'

Carra thought back to their own wedding day and the intoxicating feeling of being the girl on Duncan Finlay's arm, the girl that everyone wanted to be. She felt an unmistakeable thrill of desire and put her arms around him. 'Hello, gorgeous husband.'

'Who, me?' said Duncan, holding her tight. 'Hello, beautiful wife.'

But it felt staged. Carra hid her discomfort in a kiss, which was shortly interrupted by Daisy, who shouted 'No!' and then had to show them all the scar on Ben's eyebrow again.

Duncan laughed. 'She's right, we'd better go. I can't be late for my wedding. And you, matron of honour, better go and see to the bride.'

'Yes,' said Carra, pulling herself together. 'Elaine was very clear about everyone getting there at eleven o'clock *sharp*.'

'Bang!' shouted Daisy on their way out the door. 'Poor little weenie Benjie.'

▼▼▼▼

Lucie tiptoed into the hospital room. She carried a bouquet of boisterous yellow gerberas, interspersed with blue forget-me-nots and a smattering of hopeful buttercups. The darkened room smelled of violets and disinfectant. Its dusky pink curtains seemed to say 'Shhh'.

In the bed, under the soft, sage-green quilt, was the shape of Patricia, long and slender. The blanket was pulled right up to her ears so that only the top half of her white-blonde head could be seen. Lucie stood for a moment, searching the room for a vase.

'Hello, Lucie.'

Lucie gasped. 'Oh, goodness,' she whispered, peering through the darkness to locate the small, bald figure of Ambrose Montgomery. 'I'm so sorry, Ambrose, I didn't see you there.'

'Yes, that's a frequent occurrence,' said Ambrose with a chuckle. He had risen from his chair. 'Please, have a seat. There'll be a nurse in soon, they can sort out your flowers. How kind of you to come.'

'How is she?'

'She's tired. But she'll bounce back to keep us all in line.'

Lucie settled on a small, button-tucked chair. 'Of course she will.'

Ambrose returned to his chair and the two of them sat in the fragrant silence. Lucie had never been sure how to talk to Ambrose *Poor Rosie*, she thought.

'It's quite lovely in here,' she offered to the quiet. 'More like a hotel than a hospital.'

'Yes,' said Ambrose. 'It's the one she insists on. They have kingfish on the menu.'

'She's been here before?' Lucie wanted instantly to take the words back. 'Sorry, that's a horribly nosy question.'

'I come here periodically,' said the shape in the bed. The normal volume of Patricia's voice jarred against the susurrant soft furnishings. The bedclothes rustled and her alabaster face turned towards them. 'I have what Ambrose likes to call a "nervous condition", though probably it should just be named for what it is: clinical anxiety. Sometimes it makes me forget to breathe.'

'Well,' said Lucie, trying not to blink. 'It's very good to see you remembered again. Tell me how I can help, back home, what I can do. Water the garden, feed the hens? A St Margery's care basket?' She gave Patricia one of her prettiest laughs.

'Ooh, I do fancy some of Lurlene's lamingtons,' said Ambrose with a wink.

Goodness, he winks, thought Lucie. 'Or I could paint your front gate gold?'

Patricia drew her blankets away from her face. 'Lucie,' she said. 'I've created a monster.'

'Yes, you have, Patricia. And I think, for your own sake at the very least, you are going to have to embrace it. It's a big, lurid, clumsy old thing. Quite loveable though, and fairly harmless.' Lucie held up the bouquet of colourful flowers. 'You might find that in the end, it will brighten Nowhere River's days.'

Patricia closed her eyes and pursed her lips. Lucie realised she'd never before seen them without a delicate coating of pinkish Chanel. 'Your Nowhere People,' said Patricia, 'would have wrought significant brightening.'

'Ah,' said Lucie. 'Mere confection. There are many other schemes and projects with far more gumption. Proper fixes. Much like your presidency, Patricia.'

Patricia sighed. 'If I were to, er, relinquish my overseer position for a short time and emerge when I'm less . . . haunted, would you, as vice-president, protect St Margery's honour from irreversible harm? Can I trust you to steer this whole *espéglerie* in a seemly direction?'

Lucie leaned toward the bed and placed a hand on the quilted ridge that was Patricia's shoulder. 'Of course. I'll do my very best. It's the least I can do.'

'Thank you.' Patricia closed her eyes for a moment, then opened them again. 'It's not Monday.'

'It's Saturday,' said Ambrose.

'Why are you in Hobart, Lucie? There's a mock wedding on today, I believe.'

'I'm visiting you,' said Lucie. 'And seeing some old friends. Stepping into my old haunts. And so on.'

Patricia's eyes searched Lucie's face.

'I'm very relieved,' said Lucie, keen to change the subject, 'that your anxious turn didn't cause your heart to stop. Which is what we all thought. You gave me a terrible fright, Mrs Montgomery.'

'I do apologise, Mrs Finlay,' said Patricia with a very small smile. 'And thank you for the flowers. Quite lovely.'

Queen Mary Park was positively shimmering with romance. On the lower lawn by the river stood a white arch, draped with chiffon, adorned with flowers and tinkling with chimes. Leading to it was a long, narrow white carpet on which were scattered hundreds of pink and blue rose petals. On either side of the carpet stood alternating lines of white and gold chairs that were almost elegant, but not quite, on account of the perky carnations that adorned their shoulders.

Settling into the middle rows was a small contingent of Abigail's old folks, out for their weekend treat.

'She's not looking quite herself, our old Queen Mary,' said Swoozie Hamilton. 'Can barely see the river, and the Noey always has glitter enough, you'd have thought.'

Flo, who was helping Abigail manoeuvre the elderlies into place (a job which required strategy, patience, blankets and thermoses), looked over at the river and noted that it did seem to be twinkling in a distinctly romantic way. The surface had the appearance of silver confetti.

'Haven't Eileen and all the Thorolds done a superb job?' said Abigail.

'They've done a job, that's for sure,' said Stanton Godfrey, peering at the chandelier hanging from the beech tree to his right, and then down to the rose petals.

'There is no such thing as a blue rose,' said Bunty Partridge. 'And who has a wedding in July?'

'This morning's frost was very diamondy, though,' said Fleury, 'Quite romantic. It feels as though someone should be playing the oboe.'

On cue, there was some crackling and a squeak, followed by a soft piping sort of music that made Flo think of gardens.

Father John was there, having said (a reluctant) yes to the role of father of the bride. He paced about at the top of the white carpet, uncomfortably decked out in full morning suit, complete with turquoise cravat.

Len passed him and said with a chuckle, 'Won't Our Lord Father be affronted, his son here dressed up like a French salad, doing himself out of a job?'

'Shut up, please, or I'll arrange for a bit of sky to fall in on you. Where's Lucie?'

'Hobart, again.' Len sniffed. 'Meanwhile, I've been roped into rent-a-crowd.'

'Whisky later?' said Father John.

'Yes, please.'

By ten minutes to eleven, the white chairs were almost all taken and the park was abuzz with sparkling-wine-infused chatter. It paused momentarily when Celebrant Elaine arrived, dressed in a very snug, very short blue-and-pink tailored suit.

'Golly,' said Swoozie. 'She must be frozed. That skirt's so short I can see her religion.'

'She matches the rose petals,' said Fleury.

Elaine stood beneath the arch, faced the crowd with a beaming smile and began to speak inaudibly into a microphone.

'We can't hear you!' someone shouted.

'What?' shouted Bunty Partridge.

'The microphone!' yelled Len.

Elaine's beam turned into a daggery stare, which she pointed in the direction of her husband, Snowy, who was busy handing champagne around.

'Just twiddle some knobs,' he shouted across the rows of heads.

Len snorted, moved to nudge Lucie, and then remembered that she wasn't there.

Someone attended to the prescribed twiddling and, as the kerfuffle around the public address system continued, the groom arrived.

There was a collective gasp.

'Christ on a Segway,' said one of the Thorold girls from somewhere amid a flurry of pink taffeta. 'It's hot doc on steroids. I'm dead, he's killed me.'

'So Princess Carra is the bride, I take it?' Deidre Wagner sneered.

Gawd, Carra really is bonkers, thought Josie. *Who wouldn't want him?* She pictured Jerry, who was home trying to hide his pain and help Alex with the feeds, and then brought her train of thought to a respectful, married halt.

Oblivious to his bewitchment of the crowd, Duncan found his hand being shaken vigorously by Father John. 'Good God,' said the priest. 'You're a good-looking rooster, aren't you? I feel rather proud.'

'Steady on,' said Duncan. 'This is so bizarre. I hope they don't expect me to act. I was terrible at drama. Such a disappointment to Mum.'

'Well, that you have never been.' Duncan was surprised to see a tear in Father John's eye. Father John dashed it away, winked and said, 'Just smile a lot, you'll steal the show.'

The correct knob must have been twiddled, because Elaine's voice filled the immediate atmosphere. 'Thank you so much for helping us out with this. From here on in, we all want to be acting as though this is the real deal, n'okay? You will see our camera people at work – please pretend they are not here, and do not look at the cameras, n'okay?'

Everyone looked at a camera.

'This is a happy, happy wedding celebration,' Elaine continued. 'We want smiles, we want friendship, we want family, we want love, lots and lots of beautiful love, n'okay?'

'Oh, blow,' said Len to no one in particular. 'I was hoping for the unhappy wedding package.'

'I will be directing you at stages throughout, but if you don't hear the word "cut" from me, then please stay in character. And no acting the dick – I'm talking to you, Tameka Deakin. You and your stupid nose-ring can stay out of shot. I told you to remove it.'

'Go suck a sav,' yelled Tameka.

'The bride and her attendants will be here shortly, thank you to Carra for helping source the wedding attire, to Marceline for styling, and to our sponsors, Hobart Bridal Beautique, Romantica Hire and Say Cheese Productions. Okay, so I'm trusting you all not to fuck this up for me and Rose Quartz Weddings. This could be the future of Nowhere River. Thank you.' She ended with another beaming, photo-ready smile.

A minute or so later, the cameras began to roll as Barry Fronda's 1986 gold Falcon pulled up, frosted with white ribbons and matching hubcaps. A be-suited and combed member of the Thorold family opened the back door and out stepped Esther Very dressed in turquoise silk, followed by her fellow bridal attendants, Marceline Cash and Carra Finlay.

'Wait,' said Flo. 'Carra's a bridesmaid?'

'Oh,' said Josie. 'Who's the—'

But into her line of sight, and into her words, stepped a beautiful, petite woman, with dark, wavy hair falling to her tiny waist, and a bouquet of pink roses in her hands. There was a rumble of questions – 'Who's that?', 'Do we know her?', 'Would'ja move ya boof head, Alan?' – before the bridal party commenced their advance, and the bride turned to face the crowd.

There was a second (louder) collective gasp, a few swearwords and a 'Christ almighty' from Father John, followed by Daphne Partridge shouting, 'Bless my bloomers, it's our Sergeant D!'

A complete hush descended on the park, save the pretty call of a blackbird and the soft lap of the river. Flo craned for a better look and felt suddenly that things had switched into slow motion. Sergeant D moved towards the white carpet like a heroine in a fairytale, wearing an exquisite corseted gown of ivory silk tulle, embroidered with falling trails of flowers made from silk and shining beads. She paused to adjust her veil while Carra and Marceline tweaked her skirt. Esther Very, tottering slightly on her heeled shoes, held three smaller bouquets of roses and looked at a camera.

'What the hell?' said Josie, glancing wildly from Sergeant D to Carra.

'What's the matter?' asked Flo.

Josie closed her mouth and looked at Duncan, who was doing his best to play the perfect happy-nervy bridegroom but was perhaps overdoing the nervy bit. His expression was one of extreme bewilderment. Cameras clicked and zoomed as Carra beamed her way through the carpet of blue and pink petals as matron of honour and Father John, puffed up and in character, took the arm of the bride and led her down the aisle to her handsome groom.

Elaine, clearly thrilled by the extraordinary human specimens on display for her advertorial, led a heartfelt (if soppy) mock ceremony, complete with a little rendition of 'When You Say Nothing At All' by Ronan Keating. From prime position at the bride's side, Carra watched with varying measures of fascination, apprehension and awe as her husband took the hand in marriage of the divine and arresting Sergeant (Miss) Harmony Darling. Harmony, looking not a day older than the night of her Duncan heartbreak in a Hobart pub, smiled bashfully at her groom, then executed a convincing and stirring portrayal of the enraptured bride.

Carra knew very well that she would have to answer a barrage of outraged questions from Duncan about the identity of the bride. And she was right. Once the ceremony was over and Duncan had helped Abigail to hoist the Nuyina residents onto their bus, packed up a few chairs for Elaine and laughed off many compliments and several wolf-whistles, he took Carra aside.

'I don't get it, Carra, what possessed you to think this would be at all appropriate? Tell me this wasn't your idea.'

Carra, slightly taken aback by the vehemence in his voice but also fascinated by it, was well prepared. 'Not at all my idea,' she said. 'When I declined to be the bride and said I'd do bridesmaid at the very most, Elaine suggested Sergeant D, for obvious aesthetic reasons. And then Sergeant D said no way, but Marceline talked her around. Like you, she's very community-minded, Sergeant D, isn't she? She'd do anything for this town, and she quite liked the idea of a makeover. And you two are the best of friends these days – what's there to be awkward about? We're all adults, aren't we? It was just a bit of fun. And how incredible do you both look?' She motioned to his morning suit, and meant it when she added a 'Phwoar' for effect. 'I mean, what a perfect couple for a publicity shoot – everyone's going to want a Rose Quartz wedding.'

Carra listened to her words. There were too many of them, she decided, but she was satisfied she'd presented some solid arguments. She didn't entirely believe them, though, and she had a hunch that Duncan didn't, either. There had been moments – as his initial shock softened into surprise, bemusement and then focused into the role-playing – when the whole mock wedding caper seemed much, much more than just a bit of fun. As Elaine's fervently crafted declarations wafted over the wind chimes, Carra noticed how Harmony Darling's huge eyes locked onto Duncan's face, how they searched it and found something there, something long-held and faithful. She saw him catch on to it too, then hold it for a moment, before he let his eyes drop. It was just a flicker, as fleeting as the silverfish flashes of sun on the river. *Has he taken it with him, or let it go?* She wasn't sure if she minded either way.

Carra was spared from further inquisition by the approach of Harmony Darling herself, or rather Sergeant D, striding in with veil removed, swathes of silk over her arm and a business-like expression under her dewy make-up.

'Excuse me, Dunc, the ambos have been called to Nuyina. There's been an incident. I just thought you'd like to know.'

'Right.' Dr Finlay was back, too. 'Are you on your way?'

'Yep. Barry's going to drive me, I don't have my vehicle.'

Duncan looked at Carra and before he could speak, she said, 'Go. I'll get the babies home.'

'I'll call you,' Duncan said as he and Sergeant D walked shoulder to shoulder towards the car park.

Carra lifted Ben onto her hip, grasped Daisy's hand and tried – but failed – not to watch the part where the groom opened the car door for the bride and she smiled up at him in adoration.

Duncan and Sergeant D arrived at Nuyina in their finery to find the community ambulance crew also still in their wedding clothes.

'For the love of Pete,' shouted Daphne Partridge. 'Are we having *another* wedding?'

'No, Daphne, you ninny,' hissed Bunty. 'Cliffity's finally kicked the calendar.'

'What?'

'Cliffity, see there, lying in the garden, he's died.'

'Oh no,' said Daphne. 'Cliffity can't be dead.'

'What else is he doing lying like that in the shrubbery? Having a rest?'

Cliffity Smith, who had lived nowhere else but Nowhere River, had indeed died. His heart, having been variously grumpy, joyful, worried and restless over the last few months, had been rather exercised by the ostentations of the mock wedding, then stopped altogether.

'Never mind, Daphne,' said Bunty in kinder tones. 'He died with his boots on, with all of us nearby. And he fell among his beloved gnomes – look.'

Daphne looked, and saw that Cliffity's fall had sent two garden gnomes askew. They lay beside him, their chubby faces smiling at the sky.

'Turns out the sarge isn't the tough old bird we all thought she was,' said Len later that day. 'She cuts quite a dash in a wedding gown.'

Lucie had returned home to Riverhouse brimming with news from Hobart, but was quickly engrossed by Len's mock wedding report.

'I can't decide,' she said, 'whether it's horribly undignified or extremely noble of Sergeant D to play the bride opposite Duncan's groom.'

'I don't think it has to be either,' said Len. 'I think she's just moved on, and the whole Duncan snafu is now a non-issue.' He sighed. 'It's a shame that boy wasn't born with my bulbous nose. Those looks of his have been a lot to live up to, along with all the other incumbents and hopes we've saddled him with.' Len regretted these last words immediately, so hurried on with, 'There were eyelashes fluttering all over the park today.'

But Lucie hadn't heard. She was still thinking about Harmony Darling. 'There has to be more to it.' She thumbed her nose and looked absently at Beans, who mistook Lucie's intensity for something promising. 'She was so utterly smitten, and then clearly heartbroken. I mean, she couldn't look any of us in the eye for years, and now to be so blatant about it . . .'

'Carra scrubbed up nicely. As did Esther. Didn't think much of Elaine's sugary waffling, though. Everything was so blessèd and written in the stars and all that.'

'Perhaps she still loves him.'

'And I can't abide those terrible pop ballads. What's that one about dreams? Dreadful. Rather be in church muttering holy supplications.'

'That's it, isn't it? She still loves him. She had the opportunity to finally marry Duncan, sort of, and so she did.'

'And that swan ice sculpture, for blob's sake. They spared no expense on the mimsy.'

'All power to her.'

'"All I Have To Do Is Dream", that was it. Everly Brothers? Grievous. Sergeant D is quite the actress. She could be on the stage, Lucie. Duncan did a good job, too.'

'She didn't need to act. For a fleeting, wondrous moment, she had the man of her dreams.' Lucie hummed the Everly Brothers tune.

'They wobbled somewhat at the bit when the groom may kiss the bride.' Len chuckled.

'They had to *kiss*?'

'Well, they didn't. They sort of leaned in for one, then swerved and got the cheeks. Most awkward.'

'Oh, how embarrassing. Poor Sergeant D. Love will have us doing the darndest things.'

'Can we give her a bit of credit? I know Duncan's no stinker, but Sergeant D is a self-respecting woman.'

'Ah, but remember her back in ye olde Harmony Darling days? She was potty for him. And why hasn't she found someone else? She's very sensual, in a *Sports-Illustrated*-model sort of way.'

Len was pleased to see Lucie so present. 'You are a terrible snob, Lucie Finlay,' he said. 'Anyway, how was Hobart-town?'

'Terrific.' Lucie smiled a proper Lucie smile. 'I went and saw Patricia. She is on the mend, I think. The poor darling suffers from the most terrible anxiety, it turns out.'

'I think we're all on an anxiety spectrum, aren't we?'

'And I popped in on Mrs French from the corner! She still plays tennis! I thought, *Golly, look at you, as old as the hills*, and then realised I'm only a hop-skip behind her.' She sighed. '*It comes so soon, the moment when there is nothing left to wait for . . .*'

Len thought for a moment that she was disappearing again, but she shook herself back, tucked herself into his arm and added, 'We'd slot right back into our old traps, no trouble at all.'

Patricia Montgomery, 71

I don't like to talk about myself, it's not the most fascinating of topics. I'm sure you could find a more interesting character to talk to. Nowhere River is rather too full of them, interesting characters. But, oh well, I have two sons, one in Hobart and one in London. I have my husband and my house and a whippet named Tickety-Boo. And St Margery's, of course. All that keeps me very busy. One has to be busy in a town like this. It's very easy to moulder and stagnate and waste your life gongoozling in a riverside town. That's all I'll say, I think.

Chapter 26

Josie reached out with her forefinger and pushed the tiny sprig of green. It sprang indignantly back into place.

'They're tough little nuts,' she said to Jerry, who was bringing a hose up from the water trailer. *Microseris scapigera,* growing like babies.'

'Growing like weeds,' said Jerry.

'They're *not* weeds,' said Josie, switching the hose to a fine spray. 'Just wait, I'll change your conventional farming mind.'

'Very happy for you to do that,' said Jerry. 'But I won't be holding my breath.'

'No, please don't hold your breath. You'll die. And you've already tried that.'

Jerry laughed, then winced, then pretended he hadn't. 'Hey,' he said after a moment, slipping his arm around Josie's waist. 'Thanks for putting up with me.'

Josie turned to him and leaned in to kiss him. 'Thanks for coming back to me.'

'How could I not?' Jerry said between kisses.

'We knew you would,' said Josie, looking right into his eyes and letting grateful tears fill her own.

'Oi, is my tough-as-nails wife blubbering? No way, she is too!' He pulled her into a hug. 'Jeez, you're going to get me started.' He sniffed.

They held one another for a long moment, Josie conscious of his warmth and the familiar, living scent of him, until, in the distance, a cloud of dust caught her eye. She recognised it as Flo, on horseback.

'Here we go,' she said. 'What do you think Miss Show Girl wants this time?'

In under a minute, Flo had thundered over, bareback and at full tilt.

'Hi,' she said, sliding off before the horse had even stopped. She tossed aside her helmet and said, 'Have you seen Alex?'

'Do your helmet up or I'll confiscate your horse,' said Josie.

Flo ignored her. 'He said he'd help me put some show signs out up the highway.'

'He's picking up rocks down in the back paddock,' said Josie.

'I can help with signs if you like,' said Jerry.

'Whoa,' said Flo, as she came up the rise. 'What's all this?' She looked at the expanse of fenced-off, cultivated earth and the tiny plants within.

'This,' said Jerry, 'is your mother's mid-life crisis.'

'Hey!' growled Josie. 'It's the result of a great deal of thought, actually. Life has given us a lot of lemons lately, so I'm making goddamn lemonade.'

'Out of dandelions,' said Jerry.

'They're called murrnong, actually. Or yam daisies,' said Josie. 'And they look like a dandelion, but they're different because they have a tuber on their roots, like a small potato.'

'So you eat them?' asked Flo.

'Apparently so. It was a staple for Aboriginal people, before we, with our big clodhopping grazing animals, pretty much wiped it out.' Josie nudged Jerry.

Flo sat on the ground and gazed through the wire. 'And you found some? Yam daisies?'

'I did. Hardly any, though, and I was too late for the little seed heads. So I ordered some seeds from a specialist place and they've germinated and now I've planted the seedlings here. And if the sun keeps shining and spring hurries the heck up, they might grow and, well, we can go from there.' She glanced at Jerry, aware of her shyness in the face of his scepticism.

'As if the sun won't keep shining,' said Jerry. 'Can't remember what clouds look like.'

'Can we sell the little potatoes?' asked Flo.

'I'm hoping so,' said Josie. 'They taste better than normal potatoes, apparently. And they're really high in nutrients.'

'Like a superfood?'

'I guess so. And they tolerate drought and don't need sprays and stuff.'

'So all the vegan people will go silly for it,' said Jerry. 'And you can grow your hair into dreadlocks, Josie.'

Josie flipped the hose in his direction. He jerked out of the way and gripped his side in pain.

'You deserved that,' said Josie.

'Yeah, I probably did.'

'And maybe we'll be saving an indigenous species,' said Flo.

'Maybe,' said Josie. She couldn't help but feel if not optimism, then some upwardly geared anticipation.

The three of them watched the little plants for a moment or two, as though they might catch one growing.

Flo looked up at Jerry. 'We're not going to give up on Everston now, are we, Dad?'

'I can't promise that,' said Jerry. 'I think we need to keep our options open. But if my girls are willing to put all our hopes into a bunch of dandelions and a shitty country show, then they're not likely to give up on anything.'

Flo laughed, then gave him a gentle shove.

Josie sent a small and silent prayer into the earth-scented air.

▼▼▼

Len Finlay had a prayer as well. A number of them, in fact. They had rumbled about and irritated him until he decided that there was nothing for it but to dispatch them to their rightful place. So, in the still, cool silence that was All Angels Church on a Wednesday in the early afternoon, Len crept through the antechamber and into the nave. There, he stopped creeping, because it made him feel like an intruder – which he was, he realised, having completely shunned the Anglican faith for thirty years.

He looked at the old walls and whispered, 'Hello,' which didn't seem right either, so he tried walking normally further into the church, and sat himself down on a pew.

'Ahem,' he said, looking at the altar, and then somewhere above it. 'Right. Hello. Hello?' His words echoed around him alarmingly, so he decided instead to look at his shoes, which is what he remembered being told to do in church when he was a schoolboy.

At that moment, Father John emerged from the vestry. 'Len?'

Len jumped. 'What?'

'Oh,' said Father John. 'I've startled you. I'm sorry. I thought you were talking to me.'

'And I thought you . . .' Len cast his eyes upwards. 'I thought you were helping at the showgrounds today.'

'I wasn't needed in the end. It seems the whole town has their hopes pinned on the show. More than enough hands, and I have things to prepare for Cliffity's funeral. So you *weren't* talking to me?'

'I was— No. No, I was just, um . . . testing the acoustics. Lucie is always, you know, going on about acoustics.' Len looked at his shoes again and added, for further diversion, 'Poor old Cliffity.'

Father John moved towards Len and peered at him over his glasses. 'If I didn't know better, I would have thought you were just now having a word with the great upstairs.'

'Er, well, I . . . yes. I was . . . going to have a small word. About some things.'

Father John gave the pew a little triumphant tap.

'Don't jump to reverent conclusions,' said Len. 'I was just thinking that a prayer from the faithless might pack quite a punch compared to those that waft up from the same old people every Sunday.' He chuckled. 'But I don't suppose it works that way. He prefers his lambs, I'm told.'

'Well . . .' Father John thought for a moment. 'If you like, I could get the ball rolling, and you can add in your bits. Or I can make myself very scarce, and just let you get on with it.'

'So how does the first bit go?'

Father John sat next to Len and clasped his hands together. 'Heavenly Father'—he looked across at Len—'is a good start. My friend, your servant—'

'I'm not his servant, though.'

'My friend,' Father John said, raising his voice slightly, 'please forgive him his trespasses, calls for your guidance and spirit in this blessèd life. Specifically, he asks for your attendance on . . .' Father John bumped Len's elbow.

'On my wife, Lucie, who isn't quite herself.'

'Fill Lucie with the courage and strength we know her for, and beget her grace in the face of self-doubt—'

'She's not singing anymore,' interrupted Len. 'Not even in the shower. She used to drive Beans and I half mad with her singing. And now we want it back.'

'Lord Father, please help our Lucie to find her voice again.'

'And I want the Nowhere River Show to go so well, like old times, that it might compel her to stay here. I don't want to leave, but she's already clearing out cupboards.'

Father John took a moment or two to speak again. 'Help our Lucie through this difficult time, and to see that her place is here in Nowhere River.'

'And stop the Felicity pain, please.'

'Soothe the deep wounds within Len and Lucie, bring them strength and peace. On their saddest days, be their joy, grant them the blessing of your love—'

'And if you have Felicity there with you . . .' Len's voice stopped on a squeak. Father John put a hand on his shoulder. '. . . if you've seen her. Hold her gently.'

'Take her to you, keep her soul eternal. Send your angels to protect her.'

'Also, a bit of rain would be ideal, please. Quite a lot, if that's not pushing the friendship. Thank you.'

'In the name of God, the Father and the Holy Spirit—'

'Deliver us from weevils.'

'Len.'

'Sorry.'

'Amen.' Father John sang loudly, making Len jump in fright. He nudged Len again.

'Amen.'

▼▼▼

Having driven around most of the streets of Nowhere River, Josie finally found Carra in Tiya Street, with her bottom up, in the side garden of St Margery's. She parked the car, got out and walked over to the lawn where the twins were playing in a blow-up pool full of balls. Josie waved at them and positioned herself on the piece of footpath nearest to Carra.

Daisy waved back and screeched in excitement.

Ben held a ball aloft. 'Frow ball. Frow ball.'

Carra stood up and just as she did, Josie clicked a series of photos with her phone.

'What are you . . . ?'

'Sorry,' said Josie. 'I'm on assignment for Esther and Flo. They need photographs of all the people Lucie's interviewed for her Nowhere People project.'

'But I must look a mess. You caught me off guard.'

'That's the idea. They have to be real, and candid. And you look perfect there among the . . . what are those flowers again?'

'Camellias.' Carra looked at the mass of regal white flowers with their glossy teardrop leaves. She brushed her hair from her face, added some dirt and tried to think of what to say.

'Nice,' said Josie, nodding at an assemblage of potted flowers, waiting to be planted. 'And those?' She pointed at a cluster of blooms in various colours.

'Hellebores.'

'Right. And is Patricia okay with purple, yellow and pink?'

'I know, not really standard issue. I consulted with Lucie and she thinks we could sneak a bit of colour around St Margery's. And everything needs to be drought tolerant, where possible.' Carra tapped the stone path with her spade and tried to think what else to say.

'You're doing a phenomenal job, you know.' Josie nodded at the twins. 'When my babies were actual babies, I was lucky to get to the shop. Flo didn't see the city lights of Hobart until she was five.'

Carra smiled.

'So, that was intense the other day, Duncan getting married to Sergeant D and all.'

'Bit of fun,' said Carra with a laugh. 'Elaine's thrilled with the final video. And have you seen the posters? There's one in the shop.'

Josie thought of the misty, dreamlike image of Duncan and Sergeant D standing in one another's arms beneath the trees of

Queen Mary Park. 'Sure have. It's totally gorgeous. Duncan Finlay and Harmony Darling, eh?'

Carra glanced up to see whether Josie was laughing. She wasn't.

'Anyway,' said Josie, 'I was hoping I'd find you because a friend of a friend told me about an amazing woman in Hobart who does relationship counselling. She's saving marriages all over the place, apparently.'

'Right. Thanks.'

'So I'll send you her number? If you still have the same contact details?'

Ouch, thought Carra. She sighed. 'Yep.'

'And you'll make an appointment?'

'Possibly.' Carra picked up a plastic pot and squeezed it to loosen a hellebore.

'I mean, there's no way you're giving up on your marriage, right? I was thinking, when I first met you, that very first time he brought you to the pub to meet us all, you had the starriest of starry eyes I've ever seen. You were bananas for him. And he for you. Be. Sotted. I've never seen anything like it.'

Carra said nothing. The hellebore came free of the pot.

'Carra?'

Carra stood, the plant cradled in her hands. 'Yes, that's right. I was crazy about him. I really was. Now maybe I'm lucid about him. And not bananas. More, I don't know, potatoes. Tinned potatoes. Which are really okay only if you add butter.'

'So add butter! Make an effort. You have to work at marriage, every day.'

'I have enough work to do.' Carra placed the hellebore gently into its hole.

'So you won't even try? Come on, Carra, everyone knows marriage doesn't do what it says on the tin.'

'And everyone told me that marriage was about sharing the load. Not about one-sided compromise. I swear to God, if I share anything more of myself, or compromise anymore, there'll be nothing left of me, honestly, just dust.'

'But this isn't just about you, is it?' Josie's voice was rising. 'Look at those beautiful children. Look at them, Carra. You want to stuff things up for them? Break their dad's heart?'

Carra turned to Ben and Daisy. Daisy was throwing balls at the wrought-iron fence. 'I'll only ever do what's best for them. And I assure you, Duncan's heart will be okay.' She crouched down to pat the earth around the hellebore.

Josie sighed, then sat down on the front steps of St Margery's. There was silence for a time before she said, 'Does Duncan's poo really not smell?'

Carra stifled a laugh. 'It really doesn't.'

'Like, not even a tiny whiff?'

'Nope.'

'That can't be true.'

'Well, it is.'

'I bet if you actually sniffed his bumhole—'

'Josie!'

'You started it.'

Carra worked on while Josie pondered the impossibility of Duncan Finlay's digestive system. After a bit, she switched back to the marriage conundrum. 'Look, Flo and I can look after the twins. You and Duncan should go away together, for a long weekend. Or a week. Find your bananas.'

Carra snorted.

'Okay, so that came out wrong. Find the love again. It's there, I know it is. You can stay in a really good hotel—'

'You're forgetting, Duncan has a town depending on him. You think I haven't tried to get him away over the years?'

'So we get a locum.'

'We can't get a locum. I've tried that too. No one wants to come to Nowhere.'

'What else can we do?' said Josie. 'I don't want you to leave.'

Carra froze, and the two of them looked at one another for a long moment until Carra had to tip her head back to stop some tears from spilling over.

'Come on, Carra, please? Seriously, you have to be the luckiest women in the world.'

'No,' said Carra, letting a tear go. 'I just have to be me.'

Jeremy Bradshaw, 47

I was always going to farm Everston and marry Josie. So there we go. I don't believe in any spiritual stuff like fate or destiny or anything. I mean it's mostly about good management, and you know, doing your thing. But sometimes I wonder. I mean, can I really take credit for finding someone as good as Josie? She and I just work – we share the same values, we think the same things, we're a team. That seems like more than simple luck sometimes.

Chapter 27

On the day of Cliffity Smith's funeral, just as the bursting jonquils relieved their scent into the September air, Nowhere River woke to find that a large coterie of very pleased-looking garden gnomes had mysteriously popped up throughout the town.

Esther Very, who always rose before dawn, was the first to discover one of the cheeky visitors under her smoke tree: a gnome lying on his side, reading a book. Abigail received quite a shock when she happened upon a quartet of string-playing gnomes in her front garden. Len found a bespectacled fellow among his conifers, Marceline had one in her garden and another by the door of the salon and Sergeant D found a gnome in police uniform by her front steps.

The medical centre garden and the Pfaffs' storefront had been similarly invaded, and in the newly planted, unusually vibrant flowerbeds at St Margery's was an assortment of very busy gnomes in various poses.

Cliffity's Nuyina gnomes, meanwhile, had been cleaned up, repainted and repositioned in prominent places around the nursing home. And on the town hall's noticeboard, above a gnome carrying a fishing rod, was a sign that read 'In memory of Cliffity Smith'.

'Oh my goddy God,' said Lucie to Len when she came in from walking Beans. 'They're everywhere! The town is lousy with them.'

'What?' asked Len.

'Gnomes. Garden gnomes everywhere. It's like a sort of pestilence. This is terrible.'

'I thought you didn't mind a gnome. Cheery little things. And so spring-like after that interminable winter.'

'Patricia's going to have a full-blown conniption. She trusted me to keep things at St Margery's standards. Oh dear Lord, I thought it would be all right to test the boundaries with some colourful helle-bores, but this will have her back in the hospital as quick as you can say—'

'Balabar Muckbuckle.'

'What?'

'That's the name of our new gnome,' Len told Lucie. 'I just came up with it then.'

'I'll bet this is the work of the Shiny-town committee. It has Deidre and Ruth written all over it.'

'They might be trying to change the name of the town to Gnomeville. Or Gnomandy.'

'They're likely trying to sabotage Carra's Sporticulture. Oh, this is a disaster. What if Patricia cancels the competition altogether and withdraws the prize money?'

'If this veritable storming of the gnomes is a tribute to Cliffity Smith, what could you have done to stop it? She'll just have to embrace it. As should you, Lucie. And you know, gnomes are thought to be great protectors of gardens. And general fertility. Perhaps, with all these rehomed gnomes about, it might rain. Or some more babies will be born in Nowhere River. Or both.'

'And the show is in a week or two and we'll have all those tacky gnomes. Len!' Lucie delivered one of her best dramatic pauses. 'The gnomes could be the great undoing of this town.'

'Rubbish, they're more likely to endear us to people. It's just a bit of fun, Lucie. Poignant fun, your favourite kind. Please give me a sparkling shimmer from those beautiful eyes of yours. It was you being all optimistic about the show a few months ago.'

Lucie sank into a chair. 'I can't remember what that sort of optimism feels like.' She looked resignedly at Beans, who was hot and exhausted from his short walk and had sprawled onto the cool slate floor.

'Well, my renewed optimism isn't just for your sake,' said Len. 'I'm genuinely surprised at how enterprising young Flo has been. She's arranged all sorts of children's entertainment – there's the history display, a huge array of entries for the Hall of Industries, a sausage workshop and a lawnmower race.'

'A lawnmower race?'

'A lawnmower race. And she's asked me to be show commentator.'

Lucie sighed. 'So you'll be saving up your silliest jokes, then.'

'If there's a chance they might make you laugh, then yes, I will.'

Lucie gave him a tight smile, which encouraged Len to say, 'Will you join me on the show committee? There's a proper part-of-something feel. Remember that feeling, Madam Chief Steward? Even Jerry has been in on things, helping Flo with publicity. We should get Patricia along, too.'

'I'll have to see. I'm likely to be very busy getting our own affairs sorted out.' She looked at Len, then reached out and slipped her hand into his. 'I have a very strong homeward feeling, darling. For Hobart. I feel so encumbered here, so river-worn, like an ancient grey stone. I'm sick of gazing out these windows. Sick of these high-country winds whining through my empty.' She tapped her chest.

Len's brow gathered forlornly. 'I know,' he said after a long sigh. 'I can see that you are wilting. So I will help you to sort things out here, for our moving. And I will not put my misgivings in your way.'

Lucie looked at his face, patted his cheek and let a tear spring from her eye. 'Dearest Len,' she said. 'I'm sorry to have been so generally scattershot and wobbly. And I promised not to say it again, but I'm sorry, too, for losing Felicity.' She saw approaching thunder in Len's face and added, 'Please just let me say it occasionally. It is something of a small and temporary salve. It *was* me who lost her, after all.' She squeezed his hand and leaned in to place a gentle kiss on his lips before they could send out any contrary opinions on the matter.

'Well,' said Len, once the kiss had successfully removed his ire. 'I'd best put the sprinklers on, and hop into my funeral get-up. It starts at half past ten.' He made for the door.

'And darling,' Lucie called after him, 'I'll join the show committee, of course I will. Selfish old bag that I am.'

'That, my Lucie, would be a delight.'

'A fitting end to our time in Nowhere River.'

'Hmm,' said Len.

'And Len? Would you mind getting rid of that gnome? Beans is terrified of it.'

'Right.'

On his way to the sprinklers, Len collected the gnome from the conifer garden. 'Come on, Balabar, sorry, old chap. Lucie's not herself. Join me in the shed and together we'll think of something.'

On their way to the church for Cliffity's funeral, Len listened worriedly to more of Lucie not being herself.

'Horrible weather,' she said as they walked the short distance to All Angels. 'Typical Tasmanian spring bluster.'

'Well, it's fitting for a funeral,' proffered Len. 'Death deserves a bit o' tempest. And at least there's some sun.'

'Ah, yes, the ever-present sun.' Lucie tutted.

They found Abigail at the church gate, who said, 'Have you seen the gnomes? Oh, Cliffity would be just beaming down, wouldn't he? What a gorgeous gesture.'

'Yes, we've seen them,' said Len, trying to send a warning signal to Abigail through her gusto. It didn't hit its mark.

'There are little fly-fishing gnomes all through Queen Mary Park. So sweet.'

'Adorable,' said Lucie. 'Now we can add "poor taste" and "dinky" to our town attributes.' She hitched up the strap of her handbag and marched past Barry Fronda's hearse towards the church.

'She has a pebble in her plimsoll today,' said Len as they watched her go. 'Come on, else we'll be fighting for a seat.'

To access The Rises, it was necessary for Ambrose and Patricia Montgomery to drive through town, either along Jones Street or the High Street, to the Whistler Bridge and then on to The Rises on the southeastern side of the river. This meant that on their way home from the hospital they would be passing through the most populous areas of gnomedom. Their first hint of anything unusual was on the Pearce Highway leading into town, where a heckle of gnomes greeted them with jeering expressions. There were more at the entrance to the showgrounds, in the roundabout rose garden and lining the southern end of the High Street near the town hall, which is where Patricia demanded Ambrose turn the car around and head for St Margery's, to 'get to the bottom of this heinous tomfoolery'.

Lucie, expectant of Patricia's return, was in the office at St Margery's practising her bravest face when she heard the crunch of tyres on the white gravel of the members' car park.

'Yoohoo,' she said to herself in a bright, jangly voice. 'Here they are.' *Don't overdo it, Lucie, play it down.* 'Aren't those gnomes just too hilarious!' she said to her reflection in the hall mirror on her way to the back door. 'Donated from far and wide, and Deidre and Ruth were up half the night putting them about. A gorgeous, *temporary* tribute.'

But Patricia's expression, when Lucie opened the door to it, did not invite jollity.

'What fresh hell is this?' she asked, evidently restored to her usual self.

'Patricia, welcome home,' Lucie crooned as she opened the door. 'You look so well.'

Patricia did look well. The cool, elegant restraint and the neat purse of her disapproving lips were every bit the old Patricia. Lucie watched the curve of her left eyebrow, saw the weary face of Ambrose standing behind his wife and resisted the urge to run and hide in the linen cupboard.

'I don't know why I'm surprised to be returning to more abhorrent additions to the town,' said Patricia.

'I assume you're referring to the recent migration of those errant gnomes,' said Lucie with a manufactured laugh. 'What rascals they are.'

'Between the sundown and the night,' said Patricia, 'comes the gnoming. Very soon we will be in darkness.'

'Ha,' tried Lucie. 'Haha. How witty.'

But neither Ambrose nor Patricia joined in on her laughter – which wasn't actual laughter, to be fair.

'And what has happened to the St Margery's flowerbeds? They are a mare's nest in technicolour.'

'But I thought . . .' said Lucie. 'We all thought it might be good to join in on the general colour of things, for a bit. Show our cohesion with the community vibe.' Lucie heard the simper in her voice and loathed herself for it. *Oh come on, Lucie,* she thought, *what have you got to lose?* She watched the flaring of Patricia's nostrils, cleared her throat and said, 'I suspected you would view the gnomes unfavourably, Patricia. I don't think they need to be regarded as a spontaneous statement of the town's poor taste, but rather an incisive and salutary expression of our fondness for Cliffity. Just think, it could have been ferrets.'

Patricia, impressed by Lucie's superior vocabulary and agreeable about the ferrets, sniffed and suggested tea. Lucie took this as a small victory.

Carra yawned as she entered the Kinvarra kitchen the following morning and blinked into the light. 'Do we need *all* the lights on?' she asked.

'What?' said Duncan as he lifted Ben out of his high chair.

'It's so bright.' Carra fumbled for the light switch.

'It's the sun.'

'What?'

'It's daylight.'

Carra froze. 'Oh my God!'

'What?' Duncan looked alarmed.

'I think . . .' She stopped and thought for a second. 'I think I slept all the way through the night. Wait, I can't have. Did I? I think I did. Oh my God, what's the time?'

'Just after seven.'

'Just after seven?' Carra was shrieking now. 'I slept, wait . . .' She thought again. 'I slept for an unbroken NINE HOURS! I cannot believe it. Well done to you' – she bowed in front of Daisy – 'and to you' – she curtsied to Ben, who laughed – 'and to you, the daddy who didn't wake the mummy. Wait, who are you again? I don't recognise you without the grey veil of sleeplessness.' She planted a kiss on his smile and moved to the window. 'Oh my God, is that the actual world?' She gasped dramatically. 'Look how beautiful it is.'

Duncan laughed. 'How long since they last slept through?' he asked.

'Their whole lives,' said Carra. 'They *haven't* slept through. That was it: their first time.' She stared at him. 'Hang on, are you saying you didn't realise that every night, at least once a night, I've been settling or feeding a small human?'

'Well, you didn't tell me.'

'Right.' She turned back to the window and bit her tongue, hoping the rigidity of her shoulders wasn't visible. But also hoping it was. 'Well, thanks for dishing up the Weeties, sorting out the night nappies—'

'Oh, I didn't do the nappies.'

Carra remained silent. There was a loud-ish bang from the sink. Carra turned. Duncan was staring hard at the window, evidently trying to collect himself. Carra watched on in fascination, forgetting to be concerned. Duncan was born collected. And composed.

'Are you—'

'For Christ's sake,' Duncan said to the dishwater. Then, 'I'm sorry. I'm not so good at this parenting thing, am I?'

'Don't be silly,' said Carra. 'You're great. We just don't know what the hell we're doing, that's all. No new parent does.'

He dried his hands.

'You're just assessing yourself based on the results you achieve in everything else. You need to drop that bell curve because it's way too high. We all muddle along.'

'I don't know if I know how to muddle along.' He turned to look at her and Carra felt a twist in her heart.

She took his hand. 'Well, you're doing it. We both are. Muddling along. And look at them, you helped make them. We don't have to be perfect.' The word 'perfect' seemed to echo. *My God, he's never known what it's like to be less than perfect.*

His beautiful features were lit with a childlike perplexity that reminded Carra of being left out of playground games. *Coming, ready or not.*

Deidre Wagner, 76

I grew up in Bronte Park, not all that far from here as the crow flies. Met my Bruce at the dances when I was fifteen. He was twenty. He said he knew he wanted to marry me, made me think I should marry him. Made me think a lot of things. For a long time I thought that was romantic, him and his sureness, his strong arms. But I wouldn't like my daughters to be lined up like that. I always thought the river was exciting compared to the lakes. I've never quite trusted it, though, the river. It doesn't give two hoots about us, just rushes on by. Bruce was exciting once, too, and not very trustworthy. I was always standing in the doorway with a baby on my hip. But then he lost his hair and we could all relax a bit.

Barry Fronda, 70

For a long time, I tried to get the old passenger train up and running again between here and Hobart. But the government has their head up their arse and can't even see the usefulness of their own rectums. So then I became a mechanic. I figured with these dodgy roads, people will need me. And they do. I am the only person in the whole Colleen Valley with a reliable hearse. I still walk the old train tracks every day. I have memories there I like to ramble over.

Chapter 28

With a fortnight to go before the Nowhere River Show, a clamour of black cockatoos flew over the showgrounds and shrieked out their well wishes. But no one heard, because Walt Wallace was hammering the last of the new woodwork to the grandstand, while Barry Fronda was using a leaf blower to rid the stage of old sheep droppings. There was a cluster of people putting up an enormous marquee and another lot in the boozer shouting about beer barrels.

Carra, having planted a bed of daisies around the commentary box, went to find Sergeant D, who'd insisted on watching the twins so Carra could work in peace. Carra found them in the Hall of Industries, a large corrugated-iron shed on the river side of the showgrounds. The shed's rusty exterior belied the breathtaking spectacle inside. Carra stood gaping in the doorway for a while, taking in the walls, patchworked with paintings and photographs, the tables of handicrafts, the crowds of bottled fruit and pickled vegetables and the rafters strung with weavings and stitchings and knitted everythings.

'Oh my God,' she said.

'God is not here,' said Sergeant D, who was showing Ben and Daisy a menagerie of knitted animals. 'We worship only crafts.'

'It's the church of holey crochet,' said Lurlene Wallace, waving a doily in the air before refilling a staple gun and handed it to Father John, who was standing on a tabletop, fixing finger paintings to the wall.

Flo, from the photography section, where she stood with a clipboard and a red pen, laughed too.

'My blasphemy alarm bells are ringing,' said Father John.

'There's so much in here already!' said Carra. 'And a week to go.'

'I know,' said Flo. 'And we haven't even got the school's entries yet.'

'Or the perishables,' called Josie, poking her head from behind a screen at the back of the hall. Carra sent her a cautious wave, which was acknowledged with a nod.

'I'm a bit worried it won't all fit,' said Flo. 'We have entries from as far away as Oatlands.'

'Well, that's your fault for doing such a superb job with publicity,' said Lurlene.

'I didn't really do any publicity,' said Flo. 'I didn't call the television people, they called me.'

'The television people?' said Father John and Lurlene at the same time.

'Oops, I think I forgot to mention that,' said Flo. 'They want to come and do a story about the show.'

'Oh, Lordy,' said Lurlene. 'How excitement.'

'I knew Nowhere River would have its moment one day,' said Father John. 'People are surely craving something a bit homespun, an antidote to their digital world.'

'Ooh, the telly people are going to love Cliffity's gnomes,' said Lurlene.

There was a small Cliffity-inspired silence.

'Shame we won't have his ferret show,' said Carra.

'Stanton Godfrey has offered to take the ferrets in the grand parade,' said Flo. 'He's been looking after them for Cliffity.'

'He's not such a grumpy old bugger after all,' said Sergeant D.

'Oh, he's definitely a grumpy old bugger,' said Lurlene. 'That's his shtick.'

'Who made all this stuff?' asked Carra, wandering along the rows of exhibits.

Lurlene smiled. 'Just about everyone. Sergeant D made some adorable animals – look.'

Sergeant D held up a knitted cow. 'All the animals from around the district. There's a wombat, too. I have a lot of spare time between work shifts.' Her smile faded fleetingly. 'And I found a step-by-step tutorial. One advantage of having the best internet connection in town.' She laughed.

'They're gorgeous,' said Carra, thinking of Sergeant D alone with her knitting. *God, how I'd love that. Would I?*

'I made them for Daisy and Ben, actually.' Sergeant D smiled shyly. 'If that's okay with you.'

'Of course, that's great! I mean, really . . . sweet.' Carra inspected her words for signs of insincerity, but found none, then wondered why she didn't feel disturbed.

'And have a look at the local history displays,' said Father John. 'A triumph. Down there, with Esther and Josie.' He gestured towards the screens at the other end of the hall. 'I contributed a small water-colour. I've discovered a lot of joy in painting.'

Josie popped out again and beckoned to Carra. 'Yep, come and see. Esther has worked so hard.' Her smile was friendly. Carra walked towards it and watched it widen as she neared. She smiled back and felt the push of emotion on her throat.

'Hi, Josie,' she said.

'Hey.'

Carra turned first to where Esther stood, at a screen that displayed a series of black-and-white photographs, handwritten documents, paintings and sketches, all telling the story of a little town on a river bend. Father John's watercolour sat among them, a mass of green and brown dabs with a blurry shape in its centre, which may or may not have represented the Abergavenny ruin. A smudge of brownish red looked a little like blood.

'Oh, your painting is very good.' Carra smiled up at Father John. 'I can see the big old chimney! I think.'

'It's very abstract,' he replied. 'I've been dabbling with style.'

'Quite Fauvist,' said Esther. 'Putting the truth into the colours.'

Father John looked pleased.

'You've done a great job, Esther,' Carra said, and turned to where Josie stood, before a series of photographic portraits with accompanying notes. 'Ah, Lucie's Nowhere People. God, look at that photo of me, I'm a wreck.' She inspected her portrait: a young woman with leaves in her hair and a furrow in her brow, staring into a camera that had caught her unawares among the camellias. Despite her dishevelment, she looked absorbed, occupied and at home. Carra couldn't help comparing it to one of Ursula Andreas's shots.

'Lucie did a terrific job of collecting the stories,' said Josie. 'Esther and I just had to get the photos and pin everything up. Job done.'

'It's fantastic.' Carra turned away from her own image and quickly found herself drawn in by the words of Lucie's subjects, and the curious, enigmatic scenes they conjured. The turns of phrase and the varying tones of the voices echoed around her as she read, drawing her into a riddle of curious narratives, threading together to form a big, lively picture. 'So wonderful.' She stepped back in order to take in the whole display.

'There's still a few photos to come,' said Esther. 'I'll get to them.'

'And,' said Josie, 'we don't have Lucie's story yet.'

'That's a definite missing piece,' agreed Esther.

'I could talk to her,' said Carra, without thinking. 'Get her story, take her picture, if you're all too busy.'

'Oh that would be awesome, Carra, thank you,' said Josie. 'Do you think she'd mind?'

'I don't know. But I'll try.'

'We're like pieces of a big Nowhere River puzzle,' said Sergeant D, coming over for another look. 'I love the Cliffity Smith one. What a character he was.'

'Small Highland towns are bound to attract eccentrics and misfits,' said Father John. 'I'm one myself.'

'So am I,' said Flo.

'Me too,' said Sergeant D.

'We're all misfits, aren't we, really,' said Josie. 'I mean, here we are, living so close together, in the same landscape, by the same river, seeing different things.'

Carra stared at the space allocated for Duncan's photograph. 'Or not seeing at all, until someone puts everything in front of us to properly acknowledge.'

'That's why we're having a show, isn't it?' said Father John.

'Yes,' said Flo. 'I guess it is.'

▼▼▼▼

With a buttress of music rising behind her from the stereo in the sitting room, Lucie stood on the garden terrace gazing absently out to the river. After some moments, her mind resurfaced from her thoughts to notice, first, that the music – and her habit – had drawn her back to the river and, second, that there was something different about the day.

She stepped away from me
And she moved through the fair

It took another moment before she could place what had changed: the air, around her and up in the treetops, was still. There was no wind. Not a breath. The river, like polished glass, gazed back at her: flawless, undaunted. By the far bank, it offered up an inverted reflection of the Clyde Flats and the Abergavenny chimney, with its companion gum tree.

Lucie averted her eyes, then jerked them back again, because something on the jetty had caught her attention.

And fondly I watched her
Move here and move there

The blonde curls sat like a halo, translucent with river-shine. It crowned a little girl in a white frilled shirt and pink tutu. She sat on the edge of the jetty, her gumbooted legs swinging below her. She pointed the toes of one foot, and the tip of her boot touched the water, sending out ripples in impossibly perfect circles. Lucie put a hand into the air – as if to halt the threat of motion and the machinations of time – and began to sing along.

And she went her way homeward
With one star awake
As the swans in the evening
Move over the lake

Lucie's gaze was fixed as the swinging of the little girl's legs kept gentle time with the song. Lucie sent out the notes, filling them with her longing, her sorrow, her sorry and her heart. And a request: with a high-third harmony that singled out her voice and turned it into a resonant call, she asked the child to *please, please forgive me* and to *please let me go.*

And she smiled as she passed me
As she passed me, quite near
And that was the last
That I saw of my dear.

Lucie felt the perfect circles of solace around her move away and dwindle as the last bars of music began to fade. A docile, heedless breeze tousled her hair.

'Lucie?'

With a gasp, Lucie, turned to see Carra standing in the sitting room, by the open French door.

'Oh goodness, Lucie, I'm sorry to startle you. I was trying to work out how not to. Startle you.' Carra brushed her cheek. 'And how not to make it seem as though I was spying. I'm sorry, the door was open and I did knock, but no one came. I thought I'd just see if I . . . and then I heard . . . my God, Lucie, that was so beautiful.'

Lucie turned quickly back to the river. The girl in the pink tutu had gone.

'Yes, very beautiful, that song,' she said, with her eyes still on the jetty. 'Irish folk song. I think.'

'Your voice, though,' said Carra. 'That's what I meant. So lovely.'

Lucie was startled by a rush of pleasure. 'Thank you, Carra. I was using my full core voice, which is the one you use when you really *feel* a song.'

'Well, I don't think anyone would want to hear me feel a song. Core voice or not.' Carra laughed, and as she listened to it echo across the river, she wondered what realm of Lucie's she'd stepped into. Since viewing the Nowhere People display in the showground's hall, Carra had the peculiar sensation of being spoken to from somewhere long gone and very far away. And now, with the river – and Lucie – so reflective before her, the faraway felt closer. She felt as though there were words on the tip of her tongue, but she couldn't think what they were, so she chose instead to sit on the wrought-iron terrace seat and remain silent.

After a short while, Lucie sat too. 'It's a lovely view. I am seeing with your eyes, and I can see how lovely it is. I should have appreciated it more.'

Carra looked at the river, with its pensive stillness and reflected springtime. A hawthorn tree whispered a hint of pink blossom across the river's surface. From its branches flew a small bird, which dipped and swooped low over the looking-glass water, while in the sky, its twin flew up and over the red, time-ruined monuments of Abergavenny.

'It's really lovely.' Carra took a breath. 'Duncan tells me you're thinking of going back to Hobart.'

'Yes.' Lucie sighed. 'Of course, there are wonderful memories here, among the murky bits. Duncan has given us those. You and Duncan and the babies.'

Carra smiled, but Lucie wasn't looking, so she let it fall.

'He was always so exceptional,' Lucie continued. 'I used to find myself not talking about him in case I sounded boastful or delusional. Occasionally I made up something he'd done wrong. Someone joked once that Duncan must have hatched from a Fabergé egg.'

Carra attempted a laugh.

'I remember once telling him, in my dramatic way, when he was about ten or so, that I had Felicity's loss in my bones and that it often made me feel cold. He ran me a bath and said that it was the best way to get the chill out of bones. A ten-year-old boy shouldn't have to think about those things. I vowed then not to let him carry Felicity like that. Even so, I know that he worked very hard to make me happy. Too hard. He even sang in the school musical! He's a dreadful singer. He applied himself at school, won awards, enjoyed himself but never too much. He wasn't academically gifted but he became a doctor, for goodness sake. I think he would have preferred to join a football team, or travel, but he'd forgotten how to live life without volition. And then he brought us you, Carra – more joy, and the twins, of course. So this place has had everything in it, but also nothing. Nothing of Felicity. This was never her home, do you see?'

Carra was trying very hard to see, but her thoughts had been pinned by a thud of realisation. *I was on Duncan's list of goals.* She chastised herself for such self-absorption and dragged herself into Lucie's painful place of nothingness. The idea of losing a child, one of her darling babies, brought a crushing perspective to her preoccupations.

'I think,' Lucie went on, 'if I could go back to a place where there are echoes of the real Felicity, not the gone Felicity . . .' Lucie turned suddenly. Carra could almost feel the bright of her blue eyes. 'Do you think, Carra, that Felicity would see that as us giving up on her?'

Carra looked up into the higher branches of Len's holly tree, into the beaming yellow faces of a romping banksia rose and down to the far edges of the river. 'No,' she said. 'I think she would know that it's time you attend to being you.'

Lucie nodded. 'Yes.' She followed Carra's gaze. 'You know,' she said, 'all the wombats have gone from Abergavenny. Cliffity Smith said the wombats know when it's time to leave.'

They listened to the day for a little longer, and Carra thought of Cliffity's Nowhere People story and his missing ferret in the static muffle of the wombat burrows. The vision flickered and glitched with pictures and voices from the other stories until Carra was dizzy with them – Sergeant D's broken heart, Fleury's lonely yodel, Swoozie Hamilton's empty cellar, and the nothing part of Lucie's heart. *Coming, ready or not.* Carra's eyes found the red of the Abergavenny chimney and rested there. *All the truth in the colour.* There were words on the tip of her tongue again. She sat very still because the breeze was picking up and any chance of clarity could easily blow away.

'Anyway.' Lucie said suddenly, making Carra jump. 'Sorry, Carra. You didn't come here to sit in my doldrums and stare at the river.'

Carra smiled, cleared her throat. 'Ah, well, I'm happy to. But no, I've been at the showgrounds this morning, looking at the history displays and your wonderful Nowhere People stories, and Josie asked me for a favour.' Carra felt relieved to be steering things onto more tangible ground. 'No one got *your* story, Lucie. And it's a glaring omission. You've included Len and Duncan, and me, so . . .' Carra's toes curled, as though she were tiptoeing. 'Would you mind . . .?'

'I suppose that would be all right,' Lucie replied, taking a deep breath that seemed to bring her back to the terrace. 'Perhaps the photo first, in case I get sobby and sniffly. Should I check my hair? Yes, I'll check my hair.'

Carra watched Lucie gather herself into the mother-in-law she knew. 'Your hair is perfect. We just need you, don't we? In your natural habitat.'

'Not with the river, then,' said Lucie sharply, walking into the house. 'I mean,' she added, 'I'm not an otter. And the garden and the outdoors is far more Len's domain.'

Carra followed Lucie into the sitting room, where Beans was glad to be picked up and included in the portrait.

Afterwards, Carra let Lucie talk. She began awkwardly, but the performer in her was soon flattered and awoken enough for a whole flurry of words to unfold, which Lucie insisted must be cut back and edited where Carra saw fit. The whole interview took almost half an hour and at the end of it, Carra spontaneously gathered Lucie into a long, earnest hug.

'Oh,' said Lucie. 'My dear.' She felt herself relax a little into Carra's clean-linen scent, then patted out an ending to the hug on her back. 'Thank you.'

As she saw Carra out, Lucie took a deep breath and said, 'Tell me if you think I'm loopy, but I was thinking . . . I wonder whether Esther might . . .' She took another breath. 'Did you happen to notice anything about Felicity in the history display?'

Carra shook her head, then didn't. A collection of words and images flooded into her mind. They moved together in odd fragments, like a mosaic. *The pieces of the big Nowhere River puzzle.* She swayed a little and whispered, 'Oh gosh, Lucie, I think I did.'

Lucie looked confused. 'So, someone put her story in? And her photograph?'

Carra put a steadying hand on the doorframe. 'No. No, they didn't. Sorry, I didn't mean . . .' She was relieved to see that Lucie's mind was moving ahead.

'I was just, ah, well, it was a suggestion I was against. I rather regret it now. Just that it's probably time to make sure she doesn't turn into a fable or an embellishment. So I wondered about including her in Nowhere People. We could record it now, if you have time. She's more nowhere than any of us, after all.'

Carra stared at Lucie.

'No,' said Lucie. 'Silly idea. I'm all over the place, stupid old woman.'

'It's not, Lucie,' said Carra, trying to keep her voice from amplifying the pounding of her heart. 'It's not silly at all. Yes, yes, we must.'

It's just that, she thought, *I think I found Felicity. I think she's already there.*

Felicity Finlay, 5 (as told by her mother, Lucie Finlay)
Felicity was five years old when she disappeared on the banks of the Nowhere River. It was her first visit to the town. She had a very fun time running across the bridge and along the pathways. She loved animals and enjoyed seeing the coots on the river and the wombats on the flats. She also liked stewed apple with cream, her mother's jewellery box, her music machine, her blankie called Baah and her little brother's laugh. When she started school, she did dancing, and showed an unusual flair for someone so young. Perhaps she's still good at dancing. Perhaps she still likes all those things. I wish she could have heard her brother laugh more.

Chapter 29

As part of her Get Up and Glow project, and as a gesture of support for Flo and the Nowhere River Show, Marceline Cash was offering make-up application classes, half-price hairstyling for everyone and mobile hairdressing for Nuyina residents. She called in some favours from hairdressing friends in Bothwell and New Norfolk for extra staff, and a high-class salon in Hobart sent three stylists pro-bono after hearing about Marceline's idea and the show revival.

The end result, a few days out from show day, was a whole population made over. Flo had her dark hair cut into a blunt bob ('for confidence and energy,' said Marceline). Bunty and Daphne had their hair dyed with a balayage of rainbow colours, because 'Why wouldn't we?' Sister Julianne Poke was flattered out of her purple perm and into soft, dark-blonde waves. Lucie joined the wave of waves, accepting a dignified, Jane Fonda-esque sweep and considering it the emergence of the New Lucie. At Nuyina, even Stanton Godfrey had his moustache revamped into a perfect handlebar with twiddled ends. Notable exceptions to the made-over were Patricia (who had travelled to the same hairdresser in Hobart for her signature style every four weeks for twenty-five years), Alan Lamb, who didn't have any hair at all, and Len, because 'You can put lippy on the blobfish but he's still a blobfish.'

The other thing that happened in those days leading up to the show was the peculiar behaviour of Jerry and Alex Bradshaw. Aside from their new combed and side-parted gentlemen's haircuts, Josie felt they were just not themselves. They were frequently absent, and unusually jocular with one another. Josie found it enormously heartening but also a bit alarming. It was something she hadn't seen since Alex reached his teens and started opining on everything about Everston. After some consideration, she identified a worry that the mateship, if built too strong, would have deeper fractures to bear when next there was a disagreement. And then she put her suspicions down to hormonal negativity and dismissed them altogether.

It was the passengers aboard an early-morning flight into Hobart who eventually helped solve the Alex-and-Jerry mystery. In the pink dawn, the first fingers of sunshine pointed to the eastern side of the highest Colleen Hill, the same side that faced away from town and over the Pearce Highway. Someone on board that flight took a picture of that Colleen hillside that particular morning, because in huge, bright white letters against the dirt, were the words *COME TO THE NOWHERE RIVER SHOW*.

'I knew there was something going on,' said Josie, after word had reached her via the usual grapevine. 'I should have twigged, with all the paddocks clear of rocks and white paint on your trousers. I thought you were whiting the back fence for the horses.'

'We got paint everywhere because we had to do the painting part under the cover of darkness,' said Alex. 'For the big reveal this morning. Can't believe it's all over the socials.'

'Flo's going to love it,' said Josie. 'But you, dear husband, are under my watch and you need to rest.'

'Alex did the heavy stuff,' said Jerry. 'And I promised Flo I'd help with publicity.'

It was also around this time that Lucie stood beside Patricia in the St Margery's drawing room, watching the buzz of the High Street outside the window. Patricia tutted and harrumphed at various 'abominations', including Elaine Thorold's permed hair extensions, the cheery wave of a kangaroo paw from the front garden, the dots of gnome colour and a large overhead banner heralding *The 111th Nowhere River Show (Come for a Country Good Time – There's Nowhere like Nowhere!)*. Lucie, meanwhile, was contemplating the idea of at least mentioning to Patricia a vague notion of her departure from Nowhere River and her resignation from the position of vice-president. She was just about to speak when she overheard from Patricia a whimper of utter dismay. It confirmed to Lucie that now was not the time to discuss the future. She followed Patricia's gaze as it passed over the vision of Kirrily Kalbfell trotting along with her poodle (which had had its legs clipped into balls and its ears dyed pink) past Mr Pfaff with his beard trimmed but his bottom-crack visible above his grotty trousers, and landed upon a television camera crew.

'Heavens to God and bloody Norah,' said Patricia, evidently disturbed enough to resort briefly to common turns of phrase. 'And now this contemptible omnishambles is to be broadcast across the world. That's it, I have had it up to dolly's bow. I will crown Miss Fresh and Lovely at the show before we end up in complete Bedlamshire. Can we put word out directly, please, Lucie?'

Lucie, momentarily amazed by Patricia's 'please', pulled herself to attention. 'Of course, Patricia, I'll see to it,' and then ran-skipped over the road to where a small crowd was receiving ministrations in Marceline's salon.

The news of the upcoming Miss Fresh and Lovely announcement was all over town, and in the hands of the television crew, before Nuyina served lunch at half past eleven.

Amid the hubbub and hype, no one noticed the abstraction of Carra Finlay. Except perhaps little Ben, who wondered why he and Daisy were being hurried between Swoozie Hamilton's funny-smelling room at Nuyina to Esther Very's museum, where they weren't allowed to touch anything but had to endure their mother talking endlessly and forgetting to give them any attention. And then there had to be a lot of pacing about on the river bank. He didn't like the concentration in his mother's eyes, he could tell it didn't have anything to do with him. She seemed sad and when he tried to pat her she brushed him away. Eventually, he screamed. This was so out of character for Ben that it successfully caught Carra's attention and got him a juice box and some haste in the direction of home.

▼▼▼

On the eve of Nowhere River Show Day, when the dusk had declared to the townspeople that they'd done all they could and everyone had downed tools and turned in, the seven o'clock news headlined with the story of a little country town with a smiling river and a sign made of stones, a women's 'talent quest', a populace of gnomes and a good old-fashioned rural show.

Carra was in the Kinvarra kitchen laminating a collage when the story came on the television. 'Duncan!' she called. 'Come and look at this.'

Duncan came in behind her. 'Hey,' he exclaimed when he saw the screen. 'Look at us go!'

'Well, that'll capture imaginations at the very least,' said Ambrose to Patricia in their sitting room at The Rises. Patricia, looking at the television over her sewing glasses, raised her eyebrows as Flo appeared on the screen. 'Come to the Nowhere River Show,' Flo said in a voice turned wooden with nerves. 'You'll have a country good time there's nowhere like Nowhere.'

'Dear, dear,' tutted Patricia. 'That was far from arresting.'

'Ha!' whooped Len from his chair at Riverhouse. 'There's my girl!' He caught himself, coughed and looked at Beans.

Lucie reached to squeeze Len's hand and said, 'I must give her some more coaching before she gives her presidential speech on show day.'

Beans scrabbled his blanket and looked concerned.

In the communal sitting room at Nuyina, Bunty Partridge waved a knobbly fist in the air and shouted, 'Don't let the bastards tell us we're Nowhere.' She was rewarded with a feeble cheer and some claps.

Jerry, sitting next to Flo on the couch at Everston, squeezed her shoulder and nodded at the television. 'Look at you go, Floey Bradshaw.'

Flo huffed with embarrassment. 'Gawd, I hope people won't be disappointed.'

'I wouldn't worry,' said Alex, perching on the arm of the couch to watch and sending Flo a wink. 'No one'll come.'

Josie whacked him with a cushion.

'They have to,' said Flo to the television. 'They just have to.'

Back at Kinvarra, as the story ended with a montage of shots around Nowhere River, Duncan opened a beer and left the room, saying, 'Big day tomorrow, Carra.'

Carra distractedly smoothed a bubble from the collage, closed her eyes for a brief moment, and opened them again to an aerial shot of the town and the river. 'Yep. Big day.'

Imaginations did appear captured, perhaps to have run rather wild. Show day dawned to a great stream of vehicles coming in along the Pearce Highway from the east and a few from the Lakes Road to the west. By 8.30 am the traffic had come to a standstill a good five kilometres from the gates of the showgrounds. Inside, Flo and her committee scuttered around, unaware of the jammed vehicles and the problematic parking system that had seen Mr Pfaff direct cars in through the exit, point them in the wrong direction and call one driver a fuck-head.

'Ladles and Jellyspoons,' boomed Len's voice around the showgrounds at nine o'clock sharp. It skipped along the river, bounced off the Whistler Hills, startled the animals in their nursery and sent Narelle the ferret up Stanton Godfrey's trouser leg. Josie, who was seeing to the animals before their big day, had to scramble to catch a flustered rooster and soothe a startled lamb.

'Good grief, sorry,' said Len. 'Is that a bit loud?' There came some static fumbling. 'It's a bit loud. How's that? Ah, better. Hello everyone, my name is Len Finlay. I am your commentator for the day and as a past president I welcome you all, with great pride, to the one-hundred-and-eleventh Nowhere River Show. The gates are open, the hay bales are set, and as far as I can see – which is quite a long way from my seat in the belvedere – this is going to be the best show day in the world, is it not, Sir Barry Fronda of show sponsor Fronda's Auto Repairs?'

Barry Fronda gave Len a thumbs up from the driver's seat of his tractor, which was dressed up like a train and towing a trailer of children.

'*What in the wide world of sports is happening on the arena?* I hear you ask. Well, it looks to me like we have a lot of tossers out there limbering up for the great Nowhere River Blunnie toss.'

Lucie, who was setting out vases of flowers in the Hall of Industries with Carra, sighed and said, 'Len's having a lovely time at least, listening to himself.'

Carra smiled. 'He's made for the commentary box.'

'For our international visitors,' Len's voice continued, 'a Blunnie is a boot, a very fine boot, with some weight to it, so not an easy toss.

There's still time to get an entry in – just go and see our ringmaster. Could that young boy get out of the tree by the gate, please? We need the ambulance for the grand parade, old soldier, hop down, that's it.'

'Good heavens,' said Patricia, gliding into the hall and surveying the scene with an expression of someone who has eaten too much vegemite. 'What a cornucopia of craft. How quaint.' She turned towards the flowers. 'Ah, here you are, Lucie.' She eyed Lucie's fuchsia shirt. 'Looking *vivid* today.'

'Thank you, Patricia,' said Lucie firmly, though she knew it wasn't a compliment. A quick glance confirmed that Patricia was in full irritation bristle. Lucie looked away. 'Len was looking for you earlier. When are you thinking of making the Miss Fresh and Lovely announcement? He'd like to mention it.'

'Immediately following the grand parade and before the hall opens,' said Patricia. 'I have prepared a speech. And I've come to let you know that I am charged with welcoming the governor and showing her around. So I will bring her in here while the judging is underway to avoid the crowds.'

'Mustn't have the governor mixing with the hoi polloi,' said Lucie, noting with vague interest that she may be about to lose her temper.

'And is there any truth to the rumour that Fleury Salverson is going to assault our ears with her yodelling?'

'I haven't any idea,' said Lucie. 'But I do hope so.'

'I do hope *not*,' snipped Patricia. 'Am I the only person left with an iota of concern for this town's honour?'

Before Lucie and her hackles could reply, Len's voice burst through the tension. 'I'm looking forward to the Hall of Industries, myself,' he boomed. 'Opening after judging at around midday, I'm told. And such industry! Amazing to think of all those crafty people in our valley, frothing up their nothings to a pretty cream. And speaking of cream, I'm told the luncheon room does a very good scone, so get in there and put on your nosebag. Ah, right, and I've just had word that you should avoid the top loos, should you need to spend a penny. There's a code brown in that area, I'm told.'

'Hoary old sky,' said George Costas, who was passing through the hall towards the top toilets. 'Doesn't seem to be putting anyone off, though. The car park's full as a goog and the septic's shat itself. That's a sure sign of a good turnout.'

'By the way,' said Len into the background. 'What smells funny?' He paused for a pre-emptive chortle. 'Clown poo. And speaking of clowns, the woodchopping is about to start on the river side of the arena.'

With a small twitch of her left eyebrow and a sharp intake of breath through her nose, Patricia swept from the room.

'Gosh,' said Josie to a small lop-eared rabbit in the animal nursery. 'Len's brave, taking the mick out of the woodchop blokes.' She looked over at Alex, who was coaxing a reluctant blue-tongue lizard into view. 'Where's Flo?'

▼▼▼

Flo was all over the place, sweaty and bewildered, until she realised that the majority of her committee had slipped back into show mode as though almost a decade hadn't passed. She allowed herself a moment or two to stand in the commentator's belvedere to watch the day unfold and assure herself that all would be well.

'Quite the day you've put together, Florence Griffith Joyner,' said Len, with his hand over the microphone. 'Look at you fly.' He felt a buzz of fatherly affection and the tiny spring of a tear in his eye.

Flo smiled at him, then exhaled and smoothed her (Josie's) dress. She changed her flustered demeanour to determined confidence (which turned out a bit grumpy) and went to wait in the members' car park for the scheduled arrival of the governor. Ambrose and Patricia were already there, appearing not the least bit perturbed

by the incoming dignitary. Recruiting the Montgomerys as inter-
locutors had been Carra's suggestion. 'They're the least likely to make
silly remarks, trip over or say "fuck",' she had said. Flo thanked
the sky for the idea. By the gate, as a measure of security, stood
Sergeant D, resplendent in full formal uniform.

A bit before ten, having been waved through by a blessedly silent
Mr Pfaff, a bright silver estate car with a fluttering vice-regal flag
shimmered up through the paddock and into the members' car park.
A uniformed army man hopped out, smiled at the welcoming party
and opened the back door. Her Excellency, a slender, pretty woman
with bouncy grey hair exited the car.

'Hello!' she called. 'What a triumph for you all, look at the crowd!'

'Good morning, Your Excellency,' said Flo, in staccato. 'I'm Flo
this is Patricia and Ambrose and Sergeant D we welcome you to
the one-hundred-and-eleventh Nowhere River Show we hope you've
had a good trip.' She tried to think of the next thing. 'Don't use the
top loo. It's all bad up there.' She made a bad-smell face for just an
instant before mortification dawned. Sergeant D looked at her with
wide eyes. She dared not steal a glance at Patricia.

'Oh dear,' said Her Excellency. 'I hope there's not too much
mess.'

From the loudspeaker by the gate, Len said, 'And I'm told we
are to be graced by the presence of Her Excellency, the Governor of
Tasmania, very shortly. So please, everyone, on your best behaviour.
This is a show, remember, we are *on show* and no one by any means
is to use rude words like bottom, buttocks, bum, bollocks, balls,
bugger or bum-trumpets. Especially not bum-trumpets.'

Ambrose was startled to hear a small squeak issue from the vicinity
of his wife. It rose up, the squeak, on a freshening breeze.

'Please come this way,' parroted Flo. 'We have a very fun and
happy children's entertainment thing coming on the stage very soon
we will get you a nice drink too.'

'That sounds wonderful,' said Sergeant D, overcompensating for Flo's stilted talk.

Patricia looked eerily smiley and said nothing.

By half past ten, the woodchopping was well underway, the giant pumpkins had been weighed (a show record broken), and the tug-o'-war won. Lucie, busy with the judges in the Hall of Industries, found herself whisked away from her stewarding by a rather breathless Carra and led towards Esther's history exhibition.

'But Carra, I'm in the middle— Goodness, your hair looks nice. It's actually, you know, done.'

'Thank you. Yours is lovely, too.'

'See what a show day does? Brings out our best. But Carra, I'm needed—'

'I just thought you could have a really good look at your story project, in all its glory, while the hall is still closed for judging. They've just finished getting it all in place and it's . . . well, it's a *revelation*.'

Lucie eyed Carra's exuberance with suspicion. 'But—'

'You just really need to see it!' Carra shouted.

Lucie stopped in her tracks. 'Carra, what on earth . . .'

'I mean,' Carra collected herself, took Lucie's arm and pulled her along. 'You need to see, *really* see, what an exceptional thing it is.'

'Right,' said Lucie. 'Well, just a quick look for now, goodness me.' She shook her arm loose and walked towards the exhibit. Upon arriving, and having been manoeuvred to face the display, Lucie found herself rather taken aback. 'Oh, it does look rather good, doesn't it? The photos are marvellous.'

Carra chose some words carefully. 'The Felicity piece is perfect.'

Lucie gazed at the familiar photograph of her little girl and whispered, 'Yes. Yes it is.' She took Carra's hand, squeezed it, and after a long moment said, 'I can leave her here, I think, Carra, can't I? Among all these other Nowhere people.'

Carra let Lucie's words settle, smiled at them, and said, 'I don't think that anyone on this wall is *nowhere*, least of all Felicity, because you put them *somewhere*.' Carra fixed her eyes onto Lucie's face. 'And I find something different every time I read the stories. It's like there are stories in the stories. I mean, Swoozie talks about her grandfather's secret cellar, and Bandit finds a timeslip under the ground . . . put the pieces together and . . . what if Bandit found the cellar? I have all these funny images of a ferret drinking moonshine and getting lost on his way home through the burrows.' Carra stopped, closed her mouth on any more of the words.

'I've heard it said,' came Len's voice over the speakers, 'as true as I lie here, that there is likely to be swedge and biffo in the wool pavilion over champion fleece. There is a long and bitter rivalry between local graziers Walt Wallace and Jerry Bradshaw, so get in quick, folks, for a front-row view of the inevitable melee. Blood will spill.' Len chuckled. 'Those are my eavesdroppings, at any rate.'

'Oh, for goodness sake,' said Lucie. 'Has he forgotten we have Her Excellency here somewhere? I'll have to go and shut him up. I'll catch up with Esther later, tell her she's done a superb job.' She gave Carra's hand another squeeze and a gentle pat. 'Thank you, Carra.'

'Oh, and . . .' said Carra, but Lucie was already hurrying away.

'Cripes,' Len continued. 'I don't like the look of this wind. Some of those gusts would blow a sailor off your sister.'

Flo, accompanying the governor and the Montgomerys to the animal nursery, couldn't hold in a gasp.

Patricia's lips were white in their purse.

'Haha,' said Ambrose to the governor. 'Quite the character is our commentator Len.'

'I do apologise for his lack of grace,' said Patricia. 'Most inappropriate.'

'It's totally fine,' said the governor. 'He's very funny.'

'You're a good sport,' said Ambrose fondly. He reached out to pat the small of the governor's back in a fatherly manner, but missed and patted her upper-right buttock.

'No touching!' yelled the governor's aide.

'*Ambrose!*' Patricia shrieked.

Inda Price, who was hovering to tell the governor about the time she'd polished the floor of the Government House ballroom, burst into a loud cackle.

'Oh m-my golly,' Ambrose stuttered. 'I didn't mean . . . I'm so awfully sorry.'

The governor, who looked as though she might laugh too, said, 'Oh, don't worry. Look at those dear little bantams.'

She led the way into the animal nursery, in time to catch Josie saying, 'Fucking hell, can someone grab those fucking lizards before the ferrets do?'

There followed a cacophony of screeches from someone who'd apparently found one of the fucking lizards.

Sergeant D, poised to respond immediately to cries of help (and keen to distance herself from Ambrose's shame) ran forward and collided violently with Duncan, who had apparently spotted another lizard on his way past. The two of them grabbed one another to steady themselves, Sergeant D rubbing her shoulder as a Shetland pony trotted merrily past.

Father John, who was trying to be helpful with the rabbits, launched himself towards a pile of straw and arose triumphantly with a blue-tongue lizard in one hand and a rabbit in the other.

The lizard, apparently furious to have its freedom flight curtailed so soon, latched firmly onto Father John's hand.

'Jesus H. Christ!' he shouted.

'What in *Shrewsbury's name* is wrong with everyone?' Patricia hissed, once the governor had been steered away from the animal nursery towards the pumpkins and out of earshot. There was sweat glistening on her brow. 'Ambrose.' Patricia's hiss landed squarely between her husband's eyes. 'You have besmirched the Montgomery name. Stay here with the animals until further notice. I'll chaperone Her Excellency alone.'

Ambrose looked forlornly at a goat, who trotted over and nibbled his shoelace.

'Attention, please,' came Len's voice over the speakers. 'We have reports of a lost child, I repeat, a lost child. If anyone has seen a small girl—' Len's broadcast stopped abruptly. There was some crackling. A certain hush descended, as though the very hills were holding their breath. Lucie's eyes darted to the river.

'Ah, h-hello?' Father John's voice projected through the speakers after a bit of kerfuffle. 'Sophie Cullen, if you can hear this, please come to the green hut on the hill where your mother is waiting. Sophie Cullen. Sophie is seven, folks, she is wearing a blue hat and her mummy would like to see her, thank you.'

The speakers fell silent, and into that silence, Lucie's thoughts bounded.

▼▼▼

Lucie Finlay, 64

People tell me that I've survived a mother's worst nightmare, because my little girl went missing. But I didn't actually survive because the person I was before is not here anymore. And it's never over, the grief. I'm not all that spiritual, naturally, but I have to believe that even though Felicity isn't here, she *is* here, you know, in me. But sometimes I'm too tired to carry her. Then I pretend that she's still alive, somewhere safe and loving. I know that's silly.

Len is different. He just accepts that life is awful sometimes, and that's that. His limp came on around the time we realised that finding

Felicity was unlikely. Grief can manifest in many ways. Anyway, we have each other, and we have Duncan and things to do. We laugh, we have the babies. Daisy looks very like Felicity, I think, so there you are, she *is* still here, really. I probably shouldn't have named her 'Felicity' – it's one of the few words that rhymes with 'mystery'.

Chapter 30

Carra, having wrestled Daisy and Ben into their pram and brought them to the animal nursery, had witnessed the mayhem. From the alpaca enclosure she had seen Patricia's fury, Ambrose's disgrace, the blue-tongue lizard chaos and Flo's dismay. But it was the little parade of awkward affection between Duncan and Sergeant D as they recovered from their collision that most captured Carra's attention. Duncan had held Sergeant D's elbow with both hands for longer than seemed necessary. And there was a particular tension in the way they looked at one another. Carra had become accustomed to the easy, teasing, sibling-like friendship between Sergeant D and Duncan. But there before her in the animal nursery, as beneath the wedding arch in Queen Mary Park, there was something new. Something bashful and hesitant and tender. Duncan Finlay and Harmony Darling. *It's not new*, realised Carra. *It's something old, only just recovered and blinking in the light.* She checked in with her heart, and found it quickening with what felt a bit like euphoria.

'Caroline? My God, it *is* you. Holy shit, fancy running into you here!'

Carra spun around to see a woman wearing jeans with the knees missing. That was the first thing she noticed. *Fashion,* she thought.

The second thing she noticed was that the woman was so familiar it seemed a terrible thing to be grappling for a name, or even a memory that might give her some context.

'Hi!' Carra exclaimed, trying to overcompensate for her memory lapse. 'How *are* you?'

'Pretty good, this show is amazing! Oh, that's right, you live here, don't you? You must be so proud. Everything's so cute.'

Carra would have worried about Patricia being in earshot of the word 'cute' had she not been positively tearing through her brain for a helpful memory synapse. 'Thanks, yes, um, how are things?'

'Oh, you know, pretty good.' The woman jerked her thumb in the direction of two cross-looking children. 'They're terrified of *everything*. I bring them on a day out in the country and they can't even go near a lamb. They keep asking why their iPads won't work.'

'Oh dear,' said Carra, inspecting the woman's heavily made-up face and strangely plump lips. 'Yes, we're a thousand feet up and fifty years back here in Nowhere River.' She laughed.

'And these are your babies? Oh my God, so, so adorable. A pigeon pair, how perfect. God, Caroline, they're actually so beautiful, look at them.'

So Carra looked at Ben as he stared suspiciously up at the woman, his fist clenched protectively around a handful of feathers. Daisy, her face covered in ice cream, was trying to pop her balloon. *They are beautiful*, thought Carra with a smile.

'Are you working in landscape architecture? Can you believe it's almost ten years since we finished . . .' The woman kept speaking, but Carra didn't hear, because the correct name had just fallen neatly into place. *Ursula Andreas. Oh my goodness.* She looked again at the overdone face and the sullen children, and tried not to gape.

'And how's that gorgeous husband of yours?' Ursula was saying. 'I hope you don't mind me saying but oh my Lord I adored him back in the day. We all did. What a perfect dish.'

Carra laughed. 'He's great, thank you. And you, Ursula? I follow you on Instagram and you're amazing. I'm such a fan.'

'Oh God, don't believe a word of it. It's all a publicity thing. Works a treat for business but it's phony as. Instagram moments.' She rolled her eyes. 'Insta kids, Insta family, Insta face.' She swept a hand in front of her face. 'And look at you. You haven't changed a bit. This is what country air does, is it?' She glanced at her children, leaned in and whispered, 'I have to bribe these two to smile in photos.'

'But your gardens are beautiful.'

'Thank you. I just oversee plans now. My back is shot. So boring.'

'Oh no.'

Ben whimpered and pointed at the animal nursery. Daisy's balloon popped and both twins laughed.

'No doubt you're flat-out with your show, and I have to get these mongrels a showbag before there's anarchy. Let's keep in touch, and send hugs to glorious Duncan!' She mimed a small swoon and then tottered off on heeled boots. Carra watched her until she disappeared into the crowd, then remembered that the Nowhere River Show prided itself on its no-showbags policy.

Having settled all her animal charges back into their respective places, Josie was plaiting Bruny's mane in preparation for the grand parade when Flo hurtled into the animal nursery.

'Patricia says the show is a fiasco and a disgrace.' She hiccuped. 'She says I've invited thousands and thousands of people to witness our huge embarrassment, that I have ruined a proud tradition.'

Josie felt a burst of anger in her throat. 'My God, she's a bitch, that woman. Honestly, Flo none of that is true. Not a word of it. Look at all those people out there having a wonderful time. Patricia is just cross she didn't look her best in front of the governor.' She took Flo into her arms. 'Come on, it was Ambrose who patted Her Excellency's bum, by all accounts.'

'And poor Ambrose,' sobbed Flo. 'He didn't mean to. And Patricia's being so nasty to him.'

'I'm pretty sure poor old Rosie is used to that.'

Jerry came in at that point and said, 'You wouldn't believe it, we just clicked over eight thousand punters through the gates. It's an all-time record.'

Flo dropped into the straw at Josie's feet, put her head in her hands and said, 'See, eight thousand people witnessing my disgrace.'

'What?' said Jerry.

'Come on, Flo,' said Josie, crouching down and stroking Flo's hair. 'You're just focusing on the negatives. I've seen a constant stream of people through here who think this is the best show they've ever been to. Everyone is saying it. And they haven't even seen the Hall of Industries yet. Or the lawnmower race.'

'I think I'll cancel the lawnmower race,' sniffed Flo. 'Someone will get their leg cut off or something.'

'Hey, listen, Flo,' said Jerry. 'I've done a lot of these shows and we've never had a crowd like this. The show-jumping is going really well, people love the sheepdogs and the entire Tasmanian wood-chopping community is down in the river corner. The kids are loving it, a whole lot of people turned up dressed as garden gnomes. It's a sensation, Flo. Your sensation.'

'I have to sit in Barry Fronda's hearse for the grand parade,' said Flo miserably. 'We have a hearse, a lawnmower, an old man and some ferrets in the grand parade. Fleury Salverson is going to yodel. And Mr Montgomery patted the governor's bum.'

'Well, that's about the best thing I've ever heard,' said Josie. 'Ever.' And she laughed, then laughed some more until she had to prop herself up against a post.

Jerry laughed too. 'The hearse is a magnificent vehicle,' he said. 'A rare classic, apparently. And I doubt the governor, or her bum, minds a bit. Ambrose is about the most harmless human on the planet.'

Flo found a small smile on her face.

Carra appeared then, carrying three sausages in bread. 'Hi, Bradshaws,' she said shyly. 'I saw you come in here, Flo. Brought you something to cheer you all up.'

'Show sausages,' said Josie. 'Nothing like them. Thanks.'

'Not for me, Carra,' said Jerry to Carra's proffered sausage. 'You have that one. I'm good.'

'She's vego, remember,' said Josie.

Carra smiled. 'And you don't want to miss these sausages.'

'Oh, sorry, of course. Right, I'll take it, thanks.'

'You all right, Flo?' Carra asked.

Flo nodded and swallowed some sausage. 'Thanks. I'm glad you'll be our Miss Fresh and Lovely.'

'Rubbish,' said Carra. 'You're a sure thing for the crown.'

'Patricia hates her, apparently,' said Josie, rolling her eyes.

'I think if Patricia takes the time to tell you off, that means she likes you,' said Carra. 'She just looks through me.'

'Great sausages,' said Jerry.

'Yes, there's a reason for that. They're Everston beef. The school had them made.'

'Oh, good on them,' said Jerry.

'Sergeant D and I organised it. We donated the animal. A certain demented beast with the brand JJB88.'

Flo gasped. Jerry looked wide-eyed at his sausage and smiled.

'Oh my God,' said Josie.

'He's been a great fundraiser for the school,' said Carra. 'I gave Alex one too. Actually,' she reached over and took Josie's sausage, 'give me a bite of that bastard.'

Josie whooped with laughter. 'That's the *best* care meal I've had delivered, by *far*.'

▼▼▼

The grand parade featured far more than a hearse, an old man and a ferret. The fire trucks led the way, followed by the hearse, the town's gleaming tractors and Josie on Bruny. The grandstand was full and the spectating crowds spilled happily onto the grass around the arena to watch.

'That horse!' said the governor to Sergeant D. 'It's like watching something mythical.' They watched as Bruny, brushed to shining, danced under Josie's practised hand. Seated next to Sergeant D was Duncan, who had been wheeled out as another pleasing diversion. To his right sat Patricia, whose mood was elevated slightly by the fact that she'd managed to talk herself out of a full-blown anxiety attack and back to reasonable function. She found herself very taken and quite soothed by the Scottish marching band.

Ambrose and Len, both banished to the back of the grandstand by withering looks from their wives, sat in their shared disgrace and gazed gloomily down at the scene. Even Stanton Godfrey's comical intro-duction of Barbara, Narelle and Bandit didn't raise a smile between them. Nor did the parade of Nuyina old folks dressed as gnomes.

'How about a small whisky with our contrition?' suggested Ambrose. 'As soon as this is done.'

'That would be grand,' said Len.

But then it was time for Fleury Salverson and her much anticipated yodelling. She wobbled onto the arena's central podium, tapped the microphone and cleared her throat. 'This,' she said croakily, then cleared her throat a second time, 'this is what was described by my grandmother as "kulning". Some of you may prefer to call it "yodelling".'

In the front row of the grandstand, with her babies asleep in their pram, Carra tried very hard not to put a hand over her mouth. 'Oh, Fleury,' she whispered, glancing across at Abigail, who was nodding encouragement at Fleury and pressing her hands together with avid attention.

'Dear God,' said Patricia. 'Your Excellency, I am so sorry. This day has officially turned into farce. My deepest apo—'

But her words were interrupted by a soft and haunting note that seemed to descend from the ether. It pierced the hullabaloo atmosphere and lay it quietly down to rest, then rose back up, taking all the moments of eight thousand people and billowing them out into a single, wonder-filled consciousness.

'Hell's bells!' muttered someone from the grandstand as the sublime sound stretched towards the hills, then curved languidly back in a haunting echo. Other exclamations peppered the reverberating air.

'Oh my stars!'

'What the bajingoes?'

'Oh. Em. Gee.'

'Dickenson's aunty, that can't be coming from Fleury?'

But the sound was indeed coming from Fleury, welling up from a deep and ancient part of her that flowed in her veins and out into the atmosphere like something winged and graceful and magnificent.

'Ah,' breathed Abigail. 'Isn't it magical?'

'Incredible,' answered Carra.

The song with no words and no tune curled up and up, then whipped back on itself, dropping lower until it settled into all available spaces and hollows. It was a sound you could feel. The hairs on Duncan's arms rose, and beside him something shifted in the chest of Sergeant D. Josie, from beside Fleury, sensed a great slowing. She leaned into Bruny, who was equal parts taut with attention and lulled into stillness, and looked at the crowd. Mouths were agape, tears were flowing, hands clutching other hands. Even the wind seemed to move with the sound. Flo, who'd been slumped in the front seat of the hearse hoping no one would notice her, sat tall and listened. She wanted to take the sound in her hands, looked up to see what words it might have written on the clouds, or what fantastical beings it might have summoned.

From her high seat on the grandstand, Lucie could see the river looping the rocks of Pocket Island as though pulled by something other than gravity and tides.

As Fleury drew her impassioned call to a close, a silence descended on the grandstand, hovered for a long moment and then broke with a burst of passionate applause from Lucie. The governor joined her, as did Patricia (who forgot herself and issued an involuntary 'woohoo'), and the three of them stood in ovation. Most of the grandstand followed suit, and Fleury was left dazed and smiling into a rapturous applause, which drowned out a low rumble of thunder from beyond the Whistler Hills.

'Congratulations to our very own Fleury Salverson,' said Len, who had made his way back to the microphone especially. 'What a glorious revelation for us all. I need say no more, other than thank you, Fleury. I wish we could have heard you long before now.'

Fleury beamed up, performed a tiny curtsy and muttered to herself, 'Well, none of you sods ever listened.'

'It is now time for the show's official opening,' declared Len. 'And if you won the show girl, the pie-eating competition or the Blunnie toss, please make your way to the arena – you are to receive your awards.'

There was a general collecting of everyone's wits, and a lot of gathering around Fleury. Lucie remembered to worry about Flo and the speech she had to deliver, and Patricia remembered to stay grumpy with Ambrose. One or two others were distracted by the apparent closeness of the hills against a darkening sky.

'Well, the wind seems to have died out,' said Ambrose to the space where Len had been.

At that moment, he received a large and rather shocking splash to the bare top of his head. He looked up, expecting to see some sort of bird, the transmitter of a poorly timed evacuation procedure, but instead saw clouds – monstrous, black, looming clouds – just before a fat raindrop hit him right in the eye.

Florence Bradshaw, 16

I don't think it's true that you shouldn't get too attached to places and things. I think that when you feel at home in a place, a part of it gets put inside you, so you will always be attached.

I feel like I have these hills and this river, my house and all the old things in me, and that if I moved away from them, I'd always get pulled back. I also don't believe that 'family' has to be the people you're related to. I have family everywhere here, not just in my house. Sometimes when the sun shines low on the riverbanks I can smell that muddy, grassy home smell and I get this sad twist in my chest that maybe one day I won't be here anymore and I'll have to not be fully me. That's how I know this is where I belong.

Chapter 31

Those first sprinklings were the last of the raindrops, because very soon it was coming down in sheets. More deluge than downpour, more explosion than cloudburst and more thunderous than thunder; it had mothers drawing up their children as if a wild beast were bearing down on them. People scattered, some cried out, others scrambled for shelter, only to cover their ears to block out the pounding above them. Within minutes, rooftops ran and gutters groaned, paths became creeks, roads became rivers, and the river became something else entirely, its familiar brown lost to an angry, pock-marked grey.

From the arena, Josie looked at the sky in disbelief, but was quickly blinded by the water. Around her, what was meant to be the grand parade finale broke apart into squealing, rushing clusters of people and animals. With the kind of suspicious elation peculiar to weather-beaten farmers, she looked around for her family.

'Jerry?' she whispered, then laughed as she rushed Bruny back to the shelter of the animal nursery, happily aware of her already saturated shirt and the water dripping from her hair.

From the hearse, Flo watched the flurry of people running from the grandstand either to find shelter or their cars.

'Looks as though there's gunna be rain on your parade,' said Barry

Fronda to Flo. The pummelling on the roof of the hearse increased in volume. He peered up at the sky and said, 'Well now, that wasn't on the cards, was it?'

'No,' said Flo, panicked. 'I've been checking the weather forecast for weeks. Look, they're going into the hall. The judging isn't finished yet.'

'I think maybe that's the least of our worries,' said Barry as he watched a bulging gutter fly free of the luncheon room roof and clatter onto the verandah. 'Holy shitballs, Hughey, it's gettin' biblical.'

▼▼▼

In the deserted High Street, water streamed from shop awnings and lampposts, signs and trees. It slicked the roads, shimmered on the gold rubbish bins and brightened the faces of the gnomes. Mrs Pfaff, alone in her shop and particularly grumpy owing to a complete lack of patronage, was hurrying about with buckets and cursing the world.

The ceiling of All Angels Church appeared to be weeping, its tears streaming down one of the walls and puddling on the floor. A silver candelabra on the altar received a rhythmic *plink-plink* as rainwater dripped onto its base. Outside, the gravestones on the previously sunny side of the cemetery seemed to exhale, producing wafts of steam from the wet warmth of their stone.

At Riverhouse, Len's roses jerked then drooped under the sudden onslaught. His lobelia seedlings flinched and struggled but didn't stand a chance. His silver birches, though, shivered with delight. On the tiny verandah of the garden shed, rills of water fell from the eaves, ricocheted off leaves, filliped into flowers and pooled on the flag-stones. The whole garden looked as though it was dancing. Down by the jetty, the river had already covered the lower reaches of the lawn.

The front path at St Margery's found itself centimetres deep in water, which flowed rapidly down towards the new flowerbeds, where the clenched tulip buds held strong, but the daisies has closed themselves away and the viola flowers had sunk beneath their leaves. Inside, a low creaking fluted upwards through the walls and amplified into a mid-pitch groan, followed by an almighty, deafening crash that shook the building from attic to ground. It was heard a block away, where Mrs Pfaff rushed out with her buckets to the street in a panic.

▼▼▼▼

'Your Excellency, I regret that your Nowhere River experience has been . . . misfortunately eventful,' Patricia said as she dabbed at her face with a handkerchief. 'The rain is bound to stop soon. The sun shines at least a little every Saturday of the year except for one.' She coughed. 'I do hope that you can come back one day when we have regained our usual ataraxia.'

'Actually,' said the governor, 'I've enjoyed myself immensely. It's been a long time since I've had such an action-packed day . . . an authentic day. You have a wonderful town, Patricia.'

'I came third in the knitted novelty section,' said Father John, who had also opted to squeeze into the hall alongside huddles of other dripping people. 'I made a pair of farmyard-themed oven mitts.'

'Oh, well done you,' said the governor. 'The hall is quite incredible. All those cakes! What an engaged community.'

Patricia blinked.

'And what a blessing this rain is after such a dry,' said Father John, crossing himself.

'It probably needs to slow up a little soon,' said Sergeant D. 'Or else the run-off will take the topsoil.'

'Excuse me, ma'am,' said the governor's aide, uncomfortable in his sodden uniform. 'We are scheduled to leave shortly. I've gathered some umbrellas from the car and I suggest we press on before it gets boggy.'

'Very sensible,' said Patricia. 'Take extreme care on the roads.'

'Thank you so much for having me,' said Her Excellency. 'It will be a highlight of my term.'

Patricia motioned to disagree, but found that her throat was quite obstructed by a lump of emotion.

Outside, Walt Wallace and his trusty John Deere hauled another car out of the slurry. Lucie and Len, under a makeshift rubbish-bag cover, made a dash for the members' car park across the quagmire that had been the southern lawns. The dash, however, was hindered by Len's leg, which seemed to be worse than usual.

'Shouldn't rush,' he said, trying to lessen his limp. 'Bound to slip. You go on ahead. I'm wet anyhow.'

But Lucie slowed too, took his hand and let the sheets of water cascade over both of them.

'Lovely drop,' she said, sniffing up rainwater. 'I'm pleased for the paddocks and the crops. It feels like a sign.'

'We're really leaving, aren't we, Lucie,' said Len, blinking through the rain.

'I'm sorry, Len. I just can't see how else to proceed.' She leaned in and gave him a drenched kiss, then pulled him along towards the car. 'Come on, let's see whether Riverhouse has become the arc.'

They bundled themselves into the Mercedes and paused for a moment to rally their composure.

Lucie breathed deeply. 'I feel as though I've left something behind. Did we bring anything else?' She looked at her hands as if searching for clues. 'No, it's more like I've forgotten to tell you something.' She frowned.

Len put his hand on hers. 'That left-something-behind feeling is engraved into my bones. Has been for thirty years.'

Lucie held her breath for a minute and then put her hand on his cheek. 'I know that one. It's so familiar it's become a second stomach. This one is different. It's another sort of pester.'

But Len had stopped listening. 'A second stomach,' he said, 'in which we ruminate on our misfortune.'

The rain on the car roof seemed suddenly insolent and threatening.

'This is a proper plothering, that's for sure,' said Len. 'I hope Old Lady Mercedes from the eighties can get us out of here. We might have to walk home.'

'She's from the nineties,' said Lucie, 'and as for walking, phooey to that.' She revved up the engine, threw the car into gear and stamped down on the accelerator. The pretty gold Mercedes performed a small burnout on her rear wheels before launching forwards, skidding acutely to the left, then the right, and gliding at speed through the car-park gates.

'Blimey, don't tell me you're not a sheila from the bush,' said Len.

▼▼▼

Back in the hall, Flo, Abigail and Father John puzzled over how to bring the Nuyina residents home. The bus, which had been parked out of the way in the far lower corner of the members' car park, was utterly bogged. The three wheelchairs didn't have a hope of getting across the arena to the gates on the town side, and the ambulant members of the contingent were unsteady at the best of times. And on the torrents fell.

'We could take them on horseback?' suggested Flo.

'I think we'd have more luck asking the Almighty to send Noah,' said Father John grimly.

'We might have to spend the night,' said Abigail. 'Plenty of food, at least. We didn't quite make it to peak lunch sales.'

'What a shame,' said Julianne Poke. 'All that tidy profit for the Treats Committee down the stormwater drain.'

'Ah well,' said Swoozie Hamilton. 'The show got the gate takings. It was a cracker of a crowd.'

'And we never got to Patricia's big announcement,' said Bunty. 'Who is to be Miss Fresh and Lovely? We may never live to find out.'

'Good thing, too,' said Stanton Godfrey. 'The town has been thrown widdershins by that Fresh and Lovely business. I just want things back to normal. Pass me a scone.'

Jerry arrived then, with Barry Fronda and a solution. 'We're going to load you into the back of the hearse, four by four—'

'The hearse?' said Abigail in horror.

'It's four-wheel drive, V10, good as a tractor, 'cept carpeted.'

'It's a workhorse all right,' said Jerry. 'We've backed it up right to the verandah.'

'And Walt is here with his tractor to get the bus to the main road,' said Flo. 'So you only have to hearse it for a minute or so.'

'Don't be putting me in with Stanton and those weasels,' said Daphne Partridge.

'Well, they're not staying here to get swallowed up by the Nowhere.' Stanton ushered Narelle and Barbara under his shirt. 'Cliffity would turn in his grave.'

'Right,' said Swoozie. 'Come on, you lot, think of it as a little trial run.'

'I've never seen a set-in like this,' said Josie to Alex as they helped Phoebe secure the gate takings into a safe. 'We've got to get home to the animals.'

'I'll get Dad and Flo,' said Alex.

But Flo refused to leave. 'I have to at least make sure everyone gets out safely,' she said. 'Don't I? And what about all the animals here?'

'This isn't a sinking ship, Flo,' said Josie.

'Don't bet on it,' said George Costas, who had come looking for his wife. 'The river's moving up like stink. Hurry up, Phoebe, I need to move the goats.'

In the end, Jerry agreed to stay with Flo and keep an eye on Bruny while Josie and Alex headed for Everston. After a hairy few moments in the showground car park, Josie got their four-wheel drive out to the Pearce Highway and down into Jones Street.

'Whoa,' said Alex, as he squinted through the flat, graphite light to the sodden streetscape. On the Whistler Bridge, he said, 'Fuck.' So did Josie.

Carra and Duncan, having bundled up the babies and headed back towards Kinvarra to clear the gutters, were flabbergasted at the sheer amount of water running off the Whistler Hills. They were glistening with it, the hills, even with the thick layer of cloud between their rounded tops and the sun. The road to Kinvarra, already creviced and washed, had bedrock shining through the worst patches, with mounds of gravel sweeping in curved patterns across the softening verges.

'I've never seen rain like this,' said Duncan, slowing the car to a crawl and peering through the blurry fall on the windscreen. 'Never. Wow.'

Carra glanced over at him and was reminded that this saturated landscape, this funny little river-bend town, for the moment so transformed, was stubbornly and eternally his home. She felt a tug of fondness, mixed with guilt. She touched his rain-flattened hair and he turned his startled expression towards her.

'Look at us! Drowned rats. Let's get home.'

As they drove, Carra smiled and thought fleetingly of Ursula Andreas – whether she'd made it out and what her timid children were making of the storm. Would she post her visit to the Nowhere River Show on Instagram or would her face have run off into the gutters? Carra checked her smugness and reminded herself that Ursula had been refreshingly warm and, cosmetic enhancements aside, genuine.

She turned her attention back to the rain. 'This doesn't bode well for the gutters, does it?'

Duncan smiled. 'I'll see to the gutters, you get the twins settled inside. I'll probably have to get back to Riverhouse.'

'You think the river might break its banks?'

'If this keeps up.'

Carra thought of Lucie and Len, their beautiful house, their ill-treated hearts, and sighed onto the window. She touched the condensation with her index finger and wrote a letter F. The driving rain and the speeding windscreen wipers gave the effect of a world in fast forward.

In the back, with the sway of the slow-moving vehicle, both babies had fallen asleep.

'It occurred to me,' said Duncan over the noise of the rain, 'today at the show, that the community are looking pretty fit. Especially the ones who joined your Sporticulture group. Fit and healthy.'

'Ha,' said Carra. 'Just call me Miss Fit!'

Duncan didn't hear the joke above the rain.

'I just started them off, I think,' Carra continued. 'Most of them got sick of gardening, and went on with their own activities.'

'Well, they still had more energy because of you, didn't they? And I reckon, between that and all the revamped gardens everywhere, you'd have been crowned Miss Fresh and Lovely today.'

'I doubt that,' said Carra. 'The show itself has been the thing to really get people up and about.'

'I don't know. Did you see how mortified Patricia was?'

'But it redeemed itself, with Fleury and all.'

They both pondered the surreal delight of Fleury Salverson's performance.

'And it also occurred to me,' continued Duncan, 'that you might have come up with the Sporticulture idea because you thought it would ease my workload, being that so many of my consults are obesity related.'

Carra was silent. The idea hadn't occurred to her. *Had it?* She wasn't sure.

'I mean, I know you feel overwhelmed at times and I can tell that you wish I could be more available. But everyone says how much easier parenting gets each year. You're already through the worst part – you sailed through.'

Did I? Carra felt the old confusion begin to cloud her thoughts.

'And, well, I just wanted to say that I really, really appreciate you doing that. And I really, really appreciate you. But I will always be busy with my work, Carra. That's just how I am. I just have to be the best doctor I can be.'

You think you just have to be the best son you can be, thought Carra. *The best substitute, the best possible consolation. But all you have to be is you. It's all any of us have to be.*

'If there's time freed up, I'd love to study surgery one day. My job will always fill my working hours, and then some. It's the nature of it, it's *my* nature. You know that, don't you? You knew that when we got together. People can't just change, can they.' He folded his hand onto her cheek and smiled his devastatingly handsome smile.

It wasn't a question, but Carra silently answered it anyway. *Yes, they can. People change all the time. They're meant to, that's part of being human. I am so changed I'm not even myself.*

They turned into the cottage drive.

'Holy shit!' said Duncan. He stopped the car and gaped at the water pouring off the gutters, coursing down the driveway and pooling on what used to be the lawn. Carra looked at the garden, which seemed marginally improved by the blur of rain, like a water-colour painting: a suggestion of a garden. There were only a few smudges of green, a dab of yellow and a lot of grey and brown. She'd put her colour everywhere but Kinvarra.

Duncan opened the car door and ran to a nearby fence post, which had a rain gauge attached to it. Carra waited a moment as he fiddled about with the inner cylinder, then turned to look at her.

'Want to have a guess?' he shouted through the rain.

'Thirty mil?' she called back.

'Try sixty-three!'

'What?'

'Sixty-three. In an hour and a half. Sixty-three goddamn mil.' He looked up into the sky. 'Probably sixty-five by now.'

Carra stared at him, his hair dripping and plastered to his head and his cheeks flushed with the cold whip of the rain.

'Sixty-five mil,' she whispered. 'Oh my God.'

At Everston, once Josie and Alex had struggled the horses into the clamorous shelter of the stables, she ran to the base of the Sugarloaf. The run-off there was proving catastrophic for the still-young murrnong plants. One or two were visible through a glut of mud trapped against the fence, but most had disappeared into an avalanche of silty, soggy earth. The whole area looked pummelled, sad and weeping. Josie didn't linger. She turned away, with a low-pitched beat of tense, bitter injustice ringing through her bones.

Lucie stood at the laundry window and looked out over the Riverhouse terrace to the distended body of the river. There was something proud about it, proud and filmic, as if it were having its moment. She felt it should come with a soundtrack, and thought again of Fleury's haunting song. She could still feel the thrum of it, the tail end of its echo across the bend. The air, despite the intrusion of heavy rain, was very still. Lucie looked into the treetops and watched for signs of movement. The branches were slumped with wet, but quite motionless, as if waiting for something, and hoping it might not happen if they stayed very still.

Len opened the external laundry door, poked his head inside and said gently, 'We ought to pack a few things into the car, my Lucie. Just to be sure. I don't like the look of this.'

Beans appeared from one of the bedrooms, tilted his wrinkles of worry towards Lucie and gave a small whine.

'It's all right, Beans,' said Len, 'we'll pack you. I've a thing or two to bring up from the shed, and my office papers.'

'Don't try anything heroic,' Lucie called after him. She looked at Beans and added, 'That's when things go wrong.' She sighed and walked into the hallway to collect up the framed photographs from a sideboard. Passing a picture of Felicity as a baby, smiling from her high chair in the kitchen of Red Chapel Avenue, Lucie stopped. She lifted the picture from the wall and placed it on her pile, then moved towards the kitchen. In the mirror on the sitting room wall, she caught a glimpse of writhing river. And something else, a sudden movement, just a flicker, above the far bank. She stopped, looked again, then turned to the terrace doors.

Beans grumbled, agitating the carpet with his feet.

'Shhh,' Lucie said. 'There's something . . .' Her eyes fixed onto the opposite riverbank, in the space between the hawthorn trees. '. . . something different.'

Unsure whether it was the unfamiliar gloom, the blur of the rain or the fret wafting up from the river that added something new, she moved closer to the doors and studied the scene. After a minute (and

another two millimetres of rain), she realised it wasn't the addition
of anything announcing itself, but the omission of something. The
Abergavenny chimney – that landmark sentinel with its warm, rosy
hue and its yawning fireplace mouth – was gone.

With the rain still throwing itself onto the roof, Carra rubbed Daisy's
wet hair with a towel and listened to the squeak and clatter of Duncan
on the roof. She opened the door to the tempest just long enough to
shout, 'Please be careful, Duncan!' She listened. 'DUNCAN?'

'I'm okay,' he yelled back. 'Nearly done.'

Carra closed the door again and, after a pause, went to the phone
and dialled the Riverhouse number. She listened to the phone ring
out, then hung up.

'Wain!' shouted Daisy. ''plash, 'plash.'

'Yes, lots of rain,' said Carra, realising that the babies had never seen
rain before. She turned to the fogging window then back to Daisy, who
was sitting in a rare state of stillness, her face furrowed with puzzlement, one curved finger pointing at the streaming, formless garden.

'You really do look like Felicity,' said Carra. The name sounded
odd spoken in the Kinvarra kitchen, and Carra realised that perhaps
it never had been before. 'Your Aunt Felicity,' she added, firmly. She
followed Daisy's gaze into the watercolour world outside and felt
a pang of love, mixed with a sharp twinge of the sort of pain she
thought Lucie might carry with her every day. *Everyday pain.*

'I hope Felicity found a timeslip,' Carra whispered.

Ben tottered over with a whimper and Carra scooped him up,
gave him a squeeze. 'It's okay,' she said. 'Everything is going to be
okay, I promise.'

From where she stood on the terrace in the tearing rain, Lucie didn't hear the phone ring. She made her way down the steps, across the slurry of the lawn towards the jetty, which was just visible, submerged and rippling beneath the rush of the river. With her eyes on the opposite riverbank, she waded into ankle-deep water.

'Where's the chimney?' she whispered.

The water was cold; it sent a silver shiver of comprehension through her. She took another few steps towards the jetty, feeling the pull of a river escaped and enraptured. She braced against it, the water at her knees, her fists clenched.

The rain had brought her hair heavily down to her cheeks, so that her view across the river seemed framed by curtains. It was indistinct, the view, misted and vague and colourless but for a small puff of pink on the far bank. *Coming, ready or not.*

Lucie swiped a hand across her eyes, pushed back her hair and tried to focus. The pink blur was gone. She searched the banks for a point of reference in the anomalous world, but couldn't find one. The river's soundtrack had percussion now, beating in time with her heart.

'It's really gone.'

Swoozie talks about her grandfather's secret cellar, and Bandit finds a timeslip under the ground. Carra's words thrummed with the rain.

Lucie took another step forwards. The wrest on her legs was stronger there. With a defiance swelling within her, she said, 'Felicity?'

The river swirled on, insolent now.

'Felicity?' It was almost a shout. Lucie's blue eyes startled and blazed against their grey surrounds, as the soundtrack in her head began to chime with a series of tiny, swelling bells. They lifted and pealed, bringing Lucie's gaze back to the missing chimney.

Put all the pieces together.

A magpie sang in the distance, the river tugged and Lucie turned to run.

A few moments later Len, having been alerted by Lucie's muted call, and then urgently summoned by a gurgling groan, almost human, and a sickening crack, emerged from the garden shed in time to witness the Riverhouse jetty being torn from its piling.

'Lucie!' Len yelled from where the river had reached the terrace steps. 'LUCIE!'

Esther Very, 49

I was offered the librarian posting here six-and-a-half years ago and I took it because library jobs are pretty scarce. I don't mind being out in the country. I've enjoyed getting to know people about town, and the history. I'm very interested in history, particularly in forgotten histories. If people say, 'Ah, there's not much of a history there,' then my ears prick up. Because there always is. And often there's a forgotten history right under your nose, or out your window. And when you learn it, the view changes completely.

Chapter 32

'They're calling it a preternatural rain event,' a constable from Bothwell informed Sergeant D when he arrived to assist. 'No one predicted it. Bothwell only got an inch and it stopped after about an hour. It was so localised. You'll have the whole SES to yourself.'

'Good,' said Sergeant D, genuinely relieved. She'd had reports of a roof caving in, idiots playing in street floodwater, drain blockages, cars floating, outgoing traffic to manage and the matter of evacuating an entire town.

The evacuation had been accomplished by half past two, for the most part – George Costas had lost his footing in the knee-deep floodwater while moving his goats and was at that time clinging to a fortuitously placed blackwood tree – and the majority of the population were gathered in their bedraggled best in the relative higher ground of the town hall.

'Here we all are,' said Walt Wallace. 'Just like old days. Care for a dance, Lurlene?'

'You'll have to makeover your makeovers next week, Marceline,' said Elaine Thorold, whose pink suit had turned a nasty puce in the wet.

A little while later, the heavens relented and the skies lightened.

'The rain's stopped,' said Bunty Partridge from the town hall kitchenette. She was sipping tea in an effort to revive herself after the furore of an unprecedented storm and a premature hearse ride.

'Hallelujah,' said Father John.

'Right, I'm off then,' said Jerry. 'Gotta get home.'

'So do I,' said Flo. Both of them had been brought in under extreme duress, only acquiescing when Sergeant D threatened them with arrest and agreed to let them ride Bruny to the town hall.

Father John put down his mug. 'And I'm horribly worried about the church. And the cemetery. Awful images of our eternal sleepers floating downstream.'

Abigail whimpered.

'I wouldn't be trusting the river just yet,' said Stanton Godfrey. 'She has a million retributions to deal out on us all.'

'She's a one,' agreed Vivvy Cox. 'Steer clear while she's rizz. She'll have rhymes and reasons and won't worry none for you.'

'Please, Dad,' said Flo.

But Jerry shook his head. 'I can't risk you.'

Flo realised he looked fatigued. She closed her mouth and stayed put, in the fidgety manner of a teenager filled with flood-lit worry for her family and the hefty weight of her little-town world.

'I don't suppose there's much town left,' said Fleury Salverson gloomily. 'It's a good time for all of us to pop clogs, probably.'

'Yes, Nuyina's likely at Meadowbank Dam by now,' said Swoozie.

'We could think of it as an adventure,' said Abigail, in a voice that did not animate with any adventure.

Sergeant D marched into the hall then, wearing her best crisis-control expression.

'I would like everyone to know,' she said, 'firstly that the rain has abated, and I'm told the water's already receding.'

There was a collective sigh of relief.

'Huzzah!' shouted Bunty Partridge.

'The show patrons have departed with only a few minor incidents on the roads and, so far, both the Goodbye Bridge and Whistler's Bridge have held. And there are no reports of casualty.'

Abigail crossed herself and a few others found a bit of wood to knock.

'That said,' continued Sergeant D, 'there are a few things I need to prepare you for. I have been with the SES crew and I can tell you that there is significant damage.'

A hush descended on the room.

'The town has been inundated, not only from the skies but also from the ground up. The river has risen to about a metre above its highest point. As such, most of our houses, in particular the ones by the river, have flooded.' She looked at Marceline, whose house was at the river end of Tiya Street. 'I'm hoping the insurance policies of the past still remain.'

There was a wave of anxious mutterings.

'St Margery's Ladies' Club, I'm sorry to say, no longer has much of a roof. And there is quite a deal of interior damage. A first-floor room collapsed to the ground. There was no one inside at the time.' She cleared her throat of emotion. 'Patricia has been notified. She is at The Rises with Ambrose. They have no extensive flood repercussions up there. Pfaffs' Post and Groceries has suffered considerable water damage. It has been condemned until further inspection and will be closed for the foreseeable future.'

'Look!' shouted Bunty, pointing out the window. 'A chink of blue! I see a chink!'

'Pfft,' said Daphne. 'That's not enough blue to mend a sailor's trousers.'

'Golly,' said Elaine Thorold. 'Has anyone thought to check on Joyce Farquhar?'

'Oh, Joyce,' said Stanton Godfrey. 'Leave her where she is. She'll keep the town anchored.'

'We have,' said Sergeant D, raising her voice a little to regain control, 'a number of people to account for, who did not respond to our evacuation calls. We are making every effort to locate them and, given the brief river rise, I have every reason to believe this will end well.'

'Thank Christ for that,' said Father John.

'Thank you, blessèd Father,' said Abigail.

Father John coughed, stood and said, 'Er, yes. Perhaps we should offer up a prayer of thanks for the rain, and another for those still at large.'

▼▼▼

Len, wet to his bones, hadn't noticed the rain begin to ease. He had slipped across the submerged lawn and far enough into the river to send his roars scudding all the way to Pocket Island.

'LUCIE? LUCIE?'

There he'd stayed, clutching the hawthorn tree as the river took to the house. And there he stood as his eyes closed and the sobs took his voice and the river rose to his waist. He felt suddenly exhausted, his leg throbbed with pain until the river-chill numbed it away. The current dragged. It felt invitational, beseeching.

'Lucie.' He moaned her name and it sounded like surrender. His hand on the tree branch loosened a little.

'Len!' It was faraway, a soft peal, but it came again. 'Len!'

For a mad moment Len searched the underwater, then shook his head and turned to the house. Beans's face was at the French door, staring down at him from where he'd climbed onto the back of the couch.

'Len! Len?'

Still dazed, Len looked into the sky and saw that the rain had stopped. He waded back towards the house. 'Lucie?'

'Over here!'

Len clambered up the steps to the terrace, where the water was at his shins. From there, the river was a beast, seething and sovereign. And on the other side of it was a little waving figure in fuchsia.

'My Lucie,' Len whispered. 'Are you drowned?' He blinked.

She waved on, or was she beckoning? 'Come over here, Len! Take the car across the Whistler Bridge.'

Her words were muted by distance and damp air.

'Bring the car, THE CAR, Len, please!'

Please . . . please . . . please. . .

Still dazed, Len's eyes moved from Lucie to the sky just above her, where the clouds had parted to reveal a small patch of blue.

▼▼▼

At Kinvarra, Duncan had changed out of his sodden clothes and was preparing to leave for Riverhouse. Carra was mopping the floor in the kitchen and emptying buckets.

'It's stopped now, Duncan, we'll come too. I'd like to help.'

'It could start again, though. This sort of flash flooding is so unpredictable. And you won't be much help with these two puddling around,' Duncan nodded at the twins, dry now and eating tiny cheese sandwiches. 'You'll be safer here.'

'Sure, yep,' said Carra. She knew he was right. She watched him leave. 'Be careful.'

But as she hefted a pile of sodden towels into the washing machine, she looked at the yellow *Carra* on the wall, with its accompanying fingerprints and thought, *But I don't think I am safe here. Or maybe I'm already gone.* She imagined her unrecognisable self, floating away on the Nowhere current, leaving behind a shiny new version of herself in a perky outfit and a patient, perfect smile. *Instagram face.*

She took a corner of one of the wet towels and scrubbed the yellow paint from the wall.

It took Len under a minute to slosh through the sitting room of Riverhouse, tuck Beans under his arm and drive the Mercedes out onto Ashby Crescent.

'Come on, come on,' he muttered, unsure whether he was speaking to himself, the dog or the car. Single-minded about reaching Lucie (or the vision of Lucie, he was still dazedly uncertain which), he didn't notice the shimmering, startled appearance of the streets. But when he reached the Whistler Bridge, he involuntarily stepped on the brake because for a moment he thought he'd taken a wrong turn and ended up in a different world. The riverscape was transformed. Downstream, Pocket Island and its rapids had disappeared beneath angry swirls of water. The esplanade houses were partially submerged and the Colleen Hills cinematically bright against the retreating storm clouds. Upstream, the school was inundated and the footbridge was gone.

Beans barked. Len jumped. (Beans never barked.)

The Mercedes whizzed across the shining bridge, skidded onto the sludge of Everston Road at the top side of the school, bumped back down to the deeper water on the Clyde Flats and drew to a stop before the enormous gum tree at Abergavenny. There, standing on the rise, sodden and shivering, was Lucie.

'My God,' she said when Len hurried out of the car and in her direction. 'Len! I paddled across the footbridge and then it broke up and washed away. Mere moments. I could have . . . Oh, Len.'

But Len was very busy taking her into his arms, checking for signs of life. 'Holy sods, woman,' he said, 'I thought I'd lost you too. What the she-devil are you doing crossing that murderous river?' He found himself close to tears again.

'I saw the chimney go, and I just knew, Len.'

'What?' Len looked at the Abergavenny ruins and saw for the first time that the huge chimney was indeed gone. All that remained was a disproportionate smattering of red bricks.

'Come and see,' called Lucie, leading him closer.

Len followed, and saw. The tumble of bricks roughly bordered a large gaping cavity, dripping and dark. Part of the near side, where Len drew Lucie to a stop a safe distance from the edge, had formed a sort of lip, over which flowed a cascade of water. As they watched, more earth ruptured and fell away. The cascade turned to torrent. A patch of overhanging thistles quivered as the rush echoed into the yawning space. On the opposite side, beneath a sagging flap of torn earth, a set of stone stairs disappeared into the black. Len turned fearfully to Lucie, whose feverish eyes were fixed on the nothing.

She slipped her hand into his and. 'I think I found Felicity.'

Ambrose Montgomery, 76

I've learnt a great deal from being born and raised, married and working and parenting in a country town. How to be quiet, for instance. Quiet leads to poetry and fishing and gardening and being able to hear the perfect equipoise of a bar in a piece of music, or all the joyous little birds. There is most definitely a certain effervescence to be gained from joining in on something colourful and loud and collective, as long as there is quiet in the end. I've learnt, too, that even in the midst of chaos, if you don't rail against calamity and racket, if you squint your eyes and tip your head to a certain angle, you are likely to see the shape of things forming themselves into something new. Then you can rather enjoy the noise.

Chapter 33

The day of the one-hundred-and-eleventh Nowhere River Show saw the biggest rainfall ever recorded in the Central Highlands of Tasmania. In the first hour, over two inches of rain fell and by the two-hour mark, just shy of five inches had filled Deidre Wagner's rain gauge in Faulkner Street.

At a bit before two in the afternoon, just as authorities issued a flood warning swiftly followed by a declaration of emergency, the Nowhere River burst its banks. Around the same time, all three jetties at the fisher cottages washed away, along with the Troop Footbridge, the structural beginnings of the Pocket Island development, a chunk of the All Angels cemetery, the wheel of the old millhouse and the Riverhouse jetty in its entirety.

Nuyina stood soggy but firm, the esplanade houses were in disarray but intact, and George Costas rescued himself and squelched back home before Phoebe had noticed him missing. He lost three goats and he blamed himself for the weakened structures of St Margery's, but his plumbing work picked up. All Angels Church had some water damage, while St Margery's Ladies' Club and Pfaffs' Post and Groceries were both sealed off and declared by authorities as dangerous.

A day later, the river, having deposited its mud into carpets and crevices, up pipes and under fingernails, had retreated to its bed and lay twinkling and flirting with the town as though nothing had happened.

That same day, a police excavation began on the site gazetted as Abergavenny grain store. It was overseen by Sergeant D, engineers, a geologist, a representative of Heritage Tasmania and the SES. The Colleen–Lyell mayor was also present for a short while, but was ordered to 'Piss off out of it, you sticky-beaked, attention-grabbing blargle' by Walt Wallace, who was operating the excavator.

Lucie and Len were seated behind a barrier and given tea, but eventually retreated to the soggy Riverhouse sitting room, where the French doors were flung open to the soft, spring wind.

They were joined, at Lucie's request, by Father John, Duncan, Carra and the twins, and by Abigail and Flo, who hovered in the garden with squeegees, gin and trepidation until Len ushered them in. Beans was there too, but having been worn out by all his recent unsettlements, was snoring and twitching on the couch.

'How do you suppose,' said Lucie, over a cup of Griffiths green tea, 'one is meant to behave whilst waiting for the body of one's daughter to be recovered?'

Len winced. 'Let's not get too horse-before-cart.'

'I know I'm right, Len. It's the thing I've been not quite comprehending for days now. The Hamiltons' bootleg cellar?' She turned her eyes to Carra, who dropped hers to the floor. 'Tell him, Carra. I know you know. Cliffity's ferrets and Swoozie's poem? You were trying to tell me, weren't you?'

'What?' said Duncan. He looked at Carra.

Carra became very interested in the floor for a moment, then managed to look Lucie squarely in the eyes and say, 'You pieced it together, Lucie. If she's there, it's you who found her.'

Lucie met Carra's gaze, held it, then took something from it and packed it away. She sent Carra a barely discernible nod and a smile. From somewhere nearby came the clacking call of a plover.

'I think,' said Abigail across the subcurrents, 'at a time like this, you behave however you want to behave.' She looked at the bottle of gin.

'We could play a game?' suggested Carra, who was still feeling the prickle of Lucie's eyes.

'Watch the telly?' said Flo.

'We could cry,' said Abigail.

For a moment, they all thought about having a proper wail. Abigail almost did.

'Might be a bit premature for that,' said Lucie.

'Yes,' said Len and Duncan, with relief.

'There are a lot of bricks to dislodge,' said Len. 'Could be ages.'

'I think I'd like to sing for her,' said Lucie.

Everyone wished they had suggested this. Or brought Fleury along.

There was a stretch of respectful silence, interrupted only by birdsong and the sound of the excavator carrying across the river, followed by a throat-clear from Abigail and a shriek from Daisy.

Abigail sat straighter in her chair, cleared her throat again and launched into the opening strains of 'Ave Maria'. Father John joined her, followed by Lucie, Duncan and Len. Carra held Daisy tight, took a few steps back and listened.

From the open windows of the drying Riverhouse, the voices joined together to form an imperfect, lilting, lifting refrain that wafted out across the river to the high-vis-clad men and women gathered around the dark, earth-scented basin. Amid the sustained notes, there was a shout, and as the unlikely, mismatched chorus raised its voice for the end of the second verse of 'Ave Maria', the pale, miraculous, beautiful horror of a child's skeleton was lifted from the ground.

Felicity Finlay, Felicity Finlay, Felicity Finlay . . .

The name continued to echo – uttered, exclaimed, whispered, thought, shouted and cried a thousand times or more – throughout Nowhere River that day, and in the days that followed. Once reporters caught wind of the news and broadcast it far and wide, Felicity's name was inserted into gossip, speculation, linen parties, queues, dinners, prayers and other conversations. Parents gazed at their children, watched them sleeping, crossed themselves, counted their blessings and thanked their lucky stars.

Even before the tiny skeleton had given its precious DNA and been conclusively identified as Felicity, Lucie and Len received many letters and cards, delivered with well wishes and sympathies and all the very bests for the future.

On the third day of what Lucie considered her long-lost mourning, while the town was still drying off, a demolition crew was called in to pull apart the precarious interior of St Margery's (preserving the exterior walls). That same day, a string of journalists, photographers and camerapeople trailed through the town to the cordoned-off Abergavenny site, then back again, trawling for locals who might talk. Not one person spilled a single bean. Eventually, Sergeant D decreed that all media must come through her, and any unsolicited press requests would be subject to legal action.

The people of Nowhere River gave Lucie and Len their support and discretion, and their prayers, along with tears, lasagnes, casseroles and love. Patricia sent Lucie a peace lily and a pot of La Mer moisturiser. Not a single person dared lament the onslaught of flood, nor the smell of damp carpet, aching joints, tired eyes, lifting wallpapers or water-stained walls.

Father John, on his way to see Len and Lucie, encountered a journalist loitering at the gates of Riverhouse and lost his temper. Father John had never lost his temper, not ever, and the results were clumsy and amateur. He pushed the journalist, and then ran after him, shooing at him like one might a pesky rooster. 'Go on, get out of here, get out, you snivelling gobshite.'

Len appeared from the side door to see Father John send a sort of kick in the direction of the journalist as the latter scurried off. Father John dusted off his soft, unblighted hands and gave a little grunt of satisfaction.

'That sorted him,' said Len.

Father John looked ashamed. 'Oh dear,' he said. 'I seemed to have lost my cool.'

'Well, I still think you're *very* cool,' said Len.

'Thank you, my friend.'

'First the famine,' said Father John. 'Then the flood. And now a plague of media.'

'You forgot the sacrifice of the firstborns,' said Len.

Father John gasped in horror.

'Sorry,' said Len. 'Not one of my best.' When Father John's expression remained unchanged, Len added, 'I'll eat my shoes if God is sending us punishments. That's about as likely as stones humming and Felicity floating back to us over the hills. Life is just horrible sometimes, that's all there is to it. And the media plague is worth it just to see you turn into a ninja in the driveway. Coming in?'

Father John nodded.

'Good. But don't ask me to do any praying. Look where that got us last time.' He eyeballed the heavens.

Father John smiled. 'Len.'

'Yes?'

'I've been summoned here by Sergeant D. She's on her way. Is Lucie in?'

Len looked at him gravely. 'Ah. Should I phone Duncan?'

'I already have.'

'Right.'

At that moment, Sergeant D's four-wheel drive grumbled into the driveway. Duncan was in the passenger seat.

'Right,' said Len again.

By the time Len saw Father John, Sergeant D and Duncan to the kitchen, Lucie had stopped beating cake batter and settled herself at the kitchen table, her back straight and her hands set in front of her in a pose of preparedness. Duncan moved by her side and she put an arm around his waist.

'Is Carra on her way?' she asked.

'No,' said Duncan. 'She said it's our story to hear. But she'll come with the twins anytime if you need her to.'

Lucie nodded and looked at Sergeant D. 'Hello, Sergeant,' she said. 'I will offer you a cup of something shortly, I promise, but first I would just like you to say what you have to say. Is that all right with you, Len?'

'Yes,' said Len. 'I think that's best.'

'Sure,' said Sergeant D. She took a deep breath. 'Okay, so firstly I'll just confirm that it is indeed your Felicity. I mean, I know you knew that, but the DNA test confirms it. Also, the full report has been filed for the coroner. It's pretty clear to forensics that there hasn't been any foul play involved here. It's been recommended by the coroner that the ruling is "death by misadventure". But there are some documented injuries, consistent with a heavy fall.'

Len reached for Lucie's hand.

'You should know that there was a depressed fracture to Felicity's skull, which is the most likely cause of death. She hit her head, possibly on the flagged floor, or on one of the items found in the cellar. It's hard to say. But regardless, the fall would certainly have rendered her immediately unconscious.'

'So she felt no pain?' said Len.

'No pain. She had a fractured femur and ribs, but she would never have known about those.'

'And it was definitely some sort of contraband cellar?' Len asked.

'Yes. They found remnants of barrels and metal brewing equipment. Swoozie Hamilton says it aligns with family stories. The grain store up on staddle stones was a perfect cover for a cellar. No one would have thought—'

'Right,' said Lucie. 'Death by misadventure.'

'That's right.' Sergeant D gave them some silence in which to absorb what they'd been told.

'And so how did she come to this misadventure?' Len said. 'I mean, how would she fall into a concealed cellar, presumably trapdoored and locked in some way? She was five.'

'Well, that's still a bit of a puzzle, I'm afraid. The engineer consulting said it was most likely the result of unstable ground due to wombat burrows. The whole area was completely undermined by them. That's why the chimney pretty much disappeared. We've surmised that she may have hidden in a wombat burrow and caused the old lining of the cellar to give way.' Sergeant D's voice went wonky and her eyes filled with tears. She cleared her throat and blinked at the floor. 'It could have been any one of us kids.' She glanced at Duncan. 'We were always capering around Abergavenny, weren't we. I'm so sorry it happened to your little girl. To you.'

Lucie patted Sergeant D's hand. 'It's all right,' she said. 'It's all right.'

In the treetops outside, the flutter of a just-flown bird caught Lucie's eye. She gazed at the waving, empty branch it had left behind. The fractures in her heart shifted and sent a pain into her throat. She closed her eyes and breathed it in. *Let it gather, let it quake, let it rise, let it break. It will cry, it will call, it will whisper, it will fall.* As the pain eased to an ache, she opened her eyes, and leaned into Len's shoulder. Len stroked her hair as Duncan closed in and put his arms around both of them. Lucie's angled gaze through the window brought her a fresh-eyed glimpse of a blinking river.

'Griefs,' she said, 'are the things that send us home.'

Carra Finlay, 31

I think if you have friends and purpose and someone to care for, and a place where it's safe to be utterly yourself, then you can make great stories wherever you are. If you have a beautiful river and a nice community and some fresh air as a setting for your story, well, that'll make it better, I suppose. I haven't quite worked out my Nowhere story just yet, but I know it will be set here. Here I have family and friends and occupation and obligation. I have love and laughter and possibility. And the story is still being composed.

Chapter 34

Two major events happened in the weeks following the discovery of the remains of Felicity Louise Finlay, aged five. The first was her funeral, held at All Angels Church beside the Nowhere River.

The specially formed Nuyina Choir (a chapter of the Nowhere River Old Folks' Treat Committee) with its choir mistress Abigail Snelson and its soloist Fleury Salverson (dubbed by media outlets as 'the world's oldest rising star') led the congregation in the hymns, including 'Ave Maria' and 'She Walked Through the Fair'.

The funeral flowers were selected and arranged by the St Margery's Ladies' Club Floral Committee (directed by Deidre Wagner and Ruth Beaumont-Hudd). They were described as 'quite jazzy' by the St Margery's president, Patricia Montgomery.

In the front pew, Lucie, lovely in pale pink with a matching hat, sat with a hand on Len's shoulder, her fingers tapping out a tender adagio that brought fresh tears to those eyes near enough to see. Next to them sat Duncan and Carra and their twins. The Bradshaw family and Sergeant Harmony Darling sat close behind.

The eulogy was given by Lucie, who kept everyone's tears flowing with her sentiments.

'I hope you don't mind,' she said, 'if I address these words to my little girl, Felicity. She is gone, I know that for sure now, but she is also very much here – in this church, by this river, in this town, and in us.' Lucie sent a glance to Len, who gazed back at her through tears.

'Our darling girl.' Here, Lucie paused to steady herself. 'Our little Flossie. We are forever grateful to have known you and loved you. For the way you wrapped the folds of my skirt around yourself when you felt shy, and the way you put your tiny, warm hands on my cheeks and touched your nose onto mine. For your funny dances, that husky little voice of yours and those bouncy curls. It's said that some people are too lovely to stay in this harsh old world. I think you are one of those.'

Lucie paused again, swallowed and tried to press on. 'We want you to know . . .' Her voice veered off into a sob.

Len stood and moved to her side. He put one arm around Lucie and with the other he picked up her written notes and read.

'We want you to know that we have had thirty years to learn how not to move on. Some people think that we have to get on with things and to let time heal. But we will never heal. We wear the scar of you, and feel the pain of you, with thanks, because they mean we carry you close. No one ever tells anyone to "move on" from happiness or joy, and we will not ever move on from this sadness.'

Lucie, having taken some time to compose herself, took the paper from Len and spoke again. 'We are what we are because we had our family. We are what we are because we had you, and because we lost you. And now we will be what we will be because we found you.' Lucie removed her reading glasses and looked up at the congregation. 'So please, everyone, know that we will be sad and happy all at once. We will be moving forward, as we always have, but not moving on. And we won't move away, so there we are, you're stuck with all of us – me, Len and Felicity. And, of course, our darling Duncan, his Carra and our grandchildren, Daisy and Ben.'

Carra could feel the silent roar of emotion in the room. She imagined it forming a heavy, sodden cloud above them that might follow them all out and bring more rain. Her cheeks streamed with tears. She felt a hand rest on her shoulder and turned to see Josie sitting just behind her, her own tears bright. They exchanged a sad smile.

A beautiful white coffin, small and elegant, had been gifted to the Finlay family by Patricia and Ambrose Montgomery. Len, Lucie and Duncan bore it from the church into the churchyard, where it was buried in a sunny patch of All Angels Cemetery, close to Riverhouse. Flo watched their gentle movements and their dignified faces until her chest heaved with sorrow and she had to look away.

In the churchyard after the burial and while Len was ushering people through to the Riverhouse terrace for tea, apple cakes and cinnamon scrolls, Lucie took a moment to walk between the church and the river, crouching at the water's edge, where its tiny laps and gestures seemed shy and anxious. Its sweeping bend looked very much like a smile. She watched it for a bit, then reached out and very lightly touched the cold surface with her fingertips.

'I'm sorry,' she whispered.

The other significant event, occurring a respectful fortnight after Felicity's funeral, was Patricia's Miss Fresh and Lovely announcement. It was held in the town hall, which was still set up as a post-flood crisis centre, offering groceries and toiletries donated by the Colleen–Lyell Council.

'Cheap toilet tissue,' said Phoebe Costas. 'Typical of the council.' But she pocketed a handful of quite luxurious soaps.

'Thank you,' was all Patricia needed to say to achieve silence. 'Firstly, I would like you all to know that Ambrose and I have pledged to return St Margery's Ladies' Club to its former élan. The damage is extensive, but it hasn't affected the entire building.

Much of the original structure and many of its fixtures can be restored or replaced. Contrary to one particular rumour, we will not be converting the interior to an open-plan women's wellness centre with a juice bar.'

'A what?' said Daphne Partridge.

'We will, however, be setting aside space for a childcare area, in the hopes it might attract a younger demographic from the wider municipality.'

There was a buzz of talk. Carra raised her eyebrows at Josie.

'Furthermore,' continued Patricia. 'I will be standing down as club president. The committee needs a shift in energy. To that end, Lucie Finlay, our former vice-president, will step into the breach, along with Abigail Snelson as co-president and Josephine Bradshaw and Caroline Finlay as co-vice-presidents. A sharing of burdens as the club is rebuilt. We welcome new members, young and old.'

'And finally'—Patricia left a suspenseful pause—'I am pleased to say that the St Margery's member base is relatively strong, far stronger than it was a year ago, which is around about when I announced the Miss Fresh and Lovely quest. So, it seems, despite some impediments along the way, the scheme has been, on the whole, fruitful. And I think it's time the winner was made known.'

Another wave of exclamation fizzed across the room. Backs straightened (Elaine), hearts quickened (Abigail), lips pursed (Phoebe Costas) and eyes rolled (Inda Price). Flo tried not to appear expectant; Carra tried not to cross her fingers.

'I am pleased to say,' said Patricia, 'that I have narrowed it down to a clear winner, a proper Miss Fresh and Lovely. A person who has demanded little but delivered much . . .'

Abigail's eyes widened.

'Someone who has given this town a sense of renewal . . .'

Deidre Wagner and Ruth Beaumont-Hudd squeezed one another's hands.

'A reason to be proud, to become involved and engaged, and to celebrate its strengths . . .' Elaine Thorold held her breath.

Jerry nudged Flo and whispered, 'It's got to be you.'

'Someone who has given Nowhere River a reason to have a look at itself and adjust its values . . .'

Esther Very bit her lip.

'She has fostered community spirit, benevolence and compassion, sincerity, pride, courage, positivity and enthusiasm. She has shown us dignity, the importance of family and of friendship. And she has gifted us the perfect opportunity to be our very, very best.'

Patricia cast her eyes across the hall. 'I wish to thank every single entrant for their effort and involvement, and I encourage them to press on with their ventures and initiatives. But there is only one winner, and that is . . .'

Again, the audience bated their breath.

'. . . Felicity Finlay.'

A perfect hush descended on the hall. Not a 'strike me pink' or a 'crikey Moses' was uttered. Not an 'oh my hat' or a 'fancy that' or a 'gawd' or a 'lord'. Not a 'Godfather's ducks' or even a 'fuck'. Just silence. And then, some claps, started off by Flo and spreading around the room until every hand in the entire hall had joined in to create a resounding ovation.

Daphne Partridge, 88

What was that, dear? Ah, you must have heard enough piffle from all and sundry. Go off and sit by the river, listen to its babbles instead. And its birds! The birds have all the best things to say.

Epilogue

If you search for the town of Nowhere River – a tiny river township in the foothills of the Central Highlands on a small island at the bottom of the world – you will not find it. Nowhere River, with its watermarked streets and boarded-up cottages, its precipitous population decline, ghostly tales and snaggle-toothed cemeteries, has disappeared from the map.

It has not been swallowed up by rising water levels, nor has it been consumed by raging bushfire, desiccated by drought, destroyed by explosions of population or consumed by urban sprawl. It has, quite simply, been renamed. (Well, not so simply. As it turned out, the process was a knotty affair, given the robust opinions stalwarting about town and the tangle of red tape from the nomenclature board.)

It still has its characters and quirks, its grumbles and mutterings. Daphne Partridge is still shouting at her sister, Bunty, Walt Wallace is still swearing at his sheepdogs and Esther Very still whispers to her books. The Rises continues to dominate the southern view of the Colleen Hills and inside, Patricia Montgomery still dominates its halls. Throughout the town's streets, the gnomes remain, beaming from the gardens and Queen Mary Park has quite recovered from her unexpected dunking in the river. And the river, of course, still runs strong and clear and onwards.

The differences, though, if you wander through the streets today, are pronounced. Even if you had never visited the town before, you would notice a certain youthful crispness about it. Not at all glitzy, as the upkeep of things is well served by advice from the St Margery's Traditions Committee. (The gold rubbish bins have been repainted in French navy.) And nothing is particularly modern, either – the architecture and finishes are distinctly colonial, most of them Georgian, convict-built and classified by Heritage Tasmania. But everything has a kempt and cared-for look. Some structures are not quite there yet but display all the evidence of care – scaffolding, tradies and industry. Industry. That is a word that may enter your mind if you stroll along the High Street, past the preserved 'Life: Be In It' sign and into Faulkner Street, Lake Road, Cuttler's Way . . . the Esplanade has a new bike path and Church Street has all its potholes filled. On Tiya Street, the butchery is open and thriving, well stocked by Everston beef and Clyde Farm lamb. Inside the door is a brass plaque remembering Cliffity Smith. Barbara, Narelle, Dasher and Bandit live on in luxury at Nuyina, where Stanton Godfrey and Swoozie Hamilton bicker over who is best ferret handler. Jones Street has a bookshop and a café. The deconsecrated Catholic church is now an acclaimed B&B.

St Margery's is still St Margery's Ladies' Club. Both her roof and her dignity have been restored. Her blinds are still mostly closed, though her mind has opened a little – the childcare centre is in place and the sunroom has been converted into a community craft hub. The Management Committee is thirty-eight strong.

The Pocket Island development (which turned out to be tasteful and unassuming) has extended its holdings into Nowhere High Country Bike Trails, which have been etched into scrub above the town and declared world class by experts. Cyclists are streaming in from everywhere and filling the empty rooms of the Fat Doe Inn. It has new carpet throughout but still offers deep-fried camembert.

Pfaffs' Post and Groceries is now Overeems' General Store. The Overeem family also bought the bottom pub and are converting it into a home. Mrs Overeem is a stand-up comedian who holds monthly open-mic evenings. She and Mr Overeem have five children and two corgis.

Mr and Mrs Pfaff have moved to a smaller town, off a less beaten track. They do not wish to be found.

Miss Fresh and Lovely, Felicity Finlay, had her prize money put towards a number of community causes, including a small riverboat for Nuyina, stage lighting for the hall and an attractions fund for the agricultural show. (The Nowhere River Show was widely considered dead in the water, so to speak, until myriad requests came in from the public for more, along with a significant natural disaster entitlement from the federal government to 'assist with the ongoing preservation of the show's cultural rarities'. Her Excellency the Governor of Tasmania hosted a reception to honour the show's official relaunch.)

There have been other new arrivals to town since it 'caught the imagination of a nation' (as Abigail Snelson is fond of saying). Six families and counting. The council has installed a play-park and school enrolments have risen enough to secure its future as a district high school.

Flo hasn't gone back to school. She is finishing off her final year of correspondence school and edits the *Colleen Chronicle*, her monthly newspaper. It won a humanitarian prize for sensitive, ground-level reportage at a recent media awards. She also helps on the farm, Everston Pastoral, which has recently taken on the Clyde Farm lease because Walt and Lurlene are so busy with their Sweet Lurlene cake and confectionery shop, recently opened to much fanfare on Tiya Street.

Josie now leaves the beef business to Alex and Jerry while she tries to keep up with growing demand for her Everston Murrnong. Her last autumn harvest yielded a modest crop with a healthy seed set, and she has secured ongoing contracts with some of Hobart's most exclusive restaurants. She is now experimenting with kangaroo grass and dreams of reviving the old watermill to produce the same flour made by millennia of Tasmanians.

Father John continues to conduct services to small congregations in All Angels Church every Sunday. He no longer practises radical acceptance but hasn't given up on painting, and delivered a resounding yes to Abigail Snelson when she summoned the courage to ask him for tea.

Lucie and Len live at Riverhouse only occasionally these days. They have spent the majority of their recent time abroad, seeing the world. When they are not travelling, they are working slowly on the restoration of the Abergavenny grain store and its transformation into a cottage. Lucie joins the church choir when she can and has recently sold her Mercedes to Barry Fronda.

Beans lives with Duncan at Kinvarra, where he snoozes and watches the doorways for the raucous comings and goings of Daisy and Ben. He is suspicious of their noise, and wary of their exuberant, fumbly affection, but finds that he misses them when they are not there. His Lucie-yearns are quelled regularly by Sergeant D, who is often there, with her lap, for evening snuggles on the couch.

Carra is no longer Carra of Kinvarra. She is Carra of Faulkner Avenue, residing in a sandstone cottage she bought from Bunty and Daphne Partridge. The cottage is rundown but charming, with wonky floorboards and very twee wallpaper. Outside, Carra has forged a garden from the wilderness of Bunty and Daphne's abandoned yard. It is huge, shady and sunny, messy and neat, formal and haphazard and spontaneous. It has a bed of dahlias in remembrance of her former neighbour Cybill and another filled with runaway foxgloves beside an antique lamppost. 'A garden of lyrical disobedience,' is how the famed designer Ursula Andreas described it to her 100,000 followers. From October to March each year, Carra's Garden receives visitors from far and wide, and Carra herself has become well known for her expertise in drought resistance, her knowledge of perennials and her avant-garde use of colour. She has received several collaboration requests from her peers in the landscape architecture field, including one from Ursula, who would like her to co-author a book about Tasmania's secret gardens. Carra hasn't yet found the time to reply, as she is in the process of opening her garden shop in the old post office.

Daisy and Ben adore their new home and like to eat snails. They have been given a pug puppy by Lucie. Beans pretends to be put out but is secretly pleased.

Carra is occasionally haunted by her choices – the infliction of pain on startled, loved faces, and all the little shards of what-if. But mostly she is grateful to see the development of a different story in the mirror when sometimes she pauses to look. There are wrinkles forming in that story, but they are born of life, not puzzlement or doubt. At night, Carra regularly falls into a muscle-sore repose, sometimes entangled in the limbs of her growing children, sometimes chatting over wine with her best friend Josie and other times happily alone.

She still climbs the Whistler Hills, where she has the clearest view to the other side of her decisions. From there, she is grateful for what she sees: the evanescing reaches of a river going somewhere, a growing township she calls home, and a future of little moments – some difficult, some euphoric, others accompanied by lemon-drizzle cake at St Margery's. None of them are moments from which she wants to run.

Thank you for visiting

minanya

place of rivers (palawa kani)

Please call again soon!

Acknowledgements

I acknowledge the Traditional Owners of the lands on which this book was written and pay my respects to Elders past and present.

Thank you so much to Fiona Inglis and Curtis Brown Australia.

Thank you to my publisher Ali Watts and editors Genevieve Buzo and Catherine Hill for helping me extract this book from all the unruly words I amassed.

Thank you to Midland Typesetters for turning my manuscript into a book, and to Louisa Maggio for giving it a fresh and lovely cover.

To Lou Ryan and the PRH sales team for getting the book out and about.

Thank you to my friends at the Bream Creek Show Society, past and present, for the inspirations and for their dedication to keeping our wonderful piece of country heraldry alive and well.

And to Matt Bradshaw and Pat Bourke for answering research questions, and to Maggie Mackellar for answering all the other questions and being so vital to my process. ('Vital to my process' sounds so wanky but you know what I mean.)

To all the wonderful book sellers and to those who bought this book from them and read it, thank you for such important work.

388 Meg Bignell

Enormous thanks and love to my lifelong collaborators: Em, Mum, Dad, Dickie, Ed, Bess, Lucie and Blue for support, inspiration, laughter, patience and love.

And a small pat-on-back to me, for not deciding after the first novel that being a writer is all too hard and I should be a spy instead. Well done me.